WHERE MADNESS LIES

HEIDI K. ALLEN

INSCRIPTUS
PRESS

INSCRIPTUS
PRESS

Inscriptus Press, L.L.C.
PO BOX 522185
Salt Lake City, UT 84152

Book cover by MiblArt
Orphic egg design by Maria Alejandra Calle

Visit heidikallen.com to join Heidi's monthly newsletter and receive a free book - The Sea Blue Mane!

For Abby and Kate

I

When life itself seems lunatic, who knows where madness lies?

—Miguel de Cervantes, Don Quixote

1

Alex woke with a jolt, catching a scream in her mouth. She stared unseeing at a dingy white ceiling as the images in her mind receded like a bloody tide.

She squirmed against the thin, wet fabric clinging to her body, dread coiling in her chest as she found her forearms and ankles clamped in large brown leather cuffs with yellowed cotton lining.

Shit, she thought. *Not again.*

She took a trembling breath and slowly turned her head. Dust motes drifted in light straining through a thick, shatterproof window, barely illuminating the wall clock covered with chicken wire, caging time as only this place could. She knew the tiny room well—state hospitals all seemed to use the same interior decorator.

Alex balled her hands into fists and took several deep breaths, trying to slow her racing heart.

A pocket-sized man in a long white coat and glasses walked in carrying a file so thick it could only be hers. His long nose and the way he tilted his graying head at Alex made her think of a small bird. A woman as large as he was small followed behind, wearing gray scrubs and an exaggerated frown. She loomed behind him like a brick wall.

"Hello, Alexandra. I'm Dr. Wilcox, a relatively new attending physician here at Manhattan Psychiatric. This is Nurse Parry. Good to have you with us. How are you feeling?"

"How long have I been here?" Alex asked, her voice cracking.

"Before I answer that, we need to check your vitals. I understand from your file you don't like to be touched. May we proceed if we wear gloves?"

Alex nodded and forced her hands to relax, already longing for her own gloves and the barrier they put between her and the world.

Dr. Wilcox sat next to her and shined a penlight into her eyes, then put two of his fingers onto her wrist.

"How long?" Alex asked.

Dr. Wilcox kept his fingers on Alex's wrist, watching her face carefully. "You've been unconscious for three days," he said. "It's Wednesday."

Alex was sure the doctor felt her pulse quicken. *Three days*. It had been years since she'd been out for so long.

"Well, that super sucks," she said. Dr. Wilcox gave a thin-lipped smile and gestured for the nurse to unlock the restraints. Alex rubbed her wrists and sat up slowly, lowering her legs over the edge of the bed. Her long brown hair plastered itself to her back as the hospital gown gaped.

"I've been in contact with your psychiatrist, Dr. Arnold," Dr. Wilcox said. "She said once you came out of your catatonic state to give you these." From an inside his coat he pulled a plastic grocery bag containing some wadded-up fabric. Alex's spirits lifted at the sight of her crumpled arm-length gloves. It took all her strength not to yank them out of his hands.

"It's highly irregular, but she was quite insistent that they were part of your treatment," he said.

"Thank you so much," she said, clutching the bag to her body and sending Dr. Arnold warm thoughts. She smiled, trying to seem as sane as possible. "Can I go home now?"

He looked at her for a long minute. "I'm afraid you've had several violent fits these last few days. I'd like to keep you in observation for an additional seventy-two hours."

Oh god, no, she thought. The room immediately began to close in on her. "Dr. Wilcox, please. I just really need to get home and back to work."

"I'm sorry, but I've read your file and it's unclear to me whether you are a danger to yourself or not." He gestured with the demoralizingly thick folder. "You've had a surprising number of stays with us and other hospitals in your thirty-two years."

"But—"

"The time will go faster if you just accept it and try to understand. We are doing it for your own good," he said briskly.

Alex felt the familiar pull of the quicksand she was suddenly in. Struggle, and the days could turn into weeks, or worse.

"You were brought here as-is from the ER," he said. "So we'll give you some hospital-issue clothes to wear. You and I will talk again toward the end of your stay."

Alex nodded and they left. The door wasn't even closed before she tore open the bag and pulled on her sleek arm-length black gloves, her heart calming as she filled each finger.

Nurse Parry barged back in with a pile of white clothes, shoes, and a hair elastic, all of which she tossed on the bed. "I'll wait outside," she said in a voice like sandpaper.

Alex peeled off the sodden gown and put on the hospital clothes and ugly white plastic sandals. The scratchy, overly bleached fabric notwithstanding, it felt good to be dressed. She pulled her sweaty hair into a messy bun, grateful to have it off her neck.

When she opened the door, Nurse Parry snorted at seeing the chic gloves in stark contrast to the drab hospital clothes. She pointed down the hall. "Shower facilities are down this hall to your right. Rec room is to your left. Lunch is in an hour and a half. Follow the crowd when the bell rings." With that, she was gone.

Alex headed to the rec room. The large space had a few ratty loveseats and chairs in front of an old, corner-mounted TV, and a set of green tables with benches. Patients of varying lucidity were strewn around the room playing games, watching shows, or just staring at nothing. The fluorescent lights buzzed in her ears and down her spine. *Seventy-two hours.*

A door opened on the opposite side of the room, giving her a glimpse of greenery. Alex dashed over, desperate for fresh air. She found an empty bench underneath a row of trees standing sentry along the perimeter, not quite hiding the high stone walls, and certainly not providing shade from the irritatingly cheery September sun.

She put her head in her hands and allowed herself a moment of wretchedness before closing her eyes and beginning the mantra her grandmother had taught her for when she was scared or upset. *Breathe in...I'm okay...breathe out...there's nothing I can do. Breathe in...breathe out.*

She reached back in her memory to three days ago, trying to recall the events that had brought her here.

She'd been called in on her day off and remembered being startled by the furor of activity in a typically quiet mortuary. Theirs was the morgue/mortuary nearest to New York's Chief Medical Examiner's office, and on high volume days they often got the overflow once the city had performed an autopsy.

It had clearly been a rough few days for New York.

Her boss had rushed up and shoved a pile of files at her. "Thank you for coming. I made sure you had your end table."

Alex took the pile. "Thanks...but this looks like more than 'a couple'."

He had the decency to look a little sheepish as he shrugged. "Well, you're the fastest and the best." She gave him a flat look, feeling foolish for letting him yet again take advantage of her lack of family and social life. But it kept her busy.

Alex headed to the far side of the large morgue to her station, where she exchanged her black silk gloves for rubber surgical ones. Then pulled the first body—a middle-aged man killed in a car accident—out of a refrigerated locker and onto a gurney. After using pulleys to transfer him to the table, she walked to the left side, intentionally putting her back to the rest of the room.

Alex looked at him for a moment, taking in his salt-and-pepper hair and shaggy eyebrows. There was a reason she'd chosen a career full of corpses. For a woman afflicted with visions, the dead were safe—no future, no present, only a past. And post-mortem visions usually only took a few minutes, though she'd learned the hard way to try to get them over with before she had a scalpel in her hand.

She pulled off a glove and gently touched the man's cold, clammy cheek.

A light flashed.

Images flowed into her mind—*a child at his mother's funeral...at college, partying, philandering...working at a corporate job...laughing with a wife and children...sneaking off to gamble, taking money out of their kids' college account...arguing with his wife, humiliated and angry...a fateful car ride and a patch of ice...blackness.*

Alex took a deep breath as the final images receded. Most lives seemed to be made up of a simple cadence, interspersed with intense beats of joy or sorrow. It was these beats that primarily showed themselves to Alex, though the intensity varied, and some had more than others.

Relieved to have that part done with, she began her work. Before long he was clean, embalmed, and dressed, with special care given to his makeup and hair, combing it the way she knew he used to do it.

Alex pulled out her next body—a young woman, late-twenties, killed in an assault. She gasped quietly when she pulled back the sheet, not at the serrated gash across the neck, but at the tattoo on her face. It seemed to be a mask of sorts, with widening and thinning lines in a beautiful inky pattern of scrollwork that framed her eyes, swirling across her forehead, down her temple and over her cheekbones. It was markedly different from the gang-related facial tattoos she was accustomed to seeing. Alex pulled her glove off and hesitantly touched the young woman's cheek.

A massive, brilliant light had exploded in her mind.

And she woke up here.

A shadow covered the sun as Alex remembered that moment of panic before becoming lost in the intense, monstrous vision. At the thought, blood and screams began to surface and fear pulsed through her. She shoved it back down.

Not yet, she thought. She'd likely be forced to see it again soon enough.

A well-worn feeling of helplessness settled over her. At least it wasn't a vision from someone living, someone who would soon face such a horrifying fate. Grateful for that small mercy, she turned her face to the sun and let the light and warmth seep into her. *Breathe in...I'm okay... breathe out...there's nothing I can do.*

There was nothing *anyone* could do. She was cursed. No matter what she did, no one ever believed her.

But Alex's visions always came true.

2

Alex sat at a bolted down table in the large cafeteria, her hunger dissipating as she poked at the lukewarm meatloaf with her spork. She jumped at the sound of a tray slamming onto the table next to her, and looked over to see a portly man in a gray sweatsuit digging happily into his matching gray meat, mumbling to himself. His head snapped toward her, piggy eyes blazing.

"MY MEATLOAF! Stay away!"

Alex dropped her eyes, shoveled a few bites of potatoes into her mouth, and fled to the hopefully mostly empty showers. She grabbed an overly bleached towel, then peeled off her clothes and left them in a small pile on a changing bench, careful to hide her gloves in the middle. She stepped into the grimy stall with her plastic sandals and a prayer for hot water. She closed her eyes and rinsed away three days of sweat and fear in the warm water. She pushed the handle of one of the three receptacles bolted to the wall and wrinkled her nose at the pile of pink foamy body wash that smelled like McDonald's hand soap.

Three days, three days, three days, she chanted to herself. She was contemplating whether she could get away with just one shower in three days when she pushed the shampoo button. It smelled of rotten strawberries.

Definitely her last shower.

Alex finished and dressed quickly, relieved to find her gloves where she left them. She sighed at her reflection in the mirror, her dark, wet hair brought out the dingy grottos under her hazel eyes.

Suddenly a specter floated noiselessly behind her. She jumped and whirled, finding a waif of a human with long, blond, tangled hair. Her towel went around her almost twice, its bleached white a stark contrast against the sallow translucency of her skin. Alex could easily count the rib bones sticking out of her back. She was just noticing a strange tattoo on her inner forearm when the woman looked at her sharply with fierce, ice-blue eyes, set incongruently in her gaunt face like jewels in a skull. Embarrassed to be caught staring, Alex offered a polite smile and hurried out, feeling like a mouse running from a hawk.

She headed to the rec room, ready to narcotize herself with whatever old TV show was on. With luck, TV would be the *only* drug she'd be given during this stay. She curled up in a shabby maroon wingback chair and waited to see what was on next. When the globular bushy hair of Bob Ross appeared, Alex smiled, remembering how his magical paintbrush and happy little trees had helped fill the drawn-out days of a lonely child.

By the second episode Alex was struggling to stay awake. Bob was putting the final touches on some fluffy little clouds when a voice whispered right in Alex's ear.

"I love this show."

Alex's heart leapt into her throat and she shot up. The tall waif she'd seen earlier was leaning across the top of the wingback. Her black leggings and long-sleeved tee hung off her frame like a scarecrow.

"Yeah…me too," Alex said, breathless.

The woman put on a smile that almost—but not quite—reached her hawkish eyes. "Sorry, I didn't mean to startle you. I'm Artemis."

"Hi," Alex said, turning back to the TV.

"May I join you?" Artemis asked.

"Sure," Alex said reluctantly. She kept her eyes forward.

Artemis dragged a chair over so the two arms touched, then curled up. They watched in silence, Alex warily keeping a side-eye on the newcomer. But it wasn't until the episode ended that Artemis turned back to her.

"So, how long are you destined to be a bat in this belfry?" Her voice was a rich loamy alto, at complete odds with her long-haired-Twiggy on-crack look.

"A couple more days," Alex mumbled noncommittally. "You?"

Artemis shrugged. "I'm in and out of these places. I've been here a few weeks and I'm supposed to stay until I gather my wits, as it were." She spoke matter-of-factly as she played with her matted hair.

"Yeah, I guess that's what I'm supposed to be doing too."

"You seem pretty normal to me. Comparatively, anyway." Artemis raised an eyebrow at Alex's hands. "What's with the gloves though?"

Alex folded her arms protectively. "They…help me. A prescription of sorts, from my psychiatrist."

"Nice psychiatrist," Artemis said.

"Yes."

They sat in silence long enough for Alex to feel uncomfortable. She tried to guess Artemis' age and couldn't. She had an unusually ageless look.

They both started when a loud voice boomed into the room. "Okay everyone, that's it. Head to your rooms for lights-out!" A dark-haired man with a salt-and-pepper goatee stood near the entrance, flicking the lights on and off.

A nurse with pink hair came in and began straightening up the room. "I'd like to avoid seizures please, Thomas," she said crossly. The lights stopped their flickering.

Artemis wrinkled her nose. "And that's Thomas, our resident orderly asshole. Why is it guys like him always end up in places like this?"

Alex knew exactly what she meant. "I don't know. They're the cockroaches of the mental health industry."

"Yes! And just as impossible to exterminate," Artemis added. They gave each other small but genuine smiles. By then most of the patients had shuffled toward the door, so Alex and Artemis followed suit.

"Well hello, you're new," Thomas said as Alex walked by, his breath a fog of stale coffee and chewing tobacco. Alex kept her eyes down and didn't respond.

"Oh, leave her alone," the nurse said.

"What? All I said was hello! Get bent, Amy," he said.

Alex and Artemis exchanged droll smirks.

"Want to meet for breakfast?" Artemis asked.

Alex hesitated. She intentionally did not make or keep friends. But almost of its own volition her mouth said, "Sure." She gave a little wave and headed to her room, wondering at herself. But it would be fine, this was a safe place to make a sort-of friend, right? It's not like they would stay in touch after she left.

Alex brushed her teeth in the bathroom then stepped into her already darkening room. She eyed the freshly made bed with its thin blue blanket uneasily. Every bone in her body begged for sleep, but she knew tonight was not likely to bring rest. She ached for her cozy New York apartment. To curl up on the sofa that perfectly formed to her body, with a book or a show and a bottle of wine. To be lulled to sleep by the soothing sounds of the city.

She climbed onto the bed and rested her back against the wall, listening to the second hand click softly in the darkness.

The intruders stepped into the darkness, heading toward the laughter in the brightly lit kitchen at the end of a long hallway...

No! Alex's sagging head shot backward, banging into the wall behind her. Her stomach clenched and cold seeped into her limbs.

She'd been right. It was coming.

3

Alex woke to someone screaming as they were dragged down the hallway, echoing the screams in her head. She glanced at the clock and rubbed her gritty eyes against the indigo pre-dawn light. She'd only been dozing for twenty minutes this time. She needed to get out of this room.

Her footsteps felt as heavy as her eyelids as she plodded toward the courtyard. The air outside was cool and dewy and she perked up a little as she shivered. The courtyard was bigger and more well-manicured than she'd noticed before. She exhaled softly at the sight of several bushes of pink wild roses lining the wall, her grandmother's favorite. Alex's heart constricted and she wondered, as she often did, how she continued to survive alone in a world without her. She missed her grandmother's hugs the most, big enveloping squeezes that left no doubt how much she was loved.

She was eight when, in this very hospital, she woke to the sound of her grandmother Adamantia's voice, strong but laden with sorrow as she conveyed the awful news—her daddy was dead of a heart attack. Alex had nodded, her face crumpling. She'd known it was coming for weeks, though her desperate efforts to convince him to see a doctor had fallen on disbelieving ears. Her behavior had become so panicked and erratic he felt he had no choice but to check her into the hospital. Inconsolable, she'd clung to him with all her slight strength before the drugs kicked in, knowing this was goodbye.

Her grandmother had gathered the now sobbing girl in her arms and said she was coming to live with her. Alex's mother had died when she was two, and her father had kept his mother-in-law at arm's length ever since, so she and Alex were not very close. But this move quite likely saved Alex.

Her grandmother, whose very name meant indomitable, was a strong, no-nonsense widow who had never felt comfortable with the intense psychiatric treatment Alex's father had allowed. She immediately took her off all the drugs she'd been prescribed and soon after, Alex felt a clarity and lightness of being she hadn't known for a long time. She was able to focus, and her grandmother, also noticing how Alex had far more of her strange episodes at school than at home, took her out and began homeschooling.

This brought Alex some of the most peaceful years of her life, in their tiny, light-filled apartment, learning and living with her grandmother. She had far fewer visions during this time and clung to the calm of their home, even developing a mild agoraphobia. Adamantia, refusing to let that take hold, began taking her granddaughter on early morning walks around the park, luring her with the promise of ending with hot chocolate and crossword puzzles at the café. It became a ritual they both cherished for years.

Alex was aware how carefully her grandmother watched her. Indeed, it was Adamantia who first connected Alex's episodes primarily to touch, and had given her gloves to wear outside the home. This opened up so much more of the world to her that eventually Alex even dared to think, at her grandmother's urging, of high school and then college. Adamantia kept saying Alex needed find a way to have a career and provide for herself.

It wasn't always easy, though. Some of Alex's episodes were so severe Adamantia had no choice but to take her to the hospital. But by then Alex had long stopped trying to convince anyone of what she saw, and her grandmother was always right there to take her home when she woke.

Adamantia seemed to sense there was a deeper meaning behind the episodes, but even so, Alex couldn't bring herself to confide in her about the visions. She couldn't bear the thought of her grandmother looking at her like she was crazy. Not when she was quite literally her whole world.

Alex sat near the wild roses. It had been eight years since her grandmother's death, stranding her in a wasteland of isolation. Eight years of no meaningful human interactions. Eight years of no hugs. Alex lost herself in a series of muddled, melancholy thoughts.

The morning brightened and eventually her stomach rumbled. She shambled to the cafeteria, got a plate of dubious scrambled eggs, and found Artemis sitting alone pulling apart a single piece of toast. Alex took a deep breath and sat across from her.

Artemis smiled. "I wasn't sure you'd come."

"Me neither. I'm not that great with people," Alex said.

"Yeah, same," Artemis said. "So, what's your name, anyway?"

"Oh, sorry. It's Alex," she said, taking a bite of the rubbery eggs.

"So what do you do when you're not in here, Alex?"

"I'm a mortuary technician."

Artemis stared. "You're joking."

"Nope, I take care of dead bodies all day," Alex said almost cheerily as she took another bite.

"I've never met anyone who did that before." Artemis shivered. "I don't think I could do it. What's it like?"

"It's peaceful," Alex said. "The dead are simple. They are finished with their journey and there's nothing else for them to worry about. It's the ones left behind that need help, and I can do that by taking care of their loved one's body. I like helping people in that small way."

"And the bodies? It doesn't freak you out to be around dead bodies all day?" Artemis asked.

"No. Dying is literally the most natural thing in the world. They don't ever sit up or crawl out of their lockers or anything. I mean, if we have a zombie apocalypse I'm going to be in the wrong place at the wrong time, but I think I'll be okay," she said, smiling a little.

"Ha! Well, yeah…I guess."

"I will say that it's harder when it's kids," Alex continued. "It's hard not to think about the lives they were cut off from."

"God, I can't even imagine. I have a soft spot for kids. Not enough to have them, but still."

"What do you do?" Alex asked, changing the subject. "Great name by the way, probably one of my favorites of the Greek Gods."

Artemis smiled faintly. "Yeah? Thanks." She looked at her toast, now totally pulled apart but only half eaten. "I don't do much, actually. I've tried lots of different things, but nothing ever feels right. I live with my twin brother and I help him when he needs it. He's a geneticist. He's a lot smarter than me. I envy his place in the world."

"I know what you mean. It took me a long time to figure out what to do," Alex said. "I'm sure you will too."

"Well, god knows I've had plenty of time. If I haven't yet, I don't think I ever will."

"You're young," Alex said. "What else do you do then when you're not helping your brother?"

Artemis shrugged again. "I read a lot, watch TV, play video games sometimes, but honestly, that's about it."

"A girl gamer!" Alex exclaimed. "I play too, off and on. When you live alone it really helps to have something addicting to look forward to when you get home."

"I agree," Artemis said. They started comparing games they'd played, both lamenting the twelve-year-old potty mouths who squeed with high-pitched joy when they *pwned* you in online multiplayer campaigns.

"Well, maybe when we're out of here we can play together or something," Alex said. She froze. Why had she said that? She usually went out of her way to *not* make friends.

Artemis didn't bat an eye. "Yes, please. Want to go back outside?" She stood and picked up her tray. "I swear these fluorescent lights suck the life force out of you."

Alex nodded. They headed to the courtyard and on a whim, Alex picked a wild rose to twirl in her fingers while they walked. Her black gloves brought out the rich pink of the soft petals. They were discussing their favorite books when a deep voice interrupted them.

"You can't pick the flowers, give it here." Thomas stepped in front of Alex, a disapproving look on his face.

"Sorry. I won't do it again," she said, her eyes lowered.

Artemis piped in, sounding annoyed. "Dude, just let her have it, there are tons and no one cares."

Thomas turned his attention to Artemis, giving her a slow once-over. "Nobody's talking to you, Skeletor. Rules are rules."

"And you follow all the rules, do you…Thomas?" she asked, looking pointedly at his name tag even though she knew who he was. She crossed her arms and eyed him.

"Look, it's fine, here's your flower." Before Alex could think better of it, she tossed it at his chest and started to walk away. He grabbed her bare upper arm and pulled her around to face him. A vein pulsed in his neck as he poked her forehead with his finger. "No one disrespects me here," he said. His skin felt hot against hers.

A flash of light went off in Alex's eyes. *No!*

A petite, mousy woman running….an abandoned hallway at night…dim lights…stumbling…passing room after room…hiding…thumping footsteps…slowing…terror as a door flew open…gloating…Thomas…come here, you crazy bitch…nowhere to go…strong arms pinning her down… screaming…a blow to her head…sickening sounds…

Alex came around to find Thomas shaking her roughly, a mix of panic and fury on his face, as if she'd done it on purpose just to mess with him.

"Leave her alone, she needs help. I'm going to go get the nurse," Artemis said, sounding worried.

"I'm fine, I'm fine," Alex said. She looked at Thomas with disgust, knowing now the depths of his vileness.

As though sensing it, Thomas shoved her away. "Watch yourself girlie," he growled, stalking off.

Alex sat on the ground, put her head in her hands, and squeezed her eyes shut. *Shit, shit, shit. Breathe in...I'm okay, breathe out...there's nothing I can do. Shit.*

"You're shaking," Artemis said. She knelt in front of Alex, a peculiar look on her face. "Are you okay? Your eyes went all white and you just stopped moving. What happened?"

"Sorry, just give me a minute," Alex muttered. Her heart pounded and her mind whirled through the unspeakable horror the poor woman from her vision was going to face, and soon. Helplessness and anger flooded through her. *This* is why she never went anywhere and kept to herself. No one would believe her if she told, and she realized with frightful certainty the woman had no recourse here in this place, not as a mental patient.

Alex knew well the depths of that despair.

"Are you okay?" Artemis asked.

"Not really."

"Come on, let's get inside," Artemis said. Alex nodded and followed Artemis into the rec room. She was just about to sit when the very same petite, mousy woman she'd just seen swept into the room, dancing to music only she could hear, her dun-colored hair swaying behind her.

Alex's heart sank at seeing her in real life.

Artemis looked at Alex, then at the woman. "Do you know her?"

Alex silently shook her head.

The woman danced away. Alex felt compelled to follow. She slowly approached the woman, wondering if she should talk to her. The woman managed to sway just out of reach until, cornered, she whispered a sharp "Go away!" to Alex without looking at her.

Alex dropped into a nearby chair.

Artemis stared at her in consternation. "Alex, what is happening?"

Alex shook her head again. She couldn't explain it. The weight in her heart added to the weight of her eyelids and she suddenly felt as though she was about to be pulled into a dark, swift current.

"Sorry, I have to go," she said. She left abruptly and headed to her room, feeling Artemis' eyes on her back.

There was no escape. For anyone.

She laid down and curled into a ball, pulling the thin blue blanket over her body.

She fell asleep almost immediately.
And unfortunately, Alex dreamt.

4

The vision replayed crisp and clear in Alex's mind, blurring only slightly at the edges in that soft haziness of dreams.

Ria crept along in the shadows of the dark hallway with Jenna, moving toward the bright light seeping from an open door. The companions moved as one, silent and with deadly purpose. The smell of garlic and parmesan filled the air and they heard the murmur of voices. They stopped instantly as two deep, booming laughs echoed through the penthouse, followed by a woman's shrill giggle.

They turned to each other with concern mirrored in their eyes, the rest of their expressions hidden behind full Venetian masks. Jenna's had blood-red pouty lips and exquisite scrollwork of golds, reds, and blacks swirling around the cheeks and forehead, mirroring the black tattoo on her face beneath.

Ria's own mask was plain in comparison. It had the same lips, but the face was covered only in a harlequin checked pattern in black and cream, each square outlined in gold. Simple though it was, she loved it. When she wore it, the Madness felt more potent, more delicious.

Jenna signed to her, hands flashing in the dim light. "Did you hear that? Three people. That is not part of the plan. Do we continue?"

Ria nodded and signed back. "We do. But let's see what we're dealing with first." She signaled for Jenna to wait and slid silently down the hall, peeking into the kitchen from the shadows. Her eyes widened. She slinked back.

"It is the one we lost track of," she signed. The third man was powerful and dangerous; this could go poorly. But they could not fail the First One.

"Then it will be a challenge. I look forward to it," Jenna signed.

Ria grinned, though Jenna couldn't see it. "We will strengthen ourselves first," she signed. Jenna nodded and took a small flask out of the pack she wore tight against her back. She murmured a prayer and then drank. After a few swallows, she handed it to Ria, who did the same.

Ria closed her eyes, feeling the liquid warm her body. She delved deep into herself, following it down to her inner core, feeling it join the pulsing, undulating ball of black and red fire already in her soul.

The Madness.

She plunged in and savored the tendrils of dark fire spreading into her body, filling it with dark, frenzied energy, feeling free as all caution and reservations fell away. She never felt more alive than in those moments— focused and raw. She opened her eyes. Her vision darkened slightly around the edges but the room itself lightened. She looked over at her companion and saw the same dark light in her eyes and sensed the maniacal grin underneath. A grin she shared.

Together, they crept toward the light.

Ria lifted her hand, halting Jenna just outside the threshold of the kitchen. Waiting for the right moment could mean the difference between success and failure.

They listened in the dark.

"You're incorrigible, Sei. You know that right?" a striking blonde woman asked, slightly slurring her words. Her carefully made-up face a study in cold beauty, she stood with two burly men in a brightly lit kitchen against a white marble island. Bottles littered the top, and the dishes from dinner lay unwashed in the stainless steel sink.

"Are you a little drunk, my love?" the woman's husband asked. "You haven't had near enough to warrant that!" His blue eyes glinted with

humor and his dark bearded face had a look of wonder. He glanced at his brother, a mirror image of himself but with auburn hair.

She laughed. "I think I am! Strange! It usually takes like five bottles to get me even tipsy! But I'll take it," she said, grinning. She took a swig of wine right from the bottle.

"Classy as always, Juno," Sei said, laughing. He took a dainty sip of beer with his pinky lifted. Some of the foam stayed on his thick red beard, ruining the image. He grinned and wiped it off with the back of his hand, his sea-green eyes twinkling. "Juno. So weird to call you that again."

Juno shrugged. "Yeah, but it feels good to use it after all these years. Like I'm somehow, more...me." The men were silent, looking down at their drinks. "Silly, I guess." She took another pass at the bottle.

"Not at all," Sei said quietly. "Names have power. I'm glad for you." After a long minute he turned to his brother. "How's the rest of the family? I haven't really talked to anyone in ages."

Juno rolled her eyes and poured some wine out into a glass. "I think overall they seem pretty good," Z said. "I've seen most of them at least a couple of times this year, except for the usuals, of course." He chugged his stein of beer.

"I don't want to talk about them," Juno said, stamping her foot like a child. They both raised their eyebrows at her.

"He's allowed to ask about the family, Juno," Z said, sounding a little annoyed. "Just because you don't care doesn't mean—"

She grimaced. "I know, I know. You do."

"That's right. I love them, each in their own way. But I love you too. It's not an either/or thing," he said. It seemed like a well-worn argument.

Juno sighed. "I know, I just can't help but feel jealous of them. I never was the mothering type." A look of drunken wonder crossed her face, as though she had just made a monumental discovery about herself.

Sei roared. "That, my dear, is the understatement of the millennium," he said, laughing so hard beer splashed over his glass.

Juno glared at him.

"Sorry, but come on," he said, wiping his eyes. "This family, such as it is, is mostly only connected through this guy here," he said, jerking a thumb at his brother. "And no offense, completely in spite of you."

Juno's lip started trembling. Z looked at her in amazement and pulled her in for a hug. "It's okay, my strangely drunken wife, don't worry. You're always first in my heart." He kissed the top of her head.

"And don't we all know it," Sei mumbled into his beer. His brother looked at him in exasperation. Sei just shrugged.

The room stayed silent for a long minute, until Sei spoke up in a voice a touch too loud. "Well, that was a killjoy! Tell me the latest juicy story from your little revenge company, Juno. What's it called again? The Vengeful Vaginas?" He grinned like a teenage boy.

A devilish sparkle appeared in Juno's eyes. "Har har. You know there's no name. My business is 100% referral based. The last one, though, he was particularly worthy—"

"I know this story, I have to hit the head," Z interrupted, giving her a peck on the cheek.

Juno poured more wine and swirled it around, smiling. "This man was very dangerous. Until I was through with him, of course. He—"

She stopped short when an awful gurgling accompanied the sound of glass shattering on the white marble tile.

A dagger stuck out of Sei's throat. Blood dripped down his neck and his face contorted into shock and pain. The dagger slid out to the side, opening his throat into a horrid ragged half smile.

Ria and Jenna oozed around him and cocked their heads at Juno at the same time.

Juno screamed as Sei collapsed to the ground. She turned to run, pulling stools from under the island into their path. Jenna and Ria jumped over them with ease, moving fast.

Ria caught up to Juno just as she entered the dining hall, clamping down a vise-like grip on her wrist and yanking her off her feet into a body lock. Juno tried to wiggle away but may as well have been encased in cement. Ria moved her hand to her prisoner's throat and squeezed until she passed out on the floor.

The women turned when Z stepped out of a room down the long hallway, holding a silenced gun in each outstretched hand. The intruders looked at each other for a moment, then bent their heads and ran right toward him in a zigzag pattern, almost on all fours, scuttling forward like spiders. He started firing at the now difficult to hit targets, backing up slowly, seeming surprised to be hitting nothing but air. He grunted as Ria ran right into his torso, falling over backward like a sapling hit by a truck. As he fell, Jenna leapt over in a cartwheel and twisted the guns from his strong hands, breaking his wrists as she did.

Pain and confusion collided on his face as he bellowed, the sound cutting short when Ria landed on his chest and knocked the wind out of him. Jenna threw the guns into the other room and laid her forearms on his neck. He squirmed but was unable to shake either of them off. He ultimately passed out with a look of shock on his face.

Jenna checked his pulse and dragged him down the hallway into the dining room. She lifted him into a chair as though he were a doll then bound him to the arms and legs of the chair with zip ties and rope. She pulled him to the foot of the table, his head dangling. They lifted the unconscious Juno to the dining table and tied her spread-eagled to the legs of the table.

Ria verified Sei still lay on the kitchen floor and stalked back into the dining hall. She was not surprised to see another masked person standing over the table staring at Juno. The newcomer wore a luxurious red velvet cloak with a long hood down the back and a resplendent Venetian mask of black and white, divided by a gold line that sourced from a diamond at the crown down through the golden half-smiling lips. Gold and silver scrollwork danced around the eyes and cheeks.

Ria and Jenna knelt.

"You have done well," the figure said in a low voice.

Ria bowed her head, a thrill shooting through her body. "Thank you, First One," she breathed.

The First One turned to the captives. "Now wake them up."

Ria retrieved two glasses of water from the kitchen and threw one in each of their faces. Both spluttered and groaned, waking up groggily.

The First One grabbed Z's hair and pulled his head up. He looked up with bleary eyes and a furrowed brow. "What—" he began to ask.

"Silence. You are here to witness, not to talk. I want you to see everything that happens here and know you both brought this on yourselves."

The First One gestured to Juno, who squirmed and whimpered on the table.

"Please—" he said.

"Stop his mouth," the First One interrupted. Jenna grabbed a cloth napkin and shoved it into his mouth, duct taping it in place.

The First One moved to Juno's head and hovered over her.

Juno whimpered. "Please don't do this. Why are you doing this? Who are you?"

The First One dragged a long, bejeweled finger down Juno's cheek and neck. "The symmetry of this moment is more perfect than I could ever have hoped for. Your incessant jealous wrath is the very thing that created the beautiful monster you see before you. You have caused much pain and anguish in your long life. It is past time you reaped the evil you have sown into the world. And your husband is going to stand by and watch, as he always has."

"But I haven't—" Juno started. The First One slapped her hard across the face, drawing blood from her lip. There was a muffled yell behind her as Z cried out in anger.

"The time for words has long passed. You will die tonight, as painfully as we have lived." Juno's eyes widened and she started to tremble. The First One leaned over and whispered in Juno's ear, her voice syrupy with delight. "Lest you retain any hope, you should also know that you, my dear, are mortal, and have been for some time. Haven't you noticed a slight slowing down? An unfamiliar fatigue?" Fear and confusion warred on Juno's face. "I have been on my way to you for some time, and my ultimate gift to you will indeed be oblivion. But until then...this is going to hurt."

She stood and nodded to Ria, who shoved a napkin into Juno's mouth as well. Then Ria and Jenna positioned themselves at her arms. The First One glided backward, giving them room but remaining in complete view of the captive's face. The women each grabbed one of Juno's forefingers. Juno looked back and forth between the women in a panic. Two small popping sounds filled the room, followed by the sickening sound of tearing flesh.

Juno's muffled scream reverberated in the room.

The screams lasted for hours.

In the end, Z's strangled sobs were the only sound left in a room smelling of copper and viscera. Ria and Jenna were covered in blood, noticeable even on their black clothing. Certainly evident on the white of their masks.

"It is done," the First One said with satisfaction.

A clinking sound came from the kitchen. All the heads in the room snapped toward the doorway.

"Go," the First One said.

Ria was already moving, Jenna on her heels. They crept into the kitchen, silently moving to the area between the sink and the island.

There was nothing but broken glass and blood. The women looked at each other, flashed a few hand signs, and fanned out to search for the red-headed man.

Ria slowly headed down the hallway as Jenna moved off into an adjoining living room. She prowled slowly, letting her eyes re-adjust to the darkness, her whole body taut. She slipped through the first open doorway into an office. Its expansive bay windows were lit by the lights of the city's skyscrapers and it had walls of bookshelves, and a desk with a computer. She crept back toward the doorway after a quick search revealed nothing.

She didn't notice one of the bookshelves opening like a door behind her until it was too late. The enormous man barreled into her, carrying both of them across the room. They landed with a thud and her head hit hard on the corner of the desk. The room swam and she felt blood trickle down the back of her neck. Then a sudden crushing weight took her breath away as Sei pulled her arms across her chest and pinned her down with his knees. He leaned over her, propped up by arms like tree trunks after a lifetime of solitary sailing. He pulled a yellow diving knife out of his pocket and held it to her throat.

"Who are you?" he growled.

He went to cut the straps of her mask with his knife when she called on the Madness within, gathering its strength. She bucked him off and sweet air filled her lungs. She swiped at him with a dagger she pulled from a thigh sheath. He moved with a speed belying his bulk and dodged her attack, rolling away from her. She got up but swayed slightly and Sei kicked her legs out from under her. She fell on her face and he immediately sat on her back with his knees along her sides. He pulled her head back and put the knife to her throat. "Last chance, lady, who are you and what do you want with us?"

Then Jenna was there.

She leapt onto his back and wrapped her legs around his chest. She began to squeeze.

Sei's knife struck as he leaned back and Ria watched in disbelief as her life's blood began to spout onto the carpet in a stuttering stream.

"No!" Jenna yelled, loosening for a moment. Sei threw himself backward, landing his sizable torso onto her much smaller one, successfully knocking the breath out of her. Ria crawled forward and propped herself up against a bookshelf, using her hands to stem the flow of blood, willing her friend to end the man quickly so she could be saved.

Ria watched Jenna catch her breath and use Sei's reflexive move to her advantage, snaking her arms around his neck like two black pythons.

She began to squeeze again.

Anger and concern flashed on his face as he tried to pry her freakishly strong arms away and couldn't. He got to his knees and lumbered to his feet, a misguided move that allowed her to also wrap her legs around him. He fought for breath as he threw himself backward into a bookshelf. He was rewarded only with a grunt from Jenna, her arms and legs did not budge. He tried again and again but each time with flagging energy.

Eventually he sank to his knees and fell forward onto the carpet. Jenna waited several moments before releasing, then stood up and rolled him onto his back with her feet. She turned to tend to Ria. Ria whispered two final words as her head dropped to her chest. "Finish it."

A frenzied scream erupted from Jenna. She turned to Sei and kicked him hard, his ribs crunching beneath her foot. He stirred so she quickly sat behind his head and gripped his jaw with her fingertips while positioning her feet on his shoulders.

She pulled.

His body started to writhe, but she maintained her grip. Her arms and legs strained until there was a loud snap. The man's body went limp.

She kept pulling.

The Madness shone bright in her eyes as she tore his head off with her hands.

5

The muted morning sun strained its way into Alex's room, its sickly light guiding her out of several levels of darkness. She must have slept through the rest of yesterday and through the night. She trembled as she pressed the heels of her palms into her eyes trying to force the bloody red tide in her mind to recede. She began her mantra. *Breathe in...I'm okay...breath out...there's nothing I can do.*

She shook her head. Besides being the most horrendous thing she'd ever seen, there was little in this vision that made sense.

It doesn't matter. Not my problem. Breathe in...I'm okay...breath out...there's nothing I can do. Breathe in...I'm okay...breath out...there's nothing I can do.

Her grandmother, knowing only for certain her granddaughter was often scared and upset, gave Alex her mantra after a particularly rough episode, where unbeknownst to her, Alex had just seen the life-ending fate of one of the regulars from the café—an older gentlemen who always smiled kindly and gave her the comics section of his newspaper. Her grandmother of course hadn't known *why* Alex was so upset, only that she had just had one of her episodes, and her granddaughter hated having episodes. So while intending to have the mantra represent a kind of radical acceptance, she had stumbled onto the perfect double meaning for Alex, a little girl who had visions of things she couldn't really change.

She repeated it until the words drowned out the vision, pulled on her gloves, then slipped out to a far corner of the courtyard, hoping to avoid Artemis after yesterday's embarrassing events. *So much for seeming 'comparatively normal'.* Her stomach clenched as thoughts of the poor mousy woman and her impending assault suddenly took all her focus. Should she say something? How could she make something change when she couldn't tell anyone what she'd seen?

She was mid-thought when Artemis perched next to her on the bench, sitting as though she could take flight any moment. "Morning. You okay?" she asked. "You slept a long time."

"Yeah," Alex said wearily. "Look, I'd understand if all the crazy from yesterday was too much."

"Ha. That wasn't so crazy. I mean, strange, yes, but it takes more than strange to scare me."

Alex smiled faintly.

"Are you feeling better though?" Artemis asked.

Alex wasn't about to talk about it. "Not really."

Artemis' sleeve fell back as she pulled her hair into a bun, giving Alex a glimpse of her tattoo again. "That's stunning," Alex said, tilting her head to try to see it better.

Artemis laid her arm in front of her, displaying the design. "Thanks," she said, running her fingers over it. It was as though a forested, moonlit sky had settled onto a long arrow that filled the length of her forearm. At the top, near the crook of her arm, narrow, tapered feathers gathered as fletching, and the tip of the arrow ended in a layered triangle design just above her wrist. Along the shaft, small black crescents and circles bracketed a small sunburst, leading the way to a large, brilliant white crescent moon nestled in a graceful burst of leaves. The ink was a rich black, and the moon was a shimmery white. It looked as though she'd just had it done.

"I've had it a very long time." She gave Alex a dejected smile as she covered it again. "It's one of the few things I like about myself." Then she took an abrupt, unanticipated tack. "So, I've been thinking. Something about yesterday feels familiar. I know it's none of my business, but can I ask you a question?"

Alex steeled herself. "I might not be able to answer you, but sure."

"Well, is something going to happen to that woman? The one you tried to talk to last night?"

Alex froze.

No one had ever, in all her life, asked such a direct and specific question about a vision. She played with the fingers of her gloves as she dithered. What could it hurt to answer? It was a yes/no question. She wouldn't have to talk about anything she'd seen in the vision. If it triggered the curse, she was no worse off than she was now. If it didn't trigger…*then you can continue to look deranged and perhaps lose the first friendship you've had in years.*

Finally, uncertainly, Alex nodded.

"I knew it," Artemis whispered, her eyes gleaming.

Alex watched her face carefully for the telltale signs of disbelief, but saw only triumph. "How did you know?" she asked, cautiously.

"Let's just say I'm really good at following signs and trails," Artemis said. "What's going to happen? Let me guess, it has something to do with that asshole Thomas."

Alex nodded slowly, wide-eyed. *What. Is. Happening.*

"Okay, tell me everything," Artemis said.

"I can't," Alex said, looking down at her hands.

"Can't or won't?" Artemis asked gently.

"Well, do you believe me?"

"About the woman?"

Alex nodded.

"I think so. Yes," Artemis said.

Alex hid the small thrill that shot through her entire body. "Do you want to continue to believe me?"

Artemis looked confused but nodded.

"Then I *can't*," Alex said. She looked her friend in the eye, trying to convey everything with just the one word.

Artemis' expression turned thoughtful. "Okay. I don't understand, but I can roll with that," she said. "You seem to be able to answer questions though, yes?"

Alex gestured with incredulity. "Apparently."

"Okay, cool," Artemis said with a smile which faded quickly. "Is he going to hurt her?"

Alex winced and nodded.

"God, fuck him and the horse he rode in on," Artemis murmured, clenching her fists.

"Exactly," Alex said. "I was thinking of saying something, maybe to Nurse Parry, but I don't know yet."

Artemis grimaced. "Are you sure that's a good idea? Is it wise to get involved?"

"I don't know," Alex said. "I've been trying to think of the best way to try to help without getting pulled in myself."

"Will it make a difference?" Artemis asked, one eyebrow raised.

"I don't know that either," Alex said quietly.

Artemis looked at her for a moment. "It makes a difference to you though, doesn't it?"

"Yeah," Alex said. "It's not often I have the chance to try to help. I feel like I have to at least try. That poor woman."

"You're a better person than I am," Artemis said softly.

Alex didn't know how to respond to that.

"Alright, then I want to help too," Artemis said.

Alex's spirits rose as they worked together on what she could say. Against her better judgment, a glimmering seed of hope buried itself in her heart. She tried to ignore it.

This alliance, this friendship, could change at any moment.

But for now—for once—she wasn't alone.

6

Alex closed the door to Nurse Parry's office behind her and exhaled. It was done. The head nurse had looked skeptical until Alex mentioned Thomas' name, then she'd downright scowled.

Artemis rushed up to Alex when she walked into the rec room. "How did it go?"

Alex gestured to the outside door. They walked into a bright afternoon. The sun-kissed the autumnal trees, their green leaves just starting their glorious and colorful quietus.

"It's hard to tell. But I told her just what we planned, that I overheard Thomas tell another orderly that the woman was a good lay. She said she'd look into it."

Artemis grinned. "Good!"

Alex sighed. "I'm still shaking. She told me her name was Mary. The mousy woman. Somehow it's worse to know her name."

"You did what you could," Artemis said.

Alex nodded, but it didn't feel like enough. "I guess. I don't know, there's not a lot of time between now and tonight."

"Tonight?" Artemis asked, alarmed.

Alex nodded. She knew the way she always did, in her bones. As though her visions somehow connected her with time itself.

"Damn. Well, maybe I should say something too, it could escalate things," Artemis said.

"I think that might look a little suspicious given how much time we've spent together," Alex said.

"Yeah, probably. You can't tell if it worked?"

Alex shook her head. "No, it doesn't work like that."

"How *does* it work?" Artemis asked, a touch too casually.

Just then Thomas came into the courtyard pushing a patient in a wheelchair, looking bored. "Ew, there he is," Alex said, wrinkling her nose and neatly avoiding Artemis' question.

"Bleh. I just want to beat the hell out of him," Artemis said.

"Me too." Just the sight of him made her nauseated. Alex modified her mantra to try to settle her feelings. *Breathe in...I'm okay...breathe out...and I tried.*

They were about to go inside when they saw another orderly beeline to Thomas. He spoke and gestured to the building. Thomas looked confused but turned the wheelchair over to him and headed inside.

The two women looked at each other hopefully. Artemis' smile even reached her eyes.

They spent the rest of the day hanging out in the rec room and the cafeteria, talking or sitting in companionable silence. Alex often didn't know what to say. The skills required for friendship were still creaking back to life after years of disuse. But the air between them felt comfortable, and Alex felt grateful for the time with her.

They agreed to meet for breakfast in the morning and said goodnight. There had been no sign of Thomas the rest of the day, which seemed like a good sign. Even with the new mantra Alex hadn't quite been able to shake her apprehension. What she saw in her visions usually did end up happening after all.

But not always. She'd come to think of fate like a river, flowing down a riverbed shaped by countless actions, reactions, and inactions, all converging at once. Alex could glimpse its path, but a right-sized pebble in the right place could shift its direction, or just be lost in the torrent. It was impossible to know.

She lay still in her bed as anxious thoughts returned again and again to Mary. Was the woman about to have a peaceful night's sleep, or one of the worst nights of her life?

Alex hoped her pebble had been enough.

Breathe in…I'm okay…breathe out…and I tried.

The mantra guided Alex into a calm, dreamless slumber.

Alex stirred in the middle of the night, unsure what had woken her. She sat up at the sound of footsteps in the hallway, her heart beginning to race. The footsteps slowed as they neared her door, then kept moving, the sound fading into the night. She let herself fall back to her bed with a loud exhale, chiding herself for being paranoid.

She curled on her side and stared into the darkness, waiting for sleep to claim her again. The shadows felt heavy, as though they had swallowed something menacing and ominous. She leaned up on her elbow and squinted into the corner.

The shadows suddenly coalesced into a large, dark figure, and a strong, hairy arm pinned her down and a rag soaked in a strong, sickly sweet liquid covered her mouth and nose. "You got me suspended without pay, you little bitch," Thomas whispered in her ear.

Alex's smothered scream melted into a world already beginning to swim. He hissed as she tore at his arm with her nails.

The last thing she heard as her vision went black was her heart beating wildly in her ears.

7

Artemis lay awake in bed, her chronic insomnia in full swing. She glanced at the clock and sighed; it was three o'clock in the morning. She got up to pace, hoping some physical exertion would help convince her body it was time to sleep.

But it was her mind that was restless.

It was mostly sheer curiosity that had first drawn her to Alex—a seemingly normal girl in an abnormal place, wearing strange, arm-length gloves. But she quickly realized there was something else about her that she liked. It wasn't confidence, really, given how anxious Alex seemed. It was more like a strong sense of character, like Alex knew who she was. Artemis wasn't sure she could say the same.

But she could sense that Alex was changing things for her. She couldn't quite put her finger on it, but she could feel it. How long since she'd had an honest-to-god friend? She couldn't even remember. It seemed she and Alex were similar in so many ways, not the least in the distance they kept from the world—Alex with her gloves, Artemis through her eating disorder, anxiety, and depression. She wondered if things would have been different if she'd actually been forced to care for herself, like Alex had. Get a job, buy food, get a place. She'd depended on her brother for so much. She wondered, not for the first time, if that was part of her problem.

Her feet quickened their pace as her thoughts turned to the whole situation with that woman, Mary. Seeing Alex go into that trance had shocked Artemis to her core. Those eyes. They had danced at the edge of her memory, pulling thoughts of her previous life out of their dismal depths. A life she didn't particularly like thinking about. But…if she was right about Alex, the others were going to freak out. She smiled in anticipation.

Artemis sat on the edge of the bed. Plus, she also had to admit, it had felt good to think about someone other than herself. To try to help someone. Alex had made that happen. She thought of Alex's face, determined to at least try to help. Refusing to sit idly by.

It had been galvanizing. She liked how she felt around Alex. Plus, the thought of that asshole Thomas being booted out of the building was extremely satisfying. Alex hadn't seemed as certain, but Artemis felt sure they'd changed Mary's fate.

Artemis stopped mid-thought and surged to her feet. *Why not go check?* she thought. She threw on her clothes and crept out the door. She headed to Mary's hallway via the rec room, neatly avoiding the nurses' desk. She peeked in every door's window until she found Mary's room.

There she was, peacefully asleep in her bed, surrounded by walls of faded paper roses.

Artemis felt a thrill.

It worked! she thought. If Mary was going to be in trouble tonight, it seemed like it would be happening now, or if it had already happened, Mary would not likely be sleeping so soundly.

She had to tell Alex the good news, middle of the night or not. She snuck down the hall, knocked quietly on the door, then peeked into the window.

She gasped at the sight of Alex's empty bed with its covers in disarray. Fear sparked throughout her as she ran to check the bathroom. It was empty.

Alex was gone.

8

Alex's head throbbed as it swayed in the air. She opened her eyes to see the white of a t-shirt. The fog in her mind was still thick, and it took a long moment to realize the sharp thing digging into her stomach was bone. Thomas had her over his shoulder like a sack of laundry. She turned her head and even upside-down she recognized the abandoned hallway with its dusty equipment and hanging plastic sheets.

Panic eddied the fog.

His gruff voice startled her. "I can tell you're awake. Not that you'll be able to, but don't try anything funny or I'll break your neck and say you threw yourself down the stairs. Got it?"

Alex mumbled an affirmative, her head clearing to the klaxon of fear clanging in her chest. Thomas pushed a door open and turned on a dim overhead light, revealing a windowless room with a dingy bed pushed into the corner. There were metal restraints hung off the bedframe.

It smelled of bleach and blood and fear.

He tossed her onto the bed, causing the restraints to clink against each other ominously. Alex squirmed on the filthy sheet and sat up back against the wall, pulling her knees up.

"Look, I'm sorry for—"

Her vision swam as the mighty slap she'd been dealt rang in her ears. She felt a trickle of blood flow from her split bottom lip.

"I don't bring you crazy bitches here to talk."

Handling her with ease, he forced her struggling body straight so it was more parallel with the bed. Sharp pain ran up her arms as he put her wrists in the restraints, pinching the tender skin of her wrists along with the silk fabric of her gloves. She tried to kick, but he just grabbed her feet together like she was a pig, holding one leg while restraining the other until she was fully shackled on the bed.

"To be honest, you're a bit sane for my tastes, but since you seem to care so much, you get to take the other one's place. Then tomorrow you'll tell Nurse Parry you were lying about what you said."

It was evident he was already getting off on this. Thomas pulled his t-shirt off, revealing a thick hairy chest. He moved toward her and Alex could smell sweat and chewing tobacco as he pulled out a large pocket knife. Something clicked and she finally started to scream.

"No one can hear you in this abandoned section, missy. Scream all you want, I kind of like it."

Alex bit her cheek to stop the sound. Thomas flipped the knife open, drawing the blade across her stomach until he got to the end of her hospital shirt. He turned the sharp edge to it and cut up all the way to her neck, pulling it open to expose her heaving torso. He teased the knife back down her chest and began to cut her bra the same way.

"Hey asshole," a smooth alto voice interrupted.

Thomas spun around at the same time a strange *thwip* sound echoed in the room. Blood sprayed on Alex's face as a metal point materialized in the middle of Thomas' back. Thomas slowly sank to his knees. A dreadful gurgling sound emanated from his mouth as he toppled over and out of sight. Alex looked in confusion toward the door.

What she saw did not particularly help clarify things.

Artemis stood in the doorway, steadily lowering a large silver bow as she calmly watched Thomas the orderly die on the ground.

9

Alex watched in bewilderment as Artemis rushed in to free her of the atrocious bed, stepping over Thomas' body like he was a crack in the sidewalk. Alex felt as though her blood was turning to lead as the adrenaline seeped out of her. Even the air felt heavy and thick.

"Let's get you back to your room," Artemis murmured. She put Alex's arm over her shoulder to support her weight. Alex nodded and together they stepped around the body and headed into the corridor. Her thoughts were a jumble. How could Artemis feel so solid when she was so thin? And where did her bow go? Artemis *had* had a bow, right?

Nothing seemed real.

That arrow had been real though. The thought of its steel tip cut through her confusion. She stopped walking. "What about…?"

Artemis shook her head, her hair falling in front of her face. She pulled Alex forward. "Don't worry, I'll take care of it."

They were silent the rest of the long walk through the dilapidated old wing of the hospital, somehow managing to get back to Alex's room unseen. Artemis sat Alex on the bed then ran for a fresh shirt and wet towel.

"Let's get this off you." She gently wiped the blood from Alex's face.

Alex just stared at the floor.

"I'm so sorry," Artemis said as she cleaned. "I couldn't sleep so I thought I'd check on Mary. When I saw she was sleeping soundly I came to tell you so we could celebrate. But then, *you* weren't in your room. I knew something was up. It took me a bit to find you, but I followed the blood from that rake you gave him on his arm. I'm glad I got there when I did."

"Me too. Thanks," Alex mumbled.

Artemis nodded. "Try to get some rest now. I'll come check on you in the morning." She slipped out of the room.

But Alex couldn't sleep. Her body was heavy, but her thoughts careened in her head.

Surely someone would burst in any minute to demand answers. Or her new friend turned rescuer turned murderer would come in and demand her silence. Or make her help chop up the body.

Thomas' leering face began to punctuate each thought. She could still feel his cold knife on her stomach.

She tried to say her mantra. *Breathe in, I'm okay...* but stopped short.

It wasn't true this time.

She wished she had the energy to sob.

Alex woke to the sound of a voice in the hallway calling everyone to lunch. The events of the night before flooded back and she buried her head in the pillow. She must have finally slept out of sheer exhaustion. But lunchtime? How was it no one had woken her? Artemis must have woven some magic and had everyone stay out.

Artemis.

A vein of fear pulsed when she thought of her friend, but she couldn't pin down why. She'd saved her, after all. But she'd also killed someone. With a bow and arrow.

And there was a dead body out there, tied to both of them.

So there was that.

Alex lay in bed until she couldn't take the swirling thoughts anymore. She got up and meandered down the hallway, peeking into the cafeteria and the rec room.

No Artemis.

She approached a nurse who was tidying the game area. "Hi, can you tell me where Artemis' room is?"

"Artemis was discharged earlier this morning," she said with a smile as she walked away.

Alex sat down with a thump into one of the old chairs nearby. *What the hell?* Emotion swirled in her like a maelstrom, propelling her right back out of the chair. Every step brought a new thought. *What does that mean? Why would she leave without saying anything? Is she taking care of our man-sized problem? Does she regret doing it? Is she okay? What is happening!* she screamed in her head.

Just then, Mary swayed into the room. Alex's inner turmoil quieted with a whomp. She stared in wonder, a warm tingle rushing through her body.

Mary.

Mary was okay. And Alex had made that happen. Well, *she and Artemis* had made that happen. The thought opened up in her like a flower blooming in the sun. Her mind involuntarily flicked through the faces she'd tried and failed to help in the past. She brushed them aside and watched Mary peacefully dance across the room.

Not this time.

This time, even though it had gone in a terrible direction, it had worked. Her little pebble had changed Mary's fate. The thought helped soothe the ragged edges of her heart. She took a breath. *Ok Alex, just get through your last day here.* There was literally nothing she could do about the body or Artemis' sudden exit. She headed toward the nurses' desk to ask about her discharge time.

Alex was almost there when she overheard Thomas' name. Her heart jumped into her throat and she scurried to follow pink-haired Amy and another nurse as they walked the opposite direction down the long hallway.

"The creep get in trouble with management again?" Amy asked.

"Ha, good guess. Yes, but no. He's dead! Can you believe it?" the other nurse said.

"Really? Couldn't have happened to a better…"

"You're terrible!"

"I know. Do you know how he died?"

"Some freak accident in his apartment building or something. He fell down the stairs and was impaled on a broken piece of railing."

Amy gasped and covered her mouth. "Impaled? That can happen in real life? Jesus." She shrugged. "Well, that's a shitty way to die I guess, but I think I'm not wrong to say no one here will miss him."

"Amy!" the first nurse laughed and pushed her playfully.

Alex had already stopped dead in her tracks, staring at their backs as they continued on. A small part of her felt like she was going crazy, but the memory of blood on her face helped ground her in reality.

Last night had definitely happened. But how on earth had Artemis managed that?

Alex decided she didn't care how. Relief swept through her like a wave. Nothing was going to come back onto them.

"Alex!" Nurse Parry called from down the hallway. "It's time for your discharge appointment with Doctor Wilcox."

Alex smiled. She was going home.

10

I t was early evening by the time Alex finally arrived at her apartment. She closed the door behind her and breathed in the sweet, musty air, letting the dark blue walls and rows of white bookshelves envelop her in safety and comfort.

Home.

She stepped over a pile of mail on the floor and shed her clothes as she headed right to the shower. She needed to wash Thomas' hands and the entire hospital off her body. She scrubbed everything hard, twice, all while giving thanks for private showers, good soap, and steaming hot water.

She put her wet hair in a bun and dressed in her comfiest pair of palazzo pants and softest t-shirt, which felt positively luxurious compared to the hospital-issue clothes.

Her stomach growled. She needed—no, *deserved*—some New York pepperoni pizza. The door was still closing on the delivery man when she threw open the box and devoured a slice. It tasted like sweet, piping hot freedom. She paired it with a generous glass of Cabernet and sighed in contentment as she turned on a show. It wasn't long before her eyelids began to droop, her weary body sated and safe.

The sound of her phone vibrating on the coffee table pulled her to disgruntled consciousness. She was bewildered to see dozens of missed text messages and calls from an unknown number. Her phone had never seen so much action. They were all variations on a theme.

This is Artemis. Need to talk, can I come see you? It's important. Please. The final message read, *I know it's early, but I'm coming over. Please don't be mad.* Alex checked the timestamp - 4:32 am.

Five minutes ago.

A pit formed in Alex's stomach as she thought through the myriad of reasons Artemis could need to talk. But just as concerning, how did Artemis have her number? Or know where she lived?

Alex jumped at the sound of a loud knock on the door. She checked the peephole to see Artemis waving. She hesitated, reluctant to let Artemis—and whatever she was bringing with her—into her sanctuary. *But…she's a friend, right? Plus, I owe her.*

Artemis spoke through the doorway. "Alex, I'm sorry to just show up like this, but please let me in. I need your help."

This is probably a huge mistake, Alex thought. She opened the door.

"Hi," Artemis said as she strode in, wearing a form-fitting all-black outfit. "Sorry to just show up like this."

"Is everything okay?" Alex asked.

"No." Artemis spied the half-drunk bottle of wine on the coffee table. "May I?"

Alex nodded. Artemis swigged several large gulps right from the bottle.

"What's wrong? Are we in trouble for Thomas?" Alex asked.

Artemis shook her head as she wiped her mouth. "No. We don't have to worry about him."

"Oh good. I heard he took a fall and impaled himself. How on earth…?" Alex asked.

A ghost of a smile crossed Artemis' lips. "Long story."

Alex was happy to leave that a mystery. "Great. I was worried when you left without saying anything."

Artemis nodded. "Yeah, sorry about that. Something came up."

"How did you know where I live?" Alex asked.

"Another long story," Artemis said.

Right, Alex thought. She waited as the moment of silence lengthened.

"Do you have family?" Artemis said finally, her gaze soft in front of her.

"No," Alex said. "My mom died when I was a baby and my dad when I was eight, so I was raised by my grandmother. She died years ago."

"I'm sorry," Artemis said. "No aunts or uncles?"

Alex shook her head. Her parents were both only children. "Why?"

Artemis sank to the couch and stared at the floor. "I have a big family. We're not close, most of us. There are little groups that are, but mostly there's a lot of antagonism and we're not exactly the talk-it-out types. But everyone loved my uncle, even my harpy of a stepmother. He had a sonic boom of a laugh and it came easily. He sailed around the world on a massive boat and had the best stories. He's the only one in the family who never once made me feel like a disappointment." Her voice caught. She cleared her throat and chugged the last of the wine. It was then Alex noticed her red-rimmed eyes.

"What happened, Artemis?" Alex said softly.

"He's dead. Murdered. I still can't believe it, even though I saw it with my own eyes." Artemis spoke woodenly, her face completely devoid of emotion.

Alex gasped. "Oh! How awful, I'm so sorry!"

"It's why I left the hospital so fast. My stepmother was murdered too, and her death was particularly horrific. We think she was the target. Maybe he just got in the way. I don't know."

"Jesus, this is terrible!"

"It is totally surreal. But it's why I'm here. My brother found the bodies but there's no trace of my father. He's missing. I was hoping you could help me find him and whoever did this."

"Me?" Alex asked, her eyes bugging out. "What can *I* do?"

Artemis looked Alex right in the eyes. A piercing gaze, as though she could see right through her.

Alex started to fidget, feeling a little like a mouse again.

Artemis sighed. "I can understand why you wouldn't want to tell me. I've been trying to figure out the best way to go about this, but I think I'll just be direct. Rip off the Band-Aid."

Alex just waited, totally bewildered.

"Look, I know you're an Oracle," Artemis said.

A shiver ran from the top of Alex's head down to her toes. "A *what?*" she asked. But in the back of her head the word was already bouncing around, knocking the pieces of her life's puzzle into a semblance of order for the first time.

She pointed to all of Alex's books. "Have you read much Greek mythology?"

"A little, I always loved the myths, but I only know the most common stories."

"Oracles had the gift of prophecy. Do you know what that means?"

"They could see the future."

Artemis nodded. "And the past."

Alex's mind chugged to process the words. *Oracle. Prophecy.* Her heart pounded.

"You have all the signs. You *are* an Oracle, aren't you?" Artemis' voice was hopeful.

Alex froze. Every part of her was screaming not to answer. Talking about the curse only ever rewarded her with suffering. So she'd kept it quiet for two decades. Even her therapist thought she only had severe night terrors and OCD.

But now she had a label to cling to. She kept her face neutral while keeping a stranglehold on the wild snake of panic wriggling in her. She wished her gloves weren't lying on the floor of her bedroom.

"I have no idea what I am." She hesitated—there was no turning back after this. "But yeah, I see things," she said finally.

Relief flooded Artemis' face. She smiled, her eyes alight. "Amazing. What do you see? The future? The past?"

"Um, well, I guess I've seen both."

Artemis nodded. "Is it triggered by touch?" She gestured to Alex's bare hands.

"Usually. But not always." Alex took a couple of deep breaths, then, as though she'd been uncorked, words tumbled out of her of their own volition. "Sometimes it just happens when I'm near a big looming event. It just depends…but on what, I haven't ever figured out. I have zero control. It has made my life a living, solitary hell. I've been in and out of hospitals, had electric-shock therapy, been on all kinds of psych meds, and that's *after* having to constantly witness terrible, horrible things happening to people. It's a curse." Alex's voice thickened. Speaking the thing aloud had cut the suture of a wide and bitter wound.

Artemis' smile disappeared. "I'm so sorry," she said. "I can't even imagine. Frankly, it's incredible you're as normal as you are."

A small salve. "Thanks," Alex mumbled.

Artemis pressed on. "How have you gone unnoticed this whole time, though? Surely someone must have realized the things you talked about would actually happen."

Alex cleared her throat. "Well, that's the worst part," she said. "No one ever believes me. No matter what I do or say, or write. They don't even remember what I said. I can actually see it happen in their faces, like it's literally being wiped it out of their minds. It's unnatural. I was serious when I said it's a curse." She sank into a chair, her entire body trembling. The snake was gone, the panic it generated replaced with released nervous energy and not a little bit of wonder.

Artemis frowned. "Hmmm. That sounds so familiar..." She thought for a moment, then shrugged it off. "My brother will know, we'll ask him. Come to think of it, he might even be able to help you."

"Your twin? The geneticist?" Alex asked. "How could he possibly...?"

"Long story," Artemis said.

Alex sighed quietly. Artemis had a lot of long stories.

"So will you help me?" Artemis asked. "We could really use someone of your...talents, even if they're imperfect."

Alex looked at her friend's pleading face. The friend who had literally saved her life. She thought of her small, lonely, boring life full of books, TV, and dead people.

"Okay. I'll try," she said.

"Thank you," Artemis breathed, relief clear in her face.

Things moved quickly then. Alex went to her room to pack. She looked longingly at the bed she had yet to sleep in. But there was an electricity in her body she'd never felt before, exhilarating and stirring. She threw on some clothes, a touch of mascara, and ran her fingers through her hair, trying to tame the waves.

Artemis came in already talking on the phone. "Hey, it's me. I'm ready for pickup, and there'll be two of us." She paused. "I know, I know. Yes I do, or I wouldn't be doing it. Jesus, just get here, please."

She rolled her eyes as she hung up. "He'll be here in ten minutes."

"Who's he?"

"My other brother," Artemis said.

How many brothers does she have? Alex wondered as she stuffed some toiletries in her bag. "Okay I'm ready. Where are we going anyway?" she asked.

"Not too far," Artemis said cryptically.

Alex did a quick lap to tidy and ensure mold wouldn't take over while she was gone, when her mind finally snagged on a rather major detail.

She turned to Artemis, who was leaning on the back of the couch, seemingly deep in thought. "Wait. Artemis, how did you know that about me? And about Oracles?"

Artemis gave her a half smile. "I wondered when you'd ask that. I was literally just thinking I'd better get it all out before my brother gets here." She held out her left arm as if to put her tattoo on display. She took a deep breath, cupped her left hand as though already holding something, then twisted her wrist in two short circles, one clockwise, one counter-clockwise. Her tattoo gleamed briefly and suddenly she *was* holding something—a large, magnificent burnished silver bow, already nocked with a silver arrow fletched with white feathers.

Alex gasped.

"I've had a lot of names over the years. At some point I quit caring and went back to my given name, Artemis. The Romans called me Diana.

"I was their Goddess of the Hunt."

II

Though this be madness, yet there is a method in 't.

—William Shakespeare

11

Alex stared slack-jawed at Artemis as she held the materialized silver bow.

"I know, I know," Artemis said. "You have your visions though. I was hoping it might not be too far a stretch to—"

"Meet an immortal god? Goddess? Whatever?" Alex interrupted. "It's a stretch."

"Well, we're not gods anymore," Artemis said. She flicked her wrist and the bow disappeared. "We call it The Fall. It happened slowly, at the height of the Roman Empire, when we were at our most powerful. We were arrogant and ignored a seemingly insignificant little grass roots religion until it was too late. The short of it is once people stopped worshipping us, we stopped being gods. But apparently, and to our surprise, our immortality was not linked to our godhood. My brother has theories about how it's actually the reverse, but I don't really get into all that."

"But..." Alex said in a flat, dubious voice, "...you have a bow and arrow that appear out of thin air."

"Yeah, some things we created survived with us. We call them relics. Objects we intentionally created to stand on their own, without our sustained power. So they didn't disappear during The Fall. But there aren't many. They took a small effort, and we were careless and nothing if not lazy." She flicked her wrist and her bow appeared again. She stroked the long, supple limb. "I only have the one. I used to spend weeks in the forests, sleeping under the stars, hunting and tracking by moonlight with the animals. I always wanted her with me, so I created this little carrying case for her." She gestured to her tattoo with its crescents. Alex was reminded that in Greek mythology Artemis was also goddess of the moon.

"She doesn't come out much. If someone sees her these days, it's usually the *last* thing they see." Artemis' smile turned wolfish and her eyes gleamed for a moment. Alex squirmed as Thomas' punctured back came unbidden to her mind.

They both jumped at a loud knock on the door. Artemis opened it to a handsome, rugged-looking man with short hair and a dark beard covering a strong jaw strode in. He was shorter than his sister, but his black graphic t-shirt stretched over a solidly built frame, and he wore motorcycle boots under his jeans.

"Hey," he said in a gravelly baritone voice. Alex suddenly found herself smoothing out her hair and wishing she'd put on more makeup. His eyes didn't seem to miss much as they looked around her apartment. When they finally settled on her she fought an urge to take a step back. They were not particularly friendly.

"Thanks Hermes," Artemis said. She closed the door and gestured to Alex. "Meet Alex. Alex, this is my half-brother Hermes. Or you could call him Mercury if you want to piss him off. He never did love the Romans much."

"What the hell, Artemis?" Hermes glowered at Alex, seeming to analyze her entire being. It was unclear where she was landing in his estimation.

Alex gave an awkward wave in silent greeting.

"It's okay, I told her who we are," Artemis said.

He pulled Artemis aside. "Are you kidding me with shit? You barely know her! I just assumed we'd do the usual."

"Well, I can't exactly ask her for help and not tell her who we are. She—"

"And I ask again. Why are you asking *her* for help?" he asked, his voice indicating exactly where she'd landed.

Artemis got in his face. "Because she's an Oracle, asshole," she yelled. "God, just let me talk."

Hermes looked over at Alex in shock, immediately recalculating and clearly not used to having to do that.

Alex raised her eyebrows in as much of a middle finger way as possible. She also decided her makeup was fine just as it was.

"How can that be? Are you sure?" He seemed full of disbelief and wonder at the same time.

"I'm sure, so don't be a dick," she said, shoving him lightly. "Or at least not more than usual."

"Fine," he said. "Well, I'm late because Athena asked for a pickup first. I can tell this is already going to be a Hermes-the-taxi type thing."

Athena! Alex thought in shock. The goddess of wisdom and strategic war had always been one of her favorites from the myths.

"Deal with it," Artemis hissed. "There are bigger things on the line, yeah?"

Hermes looked down at his boots. "Yeah, I know. Just trying not to think about that too much." A thought seemed to come to him and he looked up. "Wait," he said, thumbing to Alex. "Is she the one that got you involved with the skewered dude I helped you with?"

"It wasn't her fault."

"Right. Great. God, Artemis, you better know what you're doing. We don't need any complications."

"It'll be fine. Be right back." She pulled Alex into the next room.

"Sorry about that," she said in a low voice. "Obviously we have to be pretty militant about guarding our secrets. We're bound to get more reactions like that from the fam. But don't mind him or anyone else."

"Thanks. But exactly how do I do that?" Alex asked.

"Hrm. No idea, I guess. I'm not good at ignoring them either."

"What was 'the usual' he mentioned?"

"Oh, well if he ever has to *shift* with a normal human we usually drug them first."

"Right. Wait, what do you mean *shift*?"

"You'll see in a minute."

Artemis' revelations kept hitting like a set of waves, throwing Alex off balance or just straight up knocking her over. She took a deep breath. "Look, before we go there's something else you need to know," she said. "I keep my life very small. It keeps me safe. Being around a bunch of new people makes me incredibly anxious. The chances of me getting stuck in a vision are pretty high."

"No worries, I've got you." Artemis said. "We're going to literally the best place in the world for your situation. I was serious when I said my twin brother could help you. Among other things like medicine, healing, and music, my brother Apollo was the god of prophecy."

Alex's eyes widened, and a shining tendril of pure hope coiled up her heart, refusing to be pulled out.

It was as though light and sound had been pressed out of existence. Alex was ice cold, and intense pressure slowly squeezed her whole body until she thought she would scream. A monstrous, inaudible scream. In a rush of sound and air she stumbled back into reality, falling to the grass on her hands and knees. Pre-dawn dew seeped into her clothes as the world spun beneath her.

"Just take a few breaths and walk around. It will wear off in a bit," Artemis said.

She did as suggested, breathing in the salty smell of the sea as the world righted itself. "Where are we?" she asked.

"San Francisco," Artemis said.

"Of course we are," Alex murmured as she stood and leaned against a palm tree. "Just give me a minute." It felt as though her mind was still in New York. She stared up at a massive rustic-modern mansion sitting at the top of a wide staircase, lit like a beacon in the night.

"I have questions," Alex said.

Artemis chuckled. "I bet."

Alex looked around cautiously for Hermes. "Where's your brother?"

"He went inside already."

"I thought he flew around like Superman, with his winged sandals or whatever."

"Heh, yeah, I think technically he can still do that, but I haven't seen it in centuries," Artemis said. "It's not as fast as *shifting*. We all used to be able to travel the way we just did, go somewhere just by thinking about it. It was *so* convenient. Probably one of the things I miss most from our glory days."

"If you guys can't, then how can he?" Alex asked.

"He turned his wings into a tattoo relic like mine. He really was our father's messenger so he *shifted* around the most. Thank the gods he did. He's a bit of an old trout though, so he doesn't give lifts very often."

"I noticed," Alex said.

"Come on up. I can't wait to introduce you to Apollo." Artemis began to climb the long staircase up to the mansion.

Alex followed, trying with each step to wrap her head around the new world she lived in with ex-gods, magical bows, and teleporting assholes.

12

Artemis' heart pounded as she climbed the stairs. *You're out of shape,* she scolded herself. But she knew that wasn't totally it. Finding Alex had been like finding Atlantis. Hermes had been a trial run. Introducing her to the rest of the family was going to be tricky, but also secretly thrilling. Assuming they didn't just dismiss her out of hand as usual.

She paused in front of the polished redwood door, brimming with nerves.

"Artemis, you ok?" Alex asked.

Artemis forced a smile onto her face. "Of course, come on in." She walked in and held the door open for Alex, who looked appreciatively at the large foyer with white marble floors, cream walls, and natural redwood trim. Artemis barely noticed the house's understated luxury anymore.

Her twin walked in then, brightening the room like he was made of sunshine. Physically, she and Apollo still matched in height and coloring, but these days, his hale, svelte figure only accentuated her wasted one—a depressing physical representation of his health and success versus her malady and failure. Now though, she could see through Apollo's signature kind smile to the weariness and grief around his eyes. She felt her own grief rise to meet his and smashed it down. There'd be time for that later.

"Apollo, meet Alex. Alex, this is my twin brother, Apollo."

"Nice to meet you," he said, holding out his hand.

"You too. Sorry, I can't," Alex said self-consciously.

"No problem," he said. He shot a questioning look to Artemis. "Are you ready to tell me now why it was so important to bring her here?"

"Yes," Artemis said. "I needed to make sure. And now I am." Artemis paused for effect, feeling slightly giddy. "Apollo, Alex is an Oracle."

Apollo looked genuinely shocked. "You can't be serious. After all this time? All the Oracle lines were wiped out two millennia ago!"

Artemis glared at her brother and shook her head minutely. She hadn't exactly gone into all that with Alex.

"Um, what—" Alex started to ask.

Artemis talked over her. "I'm serious. Her gift is a little bit broken and she needs your help with it, but still, an Oracle."

Apollo's face became studiously neutral. "Broken? What does that mean? You really should have talked to me first, Artemis."

Just then, Apollo's partner joined them. Henry, a professor, was like a fresh breath of academic air, tall and trim, with salt and pepper hair and black-rimmed glasses. Though he looked Apollo's senior by at least a dozen years, they were perfect together. Artemis had never seen her brother so happy with anyone, and she adored him.

Apollo gestured to him. "Alex, this is Henry, my husband."

"Hi Alex. Nice to have another human here," Henry said.

Apollo gestured for them to follow him. "Let's continue the discussion with everyone, save us having to repeat things." He led them into a long, wide redwood room, brightly lit with floor to ceiling windows along the far wall. Hermes and Athena were talking at the large glass-topped dining table that separated the white marbled kitchen from the luxurious leather-filled sitting area.

Athena stood, straightened her navy blue jacket, and beelined for Apollo. It took all Artemis had not to roll her eyes at her imperious elder half-sister. It was nearly 3 am and she looked ready to run a board meeting with her suit and perfectly twisted chignon. It made Artemis practically feel the rats making nests in her hair. Seriously, who was the woman trying to impress?

"We were just discussing the bodies," Athena said. "They've clearly been dead for days. I already have a private forensics team at the penthouse analyzing the crime scene, taking fingerprints, blood samples, and they will gather up the bodies into bags for processing once they are done. I need to communicate where to take them though. Apollo, I assume you'd like to examine them, but I also have people I trust that could at least do the initial autopsy if you'd rather not. What is your preference?" Her voice was calm and clear—used to commanding, used to obedience.

Apollo groaned, worry lines creasing his face. Henry put a hand on his shoulder. "I don't know, I probably should, since I'd maybe catch things a mortal human wouldn't. But it's been a long time and it's not usually a good idea to do it on family…"

Alex peeked around Artemis and cleared her throat. "Um, maybe I could help with that. I'm a mortuary technician, and I've performed forensic autopsies in previous positions."

They looked at Alex as though she'd sprouted horns. Hermes looked especially perplexed. Artemis suppressed a grin. Alex was the gift that kept on giving. "Are you sure?" she asked.

Alex nodded. "It's no problem."

"Well, aren't you full of surprises," Apollo said. "But yes, okay. I'd be most grateful for that, thank you. Though I should warn you about the shape of the bodies—"

Athena raised her hand. "*Stop.*" She was peering at Alex as though she'd just found a stray puzzle piece on the floor. "Who, exactly, are you?"

Artemis stepped in. This had to go well. "Athena, this is my friend Alex. She's come to help. I wouldn't bring someone here who wasn't trustworthy. She already knows who we are." Athena's eyes flicked to Artemis at that, and the air in the room suddenly felt a little more tense. "She would have figured it out eventually anyway," she continued. "Alex here is an Oracle." Artemis winced internally at the satisfaction she heard in her own voice, but she couldn't help it. She'd *never* gotten the drop on

Athena.

"Impossible," Athena whispered. Artemis could almost hear the gears in Athena's mind whir as she studied Alex. "That's impossible. I followed all the lines myself, there were none left. Where did you meet this Oracle, little sister?"

Artemis steeled herself. "At the hospital."

"Hmmm," Athena said. "So, and I say this with love, how can you be sure?"

Artemis flushed as an indignant fury disproportionate to the question exploded in her. "Screw you, Athena. Just because I struggle doesn't make me unobservant or stupid—"

"I think she is what Artemis says," Hermes interrupted. "I looked at Alex's hospital records when I hacked in to get her home contact information. It was a pretty cursory glance, but it did list her symptoms. Knowing what I know now, I have to say, they described a condition remarkably like what an Oracle would look like when in a vision. The white eyes, the catatonic state, the movable body."

Artemis glared at him again before looking apologetically at Alex, who had a troubled look on her face. "Sorry Alex, that's my fault. I was desperate to find you after you'd left the hospital." Then to the group, "I saw her have a vision myself. It was just like the old days. And the vision would have come true if we hadn't intervened."

"So, you don't really know then? That it would have come true?" Athena asked.

"And what do you mean, you intervened?" Apollo added.

Artemis ignored her brother. "What I started to talk about before was that there seems to be something broken about her gift. She said I'd stop believing her if she spoke about what she'd seen. We worked around that because I recognized the signs with the eyes and everything. I was able to make assumptions. We actually helped save a mentally-ill woman there who was going to be assaulted by an asshole rapist orderly. It was awesome." Artemis forced herself to stop, she seemed to be sounding less credible the more she spoke. She ignored Apollo's disapproving look.

"Is this true?" Athena asked Alex softly. "You see the fate of others?"

Alex nodded, looking pale and fidgeting with her gloves. Artemis held her breath; Athena was a human lie detector. Not that she was worried. Not really.

"How long have you had the gift? How does it express itself?"

"As long as I can remember. It starts with a flash of light, then I'm sucked into a vision until it's done with me."

"Incredible," Athena said. She relaxed. Everyone else did too, and the air in the room cleared.

Apollo looked thoughtful. "You say no one believes you when you tell them?"

Alex nodded.

"Regardless of what you say or how you say it?"

Alex nodded again.

"Hmm, this feels so familiar." He thought for a few moments, then his eyes widened. "*Cassandra,*" he whispered. "It has to be."

"I knew I recognized it!" Artemis exclaimed.

Alex looked shocked. Artemis wondered how much she actually knew of the tragic princess of Troy.

Athena's eyes unfocused as she appeared to look inward. After a moment she surfaced and nodded. "It would make sense. She must have had a child we didn't know about. Her line was missed, by *everyone.*"

Apollo got a pained expression on his face. "I must apologize, Alex. I'm responsible for what must have been a very difficult life, for you and who knows how many other women. We all used to be so petty and entitled. Cassandra was my priestess and like a spurned frat boy, I cursed her cruelly, to see the future but never be believed. All because she wouldn't sleep with me. I gloated when no one believed her prediction of the destruction of Troy, when she was mocked, treated as insane and put in a tower. I wonder if she ended up with child after Ajax raped her—"

"In *my* temple," Athena interjected, her eyes flashing. "Unacceptable on so many levels. After Troy fell she was taken prisoner by Agamemnon. She bore him two sons, but all four of them were killed by his adulterous wife and her lover. So it's either Ajax, or she and Agamemnon had another child not talked about on the—"

"*Anyway,*" Apollo interrupted. "What's important is that you're here, Alex, and I will help you as much as I can during this craziness, and certainly after. There are all kinds of training exercises and information I can give you. Athena, at some point we'll have to chart her family line to see if there are other women with her condition."

Athena nodded and was about to speak when her phone buzzed and she stepped away to type a message. Artemis glanced after her, surprised. It was unlike Athena to let herself be distracted, especially at a moment like this.

"I'm sorry for doubting you, Artemis," Apollo said. "You did right in bringing her here." Her brother smiled at her in a way she hadn't seen in a very long time.

Artemis could have crowed.

13

Cassandra.

With a nearly audible click, the last piece of Alex's strange life fell into place. She stared unfocused as the others talked, barely listening. The little tendril of hope swelled as she clung to the name that explained so much. She wondered what they meant about Oracle lines and women with her condition. She thought of her mother, who both her father and grandmother avoided talking about. Alex only knew she'd died by suicide when she was young, and had no memory of her. But the thought struck her—could that be why? Did she have the curse too?

Thinking of her grandmother, another piece clicked into place. She'd always wondered how her grandmother took Alex's episodes in stride, and how she'd known to watch so carefully. Maybe she'd wanted to save her granddaughter since she'd been unable to save her daughter. Alex had always honored her grandmother's wishes to avoid talking about her mother, but now she'd give anything to be able to ask the thousand questions that were in her head. She was just thinking it must skip generations when she realized Apollo was talking to her.

"Are you sure about helping me with the bodies? They're in pretty bad shape." Alex had surprised herself by getting involved, but it felt instinctual to want to help Apollo. He had an open, genuine way about him that was easy to like. And that was before he'd offered to help with her curse, becoming salvation incarnate.

"Yes, I'm sure. I've seen it all," she said.

"Thank you. I've done all kinds of work in my lab over the years, so I have the space, gurneys, and a cold room, but I don't have all the correct tools for an autopsy here. Where's the best place to get them?"

Alex thought for a moment. "It's still early in New York right? No one gets in until nine. I could borrow whatever you need from my station. Assuming…" she gestured to Hermes.

"Great. Hermes, you'll take her, right?" Apollo asked.

Hermes nodded, stone-faced.

"That's settled then," Athena said as she typed furiously into her phone.

Alex was more than glad to no longer be the subject of Athena's intense focus. For those few minutes, she'd felt like a butterfly pinned to a board, raked over, examined, and utterly revealed. It wasn't even until this very moment Alex even noticed Athena was markedly shorter than the twins. She was clearly a woman who was confident in who she was, what she was good at, and the knowledge that she was better at it than anyone else in the room.

She was, in a word, intimidating.

Athena slipped her phone into her jacket pocket. "Alright. Time for some questions now that we're together. Hermes, you're the one who talked to Father most recently. Were there any indications? I hadn't talked to him in months."

Hermes shook his head. "No. Nothing. Though I have a feeling Poseidon was just in the wrong place at the wrong time. I was supposed to have dinner with Father next week. He called to say that Poseidon had come into port unannounced, and would likely still be staying with them. He wanted to make sure I'd still come given how his last visit ended with black eyes all around from trying to break up a drunken fight between the two of them. I mostly thought it was hilarious." He chuckled once, then cleared his throat, perhaps realizing it was the last tussle he'd ever get into with them.

"What about you?" he asked Athena. "How did you know about what happened to them anyway? You never said. You just asked me to go check on them."

"The neighbors beneath them were complaining of a stain pooling in the ceiling," Athena said matter-of-factly. "They were talking about calling the authorities given the strange thumping sounds they'd heard the day before. When I couldn't get a hold of Father or Hera, I called you. Once you were back with the news, I immediately arranged for there to be a sudden gas leak in the building, giving us a chance to handle this discreetly."

"Clever. But how did you know what the neighbors were saying?" Hermes asked.

"That's not important right now. Let's discuss who could have done this. The only possibility I'm aware of currently is Hera's revenge business. She's ruined some powerful and unsavory men over the years, and given her charming personality has probably racked up a few enemies besides. But pretty much everyone liked Father." Athena's voice quivered a little at the end, though her face didn't break from its glacial composure.

Apollo put his arm around Athena. "Don't worry, we'll find him." She nodded and stood stiff in his side hug.

Hera. Alex hadn't really connected the dots yet, and it finally dawned on her for the first time who their missing father was—Zeus.

Holy shit.

"We're going to have to tell the rest of the family soon," Athena said. "Until we know otherwise, we have to operate under the assumption they know who we are. We could all be in danger."

The room was quiet for a minute as the words sunk in.

Alex got a chill, realizing for the first time that she was becoming involved in an actively dangerous situation.

Athena continued. "Apollo, are you ok with having everyone meet here? I'd very much like to watch their reactions." Apollo nodded. Athena's phone buzzed, again breaking her concentration. Artemis and Hermes exchanged puzzled looks.

"Honestly, Athena, can't your work wait?" Hermes snapped. "Also, if I didn't know better, I'd say you were talking about the rest of the family like they were suspects."

"Well, it would be illogical not to at least consider it," she said, still typing. She pocketed it and focused on the group again. "Let's put what we know on the table. Whoever killed Poseidon and Hera was strong. Really strong. They also knew the precise and only way to kill us. They must have known who we are."

Aha, Alex thought. She'd been wondering about how a few immortals had ended up dead. But there hadn't really been an opening to ask the myriad of my-new-friend-is-an-immortal-ex-god questions she had.

"Hang on, why are they suspects and not the four of us?" Hermes asked.

Athena arched a well-manicured dark brow. "I've already determined it's not likely, for various reasons."

"Like what, exactly?" he said. "Not that I disagree or anything."

"Alright, if you must know. You, Hermes, are a loner. You have, to my knowledge, never told anyone who you really are. Besides Father, you're the only one who has managed to keep a speaking relationship with pretty much everyone in the family, and while you didn't like her, you were at least cordial with Hera. You're strong, but do not have anything like the rage required for an act like this. Plus, I cannot think of a motive that would fit, even if you were to coordinate such a horrific thing and not perform it yourself."

Hermes glowered, but Athena turned away before he could say anything. "Shall we continue? You, Apollo, have no love lost with Hera, but you've spent your life in medicine and helping people, plus you have been extremely occupied of late and also have no motive." Apollo raised a brow. "You've also only told one person in this century who you are, your partner of thirty years, Henry, a good man of impeccable character whom I've completely vetted and who has not shared this information with anyone else."

Henry beamed and took Apollo's hand. Apollo seemed to be waffling between flipping her off and hugging her.

She turned to Artemis, who seemed to brace herself. "As for you, sister, you've been in your current state for far too long. You're not strong enough or motivated enough for an act of this brutality. And even though you hated Hera, you love Father."

Artemis bristled. "I'm plenty strong, Athena." She looked at Apollo for backup.

"You do need to eat more, love," he said.

Artemis looked crestfallen.

"What about you?" Hermes asked, pointing a finger at Athena.

Athena reeked of contempt. "Don't be ridiculous," she said, shaping her words into bullets. "If I'd wanted to kill Hera or Poseidon I could have done so countless times when they were least aware. While I do share an intense dislike for Hera, I also love Father. Plus, I spend outrageous amounts of time and money keeping this family safe. Without so much as a thank you, I might add. To think I would harm anyone in this family is just beyond the pale."

"Alright," Hermes said. "Though you can't expect thanks when we don't ever know what the hell you're doing."

"Hermes. Let it go," Apollo said. "Athena, I suppose those are fair assessments. But honestly, don't you think it will be the same for everyone else in the family? We all hated Hera, but who on earth would have motive enough to kill her that way? And why now?"

"Well, there are a few of us who took the brunt of Hera's brutality more often than others, but I agree it seems unlikely it was family. Nonetheless it's prudent to avoid making assumptions. As such, I'll still be watching everyone regardless."

Hermes scoffed. "And we'll watch you."

Athena ignored him. "Hera suffered greatly. Someone truly despised her."

The room was quiet. Alex wondered what could have happened to her that was so bad.

Athena's phone rang again, breaking the silence. "I have to take this." She strode out of the room. Hermes rolled his eyes.

"She's being so weird with that phone," Artemis said.

"Yeah, it's not like her to let herself be pulled in multiple directions like that. And to show all that emotion!" Apollo said.

Alex wondered if he could possibly mean that tiny tremble in her voice. "Sorry, but can I ask, how did they die?" she asked.

The room collectively held their breath. "Ah, well, it's what I was going to warn you about, since you so kindly offered to help with the autopsy," Apollo said. "Poseidon won't be so bad, his body is intact but his head appears to have been literally pulled off his body. But Hera's will be difficult, she was literally torn apart. One piece at a time. All of her."

Alex grimaced, trying to process that. And how was she going to *literally and physically* process that? It was going to be a huge job.

Wait.

His words slowly penetrated her mind, bringing images and sounds out of the dark. Familiar images. A woman's body torn apart. A man's head pulled off. Sei. Short for Poseidon? And Juno. The Roman name for Hera.

Oh god.

Her stomach clenched and her face paled.

"If it's too much for you—" Apollo started to say.

She shook her head. "I'm sure it'll be fine," she said, distracted.

There was no need to worry about how she'd react to seeing the bodies.

She'd already seen them.

14

Alex quietly drowned in dread. She had to be wrong. Wanted to be wrong. But the feeling in her stomach told her she wasn't. But how could this be?

"What's wrong?" Artemis whispered as the group kept talking.

Alex's heart was pounding as she looked at her friend. Should she just blurt it out? Or would she look crazy? It was kind of crazy. "I just have a feeling," she said. "Any chance we can go to the crime scene?"

"That's a great idea," Artemis said. "Then maybe something there can trigger a vision about what happened."

Alex nodded, letting Artemis think what she wanted. For herself, Alex just needed to be extra sure.

Artemis informed the group of their plan.

"Excellent idea," Athena said.

"Then maybe you can stop for the autopsy tools on the way back," Apollo added.

Alex could only half listen through the blood pounding in her ears.

"Hermes, can you take us?" Artemis asked.

Hermes grabbed both their arms and *shifted.*

Alex shivered as the icy black void released them into a small lobby, in between an elevator and a white and gold penthouse door. Hermes entered a code into the keypad and walked in. Artemis followed.

Alex stared at the revealed hallway, skin prickling. Her feet seemed to move of their own accord as she walked straight into the nightmare vision. The coppery smell of blood hit her nose first, heavy and thick. She could hear the murmur of Athena's forensic team in the kitchen down the hall. She glanced at the doorway on the left, where a pool of blood had crossed the threshold. There were forensic markers around it.

The office.

She stopped, not wanting to go further. "Artemis," she whispered, trembling.

Artemis turned, concern in her eyes. "Alex, it's okay, just see what you can. Do you need to take your gloves off?"

"No. Artemis. I've already seen it," she whispered. "I saw…all of it."

Hermes looked at her dubiously. "What do you mean you've seen it?"

Alex looked at the pool of blood. "This. This is what landed me in the hospital." She gestured around. "I know this place. I saw what happened here."

"What are you talking about?" Artemis asked.

Alex's mind raced. She needed to find a way to prove it without directly talking about what she'd seen in the vision. "I can't say specifics. But I know whose blood that is." She gestured to the pool on the floor.

"Hera's," Hermes said, testing her.

Alex looked him straight in the eyes and shook her head no.

"And where was Hera killed - her bedroom?" Artemis asked, following suit.

Alex shook her head.

"The kitchen?"

Alex shook her head again.

"The dining room?"

Alex nodded.

Artemis and Hermes stared.

"But the odds…" Hermes said.

Artemis squinted at Alex, as though wanting to see her more clearly. "You really saw who did this?"

Alex nodded, unable to bear the hope that bloomed in her friend's face.

"Okay. Let's get you back to Apollo. We've got to get around this curse of yours ASAP."

Hermes was already moving. "Hang on," he said.

He touched both of their shoulders and they *shifted.*

Alex sat on the edge of one of Apollo's chocolate leather chairs, under the blaze of the great room's recessed lights. The images from the vision were surfacing like a bloody red tide in her mind.

"It's okay," Artemis said. "Just take a deep breath and tell them what you told us."

The energy in the room crackled. Alex's throat felt dry. She clasped her fingers to keep from fidgeting under the gaze of four sets of immortal eyes hoping for answers. "Well, I started to connect it when Apollo said how they died. But I wanted to be sure before I said anything. And I'm sure. I saw those murders. It was so brutal the vision landed me in the state hospital. I know it seems unlikely, but it's true."

"So, obviously, we need to get around her curse," Artemis said.

"Wait," Hermes said. "How do you know it's actually a curse? Maybe people just don't believe her because it's well, unbelievable? Like it's a trick."

Alex felt her face grow hot as she sifted through responses that didn't have a swear word in them. As if she hadn't spent her whole life learning the hard way.

Luckily Athena stepped in, echoing her thought. "I'm certain she's had a lifetime to prove otherwise," she said. "Regardless, it's not worth taking the chance now and ruining such a potent lead. We'll tiptoe around it." She turned to Artemis. "You said you were able to collaborate before, how did that work?"

"Well, we used yes or no questions."

"Great, let's start there," Athena said. "Did—"

"Did you see who did it?" Apollo interrupted eagerly. Athena glared at him.

The two incredibly strong masked women came immediately to mind. Alex nodded.

"I'll take it from here, thank you," Athena said superciliously. She shooed Apollo out of the way and pulled a chair right in front of Alex. Alex's breath caught under her intense gaze.

"Did you see both murders?"

Alex nodded.

"How many murderers were there? Four? Three? Two?"

Alex nodded at two.

"Was there anyone else there?"

Alex nodded, thinking of the person they called the First One.

"More of a witness then?"

Oh, she's good, Alex thought. She nodded.

"Interesting." Athena paused for a moment. "The murderers. They were men, yes?"

Alex shook her head vehemently.

"A woman and a man?"

No.

"Two women?" Athena asked in surprise.

Yes.

"Did it take both of them to kill Poseidon?"

Alex shook her head.

Hermes crossed his arms, incredulous. "A single woman kill Poseidon? His neck and arms were the size of tree trunks. I don't think even *I* could pull his head off with my bare hands."

"Not helping, Hermes," Athena said. "But he does have a point. Truly, one woman killed Poseidon?" she asked Alex.

Alex nodded, though she understood their skepticism. What she'd seen was unbelievable. But if she was an Oracle, and they were immortal ex-gods, then was it really such a stretch that there were some Amazonian type women that existed too? She kept the thought to herself, not wanting to seem like a fool.

"Fascinating," Athena said. Her eyes lit up a little. The gears in her brain seemed to be turning fast as the mystery deepened.

"The witness, was it a man?"

Alex shrugged.

"You couldn't tell?"

No.

"Were they wearing masks then? All of them?"

Alex nodded.

"Ski masks or something?" Hermes asked.

Alex shook her head. How in the world was she going to get them to guess Venetian masks?

Athena thought for a moment. "Were they Halloween-type masks?"

No.

"Interesting," Athena said. Her eyes went unfocused again. Alex wondered where she went when she did that.

"Wait," Apollo said. "When you see a vision, it's usually through the viewpoint of one person, right?"

Alex nodded yes.

"So, who was this person?"

Alex gasped as a jolt of shock went through her body. "Oh my god, the body." She looked at Artemis, her neck and cheeks flushing bright red. How could she have possibly forgotten? "It started when I touched a body at work."

They all leaned in. Athena spoke slowly, evenly. "What body, Alex?"

"A *woman's* body," Alex said.

"A woman's body," Athena repeated. She tapped her chin as she thought.

Alex waited for the ex-goddess of wisdom to connect it.

Athena's eyes widened. "You touched one of the murderers."

Alex nodded yes, a thrill of triumph shooting through her.

"Tell us everything," Athena said.

15

Alex was thrilled to be able to talk about something not connected to a vision. She thought back to that day. "I was called in on my day off to help with overflow from the Chief Medical Examiner's office, as we're the nearest mortuary. When I process a body I always start by touching them with my bare hand to get any potential visions out of the way. Her file said she died of a stab wound to the neck. But it was her face that was surprising."

They listened with rapt attention. "What was surprising about it?" Artemis asked.

"It was covered in an intricate, delicate tattoo of scrollwork that started on her forehead. It framed her eyes and swirled down her temple and cheekbones. I've seen plenty of facial tattoos, but they're mostly gang related; nothing like this. When I touched her, the light flashed and I woke up chained to a bed three days later."

"What else can you tell us about the body itself?" Athena asked.

"I didn't see much other than her face."

Athena was already getting her phone. "Could she still be there? At your mortuary?"

Alex thought. "It's been, what, over a week? Depends if someone claimed her or not. Either way we should be able to get access to the autopsy file pretty easily. Either at my work or at the Office of the Chief Medical Examiner, since she was a murder victim."

Athena looked at Hermes. "On it," he said, walking out of the room.

Alex turned to Artemis with a questioning look.

"Let's just say back in the day Hermes was the patron god of thieves," Artemis said.

"And he's going to try to steal…what exactly?" Alex asked, perplexed. *Surely not the body,* she thought.

"Data. Like he did for me about you. Our Hermes is one of the best hackers in the world," Artemis said with a glint in her eye.

"Ah. That explains a few things."

Athena turned back to Alex. "Okay, there are probably other important things you can tell us from your vision. But we have enough to start with and this yes/no line of questioning is slow. Apollo, do you have any other ideas?"

"Well, you say the curse of disbelief manifests when you talk to someone about what you've seen in a vision. Have you ever tried writing it out?" he asked.

"Yes," Alex said. "All attempts at giving someone a written note about a vision were futile. I get the same response—the disbelief just washes over them. You can physically see it happen."

"Have you ever tried using a computer to get around the curse?" Hermes asked as he strode into the room, laptop in hand.

Alex thought for a minute. "Maybe just once," she said. "I didn't have a computer when I was young and spouting off what I'd seen in my visions right and left. But about ten years ago there was a classmate who…well, I just really wanted to help her so I emailed her a warning, hoping it would work. You know, how can a curse affect a bunch of ones and zeros?"

Hermes nodded, his point exactly.

"It did not go well."

"Same response?" Athena asked.

"Well, obviously I couldn't see her face when she read it, but it was a similar response. And she didn't remember when I tried to apologize later."

"Hmmm," Hermes said. "But you don't know for certain it was the curse. That could just be her getting upset at a receiving email like that. Most people probably would."

"I tried to write it in a way—"

"It doesn't matter," he interrupted. "I think we should try again. There are so many technologies we can try." He sat down and opened his laptop.

"And we will," Athena said. "But your top priority is to find either that body or its report. It's our most concrete lead and we're running out of time. We've only been working on this for twenty-four hours, but it's been at least a week since Father was taken. The odds are not in his favor at this point and we must start using our time more wisely." She started to give orders, quick and sharp, a general in battle.

"Artemis, call Aphrodite, Hep, Demeter, and Ares; tell them we have a family emergency and need them to join us at Apollo's immediately. Tell them Hermes will come get them. And for god's sake, start eating. We need you at your best."

Artemis gave her a dirty look and pulled out her phone. "Ares won't come, you know."

"Just try. Tell him it has to do with his mother." Artemis was already out of the room when Athena yelled, "And DON'T tell him anything specific over the phone!"

"I'm not an idiot!" Artemis yelled back.

"Hermes, yours is the only call that Dionysus will answer. Call and invite him here too. Then find that body. And be available to pick everyone up," Athena continued. Hermes saluted, muttering under his breath.

"Apollo, while we wait for the bodies, work with Alex," Athena said. "And get an inventory of what you need for the autopsy."

"On it." Apollo gestured for Alex to follow him.

"Wait," Hermes said. "Alex, does your work allow you to access their network remotely?"

Alex hesitated. "Yes, but they'll be able to see that I logged in and what records I looked at."

"Don't worry about that," he said. "Once I have a foot in the door, I'm golden. You could just save a ton of time. Log in for me." He turned the laptop toward her. The mortuary's login page was already loaded.

Alex hesitated, a pit forming in her stomach. She could lose her job.

Hermes looked exasperated. "Look—"

Athena raised her hand to forestall him. "I know it feels uncomfortable Alex, but he really is the best. And though it's unlikely, if he's detected and you are compromised in any way, we're all in positions to take care of you in any way you require. There will be no repercussions. Of that, you have my word."

"Alright," Alex said. She typed in her credentials then stepped back with a grimace and deep misgivings. She watched as Hermes opened several terminal windows and started running script after script. He lowered the lid halfway. "No one touch this," he said. "I'll go call Dionysus."

"It's early, but I, for one, am hungry," Henry said. He gestured to the floor-length windows where a pre-dawn light had backlit a distant Golden Gate Bridge. "I'll set out food everyone can munch on."

Alex's stomach grumbled at the thought. She followed Henry and Apollo into the kitchen as he pulled out various breakfast foodstuffs and started the coffee machine. She grabbed a bagel and tore into it. Then a terrible thought came to her.

"So, I might have a problem," she said to Apollo. "I'm embarrassed I didn't think of it before, but frankly the fact that people of your…um… lifespan exist has not exactly sunk in yet. I mentioned that I usually touch the bodies I work on to get any visions over with. I have no idea what would happen to me if I touched someone as old as those two. I'd probably be out for a long time."

"You just get stuck in the vision until it's over?" Apollo asked.

Alex nodded.

"Terrible," he said. "Whether or not we can circumvent your curse, I can still certainly help you control your gift."

Alex scoffed at the word through another mouthful of bagel.

He ducked his head to catch her eyes. "It *is* a gift Alex, once you're in charge. Even with that curse sitting on top of it. I promise."

Alex shrugged. She was a long way from believing that. Artemis walked back into the room texting on her phone. She grabbed a bagel too and threw it in the toaster.

Apollo continued. "To start, I have a smelling salt recipe that we used when training Oracle novices back in the day. So if you do get stuck, it wouldn't be for as long. Come down to my lab and while I make it, I can also walk you through a couple of the exercises we used to have the novices do to strengthen their mental control. Sound good?"

Alex nodded quickly, trying not to get her hopes up.

But still the tendril grew.

16

Jenna knelt in front of the shrine. Moonlight shone through the small window in her room, providing just enough light. She lit a thick white candle then opened an embossed silver box, revealing a silver knife, a small chalice, and a narrow stoppered bottle. She poured the dark liquid from the bottle into the chalice and pulled out the knife. She murmured a prayer to the horned god and performed her sacrifice.

The Madness pulsed, forbidden, inside of her. They were not supposed to use it every day, but it felt like the only thing keeping her sane. Well, sane wasn't the right word. But it did keep her from drowning in sorrow and rage. Thoughts of Ria's smiling face were now constantly replaced with the image of her head dropping to her chest, resting gently on the slowing torrent of her life's blood. It was consuming her.

Jenna put on her friend and mentor's mask, breathing in the smell of her sweat and blood. She slipped out into the forested countryside. The trees blurred as she ran on the deer trails, leaping over fallen logs and roots. The fire in her legs eventually matched the one in her heart. But not even she could outrun what had happened.

After killing that beast of a man she'd rushed over to try to save Ria. But it was too late. She'd screamed then, ragged and frenzied, magnified by the Madness throbbing inside her, hot tears burning in the corners of her eyes.

The First One had left with the dark-haired man when the fight broke out, leaving Jenna and Ria to handle it. And they had. But as the Madness waned and fatigue set in, Jenna found she could no longer simply sit in that slaughterhouse and stare at her dead friend. So instead of waiting as she'd been instructed, she lifted Ria's body over her shoulder and climbed onto the fire escape, closing the window behind her. She thought she'd be able wait for their pickup on the roof, under the cover of darkness. It wasn't her fault there had been a cat on one of the steps, or that when she tripped, she'd dropped Ria's body onto a bunch of trash cans. Or that soon after, a group of people exiting a nearby bar stumbled over her. People who had screamed and called 9-1-1.

Jenna had scrambled up and leapt to a nearby building, hiding as the authorities arrived to investigate. Eventually the paramedics loaded Ria's body into an ambulance. She made note of the numbers painted on its side.

The First One had been displeased at the loss of Ria, and furious at the loss of her body. "Find her," the First One had hissed.

It had taken two days to do so, using all her cunning to infiltrate the Medical Examiner's Office, only to find out they had sent her to a nearby mortuary. She'd been able to get Ria's body out of there easy enough, having to avoid only a tired, old guard who couldn't secure much of anything.

Now she was home, finding it almost impossible to re-enter her life.

The thoughts rampaged in her head as she ran when suddenly the First One was on the path several feet in front of her, moonlight glinting off her black and white mask.

Jenna skidded to a halt, falling backward in her effort to stop quickly. She scrambled to her knees. "First One," she said, humbly. "You grace me with your presence."

"There has been a development," the First One said. "The bodies were discovered prematurely. We need more time. You will pick a sister and execute the fallback plan. Tonight. And you have an additional objective. Someone…unexpected has joined them."

Jenna listened silently, but the Madness was blazing within her.

Yes, she thought, smiling behind Ria's bloody mask. *Give me action. Give me purpose.*

Give me vengeance.

17

Alex followed Apollo down a hallway to a door that looked like any other door until he pushed a hidden button on the wall. A down arrow lit up next to it.

Of course there's a hidden elevator, she thought. *And probably hidden tunnels and maybe treasure too.*

He seemed to read her thoughts. "I do a lot of my work here at home, and it's sensitive. So I built my lab below ground, obfuscated its entrance, and had Hermes secure it biometrically. There are only a few people with access."

"Artemis said you did genetics, is that still what you do?" she asked, wondering what needed to be locked down so tight.

"Yes, I went into medicine eras ago, a path that continues to provide the most incredible avenues of learning and growth. It suits me. For the last fifty years, genetics has held my interest most though."

"Makes sense," Alex said. The elevator dinged and the normal looking door split open. He pushed the *L3* button and the door closed silently.

"Does it?" Apollo asked.

"Well, I guess I mean if I were…you, I'd want to understand why I was the way I was."

"Ah. Yes, that was definitely part of what drew me to it. Though it's grown since then. The recent discoveries using CRISPR as a gene editor are beyond belief."

Crisper? Alex thought, wondering if she'd heard right.

"But we're not here to talk about me. Let's talk about the novice exercises. They are deceptively simple. Mastering one's own mind is a task it takes some people a lifetime to accomplish. But we can get you functioning much sooner than that. You've heard of mindfulness, yes?" he asked.

"Yes. I tried meditating once. I hated it," she said.

Apollo chuckled. "Well, I've got bad news for you then, since that's essentially what you're going to have to do the rest of your life."

They stepped out into a small foyer and at the push of another hidden button, a fingerprint reader slid out of the wall with a small click. He placed his finger on it until it beeped in acquiescence. A seamless door slid open with a whoosh as if it were opening to the *U.S.S. Enterprise.*

The feeling of being in a spaceship remained as Alex took in the cavernous lab, sleek and modern with its soothing gray walls and gleaming white counters, lit by bright white rings hanging from the ceiling like righteous halos.

Apollo smiled at Alex. "This is my happy place."

"It's amazing," she breathed.

Apollo gestured for her to sit at a table in the corner next to some strange equipment and a computer terminal. "While I'm gathering what I need for your salts, I want you to begin your first exercise. Look at this sculpture." He picked it up off a nearby counter and placed it in front of her. "Concentrate on it. Look at it. Think about it. If your eyes wander, gently bring them back to the sculpture. If your mind wanders, gently bring it back to the sculpture. Concentrate on it and be present, until this timer goes off." He pulled out a kitchen timer and set it to fifteen minutes, then walked away.

Alex obediently studied the burnished gold spiral ring, each thick ridged coil twisted, its lines curving around each other sinuously. The coiled ring sat on a black block base, about ten inches tall, with a small inscription at the bottom - 'The Double Helix - Brian King'. A delicate and complicated piece. She turned it over and the other side of the base had a plaque on it that read:

TRINITY COLLEGE DUBLIN
DAWSON PRIZE IN GENETICS
PAUL WAGNER

Alex wondered what discovery the award was for, and at the name he'd chosen for himself, assuming Apollo was Paul Wagner. She put it down gently and looked at the clock. Thirteen minutes left.

That was only TWO MINUTES? Alex thought, dismayed.

She rested her head in her hands and stared at the sculpture more. Her eyes unfocused and moved inward, thinking for about the hundredth time how insane this all was, at the sharp turn her life....*okay, back to the statue.* Alex gazed at it for another minute, then glanced over at a nearby machine, wondering what it was...*back to the statue.* She had to pull herself back over and over again. *I'm terrible at this,* she thought. It wasn't long before she wanted to throw the sculpture into the wall, feeling not unlike Daniel LaRusso painting Mr. Miyagi's fence. She took some deep breaths.

The breathing helped her remember she already did have something sort of like mindfulness. Her grandmother's mantra. She remembered her grandmother often rubbing her back as she sobbed, murmuring the calming words until Alex relaxed and the tears subsided. A warm rush of love and gratitude for her grandmother filled Alex's heart.

So she started a new one for the situation at hand. *Breath in, double helix...breathe out double helix...breathe in, double helix...breathe out, double helix.* The minutes began to flow more smoothly.

She heard something being wheeled in behind her and it took all her will to keep her eyes on the sculpture.

"What on earth is she doing?" Hermes asked in a loud, disdainful whisper.

"Practicing," Apollo said. He wheeled a cart with tools over toward a large stainless steel table. "How did you do?" he asked Alex.

"It's definitely not easy," she said, not looking up. "My mind wanders a lot, though I found a mantra that seemed to help."

"In the mindfulness world our wandering minds are called monkey brains. Our brains swing from thought to thought and we mostly just let it. It takes a lot of practice to rein that in. Mantras are helpful, as is visualizing. Spend twenty minutes a day practicing this mindfulness and you'll see a vast improvement."

"Improvement in what? I know you wouldn't have me do this if it weren't going to help, but I can't really see how. What in the world would I focus on in a vision?"

"Ah. That would be the Thread," he said as the timer went off.

"The what?" Alex asked, bewildered.

"Okay, crash course. You're familiar with the Greek myths, yes?" Apollo asked.

"Wait, wait, wait," Hermes interrupted. "Just do your inventory of autopsy tools so we can go get this part over with. I've made progress with the coroner's system and I also need to be available to go get the rest of the clan. So now's the time. Chop, chop." He snapped his fingers.

Alex felt a stab of irritation. She'd been a mere moment away from having a critical part of her very existence explained.

"Okay," Apollo said. He gestured to the variety of tools he'd gathered on the cart. "What else do you need?"

Alex shoved the feeling aside and scanned the tools. She looked at Apollo in surprise. "You just *happen* to have a skull chisel and a hammer-and-hook?"

Apollo simply nodded. "I've studied plenty of brains in my day."

"Got it," she said. Why was she surprised by anything at this point? "Okay, do you have something I could write this down with…?"

"Just say it, I'll remember," Hermes said.

She looked at him questioningly but did as he said. "I need a hagedorn needle, bone saw, breadknife, enterotome, and rib cutter."

"Got it. Then let's go get them."

"Do you know where to go?"

Hermes nodded and grabbed her gloved forearm.

They *shifted*.

18

I t was sunny in New York when they appeared at the back of the
mortuary. She turned her face to the sun for a moment, letting it
warm her freezing cheeks.

Hermes gestured to the door. "Can you get us in?"

"Yes, with the keypad, but it'll be recorded."

"Right then, we'll *shift*," he said. He reached out for her arm.

She pulled away. "Wait. Is it possible for you to mis-*shift*? Like accidentally end up in a wall or something?"

"Nope. I can just kind of feel the space I'm going to. I can tell
whether it is solid or not, or has objects or not. It's pretty foolproof."

"Okay, well, we need to go to the basement."

He nodded and grabbed her arm.

She took a big icy breath in and steadied herself in front of one of the
autopsy tables. Hermes looked around with revulsion on his face.

"Never been in a mortuary, I take it?" Alex asked, delighted to see
him so uncomfortable. She headed to her station and started packing up
the tools she needed into a bag.

"No, never. You people have such strange ways of dealing with
death."

"Us people? How so?" she asked. Then a shadow rounded the corner and Alex jumped as a security guard emerged from the hallway beyond. She sighed. Bodies never scared her, but people always seemed to.

"Alex! Oh I'm so glad to see you after your last…well, episode. I was so worried. You're okay then? What are you doing here so early? And who is this?" the elderly guard peered suspiciously at Hermes.

"George! I'm okay, thanks for asking!" Alex said. "And, if you can believe it, I have a boyfriend. He wanted to see where I worked." She grinned and reached her hand toward Hermes, who didn't even blink before stepping into character. His whole demeanor relaxed and he smiled as he took her hand, easily assuming the role of perfect boyfriend—warm, kind, and crushingly good-looking. The smile alone changed his face so completely it almost made Alex forget herself and gawk.

"When Alex told me where she worked I could hardly believe it. I just expected her to work at a library or something, not deal with death and dead bodies every day. I think she's pretty brave," Hermes said.

George's eyes lit up and he grinned. "Oh Alex, how wonderful! I'm so happy to hear this! No one deserves it more!" He turned to Hermes. "I know what you mean, she's not who I would have ever pictured to do this either. But she's a favorite among the patrons as well. She gets more thank you notes than any other technician, she's so good with that makeup brush. She's *my* favorite too; beautiful, kind, thoughtful, and certainly the nicest to me. Everyone else here is kind of…well, anyway. You take care of her, young man, or you'll have me to deal with!" he said in mock sternness.

"George!" Alex said in genuine embarrassment.

Hermes saluted. "Wouldn't think of anything else," he said. He pulled Alex into a side hug and rested his hand on her hip. Alex tried to play it cool, but found herself distracted both by the touch and the smell of his spicy aftershave.

"Okay, well, I'll leave you two kids to it," George said. He winked at Alex.

She blushed furiously. "Don't worry, we won't be here long," she said in a rush. "I really am just showing him around."

George shrugged, still grinning. "I'll just take my time on this next round, so take as long as you want. Nice to meet you, Alex's boyfriend, and see you soon Alex!" He sauntered off, humming to himself.

"That was fast thinking," Hermes said. He dropped his arm and his face returned to its normal inscrutable expression.

"God, I hope he doesn't think we're going to…" Alex said, gesturing to the autopsy table.

Hermes' eyes widened. "Surely not."

"One of my coworkers always brings his girlfriend here. Bleh. Either way, let's get out of here." She stuffed the last tool in the bag.

"Agreed," Hermes said with distaste. He reached out his hand.

"She's all yours," Hermes said to Apollo after they arrived back in the lab. He *shifted* away again without another word.

Alex exhaled and shook her head. "Man, he is—"

"Difficult," Apollo said. "But he's a good guy. You were successful?"

Alex nodded and handed him the bag.

"Great. Thank you," he said. "I've also gathered up everything for the smelling salts while you were gone. Where were we?"

"The Thread," Alex said, pouncing on the word.

"Ah, right. Are you familiar with the Fates from the myths? The three goddesses who spun the threads of human destiny?"

"A little," Alex said.

"Well, that myth is based on what Oracles see in their visions. Hesiod took the idea and ran with it. Once you know how to manifest it, you'll be able to see a delicate, luminous silver Thread running through the heart of the person you're having a vision of. If you witness the end of someone's life, as Oracles so often do, you'll see the Thread stop there."

Alex couldn't help but feel skeptical, she'd never seen anything like that in all the hundreds of visions she'd had over her life.

Apollo continued. "Strong Oracles can rise above a single person's

Thread and see how it's woven into a tapestry of sorts, how their Thread intersects with the people around them. The tapestry is made up of a solid pattern making up the past, and a more ephemeral pattern for the future; where all the most likely paths intersect with each other. Some Oracles even develop the ability to explore the less likely paths, seeing the fates that might be."

He paused, his eyes getting a far-off look. "The most powerful Oracles could rise even higher, usually with some herbal assistance, and see the pattern of millions of Threads; able to foresee major events in the world as patterns converge in such a way that tell the coming of great sadness, conflict, or joy. I've seen it only once myself. It was stunning." He sounded wistful.

Alex listened, totally enthralled. Could *she* be capable of seeing such things? If so, maybe, just maybe, it *could* be a gift. She also saw an opening for one of the questions that had nagged her all day.

"So, the Fates aren't real? Not all the myths are real?"

Apollo chuckled briefly. "No, not all of them are real. Obviously we were. Are. And we worked hand in hand with the poets of the time to come up with ideologies and doctrine for our religions to keep it all going. They wrote about our antics and made plenty of things up."

"And you were okay with that?" Alex asked.

"If it helped our cause, sure. And if we liked what they wrote, we often made it real. So some creatures and other things in the myths were real, but they disappeared in The Fall, or shortly after. We're actually not entirely sure."

"Centaurs?" Alex asked.

Apollo's eyes lit up. "Real," he said with a smile. "And super cool. Poseidon was really, really into horses. Which is funny for a sea god. They rarely interacted with humans though."

"Amazing." Alex shook her head. It was hard to imagine the world as he'd described. One of these days she was going to have to get Artemis to talk about it more.

As though summoned by Alex's thoughts, the elevator dinged and Artemis walked out. "I saw Hermes was back, so I thought I'd come see how it was going down here." She sounded stressed even through a mouthful of granola bar. "I can't believe how long the forensic team is taking."

Alex was brimming with all the information she'd just received. "Apollo just told me about the Thread and what Oracles can see. I had no idea."

Artemis nodded knowingly. "I *told* you it was a gift."

"So how do I make this Thread appear?" Alex asked Apollo.

"Well, it starts by recognizing that a vision is still just a thought in your head—"

Alex felt a surge of hard-to-identify emotion. "No way. There's no way they are just thoughts," she interrupted, failing to keep the defensiveness out of her voice.

"No, no, they're definitely not normal," he said. "I'm just trying to convey that at the end of the day you're not in anyone else's mind but your own. Our brains are incredible, beautiful, complicated instruments. Yours just happens to let you see things others cannot."

"But I can't control it. It feels more like schizophrenia or something like that. A schizophrenic can't control what he sees or hears," she argued.

"That's not the same thing at all. That is a mental disorder, something misfiring, something wrong. While someone can learn to live with schizophrenia, they can't control it without medication. But you can. The Oracle part of you is not a psychological ailment." His expression became thoughtful. "Obviously I've not been able to scientifically study this, but I suspect you simply have more neurons and synapses and maybe even some extra piece in your temporal lobe…I'd love to get you into an MRI and see—"

"Apollo." Artemis snapped her fingers.

"Sorry. Maybe someday you'll let me do some tests. But for now, just know it's a matter of focus, controlling your thoughts, and manifesting the Thread. Which sounds easier than it is, I know."

Alex nodded, letting the idea sink in that, after all this time, she had the ability to control it. It was exciting and disheartening all at once. Like Dorothy from *The Wizard of Oz* when the wizard told her the ruby slippers could have taken her home the whole fucking time. Except Dorothy hadn't even been upset. Alex was upset.

She must have done a good job keeping it from her face because Apollo kept going. "I think we need to take a trial run. We just need to find a reasonable test subject that doesn't have too much to worry about sharing and won't knock you out for too long." He drummed his fingers on the countertop as he thought. "My dog Titus might work," he said. "Have you ever had a vision of an animal?"

Alex was confounded. "An animal? Not that I can recall. We didn't have any pets growing up."

"Really?" Artemis asked. "Dogs are the best. And Titus is a great dog. He's just what I would want if I could have dogs again."

"Why can't you have a dog?" Alex asked, curious.

Artemis shrugged. "Well, you've seen me, I need to be able to take care of myself before I can take care of something else." The words sounded rehearsed.

"Well, that's not necessarily true…" Alex started to say, thinking of stories she'd read about people with depression being helped by having an animal companion.

"It's just not a good idea," Apollo said. Artemis gave him a dirty look. "Anyway, technically Oracles can see the Threads of all kinds of living creatures. Even inanimate objects that have a powerful or impactful existence. Pets don't often trigger visions because they live very simple lives. But Titus is a sweet pit bull and since he's associated with me there's a chance he will trigger one. This seems like a comparatively safe test subject."

"Okay, sure," Alex said, shrugging. A vision of a dog would not be the strangest thing to happen today.

"Artemis, take her to the library so she can do this in peace. I'll meet you there."

Alex felt overwhelmed as she and Artemis stood semi-awkwardly in silence in the elevator.

"You doing okay?" Artemis finally asked. "Sorry about my family, I told you they were a little much. And you haven't even met the rest of them yet."

"Yeah, I'm fine, it's been quite a day so far though. And they're okay, at least you have family," Alex said, jokingly. She regretted the comment immediately when she saw Artemis' dismayed face.

"No, no, it's okay," Alex said. "I didn't mean that as serious as it sounded."

Artemis only half smiled. "I bet when you went to sleep last night you had no idea you'd wake up and be thrown into a crazy, dysfunctional family of immortals."

"That, my friend, is an understatement," Alex said. She tilted her head and gave Artemis a cock-eyed Cheshire grin. "But we're all mad here..."

They laughed. "Seriously though," Alex continued, "if you think about it, if anyone were going to need therapy, it would be a bunch of immortals processing life eternal."

As she spoke the words, the doors opened to reveal Athena waiting for them. "Truer words were never spoken," she said.

"Oh come off it, Athena," Artemis said in disbelief. "*You've* been to therapy?"

"No, but I may need to soon," Athena muttered. "I wanted to let you know—"

Artemis turned her head and lifted her nose toward the great room. "Some of the family's here."

Alex wondered how Artemis had known that. Had she *smelled* them?

Athena nodded. "Your senses are returning. Good. I have not told them about Alex. I thought you'd want to since you found her."

The comment made Alex feel like a penny on the sidewalk.

"Yes. Thanks Athena," Artemis said.

Athena nodded. "I suggest waiting until after we've told them the news, so go in the back entryway. The lights are off in the kitchen, and they will hopefully not notice you until we want them to."

Artemis gestured for Alex to follow. "Time to meet more of the dysfunction," she said with a grimace.

Alex followed, her stomach suddenly churning.

19

Artemis watched the room from the shadows of the kitchen. She looked at Alex, who had her arms crossed and kept chewing her lip. She seemed nervous. But she was here. Artemis felt a surge of warmth and friendship for her. If Alex could take such huge leaps out of her comfort zone to help a bunch of strangers, she certainly could make her own efforts.

She put her hands on her stomach, wondering if it looked as distended as it felt. Even with the last couple days of eating more, her stomach was still achingly small. And she hated feeling full. Not to mention feeling so out of control. Carefully watching what she ate was one of the few ways she felt she could keep a grip on her otherwise aimless existence. But she was trying to focus on how much better her body felt. While deeply aggravating, Athena's comment had hit its mark—she needed to pull herself together if she was really going to be of use.

She looked around the room at her family as the low murmur of voices filled the room. They hadn't all been under the same roof in decades. She hated the idea of anyone in the family being involved, and she agreed with most of Athena's earlier assessments. She wasn't entirely sure about Athena's own claim of innocence—her sister was known to keep aces up sleeves no one could even see. She was also acting strange. That said, Hera's murder was not really Athena's style. Even back in the old days, Athena had never been particularly bloodthirsty. Clinical, methodical, annihilating, maybe. But not bloodthirsty.

But what about the others?

"So, who's who?" Alex whispered, breaking into Artemis' thoughts.

Artemis whispered back, "The man in the navy blue t-shirt talking to Hermes is my half-brother Dionysus. Hermes is going to be the only one happy to see him. There's no love lost between Dionysus and the rest of us. That steel-eyed woman standing behind him with the silver-haired pixie cut is his priestess Nyssa."

Artemis noticed Alex stare at Dionysus and wondered what she was seeing. Artemis grudgingly admitted her half-brother looked vibrant— clean-shaven with wavy reddish-gold hair just long enough to pass the collar of his almost too tight navy-blue t-shirt. A color calculated to accentuate both his hair and his green eyes. He seemed more at ease than normal, too. Maybe the four hundred thousand chips on his shoulder had fallen off over the last century. *But you hated Hera with your whole soul, didn't you, D?* she thought. He had plenty of rage and a bloody streak in him too. But he loved Father, and was already technically the most powerful one in the family. What would he gain?

Artemis continued, making sure to time the whispers with the swells of conversation in the room. "The guy with the cane and the muscles about to burst through his pinstripe suit is Hephaestus, we call him Hep. He's had that cane since the old days, it may even be a relic for all we know. He stayed true to his previous life, making beautiful things and working with his hands. He still has a forge on his property and he owns one of the most successful architecture firms in the world." *He also looks the most like Father with that black hair and beard,* Artemis thought with a twinge.

"The woman over there with the auburn dreadlocks is Aphrodite," Artemis whispered.

Alex looked at her in surprise. "Really?"

"Yeah, not what you'd expect," Artemis said.

"No, but she's still gorgeous," Alex whispered. "Even with no makeup."

Artemis shrugged. "I guess so." She looked at her other half-sister sitting comfortably in her colorful patched hoodie and yoga pants. Some of her red dreads were piled on her head with the rest hanging down her back, beads strewn throughout. She had earrings along the edge of her entire ear and a delicate ring hung under her nose. What irked Artemis more than her beauty was that somewhere along the way Aphrodite had actually become a good person. She was still all about love, but not the romantic kind. More the lover of all people kind, a do-gooder who was always involved with a cause. *God, I hate her,* Artemis thought, with no real energy behind it. She didn't want to acknowledge that it was mostly envy. And while the old Aphrodite had pulled off some good old-fash-ioned malice and even torture, she didn't think the new Aphrodite would.

"Why is Hep looking at her like that?" Alex asked, noticing the rancor with which he stared at Aphrodite.

"She and Hep were a thing once, back before The Fall, before it was considered gross. Aphrodite cheated on Hep with Ares, and he never forgave her. He never forgives anyone."

"Crazy," Alex muttered, shaking her head.

Artemis couldn't disagree. She looked at Hep. He was a powerful ally, but once he felt betrayed he was all stone and spikes, wielding his bitter-ness like a flail. *You have reason to hate Hera too, don't you Hep?* Artemis thought. Hera was the cause of Hep's disability. So full of rage at yet another adulterous offspring, she'd thrown him down a mountain when he was a kid. It broke his leg and she cursed it to stay that way. No one in the family had ever tried to heal him for fear of her reprisal.

Artemis shook her head at the memory. Everyone had kowtowed to Hera. Even Father, though it didn't keep him faithful. Artemis had long since accepted her father with all of his flaws, and back in the day, there were many. But he loved his kids. Her heart ached. They had to find him.

Apollo and Athena finally walked in. Aphrodite leapt from her chair at the sight of them. "Okay guys, I'm freaking out. What's going on? Is everyone okay? We never do this." She gestured at the family gathering.

Athena sat down in a corner, steepled her fingers in front of her lips and watched everyone carefully. Apollo smoothed out his face and got right to it. "No. I have some terrible news. I'd sit back down if I were you." Aphrodite sat down with a thump, a worried look on her face.

"Eighteen hours ago, we discovered Hera was murdered," Apollo said. Artemis held her breath and waited for the room to respond, trying to watch all three of the newcomers at once.

"Murdered?" Hephaestus said in a deep bass voice. "You're joking. How? Did someone actually finally cut that bitch's head off?" There were a few chuckles.

"In a sense, Hep. She was…well, she was tortured—literally pulled apart piece by piece until she died." The room was silent for a long minute.

"Well, that's horrifying," Aphrodite said with a grimace. "She was truly, and in every way, a terrible person, but no one deserves that." Everyone nodded except Hep and Dionysus. Hep was stone, his face betraying nothing. Dionysus looked disturbed as he stared up at Apollo, his body taut.

"Regardless, no one here in this room is sorry she's gone," Hephaestus said. "There must be more or you wouldn't have brought us here."

"You're right of course, Hep," Apollo said. He spread his hands wide, looking a little helpless. Athena jumped in to save him with her stoicism. "Sei was there with her when it happened. He was also murdered."

The room finally enlivened with sounds of shock, sorrow, and dismay. "No!" Aphrodite burst out. Tears immediately started to flow down her high cheekbones.

Hep sat down, looking pale, his cane falling to the carpeted floor. "How…?"

"His head was pulled off his body," Apollo said.

"Who could have cut off his head?" Hep said.

"I said pulled off. Somehow, from what we can tell so far from the evidence, someone put their feet on his shoulders and pulled his head off with their hands."

Hep's face paled and Aphrodite covered her mouth with a gasp. Dionysus sat back in his chair with a thump, the tautness leaving his body. Nyssa rested a hand on his shoulder.

"Impossible!" Hep said. "He was a bear of a man. I can't think of anyone, in any century, I would pit against him and expect to win."

Aphrodite nodded. "And everyone loved him…" A sob ripped out of her and she buried her face in her hands.

Artemis felt tears welling up herself, and stamped them down again. If she broke down now, she'd cry for days.

Dionysus nodded too, looking up at Athena as she watched the family's reactions. "Wait," he said suddenly in a strong, velvet tenor. "What about Father? If Hera and Poseidon were there, where is he? Is he okay?"

Athena folded her hands. "As far as we can tell, he was taken by whoever murdered the others."

The three erupted and stood all at once, talking over each other. "What do you mean taken?" Aphrodite said.

"How do you know?" Hep said.

"What are we doing just sitting here!?" Dionysus said, his hands balled into fists.

Athena raised her hands to get them to quiet.

"I mean we're fairly certain he was home when it happened, but his body is not there and so far none of the blood collected has been his. Though there is so much it's been difficult to process. Additionally, by the time we found them it had already been approximately a week since it happened."

"So he could be alive," Aphrodite said quickly.

"Yes."

"What is being done?" Dionysus asked. "Has there been any word from the kidnappers?"

"And why are we just now being told?" Hep asked.

"No, there has been no word," Athena said. "We wanted to process the scene to see if we could find any answers before notifying you. I have people on it—forensic teams and retired detectives dedicated to me, and they have not been idle. So far we only have a couple of leads, so it was time to make you aware and find out if there was anything you know that we don't. That, and you all need to keep your eyes open. We could be in danger as well."

"Wait, what do you mean?" Aphrodite asked. She looked dazed as she tugged on one of her russet locks.

Hermes spoke for the first time. "Think about it, Aphrodite. They were killed in literally the one and only way we can be. Doesn't that seem a little suspect? Someone knew who they were, and knew enough to know how to kill them—"

"And that someone probably knows who we are too," Hep finished quietly, staring at the floor.

The room was somber as a tomb.

"Well, that's just great," said Dionysus.

"What are the two leads?" Hep asked.

Athena gestured to Artemis. The rest of the eyes in the room followed.

Artemis took a deep breath and brought Alex into the light.

20

Alex held her breath as Artemis pulled her into the sitting area. It felt as though all those eyes were going to flay her alive.

"Speaking of people who know who we are, who the hell is this?" Hep asked, pointing at Alex. "This is ridiculous, Artemis, even for you. Of all the times to bring a mortal into things—"

Artemis jumped in. "Guys, chill. This is my friend Alex, she's here to help. She's an Oracle."

Four pairs of eyes widened at once and shock crackled across the room. Hep and Aphrodite wordlessly turned to Athena and Apollo for confirmation.

"It appears to be true," Athena said.

Apollo nodded. "Though she's not a normal Oracle. We think she comes from a line missed in the massacre. Cassandra's line," Apollo said.

A look of recognition flooded Aphrodite's face. "The poor woman you cursed? The one who predicted the whole Troy debacle?"

Apollo looked dismayed and nodded.

"How the hell can you possibly know that?" Hep asked.

"We don't, but she has the same affliction," Apollo said. "She has the gift of sight, but if she talks about it, no one believes her."

Hep looked at Alex in wonder. "I'll be damned."

Aphrodite smiled warmly at Alex. "But she can still help, I'm sure!"

"Time will tell," Apollo said. "We have to figure out how to work around her curse, but we're managing a little."

Dionysus and Nyssa were still staring at Alex. Nyssa's face was inscrutable, but Dionysus looked at her hungrily as if she might disappear at any minute. Alex suddenly felt short of breath.

Alex half waved at everyone in an awkward greeting.

"Has she seen anything yet?" Nyssa asked softly. Alex thought Nyssa's intense gray eyes didn't quite fit into her kind face. It was the first time she spoke and the room turned to her.

"Honestly, Dionysus, why is *she* here?" Hep asked.

"Because I need her here," Dionysus said. "You should know that by now, you know her."

"But why—" Hep started.

"Hep, is now really the time?" Aphrodite asked, exasperated. "It doesn't matter. And I'd like to know the answer to her question."

"The answer is yes," Artemis said. Her voice was rich with *I-told-you-so*.

Artemis caught everyone up with what had happened so far, the story punctured with gasps of incredulity and side-eyes to Alex, who felt like a bug under a magnifying glass. It also occurred to her that she was basically being outed as a witness to a murder.

"Excuse me," she murmured. She slipped out the door and fled into the hallway, craving the comfort of silence and solitude. She found Apollo's library and sank into a chair, putting her head in her hands. *Breathe in...I'm okay...breathe out...I'm okay...breathe in...breathe out...*

After a few moments she calmed, and she glanced around the room. Each wall of the sizable library was covered in white bookshelves so tall they needed a ladder, filled to the brim with books. They seemed to be mostly medical or scientific books from across the ages but as she meandered toward the back she finally started seeing titles she recognized, mostly classics. In the very back were bookshelves with thrillers, mysteries, and literary fiction. She had a feeling they were Henry's.

She reached to pull one off the shelf when she heard some fast pattering footsteps behind her. A solid, grayish-brown dog rounded the corner. He had a white patch up his chest and a big blocky head. He looked up at her in apparent hopes.

"Well, hello, are you Titus?" she asked, kneeling down and looking into his wet brown eyes. He wagged his tail at the name. She thought of what Apollo said. A test. *Maybe I should give this whole dog vision a shot*, she thought. Someone would find her eventually, and at least then she'd be doing something useful.

She sank into a black leather wing-back chair in the corner and reached out to Titus. "Come here, buddy," she said. She pulled a glove off and touched his head, relishing the feel of his fur on her skin. She couldn't think of the last time she'd petted anything. Her grandmother had been against pets so Alex hadn't really given them much thought. But as Titus looked at her with the unadulterated love of someone having his ears scratched, she realized she may have been missing out. Maybe a dog would help fill the torturous void in her life. A little friend to join her on the bitter island of safety and isolation she lived on. Someone to come home to, to talk to. Someone to love, who would love her back. Someone whose fate was simple. Her heart swelled at the thought, and she smiled at Titus.

She pulled off her other glove and scratched behind both ears, trying to imagine the flash of light that always came when she got sucked into a vision.

Nothing.

She sighed. The one time she was intentionally trying to start a vision and there's nothing. *God, it really is a curse.* Or maybe it simply doesn't work on dogs.

She leaned forward and gave him a kiss on his head. "You're a sweetheart, aren't you? You pits get a pretty bad rap." As if in agreement, he gave her a loving lick on her face.

A brilliant light flashed.

Apollo cradled a tiny Titus as he approached Henry, who was reading a thick book, his back to the doorway. Apollo lowered the puppy in front of his face, his floppy paws dangling.

"Henry, this is Titus," Apollo said. "He's for you. For us. Isn't he adorable?"

Henry set his book down and took the puppy, looking dubious. "He is. But Apollo, you know how I feel about dogs."

"I know."

"Then why would you?"

"Because you loved one once."

"Exactly. You know how devastating it was, holding her in my arms as she died. I don't ever want to do that again," he snapped. He stood and shoved the puppy back into Apollo's chest.

Apollo took the puppy but kept looking at Henry straight in the eyes, waiting, a somber expression on his face.

Henry stepped back and crossed his arms. "I'm sorry, but you knew this. You know what it did to me to lose..." he stopped, something visibly clicking in his brain. "Oh." Henry let his arms fall to the side, the anger leaving his face. "It's what I'm asking you to do...with me."

Apollo nodded. "You're not even willing to talk about the treatment. The last time it came up you gave an ultimatum—that you'd leave me before letting me try it. But I need to talk about this."

Henry raised his arms helplessly. "What if something goes wrong? What if I die in some random accident? Or get sick? What if you get sick? Or die? You have no idea what will actually happen to you once you do this to yourself...I couldn't bear losing you either!"

"But then at least we're on the same playing field," Apollo said. "We'd be living the same life, together. Caring for each other, no matter what happens. And what if nothing happens, and we're able to just grow old together! Play pinochle and smoke pipes and do whatever old men do!"

"It's not worth the risk," Henry said.

"I've done the studies, Henry, I feel confident—"

"In mice! I feel I should not have to say this, but you are not a mouse!"

"I'm aware," Apollo said dryly. "But as I've said before, mice and humans share virtually the same set of genes. And CRISPR itself has been proven in human trials now, we figured out the delivery system and it is a

one-time treatment, though it takes several days to propagate. They've almost cured sickle cell anemia, for god's sake!"

"But there have been no trials on an immortal. So you don't know. Not for sure," Henry said. He sat down, putting his face in his hands. "I'm not worth it, Apollo. Even if it works perfectly and doesn't kill you on the spot, you'd still effectively be committing a slow suicide, for me. I just…I can't let you do it."

Apollo put Titus on the floor and sat next to him.

"My love." He took Henry's hands from his face and held them in his own. "Of course you're worth it. You make me happy. I love your mind, I love your heart. You have literally helped me become a better person. You are the reason I'm doing this. Across my entire, very long life, there has never been anyone I have loved as much as I love you."

Henry sat quiet.

Apollo picked Titus up and put him in Henry's lap. "You can't ask me to hold you as you die, and then live more lifetimes without you. I won't do it."

Henry pet Titus gently, looking at Apollo with desperation.

"Plus, I'm ready," Apollo said, sitting back. "I'm weary, Henry. In my bones. I've seen countless lifetimes. I've lost so many people, even children, who I loved. The years feel like months but still after so many they begin to weigh heavy. I've done everything I have wanted, learned amazing things. I've seen the world change, watched technology bring us miracles, extending human life so much farther than ever before. I've created and completed countless bucket lists. The only thing I have yet to do, something I have always wanted to do, is grow old with someone I love. Or at least have the chance to. To truly savor life because it is precious, and fleeting. I want to be human."

Henry sighed and sat back, pulling Titus closer to him, not meeting Apollo's eyes. He cleared his throat and wiped his eyes with the back of his hand. "What about Artemis?" he asked, a seemingly last-ditch effort to stop this from happening.

"She won't understand, and that discussion is not going to be easy."

"She'll hate me," Henry said. He sounded miserable.

"No. She may hate me though, at least for a while," Apollo said. "But *at some point she has to figure out how to survive on her own. Find a purpose. And maybe it will turn out I've been hindering and not helping her in this. I don't know. But either way, I cannot live my life for her, no matter how much I love her."*

They were both silent for several moments.

"Alright," he said. He kept his eyes down and squeezed the puppy tight. "Alright."

Apollo's face lit up. "Oh Henry, thank you." He leaned over the arm of the chair and hugged him tight, squishing Titus, who yipped. The men chuckled and Henry put the puppy on the floor.

As usual Alex was totally immersed in the vision, and it was with difficulty that she mentally separated and pulled herself out of the river of emotion between the two men. Time to try to get out. She stared at Titus as he peed on the carpet, trying to remember what Apollo said about manifesting the Thread. Imagine it coming out of his heart?

Titus started sniffing his way around the house, so Alex was forced to follow him. It made it hard to focus. *Okay little guy, please help me out. Just lay down somewhere, okay?* He sniffed his way into a bedroom where he laid down and started nibbling contentedly on a pair of dress shoes.

Alex focused. She looked at the puppy and imagined a thread coming through his heart out his back. Nothing happened. She imagined it being thicker, like a rope, and thin like a filament. Nothing. Her frustration mounted as Titus nibbled. Knowing it was possible to leave a vision had changed everything, and now it felt like she was in a mental Chinese finger trap.

Okay, new tack, she thought. Apollo had called it luminous, so maybe the Thread was more like light? She tried to imagine that coming out of Titus, kind of like a Jedi's lightsaber.

Nothing but puppy.

Alex wanted to scream.

21

The shocked tension filling the great room mounted as Artemis caught everyone up on what Alex had seen and what they knew of the murderer's body.

Once she was done, Athena took over. "We're substantiating Alex's vision as we speak. Now I have questions for you three."

Artemis listened carefully as Athena ascertained everyone's recent doings and communications with Zeus, Hera, or Poseidon. All of them claimed to not have spoken to them in ages. The most recent was with Aphrodite, who had dinner with Father about six months ago but said nothing unusual was discussed. No one had a new relationship with a mortal or had disclosed anything in recent years. No one knew much about Hera's revenge business, other than she'd been doing it ever since The Fall.

Hep finally snapped. "It is starting to feel like we're being interrogated."

Athena shook her head. "I'm just fact finding. Even the smallest nugget might help."

"Has anyone reached out to Ares?" Hep spat the name. "Asked him all these questions?"

Athena gestured for Artemis to answer. "I tried. He isn't letting anyone see him and he isn't accepting calls," she said. "I left a message saying it was urgent about his mother, but frankly I don't expect him to respond."

"Well, that seems mighty suspicious," Hep said.

"Maybe, but honestly, probably not any more than usual," Athena said. "That's been his MO for decades. We're going to have to figure out how to see him to find out what he knows. And at the very least warn him."

"And where's Demeter?" Aphrodite asked. "She talks to her brothers often. She's going to be crushed about Sei."

"Demeter isn't answering either," Artemis said. "I've tried several times. We're going to have to go to her farm to talk to her."

"That's strange," Hermes said. "You tried her cell? Left messages? She's usually pretty responsive."

Artemis looked at him and blinked once, slow and deliberate.

"I'm just asking!"

"Well, someone will have to go tell them," Athena said. No one would meet her gaze. She rolled her eyes. "And we'll figure that out later, then."

Suddenly, Artemis wondered where Alex had gone to. As she got up to check, Aphrodite grabbed her arm.

"Hey," Aphrodite said. "I just wanted to see if you were okay."

Artemis narrowed her eyes at her sister. "Why?"

"Because you were at their place and saw it, right? That had to be just awful."

Oh. Damn her. "Yeah. Terrible. Brutal even for the old days. I haven't totally processed it, to be honest."

Aphrodite pulled her in for a big bear hug. "I can't even imagine. I'm sorry Artemis. This is all just insane. I can't believe Sei is gone. And poor Father!" her voice caught.

Artemis nodded. She gave her unbearably lovely sister a brief hug back and felt her eyes begin to burn. "I'm going to go check on Alex, I'll be back." She hurried down the hallway and found Alex sitting upright in Henry's library chair, with Titus curled up at her feet.

Her eyes were white.

Artemis rushed over to her friend to try to rouse her. *I've got you*

Alex, she thought. She hesitated. Everyone should see this. She hoped Alex would understand as she ran back and broke into the murmuring great room.

"For any of you still doubting, Alex is caught in a vision. You can see for yourself. Apollo, we'll need those smelling salts or whatever."

"On it," he said. Apollo rushed out of the room while the others followed Artemis. They crowded around Alex in a semi-circle of astonishment.

"Man, that's just crazy to see again after all this time," Aphrodite said.

"I never thought we would," Dionysus said, his voice full of wonder.

"And we're sure it's not just some sort of epileptic thing?" Hep said.

"I very much doubt it. Look at the iridescent sheen in the whiteness of her eyes," Athena said.

"Not to mention that she's not slack or slumped over," Hermes said. "She's just sitting there. I bet we could move her around if we wanted. Remember how we could do that?"

Artemis gave him a dirty look. "But we're not going to," she said.

Hermes shrugged. "Just saying."

"It's making me wistful for the old days," Aphrodite said.

Apollo walked in with a small vial. "Okay everyone, give her some space. Waking up to all of you staring at her will be rather unpleasant."

"She really can't get out on her own?" Nyssa asked.

"No. She's spent her whole life getting stuck like this. No training, no support." Apollo shook his head.

"Terrible," Dionysus muttered.

"Okay seriously, everyone out," Artemis said.

Hep and Aphrodite left the room. "Go ahead Nyssa," Dionysus said. "I'll meet you in there." Nyssa gave him a searching look, but nodded and walked away.

Artemis and Apollo looked at him expectantly. Dionysus was still looking at Alex. "Do you think I could…help her Apollo?"

Apollo frowned. "As in heal her?"

Dionysus nodded, not taking his eyes off Alex. Artemis felt a sudden urge to step between them.

"I don't know. I have no idea how strong you are these days."

Artemis braced herself for the inevitable humble-brag, or more likely just a full brag. It never came.

"I think I'd like to try, if that's okay with you, Artemis."

Artemis was dumbfounded. "Of course. As long as she's willing to let you. That's…nice of you, Dionysus."

Dionysus gave her a nod and walked out of the room.

Apollo shook the vial, unstopped it, and waved it under Alex's nose. He leaned back and held it at arm's length, grimacing. Artemis wrinkled her nose and backed up even further. It smelled like black licorice mixed with kale and cat pee.

Alex sputtered and coughed. Her eyes returned to normal. "Oh, thank you," she said. "It was so much worse to know there's a way out, but not be able to find it."

Apollo stopped up the vial. "I presume it was a vision of Titus?"

Alex nodded and seemed to give him a knowing and sympathetic look.

Apollo gave a curt nod and looked away from her.

What in the world is that all about? Artemis wondered.

"And obviously no luck with the Thread," Alex said. She sounded annoyed. Or dismayed. Or both.

"It's okay, it takes practice," Apollo said. "And at least now we know I haven't lost my touch with the salts." He showed her the vial and its blackish, oil-like liquid.

"Are they special ingredients? Or could I get them anywhere?" Alex asked eagerly.

"They are similar to regular smelling salts, which are mostly ammonium carbonate. In this case we replace the carbonate with anise, fennel, and a special plant called valerian mixed with Epsom salt, water, and oil. It creates a similar reaction, but one keyed specially to Oracles."

Alex eyed the bottle like it was liquid gold. "Amazing."

"I've written it all down in case you ever want more. They are accessible at any New Age or specialty herb store."

"Thanks. I'm going to wear a vial around my neck at all times and tell people how to use it for me. No more hospitals for me!"

Artemis felt a tiny surge of envy. If only she could avoid hospital stays with a single vial of liquid.

Apollo started to laugh but stopped once he realized Alex was dead serious. "It's a good backup," he said. "But don't forget you'll also be practicing how to exit a vision gracefully whenever you want."

She nodded as she pulled on her gloves. "Sure. I can't count on that though."

"Fair enough, but you will. I promise," he said. "I think it's past time we had some more food, don't you?"

Alex nodded in apparent gratitude.

Artemis touched her already full stomach and sighed.

22

Alex sat on the edge of Apollo's elevated patio, watching the longest day in the world turn to dusk. She closed her eyes, trying to let the sound of the sea below and the cooling breeze calm her ragged nerves. She'd chosen a lounge chair next to a trellis of sweet-smelling jasmine, as far from the door as possible. Away from the family's arguing and constant side-eyes.

They were all putting her on edge. Dionysus especially. She had never been the center of so much attention—certainly not from someone like him. His presence was palpable, like a dense star, pulling all nearby objects into his orbit. She felt its tug every time he looked at her, which was often. Nyssa invariably followed suit, curiosity on her face.

The patio's French doors creaked open and closed behind her. *Damnit.* She held her breath and sank lower in the chair. Artemis plopped into the chair next to her like a stone in a pond. "There you are. I don't blame you for hiding out here."

Alex exhaled. "I'm glad it's you. Your family keeps looking at me like I'm a rare exotic bird."

Artemis laughed. "Well, you kind of are. I'm sure it will go away eventually."

"What's the deal with that Nyssa woman?" Alex asked. "She's not part of the family, right?"

"Absolutely not," Artemis said firmly. "But she's been around as long. We think Dionysus granted her something close to immortality back before The Fall. She's been around since he came back from his wandering days."

"Wandering days?" Alex asked.

"Yeah. He's kind of the runt of the family—the youngest and the only one on Olympus to have a mortal mother. We were all pretty awful to him." Artemis fidgeted with her ratty blonde hair. "The only reason he was even allowed a place there was because he trudged around the world to gather up followers on his own."

Alex felt a twinge of sympathy. She knew what it was like to feel adrift in the world.

"So Dionysus became a god, and Father let him in. He had to fight for his place and we didn't. Which is likely why he lords it over us."

"Lords *what* over you?" Alex prompted.

Artemis looked like she'd just bit into a lemon. "That he's still a god, and we're not."

Alex shot up in her chair. "Say what?"

"Yeah, I figured you should know. He was able to maintain most of the cult he'd, well, cultivated, so he wasn't as affected by The Fall."

Alex fell back into the chair, stunned. "And people still worship him today?"

"Yes, if you can believe it," Artemis said. "He's not as powerful, but he can still *shift* like Hermes and do all kinds of little things we used to take for granted. Nyssa was and still is the priestess of his cult. They're inseparable."

"Incredible," Alex said. "A god." Her footing in the situation suddenly felt even more tenuous.

"Well, Apollo's theory is that any immortal could be a god if worshipped by enough people for a long enough time."

Alex looked at her sideways.

Artemis laughed darkly. "Don't worry, no one's worshipping *this*." She gestured to her bony body with a look of loathing.

Alex smiled uncertainly.

Artemis glanced back at the house and shivered. "Okay, I'll let you enjoy your peace out here. You'll need it before coming in for dinner. Meals with my family are always *super* fun."

"Can't wait. By the way, did Hermes find that woman's body? Does he need help searching the system or anything?" Alex asked.

"I'll send him out to talk to you about it," Artemis said as she walked toward the house.

"No! That's not…what I meant," Alex finished to herself. *Great.* She grimaced when the door creaked open and closed again. Vintage string lights flickered on, crisscrossing the patio and infusing the evening with a warm, cozy glow.

"Artemis said you wanted to talk to me," Hermes said curtly. He stood next to her chair with his hands in his pockets, staring into the gathering darkness. He was impossible to read—a fortress of walls, surrounded by a moat, with no sign of a drawbridge.

Thanks, Artemis.

"I just asked her if you'd found the body or if you needed help searching the system or anything."

"No. I got in fine, but found no trace of the body you described. I checked several days on either side of your hospital admit date."

"That's strange," Alex said. Without thinking, she asked, "It's a tricky system, are you sure you searched correctly? I could—"

"I'm sure," Hermes said. "I searched the date, the body description, the tattoos, and the means of death. I also saw transfer orders to and from the county coroner's office from that day and nothing."

Alex shrank into her chair. "Okay," she said.

"It's almost as if she were erased. Or, never existed." He looked at her pointedly and the patio suddenly seemed less cozy. "Are you sure you saw what you saw?"

Alex flushed and turned away, swallowing a sarcastic response. "I'm sure," she said tersely. "I'll carry it with me always."

Hermes glanced at her but didn't say anything. He just stroked his dark, aggressively tidy beard, probably thinking curmudgeonly thoughts. Alex wished he'd just go away.

"Well, it is possible someone got in and erased the record of that body," he said, finally. Alex thought she detected the smallest mote of contrition.

"It was worth a shot," she said.

He nodded. "It was a solid lead…thanks," he said, with what seemed to be some effort.

"Sure."

"Well, I'm going to get back."

Alex gave him a thumbs up, keeping her eyes forward as she listened to his boots tread heavily back inside.

When he was gone she sighed and rubbed her eyes. She was wondering if she could get away with eating dinner alone out on the patio when the doors creaked open and closed yet again.

"Thanks for that, Artemis," she said through her hands. "He's a joy."

"Hermes is definitely an acquired taste," a rich tenor voice lilted toward her from behind.

Alex whirled, her heart in her throat.

"Sorry," Dionysus said, a small smile on his face. "Didn't mean to startle you."

"It's fine," she said. "I was just—"

"Staying out of the insanity?" he asked.

She nodded. Her heart was still pounding.

"I don't blame you. This has to be a lot for any human to take in, much less someone with your…gifts," he said.

She scoffed quietly. "Apollo calls it that too."

"Ah. Fair. A gift is less of a gift when it's also a curse. Cassandra was one of Apollo's more creative and cruel retributions. We all had streaks like that back then though. Humans weren't very real to us. Not unlike how humans think of apes, I suppose."

Alex raised her eyebrows at that.

Dionysus lifted his hands as if to fend off the idea. "I don't think any of us think like that now. But back then, what we wanted was all that mattered." He pulled the nearest lounge chair closer to her and slid in gracefully.

Alex turned back toward the shadows beyond the pooling light. It was hard to think clearly while looking at him. "But aren't you still..." she paused, not sure how to really talk about it.

"A god?" he chuckled. "Yes. Especially compared to the others." He made no effort to keep the pride from his voice. "But think of it like going from the glory of the sun itself to the strength of a flashlight. It was humbling, and it certainly has changed my perspective."

"Seems like it would be better than nothing," she said.

"That is without question," he said. He paused a beat. "I saw you stuck in that vision."

Alex flushed and fussed with her gloves, embarrassed at the idea of him seeing her in that catatonic state. Hopefully she hadn't been drooling.

"I wanted to see if I could help," he continued. "I don't suppose anyone in this family mentioned that prophecy is one of my special interests?"

Alex shook her head. "I thought it was Apollo's thing."

"Yeah, he's the one best known for it, but I consider myself pretty much at his level—we shared the Oracle at Delphi and I had my own in Thrace. It was a big part of my life. Still is." He cleared his throat. "But more importantly, I also still have some healing abilities. If you'll allow me, I'd be happy to see if I could do anything to change the curse. Perhaps even remove it."

Alex looked directly at him then, shocked out of her nervousness for a moment. "Are you serious? Healing? Would you have to touch me?" It all came out in a horrifying rush.

Dionysus raised an eyebrow. "Well, no, I don't have to, though that would make it easier. Is the curse triggered by touch then?"

"Usually, but not always," she said.

"Okay, then to be safe, I'll get close enough just to get a sense first. May I put my hands on either side of your head?" Alex nodded and sat forward. He knelt in front of her and raised his hands to bracket her temples. Her face was only a few inches from his, his intense eyes locked on hers. He smelled of ivy and juniper with a hint of amber, as if he'd just walked out of the woods. The scent seemed to flow right into her blood.

Alex was just wondering if this was really such a good idea when her eyes grew heavy and closed. Gold tendrils swirled on the darkness of her eyelids, as a tingling warmth flowed from her head down to her neck and shoulders.

It felt like several minutes before she came to herself. She opened her eyes, feeling a sense of general well-being. Dionysus no longer had his hands next to her head, but his face was still close, watching her. She couldn't place his expression.

Out of nowhere, Alex felt an uncharacteristic and totally insane desire to kiss him. *What the fuck,* she thought. Her nerves flooded back with a vengeance and she sat back, quickly putting distance between them. She took a deep breath of the jasmine scented air to clear her head. "Well, that was something," she said, a little breathlessly. "Any luck?"

Dionysus shook his head and looked regretful as he reclaimed his chair. "The curse is deep in your blood and bones. Apollo was right, it would take one of us in our glory days to change something so intrinsic to your being. I'm sorry."

Alex tried not to feel disappointed. "No worries," she said. She hadn't really expected to walk away healed, had she? "Thank you for trying."

"Of course," he said. "So, what has Apollo taught you so far about your gift?"

"Well, he talked about mindfulness exercises..." she began. Dionysus rolled his eyes, though he nodded when she mentioned what Apollo had taught her about the Thread.

"I suppose the mindfulness exercises will help, as focus really is key. But it can take forever. Want a shortcut?" He grinned impishly. It made him seem boyish, like he was about to pass her a note in class.

Alex again felt the tug of his gravitational pull. "Sure, I'll take any tips I can get," she said, trying to keep her voice casual.

"Okay. But don't tell Apollo, he won't like it, especially for a novice. He's a bit of a purist."

A small dark wine bottle about four inches tall and one inch wide appeared in his hand. Its label was a field of navy with an embossed silver snake wrapped around a silver egg. "If you know anything about me, it's going to be no shock that this is wine," he said. "It's my passion."

"Right," Alex said, recalling the myths. Dionysus was the god of wine, festivities, and other things, like drama and theatre. The thought painted the moment with a patina of surrealism. Just having a casual chat with the god of wine. As one does.

"There's something just so pure and perfect about wine—how the grapes take their flavor from the earth and nature around it. This particular grape grew in one of my Italian vineyards, near where my...well, one of my Oracles had a temple. The very soil there is potent and rich with prophecy. Did Apollo mention the mineral vapors used by Oracles?"

"No. Well, I guess he mentioned they sometimes used herbal assistance. Is that what you mean?"

"Yes. The most powerful Oracles of the day used the vapors to steady and sharpen their consciousness. It made their visions more potent, allowing them better control and the ability to see more. Most Oracles didn't try them until they were past their novice state, so as not to grow dependent on it."

He paused, as though second guessing himself. "And it *is* important to develop the skill first without it. But some Oracles, especially the ones we relied on regularly, used them often, like the Oracle at Delphi. There was a reason she had her temple where it was—the vapors coming out of the earth there were the most powerful in the world. Though it wasn't exactly good for her long term."

"Why? What happened to her?"

"Well, they eventually drove her slightly mad."

"Ah," Alex said. *Lovely.*

"But I found a way around that," he continued. "Once I realized my vines were absorbing the same minerals from the soil my wife, Ariadne and I, perfected an herbal wine that gave my Oracles nearly the same experience, but in a safer form that also allowed for easy transport. With the seer's wine, Ariadne became quite an Oracle herself." His eyes went unfocused, seemingly lost in thought.

Alex caught the melancholy in his voice. "Did she die in the massacre I keep hearing about?" she asked quietly.

Dionysus nodded, surprised. "Yes. You remind me of her, actually."

"I'm so sorry." Alex felt a slight relaxing in her spine. Perhaps this was partly why he'd been staring at her all night.

He nodded. "It was a long time ago."

Alex took the opening. "What exactly happened with that, if I can ask?"

"What are we talking about?" Nyssa interrupted from behind. They both jumped. Alex hadn't heard her come out of the house. "Everything okay? I sensed you were upset." Her voice was laced with concern.

"Yes, yes, everything's fine," Dionysus said. "We were just talking about my seer's wine, and Ariadne came up."

"Ah," Nyssa said. She put a hand on his shoulder and squeezed.

"Alex, this is Nyssa, my lifelong ally and best friend. She's like a sister to me. She's my priestess and I'd be lost without her." Dionysus beamed at the woman.

"Nice to meet you, Alex." Nyssa smiled, her eyes crinkling with laugh lines.

"You too," Alex said. She couldn't place Nyssa's age, though she looked older than Dionysus with her silver hair and sharp gray eyes, brought out by the red sweater she pulled close against the sea breeze. Eyes that were still bright even in the diffused light.

"I was about to give Alex one of these," Dionysus said, holding up the little bottle.

Nyssa frowned. "Isn't that unwise for a beginner?"

"Yes, I did warn her to wait until she was more comfortable with her visions, but you're probably right." The bottle disappeared.

Alex nodded and felt a little relieved. "Yeah, honestly I'd be afraid to make the visions *more* potent at this point, but maybe someday. Thanks anyway."

"I also came out to tell you the food is here," said Nyssa.

"Okay, thanks. Be right there." Dionysus waved her off. Nyssa smiled at him good-naturedly and headed back inside. The bottle immediately reappeared in his hand and he offered it to Alex conspiratorially. "She's right, of course. Don't use it until you're stronger. But it would be a pity for this to sit on a shelf when it could be used by a real Oracle."

"Okay, thank you," Alex said. She took it carefully. "I hope it's okay if I wait. I need to at least figure out how to get out a vision on my own."

"Ah. Has Apollo talked about closing your third eye yet?" he asked, raising a sardonic eyebrow.

"Not yet."

"Well he will, he loves that analogy. But no one ever seems to know what it means." Dionysus chuckled. "In the end, it's really just about imagery. For myself, I found it helpful to simply think about opening a door and stepping out of the vision. But everyone has to find what works for them."

Alex nodded, though she wasn't really sure what he meant. "Do you have any tips for stopping one before it starts? I'd kill for a kill switch. I've been given every psychological drug known to man, but nothing seems to truly prevent it."

"It's similar imagery. For me, it was slamming the door as soon as I felt it start. Just make sure whatever image you use is strong and detailed. You're providing your mind with a vehicle, something to focus on. Eventually it will feel second nature and you won't need the imagery. Does this make sense?"

"Sort of," she said. A brief spike of frustration threatened to overwhelm her. "It's a little disheartening to think that after all this time it's as simple as imagery."

"There is nothing simple about it, and there's no way you could have intuited that without some training."

"Thanks," she said, trying to let that in.

"Well, we better get in there." He offered a hand to help her up.

She looked at it and froze. She was not going to touch an immortal, even with her gloves. "I'll be in shortly. Thanks again." She smiled to take away any potential offense.

"I'm very glad to have met you, Alex. Let me know if you have any other questions. Apollo is brilliant, but he's all about hard work and earning things. I live…a little differently." He grinned. "Plus, the chance of working with an Oracle again is too good to pass up. Though in truth, I would love to spend some time with you regardless. Call me. Please." A black business card appeared in his outstretched hand.

She took it without saying anything, and he left her in peace. Alex stared at it as she tried to corral up the strange thoughts and feelings writhing around from their encounter, a feeling perhaps influenced by the symbol on his card—the same silver serpent and egg. A single phone number was typed on the back.

"Alex, dinner's here!" Artemis called from the door.

Alex pocketed the card, took another deep breath, and headed back into the fray.

23

T he smell of warm spices filled the air as Artemis picked at her small plate of Massaman chicken curry, only half listening to her family as they discussed the situation ad nauseam. Delicious though it smelled, it was going down like sawdust. It took every ounce of will to lift her fork to her mouth and swallow a morsel, each bite seeming to erode what little control she had of her life. It didn't help that she felt like she was sitting waist-deep in shark-infested waters. Her nerves were raw and tense, waiting for the inevitable attack from her hypercritical family.

She alone heard the patio door open and close quietly above the din. Alex hovered in the shadows just beyond the bright ring of light provided by the silver orb chandeliers hovering over the dining table. She gestured to the empty seat next to her.

"So, I was able to dig up some information about the man Hera ruined most recently," Hermes said, through a mouthful of shrimp fried rice. "An upper-class New York asshole, he was powerful, dangerous. Though not so much after she was done with him. Given that, I have doubts about him being able to orchestrate anything like this."

Alex sat with a plateful of Pad Thai and gave Artemis a small, frazzled half-smile. She was perched at the edge of the chair as though she might startle and fly away at any moment. Even with her nervous energy,

Artemis was surprised how much more steady she felt with her friend there. She took a deep breath and a big bite.

"How did her revenge business work, anyway?" Aphrodite asked as she poured dressing on a predictable meatless salad. "Do we know?"

Athena pushed away a plate already picked clean. "I do a little," she said. Artemis hadn't even seen her sister take a single bite. To Athena, food was mostly perfunctory, a requirement for survival. She generally ate quickly and was done, giving whole minutes back to her day to focus on more important things. Artemis wondered idly if instead of judging maybe she should take a page out of that notebook.

"We all know Hera's feelings about infidelity, yes?" Athena asked. A chorus of groans filled the room. Artemis snorted. It was like asking if you knew whether water was wet.

"Well, strangely enough it led to her one redeeming quality—an unfailing kindness to women who had been cheated on or otherwise poorly treated by men. She could certainly relate."

Artemis thought of her step-mother and the countless times her father had been unfaithful. She'd always felt a little sorry for her—until the woman ruined any potential goodwill by being so god-awful.

"If she met a woman whose situation was particularly atrocious, Hera would take it upon herself to be an avenging angel. She'd research him, have him followed, uncover every inch of his life. Then using that information she'd ruin him, a piece at a time, in every area—job, cars, body, homes, relationships, everything. It was a complex, detailed, and systematic destruction." Athena's voice had a strange tinge of pride.

Artemis grimaced. Even if the men deserved it, she couldn't help but feel a little sorry for them. It would be devastating to be an ant under Hera's brutal magnifying glass.

"Jesus," Hep said, shaking his head, perhaps feeling similarly. "I remember hearing something about pips once. What was that about?"

Athena was typing on her phone again and didn't answer right away. Hermes rolled his eyes.

"Athena?" Hep asked, also noticing her distraction.

Man, what is with her? Artemis wondered. Athena could usually multitask like a kraken.

Athena spoke without looking up, still typing. "A pip is a fruit seed. She got the idea from a Sherlock Holmes story where the intended victims got a letter containing five pips in the mail before they died."

She put down her phone and continued, unfazed. "She loved that and since pomegranates were her favorite, she adapted it to her revenge business. Eventually it became pretty well known in the elite, upper-class circles she tended to work in. Anyone that found a small envelope of dried pomegranate pips knew they were ultimately, and totally, screwed."

"Oh, I bet she loved that," Aphrodite said in her annoyingly soft voice. "Probably recorded them getting it so she could watch their reactions later over and over."

Artemis nodded, recalling the evil gleam Hera would get in her eyes before doing something particularly shitty.

"I don't think there's any doubt this was right up her alley," Athena agreed. "We're exploring that avenue for potential suspects but as Hermes inferred, it doesn't seem very likely."

"How can you say that?" Hep asked, gesturing wildly with his fork. Bits of curry flew into the air. "These are rich individuals with tons of clout, entitlement, and ego that she just stripped away. That kind of impotence could lead to a lot of rage."

Aphrodite looked at him balefully. "You know about that. Right Hep?"

Everyone froze and Artemis held her breath. A vein throbbed on Hep's forehead as he stared daggers at Aphrodite.

Athena stepped in swiftly before Hep could explode, her voice calm and measured. "But they were almost always men. While men don't corner the market on infidelity, they are certainly who Hera enjoyed taking down the most."

"So?" Hep said, his voice a whiplash as he turned to his elder sister.

"So we know the torturers were women. I find it unlikely a man such as you just described would hire women to do this, even very strong women."

Hep deflated like a balloon, though the vein still throbbed. "That's probably true," he said. He stabbed his food so hard Artemis was surprised the plate didn't crack.

Athena nodded and Artemis exhaled in relief. Family Fight Number One averted. She wondered how long it would take to get to Number Two.

"Okay, we really need to bring the rest of the family up to speed," Athena said. "Who will go talk to Ares? I can't, given his deep hatred of me. And Hep, I suppose you're out, given your hatred of him."

"Damn right," Hep mumbled.

"We need Hermes to stay available for *shifting* as well as utilize his other skills right now."

Hermes shrugged, his eyes on his food. Athena turned to Aphrodite. "Could you go? You might have some luck."

Hep scoffed.

Aphrodite shook her head. "He and I had a falling out a couple decades ago and haven't spoken since." She twirled one of her dreadlocks around her finger. "What about you Apollo? You've no issues with each other."

"No, but I'd prefer not to," Apollo said. "We've never understood each other and frankly don't communicate well."

Athena raised an eyebrow. "Dionysus?"

"Pass," he said, sounding bored.

Artemis had successfully ignored his and Nyssa's presence until now, and apparently she could continue to. God, this family. Artemis felt a serrated spike of annoyance. "Good lord, I'll go," she snapped. "I need something to do and while he and I are not close, we've always had a mutual respect if nothing else."

The room quieted and suddenly no one would meet her eyes. Artemis looked around, baffled. "What?"

Athena looked at her thoughtfully, tapping her finger on her chin. "I'm trying to decide if that's wise."

"Why wouldn't it be?" Artemis asked.

"Well, when was the last time you talked to him?"

Artemis shrugged. "Ages. Another reason he might let me in."

"I think she's just worried that—" Apollo started to say.

"Oh come off it everyone, she's not made of porcelain," Hep interrupted. "Look," he said to Artemis. "We're just saying you're not what you used to be. And Ares has no respect for weaklings. He refuses to deal with them. You know that."

Artemis felt hot and cold all at once. She stared daggers at Hep as a flush crept up her neck and her fingernails cut into her palms to stop their trembling. She stood so quick her chair fell to the ground behind her. "Listen, you pompous, arrogant, gimpy little bastard—"

"Let's not degenerate here—" Athena began.

Apollo tried to intercede. "Forget him, Artemis," he said. Artemis scowled at her brother with hurt in her eyes. Apollo looked down at his hands.

Aphrodite gave him a dirty look. "Jesus, Hep. Was that necessary?"

"I'm just sick of everyone trying to dance around everything all the time," Hep said. He shrugged and took a bite as though nothing was happening.

They all started arguing at once. It had taken all of four minutes to get to Family Fight Number Two. Artemis turned to pick up the chair, grateful to have an excuse to hide the emotions threatening to surface. She couldn't let them see it.

Alex leaned over and caught her eyes. "I'll go with you," she said. Artemis nodded slightly and looked at her gratefully before shoving the hurt and rage into the dark recesses of her heart. She smoothed out her face and sat back down.

Somehow the group had heard Alex's offer and they each looked at her with varying degrees of concern.

"You really should stay here and practice, Alex," Apollo said. Dionysus nodded vigorously. Both looked worried.

"Maybe." Alex shrugged. "But she's the reason I'm here. I'll go where she goes."

Artemis felt a rush of gratitude.

Athena looked off to the distance, thinking. "You know, it might actually be a good idea, something to catch him off guard and keep his interest," she said.

"Great. Let's get going." Artemis pulled Alex into the hallway before anything else could be said. Let them finish their stupid dinner without her. They had gone several steps when she turned to her friend, still trying to gather her wits. "Thanks for that. But are you sure? Ares is…intense."

"He's not still a god too, is he?" Alex asked, anxiously.

"No, Dionysus is the only one. Well, maybe Hades, but he hasn't been seen since The Fall. Hades was strange because he somehow had powers but no one worshipped him directly. Anyway, Ares may not be a god, but he *is* a wicked smart sociopath and narcissist. I'm not too worried though. He won't want to do anything that would cause the family to get involved in his life."

"Okay," Alex said. "Then yes, I'm sure." Artemis desperately hoped the trust Alex was putting in her was well placed.

She heard Athena pad quietly up behind them. "What do you think Athena, she'll be fine right?" she asked, without turning around.

"Agreed, I believe she will be fine," Athena said. "You'll want to bring jackets though."

"Why?" Alex asked.

"It's raining on Wall Street."

24

Jenna watched the family eat their dinner through her binoculars. Their conversation seemed to be getting heated; she caught the burly man staring at the auburn-haired woman like he wanted to squeeze the life from her delicate neck.

Jenna smiled wickedly in the darkness. She and her sister had ensconced themselves behind the large rocks at the edge of Apollo's driveway, providing easy viewing across the elevated patio, but safely hidden from the bright light emanating from inside.

Foolish to live in a house with so many uncovered windows, she thought scornfully. The Madness roiled inside her, hungry, restless. She longed to barge in and let it loose. To wreak havoc and take her revenge.

But that was not their mission. She felt a hand on her arm and turned to her sister, who signed to her in the special language unique to them.

"This is taking forever," her companion said, her hands flying. "When do we go in?"

"Patience. We will know the time," Jenna signed back.

Her companion nodded and strapped on her Venetian mask. "For Ria," she signed.

Jenna nodded and put on her own, feeling it hone the Madness into a laser focus.

"For Ria," she signed back.

25

Alex walked with Artemis down the wide sidewalks of Broadway in the evening drizzle, shoving her hands into her jacket against the cold. Hermes had dropped them off in a quiet, unoccupied street nearby. Seeing how late it was in her own time-zone caused a wave of fatigue to roll over her. It had been a never-ending day full of revelations, shocks, and situations completely out of her comfort zone. And it wasn't even close to over. She sighed and tried to let the familiar sounds of the city soothe her—the car horns, the yellow taxis as they whooshed by, the distant sirens, the noisy night clubs bursting at the seams.

"Man, I am glad to be getting out of there," Artemis said, resentment still simmering in her voice as she stalked down the sidewalk.

Alex had to scurry to keep up. "Me too," she said. She wished she'd been able to stand up for Artemis back there, hating how they had ganged up on her.

"I mean, Hep is a dick and totally infuriating, but—and I loathe to say it—he wasn't totally wrong. Part of why I used to get along with Ares was the respect he had for my confidence and skills. I'm sure his respect for me as an anorexic sloth will not be comparable."

"But you're looking so much better!" Alex said, looking at her friend appreciatively. Artemis looked more solid, though still a bit wiry. Like someone had stuffed her sunken skin with sinew and lean muscle. "It's amazing what consistent eating is doing for you."

"That's kind of you to say," Artemis said. "I'm struggling with it, but it's nice to feel stronger. I forget how fast my body recovers when it's actually taken care of." Artemis stopped in front of a particularly tall art-deco skyscraper. Alex craned her neck. Being a self-imposed hermit, she didn't exactly make it to the Financial District on a regular basis. She was always impressed at the towering forest of stone buildings. Office lights shone out of dozens of windows on the side of the building, plenty of people seemed to be working late.

"He works here?" Alex asked.

"Yes. He lives here too. Apparently he owns the building. Only the best for Ares. Though here he's known as Ethan Bane."

"Of course he is. He was the god of war, right?" Alex asked, trying to wrap her head around who she was about to meet.

"Yeah. Not so much war itself actually, but the battles—the brutality of war. The sound of metal clashing, the smell of blood, the destruction of cities, of men fighting and screaming as they die. He lived for that shit. Ares was more like a god of bloodlust." And with that little nugget, she turned and went through the doors.

Great. Super fun, Alex thought, her stomach starting to churn a little. She steeled herself and followed.

The building's shaggy ox of a security guard sat at a wide elevated desk under a massive sign that took up the entire wall above him—*Ethan Bane Enterprises.* He looked as lumpy as he was bored, very much out of place amid the grey marble and brass fixtures. He was reading a newspaper under the light of a small brass lamp.

"Hello. We need to see Mr. Bane," Artemis said firmly, her voice echoing in the large foyer. "It's a family emergency."

The guard snorted and looked up at her over his glasses. "You know what time it is, lady? I don't care if you're the Queen of England. He's not here, and he requires an appointment, regardless." He looked back down to his paper, shaking it in dismissal.

"Thanks," Artemis said, whirling on her heel and stalking out of the door. She was already texting on her phone when Alex caught her.

Artemis' phone dinged. "Ok. Athena just gave me the address of a mixed martial arts gym nearby that Ares used to train at after work. I'm not going to even ask how she knows that. Finding him there would be even better. He'd be in a good mood after a workout and easier to approach."

Or not, if he doesn't like having people know where he is, Alex thought. But she kept her mouth shut. What did she know?

They turned off Broadway and picked their way down a narrower sidewalk for a few blocks until they found the gym. It was in a shared building with several lettered logos along the windows, including one that read *Ultimate MMA*. From the outside, it didn't seem like a place someone like Ares would train. On entering though, they found a vast, clean space, filled with red punching bags and mats and a lone pair of young men training in the back corner. Alex felt extremely out of place and was more than happy to stand back and let Artemis do the talking.

"We're hoping to find Ethan Bane here," she said to a well-muscled tattooed guy behind the front desk. He looked at them suspiciously and walked off without saying anything. A few minutes later a man channeling Hulk Hogan lumbered out, handle-bar moustache included. "I'm the owner here. You lookin' for Mr. Bane? Who's asking?" he said in a voice as thick as his neck. The desk creaked under his weight as he leaned against it and crossed his arms, causing his biceps to poke out even more.

"My name is Artemis. I'm his sister, and it's a family emergency." She seemed perfectly comfortable, her presence evenly matching that of the massive owner. Alex wondered if Artemis knew that about herself.

"You're his sister and you're having to walk around New York to find him?" the owner asked, arching a brow. A totally reasonable question.

"He's not answering his phone," Artemis said, shrugging.

"Look, Mr. Bane is one of our best customers. He trains hard and pays well for it. I don't want to risk that relationship by handing out information about him. It's against our policy."

"I get it. But this is literally life or death. It's about his father. Ethan's clearly not here." She gestured to the mostly empty room. "If I promise not to say anything about you—and I mean never again in my life—can you at least give me a clue as to where he might be? I was told this was the one place he'd likely be after hours if not at his office."

"I'm sorry. I can't."

"Okay." Alex was shocked when Artemis suddenly seemed near tears. "It was worth a shot. Thanks anyway."

The owner nodded. "I'll walk you out."

"Thanks," said Artemis, her voice thick. Alex followed, impressed at the charade.

They walked out onto the sidewalk, lit only by the neon sign of the gym and a flickering streetlight. The owner looked up and down the street quickly then leaned against the wall. "Did you know MMA was just barely legalized here in 2016?" he asked conversationally.

"I had no idea," Artemis said, a touch too dryly for a woman supposed to be struggling with her emotions. "Come on, Alex." Artemis turned away, pulling Alex behind her.

Alex looked at the man who was watching them with a suspiciously blank look on his face. She pulled back. "Go on," Alex said to him.

"Yeah, it was illegal for twenty years," he said, looking at his nails. "New York was the last state to legalize it. So back in the day there were a bunch of underground leagues for local fighters. They shut down once it went legal."

"Interesting," Artemis said, her tone implying the opposite, glaring at Alex. But Alex could feel something was still coming.

"Going legal brought about rules, regulations, referees, judges, you know the drill. Lotta folks didn't like that. At least one no-holds-barred league stayed underground—kept to the more brutal beginnings from the 90s."

Artemis finally started paying closer attention. "Makes sense," she said, nodding.

"They have night fights all over the city, I'd bet there's one right now even. But who knows," he said, looking straight ahead.

Aha, Alex thought, trying to keep an I-told-you-so look off her face.

"You know, I've always wanted to see a fight. Any idea where it might be?" Artemis asked, equally nonchalant.

"No idea. They're illegal. And bloody. I keep my distance from that sort of thing. But I *heard* they used to have them in the basement of an old shoe warehouse in Bushwick if I was looking, which I'm not."

"Smart to keep yourself out of it," Artemis agreed.

"Well, enough history lessons. You know, you feel free to come and train anytime. We could use more women fighters. If you really are Ethan's sister, I bet you've got spunk. You ladies have a nice night." He turned and trudged back into the gym.

Artemis' eyes gleamed as they hurried down the street. "Thanks for catching onto that."

"I liked him," Alex said. "And nice weepy sister act. Are we really going to an underground fight at an empty warehouse? That's not exactly the best area."

Artemis gestured to her tattoo as though a giant bow and arrow would solve all their problems. "I'm not too worried. We just have to get there. Let me see if Hermes can…actually, let's just get there ourselves, no need to worry anyone. Do you know how to Uber or whatever?"

Alex pulled up the ride-sharing app on her phone. "I've only done it a few times. But it looks like that street is only fifteen minutes away and there's a few drivers nearby. I'll have them take us to the corner."

"Thanks. I guess I need to learn how to do that," Artemis said. "I don't get out much."

Alex scoffed. "Me neither. But don't worry. I think an illegal underground MMA fight is definitely 'getting out'."

A Pakistani man with a kind face picked them up in a tan sedan. Alex's foot jiggled during the entire quiet drive, staring at the back of the driver's head. She was not at all convinced that a bow and arrow would be enough of a deterrent against a gun or whatever else they may come up against in an illegal fight club. Artemis looked cool as a cucumber though. Alex tried to absorb some of that energy.

When they arrived the driver gave them a worried look. "You ladies sure about this?"

"We're good, thanks," Artemis said. They got out and the tires squealed as he sped away.

They walked down a vacant, littered street toward the first of a row of abandoned warehouses hulking in the darkness like derelict giants. It was the fourth that caught their eye, with an worn shoe logo on the building, and a buzzing emanating from the broken windows.

Artemis grinned at her as she turned down the side to look for an entrance. Alex's heart pounded as they prowled along the dark side of the building until they found a staircase that led to a door barely on its hinges. It creaked loudly as they snuck into a vast factory lit only by the dim streetlights from outside. As they waited for their eyes to adjust, Alex rolled her shoulders, trying to steady her nerves.

The enormous rusty machines squatting in the darkness barely muffled the chanting that suddenly filled the air. They followed the sound to a rusty, corrugated staircase, lit by a single light bulb that flickered dimly as they descended. A cheer went up so loud it shook the staircase and brought dust down from the walls.

Alex gripped the railing. This was not what she'd imagined she'd be doing when she woke up this morning.

They walked down a short hallway straight into *Fight Club*—if *Fight Club* had a large octagonal cage sitting on a platform, lit with portable halogen lights. It smelled of sweat and blood and money as people thronged around the octagon, yelling and jumping. The crowd's energy pulsed, rolling over Alex in waves.

Artemis motioned for Alex to follow and they skirted along the wall trying to find a better vantage point, finally squeezing themselves onto a small railed platform next to two drunk, hollering men who barely glanced at them.

"How are we ever going to find him here? What does he look like, anyway?" Alex yelled. She could barely think with the noise.

Artemis leaned her head toward Alex's ears, yelling back, "He's about my height, with short black hair, a ridiculous pointy-ish goatee, black eyes, and olive skin. He's muscular but not beefy, and has a bold, hook nose." She wrinkled her nose. "I guess some women think he's handsome, if you're into that sort of thing."

The crowd cheered again as they scanned it for Ares. Then Alex looked up higher and her heart sank. "You mean someone like that?" she asked, pointing directly to the cage.

Artemis looked and sighed. "Yeah. Exactly like that."

A bell dinged and Ares began circling the cage, his feet strafing across each other, his fingered fighting gloves up. Blood streamed down his face and chest, and he wore a wicked grin, menacing despite the milky white mouthguard. His opponent stood in the middle, tracking him. He was shorter and stockier with red hair and had a gash on his cheek. They were both barefoot and shirtless, wearing only long shorts. They circled enough for Alex to see the tattoo on Ares' back—a large snake coiling around a blade.

She didn't know what she'd imagined when Artemis said he was intense, but looking at him now it seemed a bit of an understatement. The voices of the men next to her rang in her ears, urging someone to make a move.

Suddenly Ares lunged at his opponent, fists flying, jabbing and under-cutting. His opponent ducked and blocked, flinching as some of the blows landed. It was brutal and fast. The red-haired man took the offensive and started a similar onslaught, landing a terrific blow on Ares' face. Blood flew out of a newly split lip that caused him to shake his head, dazed.

Alex grimaced, but couldn't look away. Artemis looked bored.

The crowd roared. Ares had yet to recover when his opponent pinned him against the linked wall of the cage. They stood there for what felt like forever, each trying to get their leg under the other, until abruptly the red-haired man went down hard. Ares was on top of him in a flash. They were a tangle of thrashing limbs until the red-haired man went still.

Alex gasped in spite of herself.

An otherwise seemingly useless referee appeared out of nowhere and blew a whistle, calling the match. The crowd went wild, chanting some-thing unintelligible as the referee held up Ares' arm in victory. Ares grinned and pumped his fist, then did a standing backflip in place. The crowd lost their collective minds. Alex noticed most people seemed happy though—it seemed very few people bet against Ares. Pounding music began booming into the room and the crowd nearest the octagon seemed to be turning into a mosh pit.

The red-haired man was still on the ground. Alex hoped she hadn't just witnessed another murder. Artemis was scanning the room. "Come on," she yelled. She pulled Alex along by her sleeve as they plunged into the crowd, weaving their way through to somewhere only Artemis could see. Alex felt like she was drowning in a sea of sweaty humanity, jostled and bumped by more people in a few minutes than she had her whole life. She kept her eyes on the back of Artemis' long hair and held her breath.

They finally broke through and stumbled onto the first step of a staircase that Ares was sauntering up in a black hooded sweatshirt and sweatpants, hood pulled up. The crowd began cheering, "Ethan, Ethan, Ethan." Ares turned and waved at them with a fiendish grin. Alex felt a chill as his eyes passed by her and Artemis as they stood at the bottom of the stairs. Ares did a sharp double take, his grin frozen in place and his beetle eyes narrowing at them for a long moment. He jerked his head slightly, indicating they should follow, then whispered to a large man also on the stairwell, ostensibly there to prevent the crowd from following. He let the women pass.

They stepped out into the comparative quiet of the factory floor. Artemis started to speak, but Ares lifted his hand sharply, shaking his head. They wove through the dark dusty machinery until they were outside. Ares nodded toward a large, idling limousine. The driver opened a door for him and he got in. The door stayed open.

Alex looked at Artemis with uncertainty.

Artemis winked at Alex. "It's ok. Here we go," she whispered.

Alex took a deep breath and followed.

Best not to keep an ex-god of bloodlust waiting.

26

Artemis and Alex climbed into the well-lit, immaculate interior of the limo and sat in the white leather seats behind the driver. It was a stark comparison to the grimy basement and its bloody octagon. Artemis felt strangely alive, energized. Walking down dark, strange streets, breaking into buildings, sneaking into illegal fights, weaving through frenzied, bloodthirsty crowds—it had been ages since she'd had such fun. She found she was even looking forward to the upcoming tête-à-tête with Ares.

Her half-brother sat directly across from them past the open bar, stoically wiping blood off his face with a black towel. Artemis noticed Alex's slightly widening eyes and watched with renewed appreciation as the gaping split on his lip got smaller and smaller with each wipe, healing right in front of them. It really was kind of miraculous, for lack of a better word. She felt a sudden distress as she thought of the decades she'd abused and taken for granted that very miracle. Perhaps she ought to look at the world through Alex's eyes more often.

Ares threw the towel onto the floor and stared at her with his freakishly black eyes, saying nothing. She stared back and waited, ignoring Alex's jiggling leg. After a few long minutes, she decided to give him the win. But as soon as she started to speak, Ares held up a hand again.

"Artemis. First of all, you look like shit. Second, this discussion, whatever it is, will go better for you once I calm down." His voice was cold and clipped. "You know I value my privacy. And you'd better have a really good explanation for this." He pointed a bloody finger at Alex, who shrank back in her seat.

Artemis kept her face expressionless. "Nice to see you too, Ares," she said. "I do, actually. She's an Oracle. So just chew on that while we drive. I'll save the rest for later, as requested." She gave him a mock salute and sat back to watch him take that in, internally giddy to drop that bomb on him.

Ares sat forward and cocked a ridiculously trimmed eyebrow at her. Then he turned his dead eyes to Alex, seeming to really see her for the first time. He looked her up and down, pausing for a moment on her gloves.

"Interesting," he said. He pulled a bottle of foul-smelling green sludge out of the mini fridge and sat back to drink, looking out the window.

Artemis beamed subtly at Alex, who glared back at her.

What? Artemis mouthed. At least they were in.

They drove in awkward silence all the way back to Wall Street.

They were escorted to their chairs by a barefoot obsequious woman in a pencil skirt who offered water then literally ran to get it. Artemis took a chair in front of a prodigious black modern desk with brushed nickel accents. Behind it, the skyscrapers of the Financial District showed off its sparkling nighttime display in a bay of full-length windows.

"Well, it's more modern than I expected," Artemis whispered as she looked around the enormous room. A vaulted ceiling soared over charcoal paneled walls with espresso wood floors and white accents.

"I don't know," Alex said. "It screams power to me. What does he actually do here on Wall Street?"

"Athena said he's in corporate acquisitions," Artemis said.

Alex gave her a blank look.

"Yeah, I didn't know either. Apparently his company is top in the industry for hostile corporate takeovers. She said it's brutal and destructive, with lots of collateral damage. Perfect for him."

Alex nodded. "But bloodless, hence the MMA."

"Totally," Artemis agreed.

"What do you think those are?" Alex asked. She pointed toward a long narrow tray sitting on the edge of his desk between two succulent plants. It was full of trinkets that did not at all match the decor.

"Good question, they seem out of place." Artemis reached out to touch a gaudy class ring with an enormous ruby. She stopped and lifted her head, the light scent of soap reaching her nose just seconds before a disembodied voice spoke.

"I'd appreciate you not touching my trophies, little sister," Ares said, stepping soundlessly from the shadows. "I collect them, one way or another, from each of my business acquisitions, or as I like to think, conquests."

Artemis sat back. "Sorry." *Where the hell did he come from?* she wondered. There had been no footsteps or door sounds nearby.

Ares walked around and sat in a white leather executive chair. He wheeled it close, clasping his hands on the desk. Evidence of the brutal fight less than an hour ago seemed to have melted off him in the shower. "So," he said, "you're the first member of the family who has ever been here. What do you think?"

"It's impressive. Very you," Artemis said.

He looked at her for a beat then rolled to a cabinet and opened a small, camouflaged refrigerator. "I can barely stand to talk to you looking like that. Have one of these," he said, tossing a bottle filled with the same green liquid she'd smelled in the limo. She caught it mid-air with one hand. He nodded approvingly. "At least you still have your reflexes. That particular one is what I drink after a fight. It has electrolytes, vitamins, antioxidants, and dense nutrition, including over fifty grams of protein. In fact, take two—drink one now, and another later." He tossed her a second one.

Artemis felt a stab of annoyance. "Gee, thanks." She put them both on the floor. *Don't let him get to you,* she told herself.

"I mean it," he said. "Drink one now."

"Fine!" She winced internally at the petulance that had crept into her voice. She opened one, took a swig and spluttered. "Ugh!" It tasted of weeds and curdled milk.

Ares chuckled. "Yeah, they taste like goat piss, but they really help speed our natural healing along. Chug, chug, chug," he chanted. She gave him a dirty look but drank, pinching her nose with her free hand. She let out a big gasp when she was done.

Alex handed her one of the waters and Artemis chugged that too, letting its cool freshness cleanse her tortured palate. She wiped her mouth and rested her hands on what was now a very full stomach.

Ares turned his gaze to Alex, who seemed to hold her breath. "Alright, I am very curious about your friend here, what do you mean she—"

Artemis raised her hand in an echo of Ares. "No way, I'm done waiting. As I said, I'm here to deliver some news and ask *you* some questions. We can talk about Alex after that."

Ares blinked. He gave a wide, mocking gesture for her to continue. Alex exhaled quietly next to her.

"I'll keep it simple and to the point," Artemis said. "As you may or may not know, your mother and uncle have been murdered. Father has likely been kidnapped by the murderers. You wouldn't answer your phone so I'm here to tell you in person. If there is anything you know about any of this, please tell me. The clock is ticking."

Ares turned to stone, his face revealing nothing. "Is this a joke?"

Artemis slowly shook her head, her face just as blank.

Ares leaned forward. "Tell me."

She briefly relayed the details of what happened and what they knew. As she spoke, Ares began to pace behind his desk like a caged tiger.

"How do you know it was women?" he asked after she'd finished.

"Alex," Artemis answered, nodding sideways to her friend.

Ares stopped pacing and stared intently at Alex again. "I see," he said.

"This is unbelievable." He barked a laugh and punched his own hand in exuberance. "It's almost like the old days!"

Artemis was horrified. "Ares!" she exclaimed in dismay.

"I know, I know. It's terrible, of course. And I have no answers for you, Artemis. I haven't spoken to Mother or Father in years, but it wasn't due to any particular reason. I'm just busy and frankly, the family holds little interest to me." He started pacing again.

Artemis sighed. Great. They came for nothing.

"I know most of the family hates—well, hated—my mother. But I never really had any problems with her. She was brutal and vindictive and I admired her for it. But our very natures made it so we didn't have any kind of connection to speak of. Honestly, it was the same with Father." He paused, stroking his goatee.

"I have to say I'm the most shocked about Poseidon. He was incredibly strong. Stronger than Father, stronger than me, even. You're sure it was a woman who killed him? One woman?"

Alex nodded.

"Incredible."

"There are pretty strong women out there, Ares—" Artemis started to say.

"Oh come off it, I'm not being sexist. Of course there are strong women out there. And some of my sharpest, most cunning, and valuable employees are women. But the strength it would take to best and manually behead Poseidon would be…I don't know…unnatural." His face lit up. "Again, the old days."

Artemis gave him a disgusted look. "You'll forgive me for not being quite as excited about the murder of our family. We're all gathered at Apollo's. Will you join and help us find Father and whoever's responsible?"

"Assuming he's still alive, you mean. Hmm." Ares turned and looked out the window, folding his hands together behind his back. "No," he said finally. "I don't want to get involved. Getting sucked back into family business is the last thing I need right now. Father is likely reaping what he sowed, and if it's his time, so be it."

Disgust boiled over into outrage. "How can you say that?" Artemis yelled. "Father is the glue of this family!"

"Come on, Artemis. He may be that now for some of you, but in some ways he was worse than Hera. At least we all knew who she was and where we stood with her. With Father, you never knew which side you were going to get. The loving, protective father, or the selfish, neglectful, or brutal one. When it showed up, his dark side easily equaled Hera's."

Artemis looked down, deflated by that razor-edged bit of truth. She had mostly managed to avoid being on the receiving end of that dark side, and he had mellowed in recent years. So she'd chosen to forget about it.

Ares shrugged and seemed to read her thoughts. "I know not everyone saw it. If you didn't, count yourself lucky."

Artemis nodded and looked down at her hands, thinking about the implications of what he'd said. "I guess it's good to not make assumptions," she said quietly. "I think we have all been assuming that Hera was the target, but to your point, it could have been the other way around."

"I doubt very much that *all* of you presumed—" Ares began.

Artemis interrupted. "Fine, whatever. I'm the ridiculous one. Screw me for loving Father." To her infinite dismay, she heard her voice tremble.

"That's not what I meant," Ares said. "Again, you're just lucky."

Thankfully he'd ignored it. They all sat in silence for a minute. She just needed to think.

"We also came to warn you," Alex burst into the silence.

Artemis looked at her in surprise, but Ares just laughed out loud. Alex flushed.

"Warn me?" he asked. "What does any of this have to do with me? I already have more enemies than I can count. And as you just saw, I can protect myself. Plus I have a personally trained security team around the clock. You don't need to worry about me."

"Ares," Artemis said, exasperated. "Someone knows who we are, and knows the only way there is to kill us. And you said it yourself, they could beat you. It only makes sense to be on alert until we figure this out."

Ares began to laugh again when Artemis interrupted. "Especially if, as you say, it's like the old days…right?" She looked meaningfully at her brother.

"You may have a point there. I'll keep an eye out, but also know that should they come my way…I welcome the challenge." He broke out into a wide, ferocious grin.

"Right," Artemis sighed. She stood and nodded for Alex to do the same. "Well, we'll let you get back to your…whatever." She gestured to his office.

He walked around and she felt herself go taut. But all he did was put his hand on her shoulder. "It was actually kind of nice to see you Artemis," he said. "And you look a little better already."

"Gee, thanks," Artemis said, annoyed on several fronts. But she pocketed the other bottle in her jacket.

Ares scribbled on the back of a business card and handed it to her. "Here's my private number. Though I'm not going to get involved, I *am* interested in what you find out."

Artemis scoffed and flicked the card back at him. "Why on earth would I bother with that if you're not going to help us?"

He looked at her coldly before bending to pick it up. She didn't take it when he handed it back to her.

"Okay, how about this. If you keep me posted, with *real* information, you can call me for a favor, and my not unsubstantial resources will be at your disposal."

Artemis looked at him skeptically. "You promise?"

"On the blood of my mother," he said.

Artemis gasped, in spite of herself. "You're a terrible person, Ares." She yanked the card out of his hand.

"No doubt," he said with a shrug. He turned to Alex. "And you, Miss Alex. I didn't get to hear your story, and I very much would like to. I could use someone with your…talents. Interested in working for me?"

When Artemis began to protest, he raised his hand in the now familiar gesture to forestall her. "When this is all said and done, of course," he added.

Alex swallowed and shook her head ever so slightly. "Um, I don't think so," she said politely. "Thanks, though."

He nodded. "Well, be sure to get that number from Artemis, you call me directly if you change your mind. I could give your life a serious upgrade. And it would never, ever, be boring."

Artemis felt a sudden need to get Alex away from her pernicious brother.

"Bye, Ares," Artemis said. She pulled Alex to her feet and headed toward the door without looking back.

She felt his glittering beetle eyes follow them the whole way.

27

A lex walked alongside Artemis in silence as they wove like ants through the towering labyrinth of concrete that was Manhattan, seemingly in no particular direction. She still couldn't believe everything that had just happened. She had a wired, frenetic feeling, carrying her above her ocean of fatigue like an erratic butterfly.

Artemis was, by comparison, a walking cloud of gloom and doom.

Laughter and light spilled out of an Irish pub as a drunken man wobbled out onto the sidewalk in front of them, almost colliding with Artemis before stumbling back through the door.

Artemis looked at Alex as the sound muffled again behind the thick wood. "I think a drink is in order."

"God, yes please," Alex said.

The pub was packed with people swaying to the sounds of a lively band playing folk music. None of it made sense to Alex. *Don't these people have to work in the morning?* She chided herself, realizing she, the hermit, was not a reasonable judge of social life norms.

They found two open stools in the corner of the bar and ordered two amber ales, not talking until they'd clinked their glasses together and took their first sips.

"Ahhh," Artemis sighed loudly, trying to compete with the music. "That's good."

"It really is. You did good in there, by the way," Alex half-yelled back. "You held your own with him."

"Thanks. I told you, he's intense."

"Ha! That's an understatement. But at least it's done."

"For as much good it did us. Though that favor may come in handy." Artemis shrugged.

The music crescendoed to its final resounding note and the crowd erupted. Alex clapped politely, her ears ringing. Artemis just stared into her beer as though it were a crystal ball gone dark.

"I'm sure he'll be okay, Artemis," Alex said softly, her voice carrying easier now. "Your dad."

Artemis glanced at her. "Thanks, I hope so. I guess Ares got to me. It's probably too late. But I just can't seem to let myself go there yet."

"No, we'll figure this out. We'll find him."

Artemis nodded and went back to her beer gazing. Alex stared into her own as her thoughts drifted with the bubbles. She was not looking forward to returning to Apollo's and all the drama there, not to mention Dionysus. Her stomach flip-flopped unceremoniously as she thought how close their faces had been. She couldn't figure out how she felt about that. Or him.

"So, what else can you tell me about Dionysus?" Alex asked into the silence between them.

Artemis arched an elegant brow. "Why do you ask?"

Alex pulled out his business card. "Ares wasn't the only one who gave out his number tonight." She briefly recounted her experience with the god of wine.

"Ah, he told me he might try that. Sorry it didn't work. But be careful there. He's not exactly…stable."

"What do you mean?"

Artemis shrugged. "He's a little volatile is all," she said. "Being a god, he's used to getting what he wants. Plus, he's had a chip on his shoulder the size of Kentucky for as long as I've known him. If he doesn't get the respect he feels he deserves…watch out."

"Okay. I just wasn't sure if I should really take him up on his offer to help with my visions."

"Well, do you want to?" Artemis asked. Her seemingly knowing smile sent prickles of mortification up Alex's spine. The music struck up again, filling the room with a rich folksy beat. She was starting to feel pleasantly warm and the conversation seemed more relaxed and cozy as the ale succeeded in doing its job.

"I don't know," Alex yelled truthfully. "He's confusing. And hot." She took a long swig to cover her embarrassment.

"Ew, I guess so," Artemis said, wrinkling her nose. "It's up to you, but be careful is all. Gods are not ideal friends for humans. Stick with Apollo."

Alex nodded and raised her glass. "Noted. Thanks."

"Speaking of, what was the deal with you and Apollo after you came out of that vision of Titus?"

Alex froze mid-sip, surprised by the sudden drop into dicey waters. "What do you mean?" she asked, knowing full well what her friend was referring to.

"Well, you seemed to share a moment, and you looked particularly sympathetic. Like you were sad for him or something. I've sensed he's been dealing with something big, but haven't been up to asking him about it. I know you can't say what you saw, but—do I need to be worried about him?"

Alex squirmed. "I don't know…maybe? You two definitely need to have a long chat."

Artemis looked down at her now nearly empty glass. "Fair enough. I hate that you know something about him that I don't though."

Alex frowned. "Sorry."

"It's not your fault, it's mine. I should be a better sister to him." Artemis cleared her throat against whatever emotion was building there.

They sat in silence for a minute. Alex saw it as an opening to ask the last burning question she had. "Okay, so what the hell is this Oracle massacre everyone keeps talking about?"

Artemis grimaced. "It happened just before our fall from grace. An orchestrated, targeted attack on Oracle family lines, killing them all in one day. And when I say lines, I mean every baby, girl, and woman in hundreds of families died that day."

Alex gasped and the beer in her stomach soured. "My god, that's terrible!"

"Yeah, it was devastating. Most of us were friends with our Oracles. We consulted with them frequently, some daily. We never found out who did it, either. It's a sore spot for Athena to this day."

A terrible thought occurred to Alex. "I'm not in danger, am I?"

"Danger? No. No way. That was so long ago. And anyway, I've got your back."

Alex smiled. "Thanks. And ditto."

Artemis raised her glass of dregs to her. "And am I ever grateful for it."

Alex was just relaxing into the tipsiness floating her along the rhythm of the music when Artemis' phone buzzed.

She read the message and looked at Alex, a grim look on her face.

"The bodies are ready."

28

Alex didn't even stumble as Hermes *shifted* them back into Apollo's great room, glad to finally be getting used to his pitch black, chilling way of travel. The living room was dark and only Athena was left sitting at the chandelier-lit dining table surrounded by papers and a laptop. She was holding up her phone, apparently on a video call with someone.

"Where is everybody?" Artemis asked.

"I must go," Athena said quickly. She hung up and put the phone face down on the table. Her features remained neutral but even to Alex she gave the impression of having been caught with her hand in the till. "Apollo is in his lab. Henry went to bed. I sent everyone else home with the promise of keeping them apprised, and asked that they do the same. It wasn't difficult to see how counter-productive it would be to have everyone together. They offered their help should we need it."

"Gotcha. Who were you talking to?" Artemis asked.

"Someone from my office," Athena said. "I'm running a few key projects from here while we work on this."

Artemis paused a beat, scrutinizing her sister. She held out her hand. "I think you'd better show me your phone," she said. "Who watches the watchers, right?"

Athena's expression cooled. Alex tensed.

"I'm not showing you my phone, Artemis. It has nothing to do with this," Athena said. "I understand where you're coming from, but you're just going to have to trust me."

"If you say so," Artemis said, just as coolly.

Alex exhaled quietly, relieved they had avoided another argument.

"Anyway, I was hoping you'd go check in on Demeter while Alex helps Apollo with the bodies. You were always the closest with her." Athena looked at her watch. "Or maybe we should just try in the morning, it's getting late."

Her phone buzzed on the table, indicating another incoming message.

"Yeah, okay, I guess I'd rather be her harbinger of doom than anyone else," Artemis said.

"Great, thank you," Athena said, while looking at her phone.

Artemis waited, looking curiously at her sister. The silence grew unbearably long, with Alex looking back and forth between them. Athena finally looked up and gestured as if to say *what?*

Alex wondered too.

"Don't you want to know how it went with Ares?" Artemis asked, sounding slightly incredulous.

"Oh. Yes. How did that go?"

Athena sighed often as Artemis recounted their visit. "I suppose that's as good as it was going to get. It's good to have that favor in our back pocket. Can I have that number?" she asked, holding out her hand.

"Um, no, I think he'd kill me," Artemis said.

Athena nodded, but kept her eyes on the card. Alex had a feeling it was only a matter of time until she got it.

Alex swayed on her feet, the wiry, amped up energy of the night beginning to plummet. She'd better get down and see what Apollo was thinking with the bodies.

"Are the bodies down in the lab?" she asked.

"Hermes *shifted* them there, yes. You can head down whenever you're ready," Athena said. "And thanks again for your help with that."

"I'll have Hermes drop me off at Demeter's then," Artemis said.

"Great, thank you," Athena said, pulling her laptop in front of her. She seemed to immediately forget they existed.

"Man, she's being weird," Artemis whispered as they walked to the elevator.

"How so?" Alex said.

"Distracted, for one, and definitely it's not like her to not follow up on details," Artemis said. "Certainly not a big detail like a visit to Ares."

Alex shrugged. "She seems pretty normal to me," she said, thinking that most people had a hard time letting go of their hand-held digital fetter.

"Yeah, but that's the problem," Artemis said. "She's never been normal."

They were buzzed into the cavernous gray and white lab just as Hermes was wheeling around a cart with two cadaver bags on it, one extra-large and one extra-small. He pushed it next to a second cart holding many small cadaver bags. Too many. A pile of darkness in the spotless, brilliantly lit space.

"Where do you want this?" Hermes asked.

"Right there is fine," Apollo said. He hesitated briefly before unzipping the small bag on the first cart. Alex saw a familiar male nose peek out.

Apollo grunted.

"I know," Hermes said. "It's hard to see him like that."

Artemis put her arm around Apollo as the twins looked down at their uncle. Their resemblance was more pronounced now that Artemis looked more human than skeleton.

Tears brimmed in Apollo's blue eyes. "Actually, maybe we should start with Hera. Will you please take Sei into the refrigerated storage over there?"

Hermes nodded and wheeled the head and body away.

"Right, where are we doing this?" Alex asked.

"Right here." Apollo pushed a button on a nearby white marble counter and a long, narrow stainless steel table raised up from the floor. The tiles moved out the way to let it pass and folded back together underneath it.

"I didn't know you had that in there," Artemis said.

"There's lots of things you don't know," Apollo said gently, glancing at his twin. Artemis' face clouded over.

Not sure what else to do, Alex began moving the smaller cadaver pouches onto the steel table.

Artemis paled. "And there's my cue to go. Hermes, I need a ride to Demeter's farm please," she said.

Hermes took one look at what Alex was doing and nodded. "You got it."

"Good luck guys," Artemis said. Hermes laid his hand on her shoulder and they disappeared, leaving Alex alone with Apollo and dozens of body parts.

"What do you want to do first?" Apollo asked.

"Do you have the smelling salts with you?" Alex asked hopefully.

Apollo nodded and pulled the vial out of his white lab coat pocket.

"Great. I was thinking I could get the vision part over with if you want to lay out all the tools over there on that counter. I'm willing to stay in there for a few minutes to see what I see. Can you bring me back after, say, ten minutes? Then should we just start by properly arranging the parts tonight?" Alex yawned.

"Perfect. I know it's too late to do a full autopsy, but I can't go to bed without a preliminary look."

"Okay. Do you have an extra one of those?" she asked, pointing to his lab coat.

"Oh yes, over there." He gestured toward a row of lab coats hanging under a row of protective eye shields on the wall like a bunch of deflated scientists. She pulled one on, put her hair up, and traded her silk gloves for the surgical ones Apollo handed her. Geared up and surrounded by body parts, Alex felt truly comfortable for the first time all day.

She found the bag labeled HEAD and moved it to the top of the table. She unzipped it just a couple of inches and the familiar smell of rotting flesh belched out. "I'm used to the smell, but you may want to find some nose plugs or something. This one's going to be bad," Alex said.

"I'll be okay," Apollo said, breathing through his mouth.

"Wait, will you please remind me what you said about the thread? Maybe let's make it fifteen minutes and I'll try to practice."

"Yes, good idea. Most describe it as a brilliant white line of liquid light, going directly through the heart of the person or object you're having the vision of. Once you manifest the Thread, if you concentrate on it, it'll feel like it's sucking you in. The Thread will get big and the light will be consuming."

"Oh! That must be the flash of light I see at the beginning of one!" Alex felt a rush of satisfaction at making the connection.

"Yes. The default behavior is to get pulled in and watch whatever the Thread shows you—usually the nearest significant event. But once you manifest the Thread, all you really need to do is touch it, mentally speaking, and you can take control, using the Thread to see that person's past or most likely fate."

Alex felt a brief wave of frustration as she understood the words but couldn't comprehend their meaning. "But *how* do I control it? And how can I manifest anything when a bunch of craziness is happening in front of me? And is that how I can get out of them?"

Apollo smiled patiently. "Well, that's where mindfulness comes in, learning to focus amid chaos. Eventually you can also sort of pause it, for lack of a better word. And yes, both controlling and exiting the vision use the same mental faculties and imagery. You manifest it, then control it by whatever way makes sense for you."

"But how will I know what makes sense?" Alex asked, wincing at the exasperation in her voice.

"It's different for everyone based on their life experiences and what they are most familiar with. Back in the old days many used the imagery of pulling on an actual thread, because everyone sewed, but it may be different for you. You'll figure out what your brain connects with. Then exiting is as simple as touching the Thread and closing your third eye."

There it is, Alex thought, thinking of Dionysus and biting her cheek to keep from smiling.

"But first, you have to see it," he said.

Alex exhaled. "Right, manifest the Thread. Close my third eye."

"And keep an eye out for anything of interest," he reminded her.

"Right, okay."

She held her breath and pulled the bag open all the way. Knowing what to expect didn't lessen the horror of seeing it in person. Apollo blanched and ran his hand through his blonde hair, unable to take his eyes off Hera's face, what was left of it. Her nose and ears had been pulled off, and her eyelids sank deep into the sockets. Her lips were sunken in as well, like an old lady's. Even Alex's solid stomach lurched, saved only by her years of training.

She began her mantra. *I'm okay, and there's nothing I can do.* She took off her surgical glove and exhaled, tentatively reaching out to Hera's relatively unscathed forehead.

Nothing.

She glanced at Apollo, who was watching her in anticipation. "Sometimes it doesn't happen right away." She touched the forehead again.

Flash.

Hera in the robes of Ancient Greece, a glorious wedding ceremony... happy with her husband, a baby in her arms...weeping on her hands and knees...poisoning the water of a pregnant woman...the woman losing her baby—Zeus' baby...Hera raging, screaming at Zeus....unleashing wild animals on a poor woman...transforming a woman's whole family into birds, forcing them to rip each other to shreds...Zeus and Hera battling... reconciling...over and over...

The visions came at a dizzying pace. She couldn't see anything long enough to even try to manifest anything. If only she could get to more recent years.

At the thought, the images immediately changed.

. . .

Hera and Zeus clinging together after The Fall, powerless, scared...Hera consoling a weeping, bloodied woman...destroying the husband...finding new purpose...revenge...woman after woman...man after man...era after era...

It was still too much, too fast. *STOP!* she screamed mentally. Alex stared in shock as the vision did just that. It froze on Hera smiling with what looked like genuine happiness as she looked at a woman with a bruise on half her face, and a large, sutured wound down her cheek. The ill-treated woman looked to be weeping in relief.

Thank god, Alex thought, grateful to be looking at a single image. *Okay, now concentrate.* Alex stared at Hera, who wore a crimson Victorian dress that brought out her blue eyes and blond hair, which was piled on the top of her head in that day's fashion. Alex tried to imagine the Thread going right through her heart.

Nothing.

Okay, focus. A magical white line coming out of her chest. No problem, she thought. What came to mind first was a thick white skein of yarn, like the ones her grandmother crocheted with. In her mind it squiggled out of Hera's chest, bursting out like a mini xenomorph. She rolled her eyes at herself and imagined instead a small but powerful penlight shining through her chest. Better. She stared at Hera's well-endowed torso for what felt like forever, imagining how the light would look.

Nothing.

She started to get worried. What if she just was incapable of doing it?

She took a deep mental breath and recalled Apollo's exact description. Liquid light, he'd called it. Liquid light. The words slowly coalesced into images. She thought of her evening walks along the Hudson, catching the full moonrise over where the river meets the Upper Bay. How it created a path of pearly luminescence that reached across the water's surface right to where she stood. Just for her, beckoning. How she'd often longed to take that walk.

Feeling like she was onto something, she tried to imagine she was standing on that harbor now. This was difficult while staring at the two

Victorian women in a small parlor, but she concentrated, letting her inner eyes go unfocused. She imagined herself taking hold of that path of light, lifting it up off the sea, and folding it in on itself. Rolling it up tight until it was thin, narrow, and even more brilliant, pulsing as if it were alive. It's what she would want her own Thread to look like if she could choose—a Thread of luminous moonlight for her life to flow along. She took that image and imagined it was coming out of Hera.

Then it was simply just…there.

A cord of brilliant light impaled Hera through her heart, extending a few feet on either side of her, diminishing into the ether.

YES! Alex exulted. She imposed it on the other woman as well, and sure enough, it manifested. She looked away and looked back, still there. She glanced around the parlor and could now even see it coming out of a few objects.

Okay, now to touch it, control it. How to do that without any hands? She tried to manifest hands to no avail. She tried to focus on the Thread and tell it to move forward. Nothing. She tried to close her 'third eye' by imagining the whole room dark. But nothing.

Nothing, nothing, nothing.

The elation from a moment ago quickly faded and her focus slipped.

Suddenly an unspeakable smell permeated her mind, and everything dissolved in the fumes.

Alex gasped as the smelling salts made her eyes water. She waffled between disappointment and excitement.

"Did you see anything useful?" Apollo asked, stopping up the vial.

Alex let the excitement win. "I don't think so. But I did see the Thread!" She grinned. "I couldn't do anything with it, but it was there. I feel straight up like Neo in *The Matrix*."

"Amazing! Nice work Alex!" He beamed at her. "It can sometimes take novices several weeks to find imagery that works. Wait, who's Neo?"

Alex laughed, giddy with relief at having that part done. "Never mind." She pulled on her glove and turned to the bags containing the rest of poor Hera. She put Apollo in charge of the video recording and began.

I'm okay...there's nothing I can do. I'm okay...there's nothing I can do.

It didn't take long for Alex to sink into her usual, grisly work rhythm. She read each body part aloud as she laid it on the table, starting with the torso and upper extremities.

"I can't believe someone lived through this," Apollo said quietly. "She did live through it, right?"

Alex nodded as she laid a left upper arm and forearm next to the torso.

"Did they keep her awake then? Stimulants for when she inevitably passed out?"

Alex nodded and placed a right upper arm.

"How did they handle shock?"

Alex shrugged.

Apollo shook his head in disbelief and made a sound of disgust. "So, they must have started with the fingers, and made their way up her arm, unless they started with her toes and feet...?"

Alex shook her head. The arms were done.

"With the fingers then."

She nodded as she pulled a mottled palm from the bag as if to demonstrate the point.

Talking seemed to help Apollo think, and Alex liked that she could work while being questioned. "It was clearly about maximizing pain. Someone wanted to hurt her, badly, perhaps as revenge."

Alex glanced at him and nodded vigorously. Definitely.

"Strange though, come to think of it, if they knew who she was, which they did, right?"

A nod.

"Then they had to know that with our body's enhanced restorative capabilities, the pain would last only moments. Her body would have immediately started healing itself, starting with the nerve endings. It's actually quite fascinating to watch, I've done studies of myself under the microscope—"

Apollo froze, the gears in his mind almost perceptibly clanging to a stop. "Wait," he said, under his breath. "Wait, wait, wait." He picked up one of Hera's fingers and held it up to the light. He rummaged in a drawer until he found a large magnifying glass, using it to look at the torn flesh.

"There are no signs of regeneration here," he said. "Which is impossible. There should be signs of cell reparation immediately after the fingers were…removed." He put it down and started examining the raw edges of other body parts.

"What could possibly…?" Suddenly Apollo's face went as gray as the corpse on the table. "It can't be," he whispered to himself.

"Are you okay?" Alex asked.

Apollo nodded, distracted. "I think we've done enough for tonight, I'll put her away and we can finish this later," he said, his voice shaky. "I need to check on something. Artemis can show you to your room. Your bag is already there."

"Are you sure? There are only a few pieces left to—"

"Yes, yes, I'm sure. Thanks though."

"Okay." She grabbed her gloves and headed toward the elevator, hanging up the lab coat on the way.

"Oh and, uh, please don't say anything yet," he called to her. "There is just a possibility I need to eliminate."

Alex nodded as she pushed the elevator button. *Great, now I'm keeping secrets,* she thought. She tried to figure out what could possibly have triggered him. A memory scratched at the surface of her mind, but she was too tired to even try to put it all together.

Regardless, it didn't seem good.

29

Artemis took a deep breath of loamy air. The smell of the forest and its surrounding mist immediately calmed her heart and nerves. It was like breathing in peace. She'd spent weeks on end at her aunt's woodland farm—a safe and quiet place for her to come and get out of her own head.

Chirping crickets and rustling leaves were the only sound as a waxing gibbous moon lit the pickets of the short white gate in front of the darkened farmhouse. Farmhouse wasn't accurate though, it was more like someone had plucked an upstate New York mansion and accidentally dropped it in the middle of Nowhere, USA. Far from civilization, one had to find a hidden turnoff to find this woodland oasis, with acres of gardens and plowed fields surrounded by grazing meadows where farm animals were allowed to roam free.

As ex-goddess of earth and agriculture, Demeter had stayed true to her soul, shunning urban sprawl and focusing on her connection to the planet, responsible cultivation, and husbandry. She'd kept on the edge of technology, trying to guide the industry into more sustainable animal practices. She was tender but not overly sentimental, efficient and humane in the slaughter of her own animals if it was time.

What Artemis appreciated most was Demeter's steady presence and unwavering acceptance. She let Artemis simply be who she was, without judgement or expectation. Artemis smiled as she remembered Demeter's strong hands gently washing and combing her hair when depression had rendered her essentially bed ridden, and showering felt impossible.

The woman was an oasis herself.

Artemis was loathe to disrupt the peace here and tell Demeter the upsetting news about her siblings.

She let herself in through the gate and whistled a high trilling sound, waiting for Demeter's dogs to rush up and greet her from the back of the house. The dogs were possibly the biggest part of why she loved coming here. In the old days she'd kept half a dozen dogs as her family and companions. She missed it terribly, but felt she had to respect Apollo's wishes since she depended on him in so many ways.

When none came, she called the three dogs she loved the most. "Jasper! Camilla! Boomer!"

Silence.

A feeling of unease crept up her spine.

The feeling intensified as she reached the front door. It was slightly ajar. Demeter never locked it, but she did keep it closed against dirt, always. *Oh no,* she thought. *Please not Demeter.* Why hadn't they checked on her earlier?

Artemis braced herself and walked in.

Emptiness draped over the house like a shroud. She wandered through the first floor, checking the kitchen, living room, dining room, study— nothing. It was like walking through a dollhouse. She stood at the bottom of the wide carpeted stairs for a long moment as the silence became oppressive. She flicked her wrist to ready her bow and crept upstairs, moving slowly. Her whole body was tense as she checked each room, wondering with the opening of every door if this is where she'd find her aunt's torn and bloody body.

But again, nothing. Only silver dust motes moved as they floated in the moonlight onto her tidy bed. There was no evidence of a struggle, and there was only one set of footprints in the carpet. No one had been there except Demeter.

Artemis lowered her bow, perplexed. *This makes no sense,* she thought. The gardens in the back were the only place left to check. As she crept back downstairs, she realized she'd unconsciously saved them for last. She entered the massive mudroom, and exhaled when she saw the back door was open. She crept past all the gardening gear and bags of potting soil and stayed to the side as she looked out the door. It was quiet.

She used her bow to nudge it open. The scent of roses, lilies, and herbs clashed with the ominous feeling in her gut. Artemis walked down to where gravel pathways began to wind through Demeter's verdant botanical gardens. She knelt, looking at the ground. Someone had run here, barefoot. The moon glinted off her bow as she followed, cringing with each crunch of gravel.

The footprints led straight down the middle then skidded, turning sharply at the herb garden, heading through an opening in the hedges. Artemis peered around the hedges and listened.

As far as she could tell, she was alone.

On the far side of the lawn was a semicircle of dog houses.

Artemis no longer needed to follow the footprints, she knew where they were going.

A putrid smell wafted over to her.

Oh god, she thought.

She walked slowly across the grass, not wanting to see, but unable to turn away.

She stopped several feet away from the kennels.

"No," Artemis whimpered.

Demeter's dogs had fought here. Fought hard, and in the end, lost. It was as if a giant had picked them up and pulled them apart for sport, like a kid yanking the legs off a daddy long-leg. It was impossible to tell one dog from the next in the moonlight, their body parts scattered or heaped together, blood everywhere.

Artemis did a quick survey for any sign of Demeter and found nothing. She backed away, stumbling as she reached the hedge and dropped to her knees, barely feeling the tears streaming down her face. Images of their sweet faces swept through her, especially Boomer's. How he'd always find her and nudge his head under her hand, sweet brown eyes full of love.

They were her friends, and they had saved her in some very dark times.

And they were innocent. *THEY WERE INNOCENT!* she screamed inside her head.

It was the last straw as the weight and horror of the last few days finally broke her.

Artemis sobbed until she couldn't breathe.

30

Apollo ran to the small, hidden refrigerator embedded in the wall of his lab. He counted the vials that sat inside—a hoard of liquid treasure. Then recounted. He slammed it shut, the vials clinking together loudly.

"Goddamnit!" He banged both fists on the marble table.

His heart hammered in his chest. He'd have to tell everyone. Try to explain.

This was a disaster.

And it was all his fault.

31

A lex walked into the great room to find Artemis sitting on the dark brown leather couch with her head in her hands, lit by the soft light of a lamp. Athena was comforting her. "It's okay, we'll get them. We'll get them," she murmured.

Alarmed, Alex rushed to her friend. "What's wrong? What happened?"

Artemis lifted her face, revealing dried tears and red, brimming eyes. "Demeter is missing too. And they killed her dogs. All of them. Pulled them apart." Her voice caught. "They were my friends," she whispered.

"Oh god. I'm so sorry." Alex sank to the floor in front of Artemis and briefly touched her knee. Artemis covered her gloved hand and squeezed.

"How did it go downstairs?" Athena asked Alex.

"We got Hera halfway laid out but didn't finish. Apollo..." She paused, remembering Apollo's request just in time. "We'll finish tomorrow."

As the weight of Athena's searching look sank into her, Alex's whole body turned to lead. Her vision swam slightly. The stress of being tossed in the surf of this strange, endless day was finally taking its toll.

"I'm so sorry to bail on you right now, but I...I think I need to crash," she said.

Artemis wiped her face and looked at the clock on the mantel over the large gas fireplace. "Don't be sorry. We don't need a ton of sleep, so I haven't been keeping track. You must be exhausted. I'll show you where you're sleeping."

Alex plodded after Artemis up a set of stairs and into a comfortably furnished blue guest room with a king size bed and an ensuite bathroom. The floral duffel bag she'd packed all those hours ago sat on the thick white comforter. She stared at it, wondering how such a normal, familiar thing could exist in such a strange world.

Artemis broke the trance. "Thanks for everything today. I can't even tell you how glad I am that you came. It's just so nice to have a friend here. Nothing like family to make you feel like a total piece of shit, right?" She smiled faintly.

"I'm glad I'm here too," Alex said. "And you're great, forget them."

"Well, you still don't know me very well, but I'll take that, thanks."

"Are you going to sleep too?" Alex asked.

"Eventually. I'll probably wait up for Apollo then crash too."

"Alright, goodnight," Alex said.

"'Night," Artemis said as she closed the door.

Alex quickly changed into her pajamas, brushed her teeth, and climbed into the luxurious bed with a sigh. She curled up on her side and closed her eyes, welcoming the near instantaneous oblivion.

32

Apollo paced, his mind whirring as fast as the white centrifuges he was waiting on, though he dreaded their damning results. *How long had it been gone? Had they used it on Hera? Had they used it on Father? How am I going to tell the family?*

They would not understand. He had not intended for anyone to know until he had used it on himself. He hadn't gotten much further than that.

The first centrifuge dinged. Two sets of data appeared on a nearby screen as he compared the DNA from Poseidon's body to the sample he'd taken years ago. They matched exactly. A tiny spark of hope kindled in his heart.

The second one dinged and he pulled up Hera's DNA charts for comparison.

Her genes were changed, modified.

He groaned, the spark of hope squelched in the tide of bile rising in his throat.

The scientist in him couldn't help but wonder if Hera had felt any different, more sluggish, more...human. Apollo froze as the thought permeated. He himself had been feeling a little off. Not ill, he was never ill. But definitely off. In a rush, he scrambled to find a syringe to take a sample of his own blood. He would have to get samples from everyone!

Oh no, oh no, oh no.

Just as he was tying a tourniquet around his upper arm, the power went out, sinking the lab into a blinding darkness. A moment later, LED emergency lights flickered to life, illuminating the floor every few yards. Apollo looked around in confusion. He certainly hadn't been doing anything enough to trip the power.

The hair on the back of his neck lifted as he heard the faintest shuffle behind him in the sudden silence.

Someone was here.

His heart pounded loudly as he turned around.

At the end of the aisle two figures stood side by side like a pair of revenants, their Venetian masks almost glowing in the dim light.

As one, they cocked their heads to the side. Apollo only managed one step back before they were on him. One swept his legs out from under him and he landed on the cold, tile floor with a grunt. The figure grabbed his arms and pulled them over his head, holding them in place. The second one sat on his chest and covered his mouth with a cold, gloved hand. A stab of icy fear filled his stomach.

The Venetian sitting on him leaned over. "Who have you told?" The voice was slightly muffled by the black and white checkered mask, but Apollo thought it was a woman's. He struggled against her grip, but her hands were like a vice. Her eyes reflected the light of the nearest LED. Apollo squinted his eyes to see. They looked...wrong. *How could something like that be physically possible?* he wondered, ever the scientist.

She punched him in the face. The world exploded into bright points of light. "Who else have you told?" she hissed.

He groaned. "What are you talking about? Who are you?"

"Who else knows about your little serum?"

"Where is my father?" he asked.

The woman punched him again, harder. He felt his jaw crack, the sound resounding in his ears as thick, coppery blood filled his mouth.

"I'm asking the questions," she said.

Apollo brought a knee up to her kidney and spit the blood in her face. She grunted but didn't move. His own blood dripped down the white porcelain back onto him.

"I will only ask one more time, then my sister will tear your head from its perch. Or…it may be, we no longer need to do that." She pulled a strange spear-like dagger out of a sheath buckled around her thigh and twirled it expertly in her hand. "Perhaps you already have the wish of your heart." Apollo could hear the grin behind the mask as she spoke.

The cold pit in his stomach spread, numbing his fingers. "What do you mean?" he asked. His jaw ached with each word.

"Don't play dumb with us," she replied. "You know." She giggled. A terrible, maniacal sound.

"How—"

She punched him again. He groaned. His vision blackened for a moment.

"No more questions!"

"Sister," whispered the one holding his arms. "Someone could come at any time. Let us be done."

The woman on his chest held the knife to his throat. "Surely you don't expect us to believe you have not told anyone?"

Apollo just shook his head no. "No one."

"Not even that husband of yours?"

Panic shot through Apollo at the thought of them hurting Henry. He began to buck against her, unsuccessfully. "No! Leave him alone! He doesn't know I finished it!" he yelled.

She giggled again. "We shall see. He is not part of the plan, for now. It is all by the grace of The First."

He kneed her again with all his strength and was rewarded with only another grunt.

"Enough!" She dragged the flat edge of the knife across his throat, teasing.

"Sister…finish it," urged the other one.

"I will, Sister, I will." She kept her eyes on Apollo. "Answer my question, and maybe I'll make sure no one else gets hurt. Maybe."

"Look, no one knows. No one. I didn't want to tell them until I'd done it already, and I've been sitting on it for weeks, trying to work up the courage. I swear."

She cocked her head at him. "What about your sister?"

"Especially her!" Rage replaced the panic and Apollo head-butted the

Venetian as hard as he could, cracking her mask. She gasped and sat up, pulling it off to reveal a tattooed face with a line of blood where the porcelain had cut her. He twisted his body and kicked the lab table next to them, causing a large set of hanging test tubes to fall on her head in a loud crash. She fell back, dazed.

"Sister!" the other exclaimed, still holding Apollo's arms. He writhed, trying with all his strength but unable to escape her grip. It had bought him nothing. The spike of rage faded as panic set back in, careening wildly around in his chest.

The house's intercom buzzed, startling everyone. "Apollo," Athena's voice rang through the darkened lab, sounding impossibly calm. "We have news of Demeter, come up soon please." His heart withered inside him hearing her voice. Clearly the house still had power—they had no idea anything was wrong. He never thought he'd regret having the lab on a separate circuit.

Apollo rolled his legs back over his body, trying to kick the Venetian holding his hands, but she dodged him easily.

"Sister, recover yourself," she said. "We must hurry. They will come soon when they do not hear back."

His assailant shook her head, collecting herself. She crawled toward Apollo, climbing across the floor and up his body like an insect, pinning him back down.

"You're lucky we are out of time," she said. She traced the knife down his cheek and throat, then held it perpendicular over his heart. "The First One wishes you to know that because you have shown much good-will in your life, this is not desirable. It is, however, unavoidable. But we were instructed to grace you with a death kinder than our usual methods." Her eyes shone with madness.

"Please don't," Apollo pleaded with her. His breath was fast and quick. His dreams of mortality and a life with his husband shrinking in front of his eyes until it was a mere pinprick of light. He never thought it would end this way.

Apollo's grief-stricken scream filled the lab as the Venetian slowly pushed the knife into his heart.

"Shhhhhhhh," she whispered.

33

Alex jolted awake to the sound of a fire alarm blaring, confused about where she was at first. Heart pounding, she scrambled out of bed and ran out into the moonlit hallway, expecting to smell smoke.

What she saw instead froze her blood.

Two women in Venetian masks were crawling up the stairs like grotesque, malformed spiders.

Alex gasped and ran back into her room, locking the door behind her. She looked around, breathing hard, her brain totally blank. There was nowhere to go except the closet or the window.

She was running to the window when the door behind her splintered apart. The Venetians stood side by side in the doorway, plucked straight out of a horror movie. As one, they turned to look down the hallway, hearing something Alex couldn't. They quickly signed to each other and one disappeared, leaving the other with Alex.

One was still plenty to worry about. Alex's heart was in her throat.

The Venetian's mask was cracked and dripping with blood. It's painted smile mocking her as the woman skulked into the room.

"What do you want?" Alex yelled over the sound of the alarm.

A gunshot rang in the hallway. The woman paused, cocking her head, listening.

But only for a moment.

She took another slow step, pulling a knife from her thigh sheath.

It had blood on it.

Oh no, it's actually happening, Alex thought. Her heart filled with regret. Death had been a lifelong companion, and she always thought she'd face her own with grace and courage. But now her boring, precious little life was about to be extinguished, and a swath of outrage entwined with the fear pulsing through her. "Go to hell!" she yelled. "I know what you are, you coward." *What are you doing?* she thought frantically.

The Venetian paused and cocked her head again. "You know nothing about me, little Oracle," she said, the words slightly muffled through her mask.

"I know all about you and your Madness. You hide your insanity and brutality behind those beautiful masks. As if anything could truly cover the ugliness you have inside." The Venetian stepped into the moonlight streaming through the window, reflecting off the white of her mask. It struck a chord of recognition in Alex and she took a wild stab. "I also know one of your sisters is dead because of you."

The woman's eyes narrowed at Alex and she went down to a crouch, her every muscle tense, ready to pounce. "You see much, little Oracle," she finally whispered. "No wonder the First One wants you dead."

Alex forced her face into a semblance of composure, certain the Venetian could hear her heart hammering. "Look, I've lived with death my whole life, and I am not afraid," she said. "If you're going to do something, just do it and get it over with."

The woman chuckled. "You would have made a wonderful Chosen. But very well, little Oracle, let us end this."

She pounced.

Alex closed her eyes, waiting for the imminent explosion of excruciating pain. Instead, two arms grabbed her from behind, pulling her backwards and out of reach just as the woman leapt.

She gasped and braced herself for impact but felt only icy darkness.

Athena lay in bed looking at her phone when the fire alarm began to blare. She scrambled off and rushed into the dark hallway, freezing when she saw two strange creatures crawling up the stairs. Demons with white, patterned faces in the moonlight.

The women in masks, she thought, fear flaring bright and hot as she quickly made the connection. Certain they had seen her, she ran back to her room and shut the door as quietly as she could. She dug into her travel bag and pulled out her black and silver .40 caliber Kahr, its familiar grip immediately bringing focus and clarity as it became an extension of herself. She savagely shoved the fear from her mind and planted her feet in front of the door, gun raised. She took deep, even breaths as she stared at the faint light coming in underneath.

Two shadows passed by her completely. Perplexed, she crept to the door and pulled it open an inch, keeping the gun raised as she peered through. The demons were standing in front of a door several feet away.

Alex, Athena thought, her stomach clenching.

She ran to her phone, swiftly sifting through options. *Based on what we know of them it is not likely I would survive an engagement with both of them. One, perhaps.* The thought conjured Sei's bodiless head and she changed her mind. She needed help.

She called Hermes, but it rang to voicemail. Artemis never had her phone, and Apollo was too far away, and probably already trying to fight the fire. If there even was a fire.

She hesitated, realizing there was only one last disagreeable, but logical, option. Decided, her fingers flew as she typed a message. *Murderers here. After Alex. Upstairs guest room next to Apollo's. NOW!*

She held her breath, waiting for what felt like an eternity until she got a reply.

Omw.

Okay, she'd done what she could there. She needed to distract them. Perhaps she could shoot at least one of them before making them aware of her presence. She slowly opened the door wider, but a squeaky hinge betrayed her. They both looked her way, and signed in rapid fire to each other. That didn't bode well.

So it begins, Athena thought.

She flung the door open and fired. But the one she'd aimed at was already moving, fast. The shot missed and she only had a half second to fire another one before the creature was barreling into her, knocking the gun out of her hand. Athena grunted as she hit the ground. At least she had succeeded in separating the pair. Athena was surprised to see the mask was Venetian, with gold, red, and black flowers across its face. She sat on Athena's abdomen and snaked both hands up around her neck. The woman leaned forward until their faces were only inches away, adding her upper body weight to the strangling effort.

"You are not part of the plan, but I think I would not be punished for accidentally popping your head off," the Venetian whispered as she squeezed. Athena scrabbled at the hands on her throat, gasping for air.

Then she went calm, letting her arms drop to her sides—and grinned.

Her assailant cocked her head again, seemingly confused at the response.

In a blink, Athena moved. She put her right hand on the woman's right wrist, a left hand up on her tricep while her left leg wrapped around the woman's right leg. Then she pushed hard, flipping the Venetian woman to her back. Athena rolled too and was now on top, leaning over as she began her own rapid assault.

That's. How. You. Do. A. Full. Mount. Choke. De. Fense, she said to herself in time with the rhythm of each blow. An elbow to the woman's face broke her mask and sent it flying, revealing a facially tattooed blonde with a now bloody lip and a surprised expression. Adrenaline pulsing in her veins, Athena kept moving, hitting her with all her might in the trachea, then sitting up to punch her several times in the stomach. The woman grunted.

Athena noted with growing concern her attacker was not becoming incapacitated. These blows would have taken out a man twice her size. The Venetian's breaths were wheezy from the trachea hit and she tried to buck Athena off between blows. Athena tightened her legs and remained on, barely. She leaned forward, keeping the woman's arms pinned as she scooted to the side. She got in a kidney punch and stood quickly to deliver a more damaging kick when the Venetian rolled away just out of range, then leaned onto her arms and pivoted, flying into a whole body kick with both feet thumping into Athena's abdomen.

Athena heard something crack as she flew back several feet into the wall behind her, leaving an indentation the shape of her back and head. Dazed, her vision began to fade but Athena held on, forcing it back. She righted herself. She would face her fate with eyes open. She tasted blood in her mouth and grinned. She hoped there was blood on her teeth.

The Venetian crawled toward her, loathing in her strange, tattoo-encircled eyes.

Suddenly her companion appeared. "Sister, no, we must go. The Oracle has escaped. We must not make any other mistakes."

The woman stared wildly at Athena, as though she were an unfinished meal. Then she nodded, silently picked up her broken mask, and they both slipped out of the room.

Athena exhaled and let the darkness take her.

Artemis was dozing lightly in the great room when the alarm went off. Heart in her throat, she ran into the hallway looking for signs of fire. Her sensitive nose caught only a light scent of it. *There's only one place that could contain the smell so well.*

The lab, she thought. *Apollo!*

She raced toward the emergency stairway leading down to the foyer of the lab. As soon as she opened the door, the smell of smoke quadrupled, doing the same to her fear. Hair flying behind her, she ran down the stairs calling for Apollo. Hermes *shifted* in at the bottom of the stairs out of nowhere, narrowly avoiding a collision with Artemis as she leapt the last five steps to the landing.

"Move!" Artemis yelled over the sound of the siren. Hermes yanked the door open, getting out of her way. Smoke billowed out of the lab's open door. She tried to pull the door open further and yelped when her hand burned.

"Artemis, you're barefoot!" Hermes exclaimed.

"I'll heal!" Artemis yelled. "Apollo isn't responding. We have to get in there!"

Artemis dropped to all fours and crawled under the smoke. The fire was already consuming one wall in particular but was also burning several pieces of lab equipment. "I'll try to get the sprinkler system on!" Hermes yelled.

"Apollo!" Artemis screamed as she crouch-ran through the once-pristine lab. The smoke obscured everything. "Apollo!" *Maybe he's in the refrigerator room,* she thought. She turned a corner and saw a prone form laying on the floor with flames perilously close. Her heart plummeted. "No!"

She flew to her brother, trying unsuccessfully to ignore the pool of blood next to him. She grabbed his arms and pulled him away from the nearest flames. Her stomach clenched as she noticed the gray pallor to his face and lack of movement in his chest.

Not him. Not him. This can't be happening, she thought. She noticed the bloom of crimson on his shirt and pulled it up, causing blood to pool out of a deep gash in his chest. She felt a spark of fury and confusion amid the panic. *This should be healing,* she thought. Maybe the smoke inhalation was affecting him somehow. She pulled him along the wall toward the door, struggling to pull it open and pull Apollo through at the same time.

Then Hermes was there. He took Apollo in at a glance, his face showing what Artemis felt—confusion, anger, and panic. "Oh shit, Apollo! I had to reset the whole system; the sprinklers should come on any minute."

"Just help!" she said. Hermes *shifted* them up to the living room where Artemis laid him down on the carpet, coughing.

He knelt beside Apollo. "Did you see anyone else in there?" he asked as he felt around the wound.

"No," Artemis answered. "But why isn't he healing? Apollo, you ass, wake up!" She put her head on his chest next to the gaping wound.

She focused. Really focused, like she used to back in the old days. One by one, she shut out the siren, Hermes' ragged breathing, the smell of smoke, the pain in her feet and hands, the panic in her belly. She exhaled slowly through her nose and closed her eyes, and listened for a slow heartbeat, or the sound of blood sluggishly moving through his veins, any sign of his body struggling to heal.

The quiet of his body was deafening.

She felt bile rising in her throat. She cupped his face in her hands and looked into the icy blue eyes they had both inherited from their mother. They stared past her, already graying.

He was gone.

Artemis howled.

34

Warm air rushed past her as Alex landed hard on her back, colliding into someone's solid chest. The strong arms holding her let go abruptly and she rolled over onto her hands and knees, taking deep, shaky breaths. Her heart was still beating wildly as her mind and body adjusted to the fact that she was not being stabbed to death at the moment.

In fact, she seemed to be kneeling on a grassy hill of some sort, which made no sense. How was she not dead? She glanced over to thank Hermes when the bright moonlight revealed wavy red-gold hair and a long, lithe body.

She stared at Dionysus, begging her brain to catch up. "Dionysus? How…?"

"Athena messaged and told me to get you to safety," he said simply.

"Oh," Alex said. "Wait, what about the others? We need to go back!" She flew to her feet.

"We can't go back right now," he said.

"But they might need help! You could help them!"

"My priority is keeping you safe," he said. "They'll be fine. They always are."

"But I *am* safe! Please go help them! You have to!"

Dionysus tightened his mouth, then nodded. He disappeared.

Alex sank to the ground, trembling. She wrapped her arms around her body as a light wind picked up, cutting through her thin tank top and pajama bottoms. She barely felt it. Her emotions were roiling, turbulent. Her own murder was not supposed to be part of the deal. And what was happening back there? Those freakish women were still there with her friends.

The same freaks who, apparently, were after her now.

Alex wanted to scream.

She jumped when Dionysus suddenly reappeared beside her, looking shell-shocked. "Let's get you inside," he said, holding out his hand. She eyed it with alarm as she realized she didn't have her gloves.

Ignoring his hand, she stood on her own. "What happened?" Alex asked. Dionysus hesitated, distress on his face. A pit formed in her stomach. Someone else was dead. *Please don't be Artemis, please don't be Artemis,* she thought. Which made her feel like an asshole, of course she didn't want it to be anyone.

But please not Artemis.

"Apollo's dead."

Alex's hand flew up to cover her mouth. "Oh no!" she gasped. He had been so kind and wonderful, and poor Artemis! "What about...everyone else? Please take me back."

"No. No one else was harmed, but Hermes asked if you could stay here for a little while. Artemis is wild with grief and there's nothing anyone can do. He asked me to keep you safe."

"Oh, Artemis," Alex whispered. She felt a deep pang for her friend. She knew well the bottomless sorrow of having your closest family torn away—of being left alone in the world.

"How did he...?" She couldn't finish the question.

"A knife to the chest. Which should have injured him, but not killed him."

Alex shook her head. The tempest was slowly oozing out of her into a blank void. She stared unseeing, welcoming the stupor.

"Well, I insist you stay here," he said. Alex was too numb to disagree. The breeze picked up, its chill bringing her more to her senses. Why were they standing outside on a hill anyway?

"Where is here?" she asked.

Dionysus gestured behind her. "I should have just *shifted* us right to my home, but…I wanted you to see this. Silly under the circumstances, I suppose."

She turned. She stood on a hill that overlooked a lush valley, with acres of vineyards surrounded by cypress trees, and a well-lit complex with several white buildings nestled in the bottom. Standing tall in the center was a Pantheon-looking temple lit with bright lights.

Brilliant white jewels in a sea of emerald.

"Oh," Alex breathed.

"This valley is our sanctuary, and the complex, our home. It can be your sanctuary as well while you're here."

"But where are we?" she asked again, sure they were in some Grecian or Italian countryside.

"Northern California," he said.

Alex stared at the valley uncomprehendingly. California?

He seemed to wait for a moment, but she couldn't focus. Her mind felt like mush.

"You must be exhausted. Let's get you inside and back to bed," he said finally.

Alex nodded, her eyes and heart were heavy.

He grabbed her bare hand.

She didn't even flinch.

35

Artemis insisted they lay Apollo out on his bed. She and Henry curled up on either side of him, weeping until exhaustion overtook them. She slept only a short time, her eyes flying open to behold the nightmare of his cold, pallid face, made worse by poor Henry, still sleeping next to him, clutching Apollo's stiffening hand to his chest. She fled to her bungalow in the pre-dawn, slipping on the dewy grass.

She stalked through the clutter of her house up to her bedroom, where clothes were strewn everywhere and several coffee cups sat on the dresser and nightstand. She picked one up and hurled it against the wall over her unmade bed, shards of porcelain and dried coffee scattering onto her sheets. She was sinking into a tormented, seething mass of raw emotion. Her brother, who didn't deserve even a paper cut, was dead. How could they have done that to him? A sob escaped her lips as she thought of everything that would have to happen next, of his poor body cremated, organizing the wake Apollo deserved.

Well, someone else would have to do all that, because she had something else to do. Find those women. Skewer them with a thousand arrows.

Yes. Hunt. Those. Bitches. Down.

The thought surged through like a bolt of lightning, filling her with clarity and purpose. A lifeline in the maelstrom of grief threatening to consume her.

She pulled off her bloody, singed clothes and ran to the ensuite shower, stopping short at the sight of her body reflected in the trifold mirror. She stared as though seeing it for the first time, reflected on all sides. She grudgingly admitted she looked a tad healthier, but she was still a far cry from the hale hunter of her glory days. Who was this wisp of a woman? How had she let go of her own destiny? A leaf falling down from the tree of their previous excellence, fluttering and flailing, kept aloft only when her brother temporarily blew life into her.

Now she was alone. No brother to keep her afloat. And worse, she had failed him. She'd become something else for him to deal with, to take care of.

No more. She was going to take care of him for once.

"Too late, though, too late," she growled as she flung herself into the shower.

She scrubbed until her skin was raw. Then she attacked her hair—washing out the smoke and with the help of half a bottle of conditioner, combed through the worst of the knots that had made their home there over the years. Part of her wanted to sit in the shower and cry until she had no tears left.

She told that part of her to shut the fuck up.

She dried off and took precious minutes to put on her old smokey eye makeup and weave her wet hair into a wide, intricate braid, her fingers remembering the rhythm and pattern before she did. She threw on a black t-shirt, leggings, and sneakers, then pulled out her favorite black leather jacket. It was double-collared with a hood and lots of pockets, old and stiff from disuse. She shrugged into it and stood in front of the mirror again.

She looked more like herself than she had in years. She desperately wished her brother could see it.

But he couldn't.

Her blue hawk-like eyes flashed as she flicked her wrist, bringing forth her great silver bow.

Time to go hunting.

III

It is only through mystery and madness that the soul is revealed.

—Thomas Moore, Care of the Soul

Alex lay in the large, unfamiliar bed, willing herself to sleep. She had been staring at the ceiling for who knows how long as dark thoughts ricocheted in her head. Unable to lay still any longer, she threw the blue velvet covers off and slipped out onto the balcony.

She took deep breaths of cool, earthy air, as early dawn's burnt orange hues highlighted the dark contours of the hills surrounding the valley. Her life had taken on the strange quality of dreams, where people and places were fluid and little made sense—where bad things happened as easily as good.

"Can't sleep?"

Alex whirled, nearly jumping out of her skin. Dionysus leaned against the doorframe, watching her. "I'm sorry for scaring you. I just didn't want to be here and you not know, now that you're fully awake."

As opposed to when I was asleep? she thought, unnerved. How had she not realized he was in her room? "What are you doing here?"

"Hermes told me to keep you safe," he said, as if that answered the question.

"Am I not safe here?" Alex asked.

"You are. You just seemed to be in shock. So I stayed to watch over you as you slept."

She turned to hide her frown.

Dionysus came out and leaned on the white marble balustrade next to her. "In truth, I couldn't sleep either," he said. "Apollo and I had our differences, but he was one of the few in the family that was kind to me."

Alex felt a pang of sorrow. "I'm sorry for your loss," she said, wishing for the thousandth time there was something better to say than that paltry phrase.

Dionysus nodded. "It doesn't feel real."

"None of this does."

The moment drew out as they watched the dawn approach. "Thanks for getting me out of there," Alex said finally, glancing at him.

"Of course. I'm just glad Athena texted when she did."

"Me too," she said. Then she blurted out the burning question that had kept her up all night. "How do you think they knew about me? Those Venetian women. They even called me an Oracle."

"I have no idea," Dionysus said. "Apollo's house must be compromised in some way. Though I can't imagine how. Or why. It's definitely concerning."

Alex shivered, and not just because the breeze cut through her thin pajamas.

"Here, wear this." He held out a black hoodie, materialized out of thin air. She pulled it over her head, breathing in its woodsy smell. It was clearly his. She shoved her hands into its front pockets, grateful for the warmth and extra layer it gave her against the world. She missed her gloves. And clothes, for that matter.

"Are we really still in Northern California?" she asked, turning back to the valley. "This feels more like Italy or Greece."

Dionysus nodded. "That is intentional. I love the old countries. I even took the design for this complex straight from the ancient city of Heliopolis. But America has a special place in my heart. It's certainly the heart of my cult, though we are worldwide."

"Why?" Alex found she was genuinely curious. Plus, it was nice to think about something else for a minute.

"Well, America has the most fertile soil in the world for religions and cults. It's been growing them like weeds since its colonization. California became particularly high-yielding—Manson, the Moonies, Children of

God, Symbionese Liberation Army. I could go on, but you get the drift. I mean, cults exist everywhere, but not quite like here."

"So…it's a cult instead of a religion then?" she asked, treading carefully.

"Tomato, tomahto. Religion is simply worship directed to a specific person. With a cult, the person is usually alive as opposed to some invisible god, but they don't have to be. Sometimes that worship is misguided—Jones, for instance, was a narcissistic asshole and everyone in Jonestown died because of it. Obviously that is less than ideal."

Alex scoffed quietly. Immortals seemed to have a gift for understatement.

"I, for one, need my people alive to maintain my powers. To that end, we have been very careful about how we constructed the theology of Orphism. It's based on worship and sacrifice, mixed in with some legit miracles, a dash of fear, and an overall improvement of life. It's a delicate and perfect blend, sowed and reaped over the centuries." He spoke matter-of-factly, describing mass manipulation as though it were a sangria recipe.

Alex closed her eyes against the light of the sun as it fully escaped its mountain prison. She let the name roll around in her mind—*Orphism.* "The 'we' you mentioned, is that you and Nyssa?" she asked.

"Yes. She oversees the daily running of the Orphics as well as the extremely selective recruitment process. She loves it. Me, less so these days. Now I mostly just show up, act godly, do some miracles, and go. It gives me plenty of time to work with my grapes and perfect my wines."

Alex felt zero sympathy for him. "Seems like it's a good arrangement."

Dionysus nodded. "She's my confidante and friend." He seemed to give an ever so slight emphasis on the word friend. "I'm sure you'll like each other."

"She's okay with me being here then?" Alex said.

"It's fine. She was hesitant, we are obviously very private. We don't invite strangers here, ever."

"I don't want to cause any trouble."

Dionysus turned to face her. "Alex, I told you I wanted to spend time with you. You're not trouble."

"Okay. Thanks." She began to feel a little befuddled as she felt his gaze on her while breathing his scent in from the hoodie.

"Um, can I ask a favor?" she asked.

"Anything."

"Would you be willing to *shift* me back for my bag and things? I'm desperate for my gloves. And clothes."

"I'd rather make it so you didn't need them," he said.

Alex looked at him askance, an uncomfortable flush creeping up her neck.

Dionysus grinned impishly. "Your gloves, I mean, of course."

Alex forced a laugh. "Oh, haha."

His face sobered, but his eyes still gleamed. "I'd like to help you with your gift while you're here. If you'll allow me. Especially now that Apollo can't."

This time the pang Alex felt was a selfish one. "Oh. I hadn't even thought of that yet." Knowing what she knew now, the idea of going back to a world where she had no control over her "gift" was unacceptable. "Yes, please."

He nodded. "I cannot, however, allow you to go back. I'll go get your things."

Alex cringed at the thought of Dionysus touching her clothes and toiletries. "No, no, I just want to gather it up. Can you please just take me?"

He relented and held out his hand. "Very well."

She eyed it warily. "I feel like I've tempted fate enough today. Will you grab my arm or something instead please?" She held out her elbow.

"Or something," he said. He smiled that devilish smile and put his hand on her hip.

Alex's pulse quickened. They *shifted*.

Apollo's house was eerily quiet as the morning sun peeked through the windows. Alex felt a wave of nausea at the sight of the broken door on the carpet. Until now it felt like a nightmare. But it was real.

Alex pulled on her gloves with relief and quickly gathered her things.

She tiptoed over the broken wood to peek out into the empty hallway. Now that she was here, she felt a strong urge to find Artemis.

"It seems okay here now," she whispered. "I'm going to just go down and see if Artemis is here. I won't stay, I just—"

"No," Dionysus interrupted, motioning her back.

"I'll just be a minute." She turned toward the door.

"I said no!" His hand touched her shoulder and *shifted*.

"Hey!" she sputtered as Dionysus returned them both to the guest room. "You can't do that!"

He lowered her bag to the ivory carpeted floor. "I said I'd keep you safe here, and that's what I intend to do. Plus, I'm not ready to give you up yet." He lifted his nose to the air. "I smell breakfast. Nyssa makes wonderful pancakes. Will you join us?"

"Actually, I don't have much of an appetite—"

"You must," he said. "It will be good for you. The stairwell is down the hallway to the left and around the corner. Then the main hallway takes you right to the kitchen. I'll see you there." He smiled at her then closed the door behind him.

Alex stared at the door as a tangle of nerves formed in her chest. She was stuck. With an extremely powerful person who caused extremely conflicting feelings in her. She took some deep breaths and started her mantra.

I'm okay and... she paused, shaking her head.

It's time for a new fucking mantra.

37

Alex showered and readied quickly, choosing a shirt that made her eyes pop and running her fingers through her waves. She stepped out into a luxuriously appointed hall where thick Persian rugs masked her steps and huge arrangements of fresh flowers sat on mahogany tables. It seemed surprisingly normal, with no signs of religious iconography anywhere.

Following his instructions, she took the stairs and entered into a main hallway of travertine tile. Soaring columns lined the walls and lofty oval windows sat between each one like sunlit jewels.

Alex followed the rich smell of coffee to an airy modern Tuscan kitchen, complete with dark cabinets, modern stainless steel appliances, granite countertops, and a massive wine rack embedded in the wall. The sun shone through a bay of windows onto a rounded polished cherrywood table where Dionysus sat, surrounded by breads, jams, syrups, and coffee. He gestured to the seat across from him. Alex sat as Nyssa put a plate of pancakes on the table. "Nyssa, you remember Alex," he said.

Nyssa smiled, her gray eyes friendly and warm. She wore an apron over a simple green t-shirt and jeans. "Of course, hello. Dionysus told me what happened, I'm so sorry. I'm glad you're okay. Pancakes?"

"Sure. Just one please, I'm not super hungry."

Nyssa put four on her plate and Dionysus passed over a carafe of warmed maple syrup. Alex stared at the stack for a moment then sighed quietly and took a bite.

"Delicious, thank you so much," Alex said. They melted in her mouth. She found herself taking a few more bites.

"Of course," Nyssa said. She pulled off her apron and sat next to Dionysus at the table.

"Mimosas?" Dionysus asked. "My champagne has been coming out splendidly in recent decades."

"God, yes," Alex said, anxious for anything that could help smooth the sharp edges of her nerves.

Dionysus gestured and three bubbling flutes appeared on the table, one in front of each of them.

As one does.

Dionysus raised his glass. "To Apollo," he said somberly. "One of the good ones."

"To Apollo," the women said, raising theirs. Alex tossed back the entire glass, glad to taste more champagne than orange juice. She put it down and the glass filled right back up.

Dionysus grinned at her. "Glad you like it."

"It's really good," she admitted.

"What do you know about champagne?" Dionysus asked.

Alex took another drink. "Not much, I'm more of a wine person," she said.

Nyssa gestured to the prodigious wine rack. "Oh, you'll fit right in around here. And that's just to keep on hand, you should see the cellar."

"Wine. My one true love," Dionysus said. "I have vineyards all over the world as different grapes grow in different climes. Here I make Cabernet Sauvignon, Merlot, Pinot Noir, Chardonnay, Sauvignon blanc and Syrah. Do you prefer red or white?"

"Mostly dry reds. Cabs, Malbecs, that kind of thing."

"Excellent, maybe we'll do a tasting later," he said.

"Yeah, maybe," she said. She finished the mimosa and picked at the rest of her pancakes, wondering how long until she could make her excuses and go back upstairs to rest.

"Alex, I have a favor to ask," Nyssa said. "This is the first time in...

well, a very long time Dionysus has brought anyone here not a part of our society. I don't expect you'll see much while you're here, especially if you stay here in the house. But I'd appreciate you keeping anything you do see to yourself."

Alex nodded. "Of course." She was *definitely* staying in the house.

"Was that necessary?" Dionysus asked.

"I'm just being cautious," Nyssa said. "That's not to say you're not welcome Alex, you most definitely are." She smiled again, but this time it felt a little forced.

"It's okay, I understand. I won't say anything." Alex took a sip of the miraculously refilled drink. She closed her eyes for a moment, holding the effervescence in her mouth as the warmth of the champagne flowed through her. Truthfully, she wanted to drink the whole bottle, wherever it was, and embrace the temporary oblivion it contained.

When she opened her eyes, she was surprised to see Dionysus slumped in his chair, his eyes half-lidded.

"Dionysus?"

"He's okay, he does that sometimes," Nyssa said, gesturing to him with a fork full of pancakes. "He doesn't need much sleep, but he's been pushing hard these days. And I don't think he slept much last night." She raised an eyebrow at Alex.

Alex lifted her hands. "Hey, I didn't even know he was in there until he scared the shit out of me this morning."

"Ah." Nyssa nodded.

"How long will it last?" Alex asked, peering at him.

"Just an hour or two while he...recharges. Let's leave him to it. Would you care for a walk outside?" Nyssa took off her apron and laid it over a chair.

"Actually, I think I'll—"

"Please," Nyssa said.

Alex exhaled. "Okay, sure." She finished off her third mimosa then followed Nyssa out to an expansive manicured lawn ringed with gardens. The white columned temple loomed in the near distance, dwarfing the villa. She could also see a few of the other white buildings in the complex, though not how they connected to each other. If they even did.

Nyssa led them down to a path under an arbor of purple wisteria that wound along the perimeter of the garden. The scent of the flowers was light and delicate in the air as the filtered sun made patterns on the gray flagstones.

"Pardon him, but we have our biggest ceremony coming up this weekend. It only happens once every seven years when there is a lunar eclipse over our temple. It's quite involved and requires a lot of his power."

"Sounds intense," Alex said.

"It is. In all the best ways," Nyssa said with a glint in her eye.

Alex gave a faint smile as the champagne began softening the rough edges of the warm morning.

"I heard you work with the dead, is that true?" Nyssa asked.

"Yes, I'm a mortuary technician." Alex said, grateful to move onto a safe topic.

"And how did you end up in such an unusual career? It is unusual, yes?"

"Yeah, it's fairly uncommon. I was always interested in science and medicine, and it seemed a comparatively safer career with my curse. Plus, I like helping people. In this case, by taking care of their loved one's body."

"Ah, you have a kind heart. Death has always fascinated me. You're so close to it—do you think there's an afterlife?"

So much for safe topics. "Ummm," Alex stalled, trying to think of an answer that wouldn't offend the religious priestess walking next to her. She couldn't, so she finally just said so. "I don't want to offend you."

Nyssa threw her head back and laughed, her eyes crinkling. Her face suddenly youthful and joyous. "You can't offend me, Alex. I've quite literally heard it all."

"Okay. Then, I'm agnostic, bordering on atheist," she said. "I do sort of believe in karma and energy—that the energy you put into the world matters. But I don't believe there's a robed, bearded man in the sky keeping a ledger of all your doings. There's no heaven or hell to earn your way into."

Nyssa nodded, thoughtful. "So when you die, nothing?"

"I don't know for sure, hence the agnostic, but I very much doubt it."

"Just slipping into the darkness," Nyssa said. "Then, I presume, you do not believe in the soul?"

"Not in the way you probably do," Alex said.

Nyssa leaned over conspiratorially. "Actually, between you and me, I tend to agree with you, though you mustn't tell our followers that. The most significant tenants in Orphism involve big rewards in the afterlife."

Alex wondered briefly if there were *any* cult leaders out there that actually bought their own bullshit.

"Can I ask you another question?" Nyssa asked.

Alex reached out to touch a low-hanging strand of wisteria. "Sure."

"What are your intentions toward Dionysus?"

Alex looked at her in shock, sure she'd misheard. "Sorry?"

"What are your intentions toward him?" Nyssa repeated. Her tone was still light and airy, but the air around them suddenly seemed a little thicker.

"I have no intentions toward him. I barely know him."

"He likes you, I can tell. At Apollo's he couldn't take his eyes off you. And now you're here."

"I didn't ask to be here. I mean, I'm grateful—"

"Oh I know, dear. But, just as a favor to me, be careful around him, okay?"

Alex was startled at the echo of Artemis' warning. "What do you mean?"

"Well, unless I'm mistaken, you like him too, do you not?"

Alex flushed. "I don't know. Frankly, there are bigger things going on to deal with. And again…I don't really know him."

"Well, I have a feeling he has a mind to change that. You really do look remarkably like Ariadne, his dead wife. He's had plenty of women over the years, but she was his one true love. He's never quite recovered from losing her."

The smell of the flowers was beginning to feel oppressive. "Oh, I heard about her," she said. "So sad."

"What did you hear?"

"Only that she died in that awful Oracle massacre."

"Ah, yes, it was truly tragic. They had a connection unlike I've ever seen. Anyway, I'm not trying to tell you what to do. But I can't recommend enough that you keep your distance. As a mortal you would eventually leave him one way or another. Plus, he is clearly very distracted and this is an important time for us. He really needs to be focused."

Alex tried to suppress a flash of annoyance. "Sorry, but have you talked to him about any of this?"

"Ha! Hardly." Nyssa smiled and the tension seemed to dissipate. "He would kill me if he knew I was talking to you like this. And please, forgive my directness. Big sister type here. It's an old habit, protecting him. He's still innocent in so many ways."

Innocent was not a word that seemed to fit Dionysus but Alex kept the thought to herself. "It's fine," she said instead. Tipsiness was quickly dissolving into a deep fatigue. "Thanks for the walk. If you don't mind, I think I might try to get a few hours more sleep."

"Of course. Thanks for the chat," Nyssa said.

"Thanks for the pancakes."

Alex retraced her path, pausing to look at Dionysus as he dozed at the table. Resisting an urge to tuck his red-gold hair behind his ear, she scurried past him, shaking her head at herself as she fled to her room.

She closed most of the curtains, flopped into the bed, and with a grateful sigh, let sleep take her.

38

Jenna knelt in her room with her head down and hands clasped to her chest, both in reverence and to control her trembling. Crimson robes swished furiously on the floor in front of her as the First One paced.

Jenna had heard the stories. Things did not usually go well for Chosen Elite who failed. "Forgive me," she said finally. "I spoke to her a moment too long. I had no idea—"

"You are not to blame," the First One interrupted, the malevolent tone belying the words. Jenna flinched.

"It was a…miscalculation," the First One continued. "But we must try again. They cannot be allowed to interfere. Let them relax. Think they are safe. They do not know the length of our reach."

The First One's pacing stopped unexpectedly. Jenna held her breath, expecting the hammer to fall any second.

"Replenish yourself with the wine," said the First One. "Meet your other sisters in the traveling room in two hours."

Jenna nodded. "How many?"

"Six."

Six Elite! Jenna thought. An infiltration unlike any before.

She would redeem herself.

The Madness began to throb in her like a drum.

39

The sun had fully risen when Artemis headed back toward Apollo's house. She took the loping stride of someone who used to run often, her muscles creaking to life until they melted and gave her what she needed.

She ran straight into the kitchen and pulled the other shake Ares had given her out of the fridge. She chugged it, willing it to fuel her body and fill out her muscles. Sunlight poured warmly through the windows as she searched for other food, more protein.

All she could find was eggs. She could barely pour cereal, but how hard could it be to scramble eggs? *Cooking, of all things,* she thought. *My brother will...* she caught herself. *Goddamnit.*

As she broke eggs into a bowl, a throat cleared nearby. Artemis looked up in surprise. Hermes sat next to a prone Athena laying on the couch in the living area of the room. She'd been so focused, she hadn't even noticed them.

Both were looking at her in surprise. Artemis gave them an annoyed look. "What?"

"It's just...really nice to see you, Artemis," said Hermes. He gestured to her changed appearance. Athena nodded.

Artemis shrugged the compliment off. "Apollo..." she faltered.

"It's already handled. He's in the cold storage room with Sei. Most of the lab is destroyed, but thankfully that room was sealed and untouched. We tried to get Henry to leave, but he won't. He's upstairs with Titus."

Artemis nodded in thanks. Hermes came over as she continued to break egg after egg. "What are you doing?" he asked.

"I need strength," she said curtly.

"Okay. I just wanted to let you know I have Alex squared away with Dionysus. She'll be safe there."

Shit, Alex! she thought. Artemis gave Hermes a stricken look. She hadn't even once thought of her friend.

"It's okay," he said. "He'll take care of her."

She glanced at him doubtfully as she whisked. "Are you sure?"

"I trust him," Hermes said, shrugging. "Plus, seems like a better place than here."

She nodded and he went back to Athena.

Artemis poured the egg mixture into a skillet and stared as liquid turned to solid. *That's exactly what I need to do,* she thought. Solidify, firm up. Reclaim her best self—strong, fierce, patient, and relentless. A master tracker and unparalleled archer. She'd felt this occasionally over the years, a yearning to return to herself, but had never seen a reason to. What was the point? What was she going to do with all those skills in today's world? She had no interest in law enforcement or military. Her brother tried to tell her there were other possibilities, but she'd been unable to overcome her depression and self-loathing to really listen. She'd tried fleeting, meaningless work, but it seemed that nothing of her true self made any sense over the centuries.

The eggs tasted like sawdust as she shoveled them in. Her stomach strained to hold both them and the shake. She ignored it.

Athena and Hermes quietly watched her.

"Artemis, the loss of Apollo is staggering. We're all so—" Athena started to say.

She had no room for condolences. "So, how are we going to find these bitches?" Artemis interrupted, taking a bite.

"We were just talking about that," Athena said, taking her lead. "We obviously need a new place to work from. I think, unfortunately, it makes the most sense to use one of my homes," she said with reluctance. "At least I feel fairly certain the rest of us are not really in danger. This seemed to be specifically targeted at Apollo and Alex. Those Venetian women only came at me once I tried to interfere."

Artemis stopped chewing, her blood freezing in place. "They went after Alex?"

"Yes."

"And you saw them? Is she okay? Wait, are *you* okay?" She only just realized Athena hadn't gotten up from the couch and was clutching an ice-pack to her stomach.

"Yes," Athena said. "I will be, anyway. I saw at least two of them. There were maybe more depending whether my interactions with them were at the same time as what happened in the lab, or after." She briefly recounted her experience with the Venetians.

"Jesus," Artemis said. She pushed her plate away, her appetite was lost in another layer of guilt at putting her friend in danger. "Thanks Athena…for trying to protect her."

"Of course," she said. "Their strength is astonishing. I'm lucky to only have a few broken ribs and whatever is bleeding internally. It will probably take a few days to heal completely."

"I'm so sorry. I'm so glad you're okay though. Do you…do you know why Apollo didn't heal?" Artemis asked.

Athena's face closed up like a trap. "Well, I don't know for certain, but I have a theory," she said carefully.

"Well?" Artemis asked, when her sister paused.

"Had Apollo mentioned being sick lately?"

Artemis gave her a bewildered look. "Sick? Like the flu or something? No. I mean, we don't get sick, do we?" Her face darkened. "Or do we?"

Athena thought for a moment, looking around. "I'd better not here, just in case."

"Good call," Hermes said. Though he also looked perplexed at her question.

"What do you mean?" Artemis growled. She had no more patience for cryptic comments.

"Think about it, Artemis, how could they have known to go after

Alex? This is the only place we've talked about her outside where you met her. It's likely we're being watched or listened to," Athena said.

Artemis shivered as her hackles rose. "Great. Just great," she said.

Athena seemed to make a decision. "Okay, gather whatever you need from here and we'll go to my primary home. I have multiple safeguards there. But one thing first," she said, looking intently into each of their eyes. "You must not speak of what you see there to anyone, especially the rest of the family. Swear to it."

Hermes and Artemis looked at each other in surprise then back at her. "I swear it," Artemis said. She couldn't care less right now about anything Athena could possibly be doing there.

"I swear. You have nothing to worry about from us," Hermes said slowly.

"What about Alex?" Artemis asked.

"Hermes can collect her later today and bring her to us. Dionysus is NOT allowed in my home, just so we're clear. Be prepared to back me up on that should he press."

"Wait, he can't come to your house but we're all okay with Alex being at his?" Artemis asked.

"Yes. I am not worried about her. It might, in fact, ultimately benefit us," said Athena.

"What the hell does that mean?" Artemis asked. Athena was at her most irritating when she was several steps ahead of everyone else. So basically, all the time. She also didn't like how it made Alex sound like a pawn.

"It's just a theory," she replied.

Artemis groaned. "Well, before I go anywhere I want to see if I can find how they got in and if there's any evidence left behind," Artemis said.

"Excellent idea," Athena said. "I was going to get a forensics team here, but since you're…well, on your way to being you again, you could save a great deal of time."

"The lab's trashed," Hermes warned.

Artemis shrugged and walked out of the room. *They had to have left something somewhere.*

She began by checking the perimeter of the house. She walked slow, looking at the ground, the walls, and the windows for any signs of entry. She found it at the back of the mansion. A screen was set neatly on the ground, leaning against the house underneath an open window.

She found small footprints in the ground and a scrape of dirt on the wall where they'd climbed in. She followed and landed in a rarely used storeroom, with footprints leading through the dust into the house.

There had clearly been only two intruders.

Dreading each step, Artemis tracked them to the stairs going down to the lab. She took a deep breath and opened the door, choking on the smell of burnt plastic and wood.

It didn't take long to surmise she would not find much amid all the rubble and soot. Anxious to leave the lab and the pool of blood on the floor, she hurried upstairs to the main floor. She picked their trail back up again when she found the same small footprints in the lush carpet on the stairs going up to the bedroom. Oddly enough, handprints too. They moved strangely, these Venetians. The prints confirmed Athena's story, first moving to Alex's room, then just one moving back toward Athena's room.

Her heart sank when she saw the broken door of Alex's room but found nothing within but splintered wood.

If she was going to find anything it would be in Athena's room. A hair, a blood drop, *something* had to have fallen during their struggle. She touched the indentation in the wall made by Athena's body, deeper and bigger than she'd imagined. No wonder the woman was lying down.

She scanned the area in a grid pattern. She was beginning to feel disheartened when she caught sight of something white underneath the nightstand. She grabbed a tissue to pick it up and looked at it closely. It was a piece of porcelain, about two inches wide. It had blood on it.

"Got you," she whispered.

She folded it in the tissue and ran back downstairs to the others. She cradled it as though it was the most precious thing in the house.

And at this point, it was.

40

Alex turned her face to the early afternoon light reaching through the one uncovered window, forcing her nightmares to flee. She stretched languidly, in no rush to get up.

There was a knock on the door, sounding suspiciously like it came from inside the room.

Sure enough, she rolled over to find Dionysus standing next to it. "I didn't want to scare you this time," he said.

"Were you watching me sleep again?"

"Guilty." He smiled as he threw open the curtains. Alex squinted. He'd clearly showered and now wore jeans and a forest green t-shirt. He sat on the edge of her bed.

She froze, feeling a bit breathless. He was always just so close. She sat up against the carved wooden headboard, trying to scoot away without being too obvious.

"I'm sorry about breakfast. Nyssa told me I crashed. I didn't mean to just abandon you."

"No worries," Alex said. "Had a nice chat with her. What time is it? Have you heard from anyone yet?"

"It's after one. And no, not yet. How are you feeling?"

"I don't know. Better with some sleep, I guess. Thanks."

"Good. What did you and Nyssa talk about?"

"You know, casual topics, like death and the afterlife," she said.

Dionysus cocked a brow.

"Seriously," Alex said. "She asked about my work and it went from there."

"Ah," he said. "Nothing about me?"

Alex shrugged noncommittally, avoiding his eyes by picking at a thread in the blue velvet comforter.

"I suspected as much," he said, mildly chagrined. "What did she say?"

"You'll have to ask her," Alex said, wondering briefly if perhaps this was actually a cult of high-schoolers.

"Fair enough. Do you have someone, Alex?" he asked. The non-sequitur slid into the conversation like a blade.

A fluttery, nervous feeling rose in Alex's chest. Touching and dating quite literally went hand in hand, so she'd dated very little. The risk was simply too great, it was too easy for some asshole to take advantage of her. Her grandmother had tried to convince her she'd find someone some-day, but she had long ago reconciled herself to a celibate life. As long as she didn't think about it too much and avoided rom-coms like the plague, she got by.

She was finding it hard not to think of it now.

"No," she said, fiddling with her gloves. The very symbols of her isolation from the world.

"You must be so lonely," he said with horrifying sympathy.

Emotion welled up in her throat as his words struck a painful chord. She turned to hide her face in case it spilled over. His hand touched her chin and he pulled her face back toward him. He had moved even closer. She pushed his hand away forcefully. "Don't touch me! What if I—"

"I'm not worried."

His flippancy and constant disregard for her boundaries finally broke through her politeness. "How nice for you," Alex said. "But I am. Who knows how long I'd be out with someone like you! I'd be completely vulnerable. And I don't have the salts with me."

Dionysus didn't even blink. "What if I told you I could prevent you from going into a vision?"

Alex frowned. "You could do that?"

"I think so. Though actually, it would probably be better to get you into one and help you from there."

"What do you mean? How?"

"We kick a vision off. Once you're in my Thread, I can connect with your mind and meet you in there."

"Connect with my mind? What the hell does that mean? Can you read thoughts?" Alex asked, completely unnerved.

"Only if I try really hard," he said.

Alex glared.

"And I'm not trying!" He laughed, lifting his hands up in defense. "It really does take a lot of effort and is rarely worth it, in my experience."

"If you say so," Alex said dubiously. "Aren't you worried about me seeing something you'd rather I didn't?"

He grew serious. "I'm fairly certain I'll be able to pause the vision once it's started. Either way, I'm willing to take the risk if it will help you."

Alex was surprised at his willingness to be so vulnerable. "I'm thinking," she said. She let her eyes wander everywhere but him as her brain seemed to race around in circles. She would be vulnerable, potentially dangerously so. But what if he really could help her? Would it be worth whatever happened if she could learn how to control her visions? He seemed to really want to help her. What if she was just misreading him?

"Okay," she said, her mind made up. "Let's try it, just let me get up and—"

Suddenly he was there, cupping her face with both his hands, his warm mouth on hers, his woodsy smell washing over her. She froze, sharp terror exploding in her chest. His lips were deft, parting her mouth slightly, his tongue lightly touching hers. Years of deeply-ingrained self-preservation and fear warred and mingled with a slowly rising exhilaration. The fire in her lips shot straight through her and it felt as though her whole body had a pulse. Her body betrayed her and short-circuited her brain, sweeping away all coherent thought. She leaned into the kiss. She felt clumsy, but he responded to her in kind and the intensity escalated. One of his hands started to wander slowly down her neck.

For once in her solitary life, she was no longer thinking of what could happen, only what was happening. His hand wandered down, cupping her breast. He pulled her t-shirt over her head, revealing her simple black bra. She moaned softly as his hand caressed the strap off her shoulder, his mouth leaving a fiery trail on her skin as he kissed his way down. He reached the edge of her bra and unfastened the hook in the front. It sprang open and he slowly pulled it away, exposing the soft, rounded skin.

"Perfect," he whispered. He kissed her on the mouth briefly and started his way down again. She arched her back slightly, giving him more access.

She gasped as his mouth closed on her.

A brilliant light flashed.

No! she thought.

But she was already gone.

41

lex entered a world on fire.

Dionysus wept openly over the body of a woman lying on a cold stone floor, paying no heed to the inferno raging around them. Her waves of sable hair lay in a pool of blood seeping from the angry wide gash in her throat. He pulled her body into his arms and cradled her, rocking back and forth, covering himself in her blood. "I'm sorry, I'm so sorry!" he wailed.

Suddenly, Nyssa was there in long white robes. "Dionysus," she said.

"Leave me alone!" he screamed.

"Dionysus!" she said more urgently. "We have to leave!"

"She's gone!" he sobbed. "This was never—"

The vision stilled into silence mid-sentence. The Dionysus she knew walked into Alex's line of sight, his jeans and t-shirt a marked contrast to the tunic and robes of his former self.

"I think that's enough of that," he said in a strained voice. His face was neutral but his whole body was tense as he looked at the scene. He exhaled and turned his back on it.

"Are you really here?" Alex asked. She was startled by the sound of her own voice in the void as it resonated and echoed slightly. She'd never tried talking in a vision before.

"Indeed. I couldn't help but notice when you slipped into the vision. Very unfortunate timing, by the way," he added with a wicked smile.

Alex felt herself blush crimson, then wondered if it was even possible to blush in this peculiar mental space.

"I'm so sorry about her," she said, gesturing to the scene behind him.

Dionysus nodded, his eyes tight. "Thanks. It was a long time ago." He cleared his throat. "I suppose it's not surprising you were drawn here, given how much you remind me of her. Let's go somewhere else along my Thread. Can you manifest it?"

She looked at the grief-stricken Dionysus and imagined the liquid line of moonlight coming out of his chest. It appeared briefly before faltering into nothing.

"It was there for a minute," she said, a little desperately. "I've only ever done this one other time."

"It's okay, take your time and try again."

She took a deep mental breath and did so, getting the same response.

She needed a mantra to help her focus and settle her nerves. *A Thread of liquid moonlight...liquid moonlight...liquid moonlight.*

She manifested it again and this time it stayed, impaling the grieving Dionysus through the heart.

"Good!" Dionysus said. "Now reach out and touch it."

Alex didn't want to go closer to the grisly scene and wished the Thread were longer. At the thought the thread reached out toward her. She looked at him, amazed. "There is no spoon!" she crowed, thinking again of *The Matrix*. For a brief moment she was covered in a patent leather bodysuit with a trench coat and sunglasses.

"What?" Dionysus asked, confusion in his face. "Spoon? And what are you wearing?"

"Never mind," she said. She quickly changed back to herself.

"You must exercise control here, you can get into trouble with stray thoughts," he warned.

"What do you mean?" she asked. "How can I get into trouble?"

"One thing at a time," he said. "Just stay sharp."

She reached out to touch the Thread and her hand went right through it.

"Eventually you won't even need these metaphysical actions. You'll just think it and it will happen. But for now, focus on the details, whatever they are to you. What would help you feel like you're able to touch it?"

She looked at it again. How exactly does one hold light? It dawned on her that it doesn't have to actually *be* light, it could just *look* like light. She imagined it was solid, like a long, radiant cable.

Her hand connected with the Thread.

All at once her perspective changed. She was no longer inside the vision as an unwilling participant, but viewing it from the outside—a shining cinema vérité in a vast Stygian space. The Thread had become a broad, pulsing ribbon stretching off into the ether on either side.

Alex was dumbfounded. If she looked down the Thread to the right, she could see an image of Dionysus standing with Nyssa in front of a statue honoring his dead wife. Looking to the left showed him standing in front of a bunch of wildly cavorting women in the night.

Without even thinking about it, she swiped left with her right hand as if using her smartphone. The vision followed her guidance and blurry images slid past her as she slid forward in time. It slowly settled on an image of a still Ancient-Greek Dionysus kneeling on the earth in front of a grapevine, his fingers in the soil.

"And now you see," he said from behind her shoulder. "You're in the Thread."

"It's incredible," she breathed.

"From here you can go wherever you want. Go to a specific date, just by thinking about it. Or think of a specific person in their lives and start seeing scenes involved with them. As you spend time here you'll eventually be able to see echoes, the less likely fates branching off from particular decision points, and transverse those a little way. Perhaps someday even elevate enough to see the Tapestry, have you heard of that?"

Alex nodded and without thinking she reached out to touch the image in front of her. She felt a tug and was pulled into where the sun blazed as Dionysus walked between rows of leafy vines bursting with grapes. His sandals left footprints in the soil and his hair was pulled back with a leather string. He reached out to examine the fruit and murmured as he did, almost as if he were talking to them.

"This is amazing," Alex said. "Were you talking to the grapes? Never mind. How do I get out of here? How can I use all of this to return to the real world?"

Dionysus stepped into view. "Same concept. Visualize whatever makes you feel like this is at an end. That you're stopping it, closing it. Whatever resonates with you. Then make it so. I was always partial to the imagery of the Fates with their scissors."

She tried to think what that would look like to her. She started by imagining a door in between the rows of vines. The shape of a wooden doorframe shimmered into being, with a soft white void where the door would be. The whole thing looked insubstantial, like she could almost see through it. Hopefully it was good enough. As she stepped toward it the stray thought occurred to her that she would look awfully foolish in front of Dionysus if it was actually solid and she ran into it.

So of course that's exactly what happened.

She fell onto her backside and rubbed her nose gently where it had run into the now hardened white wood of a door. The whole thing dissipated into thin air. Her face felt hot.

Dionysus chuckled as he helped her up. "Be patient, it takes time. And…as you just saw, it's essential to control your thoughts. Hence Apollo's boring mindfulness exercises, which you should in all seriousness practice. Now. Try again."

She pushed aside the fact that Dionysus was watching and let her eyes unfocus as her mind sifted through ideas and images. Her quality of life was on the line.

Okay, close my third eye, step out, end this, turn it off. Turn it off, step out, end it, turn it off…

What did she connect with? She didn't have much of a life, just work and home, home and work. So what was at home? She watched a ridiculous amount of TV, maybe clicking the TV off and the ensuing darkness? Or dying and re-spawning in the RPG video games she played? Or what about her books? Reading was her true passion, and she still preferred the tangible item as much as possible—a whole universe encapsulated between its covers, the feel of the paper, its soft sound as she turned the page, the sweet, musty smell of lignin as they aged.

She was getting closer. Perhaps a large book being slammed closed? The thought first brought to mind a cherished movie from her childhood, *The Neverending Story.* The moment Bastian realized the Childlike Empress could see him as he read her story, he'd slammed the Orrin-covered book closed and threw it across the dingy attic, causing the candles to flicker.

Getting closer.

She thought of the moment she finished the final book in a series she'd particularly loved. Savoring the words of the last few chapters, lingering on the last page. The characters had completed their journey, met their fates, and it was done. She'd close the book and clutch it to her chest, knowing she would miss having them in her life every day. But then also knowing, and loving, how she had their whole world in her hands, and could visit whenever she wanted.

But here, in the Thread of a living person, the journey was not complete, and fate was still a question.

She smiled to herself. She had it.

Ancient Greek Dionysus stopped mid-stride as Alex paused the vision and manifested a long Thread through his heart. Then she manifested a large leather-bound gold leaf book in her hands. A grimoire not of spells, but of life. Embedded in its cover was a burnished metal carving of a thick leafy vine with clusters of grapes, cradling a full moon. She opened the book to the middle, its pages filled with loose, unreadable script.

She held the book up to the Thread, laying it right in the middle.

A bookmark of liquid moonlight.

Alex closed the book.

42

Alex gasped and shot up in the bed, grinning wildly. She glanced down quickly, relieved to see her bra had been put back in place while she'd been out.

Dionysus sat beaming next to her on the bed. "Nice imagery," he said. "You have a lovely mind."

"Thanks," Alex said, breathing hard. The magnitude of what she'd just accomplished seeped through her, radiating out until she could almost touch the life she could have now.

"I can't believe it," she said. She couldn't stop grinning.

"You should always smile like this."

"Thank you. Thank you so much." Before she knew what she was doing she crawled over and threw her arms around his neck. She gave him the biggest, tightest, most carefree hug she'd ever given anyone—the dread of human touch muted for the first time in her life.

His arms slipped around her and he hugged back, tight. It was intoxicating.

"I'm glad I could help," he said into her hair. "Just remember it takes practice and be patient with yourself." He pulled her around so she sat on his lap facing him, her legs positioned around his hips.

"Shall we take these off?" he asked, lifting up her gloved hands. She froze. Could she? She trembled as he slowly peeled them off. He threw them on the floor, then took her bare hands and kissed her palms. Alex closed her eyes and sighed.

He kissed her then. His mouth felt even more electric than before and his hands wandered in all the right places. The intense physical connection was propelling her joy into near ecstasy. He had just started fiddling with her bra again when a voice spoke from the doorway.

"Dionysus. A word, please," Nyssa said, her voice a study in neutrality.

Alex was facing the door and caught the full brunt of her decidedly unfriendly stare.

Dionysus tightened his hold on Alex. "Not now, Nyssa," he said.

"Yes now. It's important," she said.

Feeling like a teenager caught in the act, Alex climbed off of Dionysus and sat next to him on the bed, gladly turning away from the door and Nyssa's accusing eyes.

Dionysus sighed and cupped Alex's chin, turning her face to him. "I'm sorry." He gave her a thorough kiss then stood and walked out with Nyssa, closing the door behind him.

Alex laid back on the bed, beaming at the ceiling. She was free. For the first time in her life. Nothing could dampen that. She couldn't wait to tell Artemis.

The thought hit like a dark bolt of guilt right to her stomach.

Artemis.

How could she be so full of joy when her friend was so full of grief? Her euphoria waned slightly. She pulled her t-shirt back on and headed to the bathroom. She looked at herself in the mirror, surprised at her still-smiling reflection. It was as though a shroud of horror, fear, and self-imposed isolation had lifted, revealing a luminous woman of hope and joy.

The little logical voice in her mind told her it was just one success. There were bound to be failures and situations still totally out of her control.

But hope is powerful, a lifeline and anchor of light.

It radiated from her.

On hearing the door open, Alex returned to the bedroom and was disappointed to see Nyssa there instead of Dionysus. Nyssa had a smile plastered on her face.

"Dionysus is calling Hermes," she said. "I think it's time you were reunited with your friends. Don't you?"

Alex felt another stab of guilt at not feeling quite ready to trade this joyous moment for more peril and sorrow.

Dionysus walked in and shooed Nyssa away but left the door open. "Hermes is ready to pick you up and take you to wherever they are going next. He wouldn't tell me where," he said sourly.

Alex nodded. "Did you hear how Artemis is doing?"

"No." Dionysus didn't seem too particularly interested. He pulled her close and her arms snaked around his neck of their own volition. She relished the feel of her bare arms touching his skin.

"Stay," he said. His voice was quiet and urgent. "They don't really need you. But I do."

Alex scoffed gently. "You don't need me. And what about your father?" she asked. "Don't you care about finding him? Or about finding who did that to Apollo?"

Dionysus just shrugged. "It's complicated with him. With all of them. Honestly, you are far more important to me right now." He kissed her.

Alex pulled away, but he held her tight. A feeling of unease settled in her. "You don't even know me though. And I really should get back," she said. "I want to help them. Help her. She's my friend."

"Getting to know you is literally all I want to do right now," he said. He kissed her again, his mouth urgent. She couldn't help but respond. "Plus," he said between kisses, "think of the work we could do together—your gift, my wine—"

"And I'm sorry, but that's why she has to go, Dionysus!" Nyssa said from the doorway again. "You have other crucial and imminent priorities."

"Nyssa. Seriously. Go away," he said.

"Alright, alright." Nyssa disappeared from the doorway again, though Alex was sure she hadn't gone far.

Dionysus sighed. "Unfortunately, she's right. The Mysteries start this week. Our biggest ceremony, it only happens once—"

"Every seven years, with the lunar eclipse," Alex finished. "Nyssa mentioned it."

He smiled. "Ah. Well, at the end of the day I'll be of better service to my people, and to you, if I can maintain my power."

"Makes sense," she said. *And probably for the best,* she thought. She couldn't think clearly around him.

Dionysus grunted and finally let her go. "I hate this. Plus, I feel like sending you back puts you at risk." He thought for a moment and his eyes lit up. "You should come!" he said, grabbing her hands.

"What?" Alex asked. "Come to your ceremony?"

"Why not?"

"Um, I'm not too big into religion," she said stupidly.

"No, no, no, you don't have to do anything, or worship…anybody. But I'd love to have you see it."

"ABSOLUTELY NOT!" Nyssa said, striding back in. "She will be far too distracting, and you need to be on your A-game. You know this."

Dionysus turned from Alex, but held onto her hand. He looked at Nyssa for a long, uncomfortable moment. "I think I'm quite able to invite whomever I want," he said finally.

Nyssa walked to him and put both of her hands on his shoulders. "Of course you can darling, but you know we need this. *You* need this. And you know that inviting her will cause problems."

For once, Alex felt completely fine being talked over. She was actually on Nyssa's side.

"At any rate, I think Hermes has waited downstairs long enough, don't you?"

Dionysus nodded.

"He's here? Waiting for me? Why didn't someone say so?" Alex asked, flustered.

Nyssa turned to her. "I just did."

Alex threw her things back into her bag and put her gloves back on, her new skills too new and fragile to face the real world without them. Dionysus handed her his sweatshirt. "So you can remember me," he said. "Though you better not think this is goodbye." He flashed her a dazzling grin.

They went downstairs where Hermes stood quietly looking around the airy foyer. At the bottom of the stairs Dionysus grabbed Alex and pulled her in for a deep, thorough kiss, right in front of Hermes. Alex's cheeks flamed red as they pulled apart.

Hermes gaped uncharacteristically.

"Bye Alex," Dionysus said quietly. He turned to Hermes. "Please take care of her H, I *will* see her again."

Alex sighed in frustration at the certainty in his voice. She reached up on her tiptoes and kissed his cheek. "Thank you, Dionysus. For helping me. I will never forget it." He looked at her in confusion and tried to catch her hand again but she slipped away. Hermes seemed to have an eyebrow permanently arched at her.

"Oh wait Alex, this is for you." Nyssa handed her a bottle of cabernet. "We never did get to do a wine tasting. Please accept my sincerest apologies for all this. I do hope you'll come back after we get through all the craziness here."

Alex gave her a small smile. "Thanks Nyssa. I understand. It's probably for the best anyway." She glanced at Dionysus, who frowned. "Good luck with everything this week."

"Yeah, hope it all goes well Dionysus," Hermes said. He reached out to grab Alex's forearm. "We'll keep you posted."

Dionysus was staring intently at her when everything went black.

Hermes dropped her off in Athena's massive Bostonian great room. The room was as tall as the entire house, with a spiral staircase in the corner leading up to a balcony on the second floor. The walls were white with brown hardwood floors and gray furniture surrounding a large stone fireplace. The whole space was expensive and immaculate, without being exorbitant or flashy. A faint scent of furniture polish permeated the air.

In the corner of the room stood a full length marble statue of Hellene Athena. The sculptor had brought her flowing robes, helmet, and shield to life from the stone, making her seem soft and strong all at once. It belonged on the cover of Edith Hamilton's *Mythology*. Or in the Louvre.

A somewhat sobering reminder of who these people really were.

"Hey Alex," Artemis said. Alex marveled at the lithe, athletic woman who stalked in like a jaguar, her yellow hair woven into an intricate braid that shone against the black of her leather jacket.

The emaciated, gaunt woman she'd befriended in the hospital was totally gone, replaced by a trim ex-Goddess of the Hunt. It was the first time Alex felt truly out of place, the only weak human among a group of powerful immortals. She hadn't realized the shelter Artemis had provided until that moment.

All those thoughts melted away as she saw the raw pain in her friend's eyes.

"Oh, Artemis," Alex said. She ran over to her friend and threw caution to the wind by putting her arms around her. "I'm so sorry about Apollo, I can't even imagine…"

Artemis seemed shocked at the contact, and it took a moment to return the hug.

"Thanks," she said quietly. She pulled away. "How can you—"

"She and Dionysus got awfully cozy," Hermes answered for her, folding his arms and leaning against the wall.

"What?" Artemis stepped back, her eyes narrowing.

"He helped me with my visions," Alex said quietly.

Hermes scoffed.

Alex gave him a dirty look. She turned back to Artemis, who was looking at her with hurt and confusion.

"He came on pretty strong," Alex said. "But he helped me have a huge breakthrough with my visions and…none of it was my intention. It just felt amazing to be able to touch someone. To hug someone." She spoke quieter and quieter. It all sounded so lame.

"Hugging." The word felt flat out of Artemis' mouth.

"I mean, it was a little more than that, but not much."

"My brother is stabbed to death and you're getting it on. With Dionysus, of all people," she said in a monotone voice.

Alex looked down as lava-hot shame filled her whole body. Her words fell out in a jumble. "I'm so sorry. I begged him to bring me back several times and tried to find out what was happening with you all often. But he was just always there, in my room. He asked if he could help me with my visions and once I agreed he kissed me. And it's just been so long…years, since…well, I got caught up in it," she said. "And then of course I got sucked into a vision. He helped me learn how to get out, which is pretty life changing for me." She paused and took a breath. "I've been thinking of you though," she finished lamely.

"Yeah, you've clearly been distraught," Artemis said. She turned and strode out of the room.

Alex stood there looking at the empty doorway, her emotions sinking into a grey, messy heap on the floor.

"Sorry," a gruff voice said from beside her.

Alex jumped; she hadn't noticed Hermes still standing there.

"I didn't handle that well," he said. "I know Dionysus. Hell, I raised him. He can be a bit pushy and selfish. And someone in your situation… well, you wouldn't have had much of a chance."

Alex gave him a black look. "My situation?"

"We forced you over there. And then I just meant, the way you talked about it just now, how your life has been. I didn't think. I'm…sorry I caused an unnecessary problem between you and Artemis."

"Well, thanks," Alex said. She sank into a nearby chair and put her head in her hands. She really didn't think she could handle a suddenly nice Hermes right now.

He turned to leave. "I'll talk to Artemis."

"No! No, thanks though. I need to fix it with her," she said.

Hermes nodded and looked at her a long minute, as though trying to sort her out again. Eventually he just walked out. She put her head in her hands again.

All the light and joy she'd felt just minutes ago was gone…sucked into an enormous, Artemis-shaped black hole.

43

Artemis paced in the expanse of Athena's basement. It seemed more like a secret museum than a basement, with bookcase lined aisles containing perilously old books, alcoves of statues, paintings, jewelry, and god knows what else. She stalked up and down the rows, not really noticing the millions of dollars in antiquities around her.

She was trying, unsuccessfully, to sort her feelings. Logically, she knew she couldn't fault Alex, who had been given no choice in going to Dionysus…who, as they all knew, tended to get what he wanted. Plus, it was her fault Alex was here at all and in danger in the first place. And she was glad her friend was safe and had experienced a breakthrough.

Nevertheless, rage streaked red and raw just under her skin.

She also knew her interaction with Alex was not the real reason.

She marched into a large room with lights that flickered on at her entry, illuminating the white walls and the myriad of shelves, chock full of statues, busts, and urns of her family from ancient times. She stared. It was clearly the crown jewel of Athena's collection. She slowly walked around. It seemed to be organized by person. She passed artifacts of Ares, Demeter, Hephaestus, and suddenly stopped in front of one about herself.

The story of the hunter Orion, her lover. How Apollo had tricked her into killing him. God, she'd been furious at him. She had truly grieved, and though their powers weren't great enough to rearrange the stars, she had ensured that particular set was named after him. She still thought of Orion occasionally, mostly in the fall months when his constellation was overhead. It was also a perfect example of how humans inevitably got the short end of the stick.

She moved on, not wanting to see any more of her own stories. She scurried past Apollo's, her heart constricting. Athena's section was next, the most prominent in the collection, of course. There was one about Athena competing with Poseidon for the city of Athens, its people choosing her gift of the olive tree over his of the horse. The weaving contest with Arachne, who after besting Athena was transformed into a spider. Athena helping Odysseus on his quest.

Artemis rolled her eyes at that. They had loved their heroes—what sport they had been! She remembered taking bets on each of them and their expected successes and failures.

She and her family had been brutal, callous, and glorious.

She continued her walk of remembrance until a painting of her father and Athena sucked the breath right out of her. It was a classic painting, with idealized rounded bodies and vibrant colors. The artist had captured her father surprisingly well though, with his black hair and bearded square jaw. But it was the look on Zeus' face that had stopped her—a look of love and adoration for his favorite daughter. It was a look she'd seen herself a few times. Seeing it now caused emotion to well in her.

She suddenly, desperately, wished he was here.

Artemis had never cared that Athena was his favorite. He'd always given her enough. She thought of the times they'd been close, of how, when she was little, he threw her into the air so high she thought she was flying. Maybe she even had been. How he patiently taught her and Apollo how to use their powers. How to shoot a bow and arrow. She remembered him delighting when they both took to it, but truly relishing when it was she who made it her own, ultimately surpassing both her brother and her father in skill.

She thought of his rare but intense bear hugs, and the concern over the centuries at her depressed state. How he would reach out to try to break through and connect—how much that meant to her. And how he never made her feel like a disappointment to him, though of course she was.

Her stomach clenched and a feeling of urgency came over her, reminding her there was more at stake than revenge. She couldn't lose him too.

She turned to go and was confronted by a massive painting of the whole Olympian family hanging over the doorway. It was rare to see everyone all together in one painting. It had clearly been commissioned in later centuries, and it must have been under Athena's direction because she'd never seen one before where they each looked so close to their real selves.

She stared at the image of her family in all their glory, incandescent and dazzling. Her heart sank. How was it they had all managed to come through the millennia so well when she had collapsed and come to such a complete pile of nothing? How had she failed so completely? Was she so different than they?

She turned in a circle looking around the room, feeling the eyes of her family boring into her, seeming to judge her from their transcendence. The room started to spin on its own and she could feel the hot sting of tears in her eyes. She screamed, flicking her wrist and in quick succession sent three silver arrows into a bust across the room.

Trembling, she walked over to find she'd skewered a two-thousand-year-old stone bust of Aphrodite's beautiful face, now cracking and falling apart. She smiled a little, feeling she'd improved upon it.

"I never liked that one of her anyway," a voice came from behind her.

Artemis whirled to find Athena standing in the doorway, her arms crossed.

"Sorry Athena," Artemis mumbled. "I just—"

"It's okay," Athena said. She limped forward and folded her taller little sister into her arms. Artemis was surprised and stiff; Athena was not usually physically affectionate. But Athena held tight and as usual, seemed to read her mind.

"You know, none of us have weathered the march of time unscathed," she said quietly as they separated. "We've all faced our own battles."

Artemis scoffed. "Ha. It doesn't seem like it. Everyone else seems to have it pretty well together."

"We just hide it better. Your gift just causes you to wear your struggles more visibly."

"My gift?" Artemis asked.

"Yes. You feel things deeply, and you wear your heart on your sleeve. It's why you were the protector of children even though you never wanted your own. It's why you connect so well with dogs and other animals. In the old days your empathy served you well, and you were confident in it. You had a lovely balance of mind and heart guiding you as you maneuvered through the world. Not all of us are good at that."

If she didn't know any better, Artemis would have said Athena sounded wistful. Which couldn't be right since if anyone maneuvered through the world well, it was Athena.

"In short, you, Artemis, in my opinion, were the best of us."

Artemis gaped at her.

"Which is why, when you didn't easily find a new purpose after The Fall, you may have hit the ground hardest. Your gift turned on you and it ate at you. And you let it."

Artemis looked down and flushed, feeling the rebuke hit home. She knew after all her time in and out of hospitals that clinical depression is a true disorder, out of the control of those afflicted with it. But that was not what had plagued Artemis. She'd let herself wallow in self-pity until it began to feel more real than anything else.

"You know, you don't have to be a god to have power," Athena said. "To carve out of this world an existence that's full of meaning and happiness. It can take time, and sometimes several false starts. But in the end, all it takes is grit. Something you have in spades."

Artemis shook her head. "Not anymore. I just never seemed to fit."

"But, my dear sister, somewhere along the way, you stopped believing you could make it fit to you," Athena said gently.

The words sat heavy in the air, almost visible as Artemis saw the truth of them. She nodded and let her heart slowly absorb the thought. She'd been talked to like this before, probably even by Athena herself. They'd all tried their hand at it, she'd just never been in a place to hear them. She felt a surge of anger and self-reproach that it took the death of her brother to perhaps, just possibly, save herself.

Athena gave her sister another short, tight hug, wincing slightly. "Just do me a favor and keep that in mind, once this is all done, and your current righteous purpose is complete, okay?"

Artemis shrugged. "If I'm still here after skewering every one of those Venetian bitches, I'll try."

"Fair enough," Athena said, nodding. "Shall we?" She gestured for Artemis to follow as she walked out.

Artemis took one last look at her overly idealized family, captured as they were in all their glory and perfection, flipped them off with both middle fingers, and turned off the light.

44

Artemis found Alex sitting at Athena's immaculate grey driftwood kitchen table. She was playing with a small leafy twig likely pulled from the long table garland of silver-leaf eucalyptus and delicate white flowers. The golden light of late afternoon highlighted the misery on Alex's face. Artemis felt a pang of regret.

As soon as Alex saw her, she stood. "Artemis, I'm so sorry. I totally understand why you're upset. I really value your friendship though and don't want anything to ruin it."

Artemis pulled Alex into a quick hug. "It's okay. I'm sorry too. The only reason you were there is because of me. And I'm thrilled you got help. And mostly, I'm so sorry you were in danger at all. I'm just all over the place right now and I wasn't prepared for that extra little nugget."

"Given everything, you're more than allowed," Alex said, sounding relieved.

They sat and spent the next half hour catching each other up on what had happened since they'd separated. Alex's face was open and full of empathy as Artemis briefly went over highlights of that hideous night. She grabbed Artemis' hand, seeming to hear everything unsaid.

Alex in turn told her about the harrowing experience with the Venetian, and her surprising time with Nyssa and Dionysus. Artemis could tell she was holding a few things back as well as she twirled the twig anxiously. But as they talked, the tension in the air between them slowly dissipated.

"So now what?" Alex asked.

As if to answer the question, Athena strode into the room with Hermes already in discussion. She flipped on the bright lights of the kitchen as she passed the massive marble island in the middle of the room.

"You have to tell her, Athena," Hermes said urgently. He'd changed into jeans and a black t-shirt that looked exactly the same as the one he'd been wearing. At least he no longer smelled of smoke.

"I know!" Athena said, exasperated. She was dressed as casual as Artemis had ever seen her, in jeans and a blouse, her long brown hair down out of her usual chignon.

"Tell me what?" Artemis asked.

"I heard back from my geneticist."

"And why are we talking to geneticists?" Artemis asked wearily.

"It's about Apollo. And I'm afraid you're not going to like it."

Artemis went cold all over. "Great. Just spit it out."

"Okay." Athena assumed her matter-of-fact manner. "You know Apollo mapped our genome, right?"

Artemis nodded, remembering how he'd collected DNA samples from the whole family over a decade ago.

"Well, Apollo used that map to create a virus. A virus containing gene-editing technology to turn him mortal."

A wave of confusion washed over Artemis. The words were practically nonsensical.

Athena watched Artemis carefully, as though waiting for an outburst. When none came, she spoke more plainly. "He was tired of being immortal, and wanted to grow old with Henry."

Artemis felt the blood in her body constrict and her extremities went numb. *There's no way. There's no way he wouldn't tell me,* she thought. "How do you know? He told you all this?"

Athena nodded. "Not at first, not until I approached him directly about it."

"*You* approached *him*?" Artemis asked. "How did you even know?"

Athena glanced at Hermes for some reason, who looked suspicious. "I'll tell you about that later. The important thing to know now, and what my geneticist just confirmed, is that Apollo was already mortal when he died. He'd been subjected to his own virus. That's how they killed him with a simple stab wound."

Artemis was stunned. Alex gasped behind her. "Bullshit. He would have told me," she whispered.

"You had enough on your plate, he never wanted to—" Athena began.

"BULLSHIT!" Artemis yelled, standing suddenly.

"It's true," Alex said quietly. Artemis turned to her, barely noticing Alex flinch at the raw expression on her face. "I saw something about it in the vision I had of Titus. But I didn't connect it to what happened until now. I'm so sorry."

Artemis fell into her chair and put her head in her hands. "Why didn't he tell me?" she asked miserably.

"He didn't know how to tell you," Athena said. "He was afraid of what would happen to you."

Artemis scoffed softly, filling with serrated self-recrimination. "I bet. He was my twin. I should have known, I should have been there for him."

"He would have told you eventually. And you'd have had years to come to terms with it, as he lived out his last life with Henry," Athena said.

Artemis saw it then. Apollo loved Henry more than anyone she'd ever known him to love. She imagined them aging together, enjoying a lovely and precious life as tottering old men doing crosswords together. Apollo would have been happy.

Would have been.

She took a ragged breath. "But someone took that away," she said. The fire in her eyes vaporized the tears brimming at the edge.

"Yes," Hermes said. "And we're going to—"

"Wait," Artemis interrupted, looking at Athena. "I need to know how." Anger and sorrow boiled together in her stomach in a vile, sour concoction.

"How what?" Athena asked.

"How did you know about it? I need to know how you knew before me. You've been acting weird and distracted this whole time. What else aren't you telling us?"

Athena's face closed up fast as a clam. "How do you mean?"

"I think you know what she means," said Hermes, joining in. "And I agree with her assessment. I want to know how you knew also. And how you knew about what happened to Hera and Sei so soon too. And frankly, how could your geneticist confirm that without any other genetic information about Apollo to compare it to?"

Athena looked out the windows as though the sculpted hedges beyond held the answers. Artemis could see the telltale sign of her sister's remarkable brain quite likely doing a cost-benefit analysis of telling them what they wanted to know, versus her idea of what they needed to know, versus avoiding it completely and deflecting.

The tension mounted and just as Artemis was about to violently shake the answers out of her, Athena sighed. "Very well. It's quite involved, but I'll endeavor to keep it simple for brevity's sake. The answer to the first question is that I've set up monitoring for all of our family's networks and devices, as well as those of the people that live and work around us."

Everyone stared, and Hermes spluttered as she continued. "Obviously, I don't have the bandwidth for actual daily monitoring of so much data, so I have alerts set up based on keywords. I also have machine-learning code set to alert me on unforeseen threats. I use speech recognition to convert phone calls and other conversations into text and add them to the data set. Which is how I learned about the neighbors' intentions. I flag anything regarding the police or other authorities of any kind."

"Unbelievable," said Hermes. His jaw clenched under his dark beard. "That explains your little comment the other day, about 'spending outrageous amounts of time and money keeping this family safe'," he said, miming quotations at her.

Athena nodded. "Precisely. It's for the good of this family."

Hermes scoffed. "And let me guess, you do nothing with it, typically letting events take their natural course."

Athena gave him a long-suffering look. "Don't be ridiculous. Of course I intercede. Look, whether you approve of it or not, I'm in the business of information. It's the currency of the world and is certainly the currency of our family. I have spent millennia building networks of people who report to me, and in the last hundred years have employed more technological means of obtaining and evaluating the petabytes of data people around us share, freely, without even thinking. I've prevented all kinds of leaks that would have exposed our family. And while I can appreciate you not loving the idea, there is a need."

Hermes shook his head, scowling. Artemis could scarcely believe what she was hearing.

"I mostly do it to protect our identities and ensure no one breaks the rules or does anything stupid in such a way that would endanger all of us. At some point the algorithm alerted me to something Apollo was working on called Project Amaranth, which is a flower named after the Greek word for unfading. It was an unusual word to constantly show up in his records, so eventually, it flagged. I started digging into what he was doing and found project journals on his laptop. It's a good thing I did though, is it not?" Athena asked, eyebrows raised.

Artemis and Hermes stared at her with incredulity. Artemis' self-recrimination quickly turned into a cold rage. "How dare you!" she yelled. "Those are his private journals! What else have you seen? Have you read mine?"

"No." Athena thought for a moment. "Well, not very much," she admitted. "And I only read a portion of his, only the entries referencing Project Amaranth."

"So wait, you knew all along about this? Why didn't you say something earlier?" Hermes asked, his brown eyes flashing.

"Maybe this is all your doing!" Artemis piled on. "Did you tell someone about it? Or, or are you behind all this? Did you try to stop him to 'protect the family'? WHAT IS HAPPENING?" She stepped forward, towering over her sister as she flicked her wrist, the bow appearing in her hand. Hermes moved to separate them but Athena raised a hand to forestall him. She looked up at her sister with a calm face. "Artemis, it was not me. Why would I tell you about it if it were?" She pinched the bridge of her nose and closed her eyes. "If anything, I was deeply invested in his project," she said with a resigned sigh.

"Prove it," Artemis said.

"I will. Then you'll understand everything." Keeping her eyes on Artemis, Athena pushed a button on her watch. "Bring her in, please," she said.

Artemis narrowed her eyes, and Hermes crossed his arms. Then Artemis smelled and heard someone coming, their footsteps light on the floor. No, it was two someones.

A young woman walked into the room carrying a little girl wearing a pink dress with wide brown eyes that matched her hair. She couldn't be much more than two. The young woman handed the toddler to Athena, who snuggled right up to her.

Athena gave the girl a kiss on the cheek. "Hi, sweetheart," she murmured. Athena turned back to the room with the girl on her hip.

Artemis was shocked into stillness, the cold rage quieting with a loud thump. Hermes looked as though he'd just seen a Gorgon.

Athena took a deep breath. "Everyone, I'd like you to meet my mortal daughter, Sophie."

45

Alex was mystified as to what about a little girl could be so shocking. It clearly was though, given how most of the jaws in the room were practically on the floor. The little girl giggled and reached out to Artemis, who, looking totally stunned, flicked her bow away and gathered the girl into her arms.

Sophie pulled on Artemis' long braid. "Yewwo!" she said, delighted. Artemis stared in wonder as she looked down at the adorable mini-Athena in her arms, her short dark brown hair forming a wild halo around her head.

"But—" Artemis started.

"I know," Athena said. "I'm probably literally the least likely person in the universe to have a child."

Hermes looked at Sophie as though she were a scorpion instead of a beautiful child. "But the Pact." His voice was low and menacing as he looked meaningfully at Athena. "*Your* Pact."

"I know. I thought, and I still do think, that it's what's best for our family."

"Then what. The. Fuck?" he seethed.

"It's kind of a long story, Hermes."

"I bet it is," he said.

"Look, if I had my way you'd never have known about this until much later, if at all. But recent events have changed things."

"If at all?" Artemis echoed quietly, giving the girl a squeeze. Sophie giggled and started squirming. Artemis handed her back to her mother.

"Well, I feel like such a hypocrite. And it hasn't been easy. I was… am…angry for putting myself into this position."

"And what position is that, exactly?" Hermes demanded.

"Of doing exactly what I try to keep everyone else from doing. Of being careless. Of, when I found I was pregnant, taking a chance. And losing. I can't bear…" Athena choked with emotion. She cleared her throat. "I can't bear the thought of losing her someday, that I'll have to watch her…" No one in the room had to guess what she was going to say.

"Right! Not to mention the risks for all of us if it had gone the other way!" Hermes yelled. "You *are* a hypocrite! Someone should have been watching YOU!"

Sophie stuck her bottom lip out at him and started to wail. Athena kissed her again and handed her to the young nanny, who had been hovering near the doorway to the next room. "Time for her to go to bed soon anyway, thanks," she said.

Artemis punched Hermes in the arm. "Nice one. It's not the girl's fault."

"No! It's hers!" he yelled, gesturing to his elder sister as she returned. Athena waited until the sound of Sophie's crying diminished entirely. Then she stood as tall as she could, managing to look imperious even though she was shorter than both of them. "Look. I, more than anyone here, know it was unwise. But it happened. It's done. And I'm not sorry. I will never be sorry to have that little girl in my life. I've already beaten myself up plenty about it. But it's also the best thing that's ever happened to me."

Hermes glowered another moment then exhaled loudly, as though trying to physically expel his anger. "I know. Children are truly the greatest gifts," he said, his voice suddenly soft. Alex looked at him sharply; this didn't at all jive with the curmudgeon she'd briefly come to know. "I guess it's only fair you had a shot at it too, since most of us did at one time or another."

"Thank you. And now I also understand you more as well," Athena said. "So I'm sorry, *especially* to you, for breaking the Pact, when I know honoring it's been difficult for you."

He nodded. "Yes, but in some ways good too. No one should have to outlive their kids." A dark realization dawned on his face. "Which is why you were so interested in Apollo's work."

"Precisely." Athena's lip trembled.

"Jesus. This just keeps getting worse and worse," Artemis muttered. "Are you considering becoming mortal too?"

"I…I was still working that out," Athena said, her shoulders slumping. "I don't know what to do. I copied Apollo's work and sent it to my own geneticist. He's working on a virus with the opposite genes targeted, just in case. Though I didn't tell him what the genes did or what the project was."

"And I bet you didn't tell Apollo," Artemis said.

"I didn't want to burden him—" Athena started to say.

Artemis snorted. "Bullshit. Again. You spy on all of us, making decisions on our behalf without our consent, while you're doing whatever you want totally unchecked!"

"Wait a second," Hermes said. "Let me get this straight. You used Apollo's research to have someone, a human, create a virus that would make a human immortal?"

Athena grimaced.

"Are you insane?" he yelled.

He and Artemis laid into their sister, while Alex tried to make herself as small as possible, not sure whether it was best to leave or stay, deciding in the end to just not draw attention to herself at all.

Athena stood tall and silent against the barrage until she suddenly covered her face with her hands and started to cry. It stopped both of them mid-sentence and they looked at each other with wide eyes.

"Yes, Hermes. Apparently I am insane. I feel like I've lost complete control of my faculties over the last twenty-eight months. I wade around the world in a crazy emotional state all the time. I've never understood how the rest of you do it, and now I'm drowning in it. I do not have your gift." She gestured to Artemis. "I can't seem to get myself together. And

I'm making decisions I know are logically unsound and sometimes even ridiculous. But I can't…seem…to…stop," she finished, each word a sob.

Artemis rubbed her eyes. She pulled Athena into a hug. "Oh Athena, you're a mom now. You're probably going to be more emotional for the rest of your life. Your heart is now outside of your little Spockish body and running around on two legs. You're living a new normal where you'll do anything to protect her. And, just so you know, so will I. I'm glad to know about your daughter. She's adorable." She smiled down at her big sister.

That just made Athena cry harder and grab Artemis with both arms, squeezing hard before pulling away. "Thank you."

Hermes stared at Athena as though imprinting the image of an emotional Athena forever in the annals of his memory. "Okay, fine. It makes sense you wouldn't know what to do with all of…this." He gestured to her puffy red face. "But ironically, what *you* have done is perilous for us all. Both you and Apollo. And it's no surprise someone has started using it against us." His eyes widened as a terrible thought came to him. "Wait, were Hera and Poseidon infected too?"

"Not Poseidon, but it seems Hera was, yes," Athena said, pulling away. She wiped her eyes.

"Goddamnit!" Artemis punched a fist into her opposite hand. "Is that stupid virus at the heart of all this? Is it why Apollo died?"

"It's hard to know for sure yet, it feels like there are multiple things going on. But the dots are leading that way. Dots I didn't connect initially because of the way Hera and Sei died. But yes, someone else clearly knows about Apollo's work. "

"But how?" Hermes asked.

"I'm not sure yet," she said.

"Wait, you said you only knew about his project because you were in his system, right?" he asked.

"Right."

"But how, exactly, did you get into his system? I mean, it stands to reason that if you were, someone else could be too." He crossed his arms as Athena turned to him, clearly bracing herself for another barrage. "I'm not going to like the answer am I?"

"Probably not," she said. "You designed all of our networks, yes?"

His eyes narrowed. "Yeah…"

"Well, remember when you were working on upgrading most of us to dark fibre, and you wanted a second set of eyes on the optical router configs?"

The blood started draining from his face. He nodded.

"Well, I may have written in a back door before I gave it back to you. A tap that would send a copy of all the data to my network where it could be aggregated."

Hermes trembled with anger. The color flooded back onto his face like a cartoon. "You've compromised us all. We are all vulnerable."

"No!" she said. "I'm the only one who knows about that, and it's obviously not here. There's no way anyone else exploited it."

"You sure about that?"

Athena nodded.

Hermes arched an eyebrow.

Athena cleared her throat, her mind clearly racing ahead. "Very well, it's a possibility and it would make sense. We don't have time to confirm it, so let's operate under the assumption that, one way or the other, the answer is probably yes. Especially given that someone used Apollo's work against him and the rest of our family. We should all get tested, by the way. Has anyone felt strange lately?"

The question landed like a live grenade.

Hermes and Artemis turned ashen. They glanced at each other and shook their heads.

"I'll get samples from you to send out for analysis just in case. But actually, the key to this is that the intruders knew about *her.*" She pointed to Alex, who grimaced, not wanting to be part of this discussion at all.

"Hmmm, true," Hermes said. "It seems unlikely someone in the family talked about it."

"I agree. We have to consider the idea Apollo's place was bugged, perhaps after they found out about Project Amaranth."

"Hmpfh," Hermes said. "Well, we could sweep the house and see if we can find something that's sending data…" He stopped mid-sentence as another thought clearly came to him. "Wait. When Apollo built the lab he had me install cameras all over for the purposes of tracking his scientific methods and results, or whatever. It sends a video feed to an external cloud server. It's been years since I looked at the setup, but I bet he still used it. Not only could they have tapped into it, we certainly talked about Alex there, and it could show us what happened to Apollo!"

Artemis practically pounced on him. "Go! Go find it!"

Hermes nodded and *shifted* away.

Athena's phone rang and she picked it up, answering it using another name Alex didn't quite catch. She turned her back to the room and spoke for a few minutes.

"My forensics specialist just got back to me with the print and DNA results from the piece of mask you found, Artemis."

Artemis' eyes lit up.

"No hits."

Artemis rolled her eyes. "Say the second part faster next time, please."

Athena turned to Alex. "Do you think you could touch it and see something? Sometimes objects can have a Thread of their own."

Alex nodded, an unexpected thrill of excitement going through her at the prospect of trying her new skills. "I'm willing to give it a shot. Can we get the smelling salts out just in case, though? If it goes too long I want someone to be able to get me out."

"Great. Yes, I grabbed them along with the note Apollo left you listing the ingredients," Athena said. "Let me see if Hermes can pop over and grab the mask so we can go down both paths at once. Artemis, the salts are in the spare room I set up for Alex," she said as she sent a text message.

"On it," Artemis said, loping up the stairs.

Hermes *shifted* into the room and held out a forensic bag to Alex. She took it and he disappeared again.

Alex peered at the piece of Venetian mask through the plastic. It was only just smaller than her palm, with part of the red painted lips on it. It was covered in fingerprint dust. When she turned it over she could see the blood stain.

"Is there somewhere else I can go, so I'm not in the way down here?"

She gestured to the wide open room. She didn't like feeling so exposed when she was so out of it.

"Yes, my office is down the hall on the left. Feel free to open the bag, they got what they needed from it."

"Thanks."

Alex found the large spotless office and sank into a soft grey sofa with colorful pillows near an extremely tall window. This was clearly where Athena spent a lot of time. The large, espresso desk across the room held two monitors and stacks of well-organized papers on the sides, and the grey executive chair in front of it looked well-worn. On the wall hung a bunch of technical diagrams between colorful abstract paintings.

She glanced out at the setting sun and experienced a brief, unsettling sensation of being unmoored, of losing more than just time as she bounced back and forth across the country. She shook herself and got to business. She took her gloves off and opened the bag, pulling out the piece of porcelain and placing it gingerly in her palm, bloody side up. Her fingers touched slowly all over. Nothing.

She tried to remember what Apollo had said about being able to detect the Thread in people and things from *outside* a vision. But he'd never really said how.

She rubbed her finger on it, trying to imagine what it looked like whole. And then, more importantly, what it would look like with a Thread coming out of it.

There, she thought. A slight echo of a Thread vibrated through her senses. The mask had something to show her.

She willed herself into the light.

Flash.

46

Artemis found Alex's vial of salts on a nightstand in a sumptuous spare room on the second floor, its viscous black liquid seemed to absorb the dusky light from outside. She looked down at the expansive manicured lawn with its modern patio and old growth trees along the perimeter. From this vantage point she could see the outline of M.I.T.'s iconic buildings in the distance, where her overachieving sister sat on the board in addition to her other job as secret majority shareholder of several high-tech firms.

She closed her eyes. The revelations of moments ago had sliced through her, each one leaving a raw, weeping wound in its wake. The image of Apollo growing old with Henry cut deepest, only slightly more than the one of him keeping it a secret. She wished he'd been able to talk to her.

She wished for a lot of things.

She opened her eyes and realized with a start that night had fallen. She must have been wallowing for several minutes. She turned to leave when movement on the grass below caught her eye.

Dark forms oozed from between the trees like shadow demons, the light from the house glinting off the white of their vibrant masks.

Alarm erupted in Artemis, shooting tingly jolts throughout her limbs. Her heart started pounding.

Oh god, they're here, she thought.

Artemis took a precious moment to inhale deeply. She used the fear's barbed energy to bring clarity. She flicked her wrist to bring forth her bow.

They'd soon find they were not the only hunters here.

She yelled as she flew down the stairs. "The Venetians! They're here!"

Athena ran into the foyer, a stricken look on her face. "Impossible! How many? Do you have your phone? We need Hermes! Oh god, Sophie!" It all came out in a panicked rush.

"Several. No, it's in my room. Where's Alex?"

"She's still in my office, in a vision, we—"

The sound of several windows breaking all at once came from the great room.

"Come!" Athena grabbed Artemis by the arm and dragged her into some sort of study. She ran to a set of bookshelves on the wall full of books and other accoutrements, lifted the lid of a small decorative box, and pushed a button inside. Artemis gasped as the bookshelf slid soundlessly to the right, revealing a narrow, dark, cinderblock passageway with exposed wooden beams. Athena gestured for Artemis to follow her in, then pushed another button to slide the door back into place on well-oiled gears.

"Athena, what the—"

"Shhhh!"

"Okay, but are we really going to just run and hide?" Artemis whispered.

"No. But they're too strong, too fast. Our best chance is to use guerilla tactics. Keep them at a distance, do what damage we can from the walls. In and out. These passageways go to many rooms in the house, and they are marked. There is a door to my office that way." Athena pointed toward the narrow passageway behind Artemis then continued in an urgent voice. "You go get Alex and pull her into the wall. You'll have to move fast. I'll get my daughter and her nanny, and my guns. Then I'll try to get a message to Hermes to get us out of here. There is a panic room in the basement. If you don't see Hermes, find the stairs going down around the corner. Meet me there with Alex."

Athena pulled her into a fierce hug. "Be safe," she said. Then she raced away.

Artemis crept down the passageway holding her bow in front of her so it didn't scrape against the wall. She found the door marked 'Office' and put her ear up to the wall to listen.

"Here, there's one here!" said a female voice through the wall.

"Good. The rest have to be here somewhere," said another. "Spread out. Remember, do not harm the male."

Artemis frowned. Why not Hermes? She closed her eyes and listened. One set of footsteps walked slowly into the room as several others pattered away into the house.

"Look at you, little Oracle," a voice said. "Doing your thing. I wish you were awake so you could know what was coming. You escaped me before. But not again."

Go to hell, you masked freak, Artemis thought.

She lifted her bow and pushed the button on the wall.

lex let the vision take her where it wanted at first, a woman seemingly in her early twenties choosing the mask out of dozens on a wall.

"Just find the one that speaks to you, Gwen. You will know," a barefoot woman said from behind her, wearing a soft, creamy tunic with fringe just above the knee. Nothing else. The scrollwork tattoo on her face shimmered, as though the vines could at any moment come alive.

Gwen found she was drawn back to one particular mask over and over. Its ivory face was graced with gold, red, and black flowers around the upper half and a large pearl set in the middle of the forehead. Its full red lips were painted into a small, knowing smile. She pulled it off the wall and put it up to her face. She sighed. "Oh Ria, I think this is it! When I put it on, it feels like home and...I don't know, makes me feel more like me, somehow."

"Excellent! It is beautiful!" Ria clapped in delight. "You have been a worthy follower and pleased your god. He himself recommended you take the next step in your spiritual journey, one reserved for only the most special of women."

"I am honored and blessed."

Ria nodded. "Your parents will be proud. Now that you have chosen your mask you may begin studying the ways of The Chosen, our god's most ardent worshippers. Once you have completed all the steps you will receive your own garland of ivy, drink the sacred wine of The Chosen, perform your sacrifice, and join the Sisterhood.

"When? And does it... does it hurt?" She touched her bare cheek.

"A few short weeks. It does not hurt. You will see."

"Thank you Ria. I am so grateful for your mentorship, and lucky to have you for my guide."

Ria smiled. "Don't tell, but you and Jenna are my favorites," she whispered.

Alex paused the vision and stared at Ria, the woman whose body had started this whole thing. Whose life blood she'd watched spill from her neck. It was like seeing a ghost.

Alex shook herself. She tried and failed to manifest the Thread onto Gwen several times, panicking until she remembered with a smack to her mental forehead that it was the *mask's* fate she was following. She imposed the Thread onto the mask and there it stayed, the cable of light impaling Gwen's face. Alex sighed in relief. She reached out and took hold, grinning as her perspective changed, giddy at her success so far.

Alex grinned as her perspective changed to the side, giddy at her success so far.

She slid the vision forward, trying to find something helpful. Her mental pulse quickened when she recognized the First One. She slid back to beginning of what looked like a ceremony.

At least a hundred torches created a circle of soft light in a forest clearing, providing light to the dozens of tattooed women standing in a semicircle three people deep. They were bare-limbed and wore the same soft cream-colored tunics. In front of them stood five women wearing their masks and what looked like gray and brown deerskin. Gwen stood in the middle.

The First One stood in front, wearing a familiar mask of half black and white with large dark red feathers around it like a mane. "Welcome, Initiates," the First One chanted. "You have studied and learned the ways of the Bacchae, and now, clad in nature and wildness, you will drink of the sacred Wine of The Chosen, allowing the breath of Bacchus to enter you. Allow it to seep into you as you offer your mind, your heart, and your body to your god. As you become one of us. One of the Bacchae. One of his Chosen. Praise Bacchus."

"Praise Bacchus," the women intoned. The First One stepped back and gestured to the sky.

"Grace us with your presence, oh horned god."

A sound of deep rolling thunder filled the clearing and a flash of light blinded everyone momentarily. When the light faded, a man stood in front of them. He wore a dark suit with a dark gray shirt, and a golden three-quarter mask with the large curved horns of a bull sprouting off the forehead.

"Chosen," his voice boomed. "I am come."

The women fell to their knees, laid their arms in front of them, and chanted. "Bacchus, Bacchus, Bacchus."

"You may rise," he said. "I am come to witness and bless the metamorphosis of these women, these Initiates, as they become Bacchae, my Chosen. As you join my innermost family, I welcome you to my constant presence and your True Life."

"Praise Bacchus!" the women intoned.

"It is time for you to drink of the wine I create special for my Chosen. It gives a gift unlike any other gift in the world—liberation from your conscience, from your constant worries. Its fire will fill your bellies with health, and strength, and a way of seeing the world through the eyes of the free, in every sense of the word. Eyes of the passionate, the frenzied, the enthused. It is a glorious delirium, but instead of losing your senses, they are heightened."

"Praise Bacchus!" they chanted.

"Once consumed, it will become a part of you, sustaining you as long as you honor and worship me, your god, in all the ways of the Bacchae. And in return, I will heap blessings upon you."

"Praise Bacchus!"

Bacchus lifted his hands and a stone fountain appeared beside him. The women murmured in appreciation. Cascades of rich, dark wine flowed over two stone bowls into a larger basin brimming with the crimson liquid. The air filled with its pungent smell. The basin was carved into the face of a bull. On the edge of the basin stood five pewter goblets.

"Come, Initiates, remove your masks and become one with me." He gestured them forward.

Moving in unison, the women glided across the grass, each removing their mask and filling a goblet. They drank as one and returned the cups to the basin. Their chests heaved as the wine permeated their bodies.

The horned god smiled. He gestured again and the women gasped. Dark furls of ivy crept over each of their faces, covering their foreheads and cheeks. They made sounds of joy and exclamations, feeling each other's slightly raised skin.

"You are now wreathed in my glory, wearing forever my most potent symbol, the ever-green ivy. It represents my triumph over death, my vitality, and my divinity. All of which I now share in part with you."

The women fell to their knees. "Praise Bacchus!"

"Rise my Chosen, my Bacchae, it is time to celebrate!" He stepped back and music filled the clearing, a wild, pounding rhythm. The newly initiated set their masks on the edge and began to dance to the rhythm, swinging and swaying and twirling.

"Dance, Bacchae, dance! Exhaust yourself for my glory!"

The other Bacchae joined in and were lost to the night.

48

Artemis slipped into Athena's office with her bow already pointed in the direction of the Venetian's voice.

Alex was clearly still in the vision. Her eyes shone in an eerie, pearlescent white, not reacting at all to the fact that a Venetian was standing behind her, hand on forehead, holding a knife to her throat.

No! Artemis thought. She knelt, took aim, and fired twice in quick succession.

The Venetian's head snapped back as arrows pierced the small eye holes of her mask. She toppled silently backward, her body crumpling across the open doorway with a thump.

Artemis crept over and pulled the corpse all the way into the office, closing the door behind her.

Alex's head had remained in the terrifying position the Venetian had put it in. A small rivulet of blood ran down her neck.

Artemis shook her friend. "Alex!" she whispered. "Wake up!" She flicked her bow away and searched her pockets frantically for the vial of smelling salts.

"Any luck?" a voice said from down the hall.

Artemis froze.

"No, it is strangely quiet," a second voice said.

Shit, Artemis thought. She curled her arms under Alex's arms, dragging her toward the hidden door. She glanced behind her and was horrified to see the hidden door was closed, covered by an enormous black and white painting of an owl.

"Same here," a third voice joined them. "Though I feel they are here."

"As do I. They must be hiding."

No, no, no! Artemis thought. She let Alex slump to the floor and fumbled around the edge of the frame. *There has to be a button here,* she thought. The frame was maddeningly smooth.

Damn you, Athena! Artemis crept back to Alex and pulled her behind the grey sofa to hide her from immediate view. She feverishly scanned the room for another place Athena would have hidden the stupid button. She finally spied a dark paperweight owl on her desk. It had a hinge.

Owl painting, owl statue.

"Where is Jenna?" one of the Venetians asked. "Surely she is done with the Oracle."

"You two go check, she probably just started to search as well."

Artemis dove behind the sofa, thankful that it had enough space for both of them. She flicked her wrist and held her breath.

She stared at Alex as her pulse raced. *Please don't wake up now,* she thought.

The door opened. "Jenna! Noooo! Our sister is dead!" the Venetian keened like a banshee.

The others took it up and the strange, loud wailing filled the house.

Then a gunshot cut through the sound.

"Go!" one of them hissed.

Artemis waited as the footsteps ran off toward the sound. She began to slowly peek her head up over the edge of the sofa when a floorboard creaked.

She silently dropped back down. Her heart thrashed in her chest like a bird trying to escape its cage.

At least one of them had stayed.

49

lex's mental skin prickled as she watched the ceremony of the Bacchae. She sensed she was seeing and hearing important things and desperately wished for more context. She had a feeling if the others saw this, they would already have answers. She skipped through the revelry, feeling her mental self blush as many of the Bacchae removed their clothes. They were so unabashedly free!

She swept the vision forward, wanting to check for anything else useful while trying to be mindful how long she'd been gone. She stopped short at the sight of a group of masked Bacchae standing in a semi-circle around Gwen's bed. It was the middle of the night. Strange. She slipped into the moment.

"Sisters, what are you doing?" Gwen sat up in the bottom of a metal bunk bed in a spartan white room. The upper bunk appeared to be empty.

One of the Bacchae spoke. "Sister, you have been selected to be part of the Elite. The Chosen Elite. An inner circle of Bacchae that serves the full measure of our god's needs."

"Ria? Jenna? Anne? What do you mean?"

"He needs our help," Jenna said. "But he cannot ask it of all his Chosen. Only those with the strength to give their all."

"If he needs help, I am here for him," Gwen said reverently. "Anything."

The women nodded together.

"We are not called often, only when there is great need. And there is such a need now. We must help him conquer his enemies."

"He has enemies?"

"Yes. Old and new," Ria said.

"Then I want to help," Gwen said. She swung her legs out of the bed and grabbed her mask from the nightstand.

"Wait. If you mean to serve as a member of his Chosen Elite, it must be as secret as it is sacred. For you will receive training not given to the rest of the Chosen. There are only a couple dozen of us and right now only we three know you have been selected to join our ranks. If you choose to join, you will be marked so as to be known amongst the other Elite. Do you swear on the horned god's name to keep this a secret?"

"I swear," Gwen said. "Praise Bacchus."

"Praise Bacchus," the women echoed.

"Now we must alter your tattoo," Ria said. She pulled off her own mask and pointed to two small filled in leaves hanging like commas off the lowest curving line of her facial tattoo. "This is how you will know your fellow Chosen Elite."

The other two women pulled their masks off as well. The ivy leaves were noticeable once you knew to look for them.

Ria pulled out a tattoo gun and put on surgical gloves. "Apologies, Sister, this will hurt a little." She inserted the ink cartridge and started it up. Gwen winced as the needle slid over her skin, giving shape to the leaves. It didn't take long.

"Welcome to the Chosen Elite," Ria said when she was done.

"Praise Bacchus," Gwen said.

"Praise Bacchus," they replied.

"Now. Here are our latest directives from the First One." She handed Gwen a piece of paper.

Gwen read it, then looked wide-eyed at her sisters. "But, this is..."

"What is needed," Ria finished for her. She handed Gwen a strange looking knife with a pinecone on its hilt.

Ria smiled. "Fear not. The wine provides and the wine forgets."

Alex felt a thrill of discovery. She couldn't wait to share what she'd seen. The thought of conveying so much with yes/no questions was daunting, but she'd do what she could.

First, she had to get out. Here's hoping it worked the second time around. She mentally crossed her fingers and manifested a large book unique for this Thread, covered in ivy and the mask's gold, red, and black flowers engraved on the cover.

She held it up to the Thread and closed it.

50

Artemis closed her eyes and held her breath, carefully shutting out the sound of her heartbeat to really listen.

There it was again, a quiet footfall. Closer this time. They were stealthy, these Venetians.

Artemis had only one chance to use the advantage of surprise. She ran through her options as she sat with Alex in the wide space between the sofa and the wall. She had mere seconds, and she couldn't tell which way the Venetian was coming. By the time she heard the next footstep, it might be too late.

She figured she had a fifty-fifty chance, and prayed she'd catch the Venetian on the opposite side of the couch, giving her the space to fire. She bunched her legs under her then shot them forward, exploding herself from behind the sofa with her bow raised and bowstring pulled back.

She'd guessed wrong. The Venetian was only two feet away. She dove on top of Artemis before she could get a shot off. In a single move the Venetian knocked the weapon out of her hand and jammed a knee into her stomach, knocking the wind out of her. The silver bow and arrow went skittering back behind the sofa.

Artemis groaned and would have doubled over if the Venetian hadn't sat on her, pinning her arms to her side. Artemis struggled, but it was like trying to wiggle out of a straightjacket.

The Venetian glowered, her eyes blazing through the holes in her mask. "You killed my sister."

"Well, she was about to kill my friend," Artemis wheezed. "Why are you doing this? Why did you kill my brother?"

"Less talking, more screaming."

Artemis panicked as she felt a sudden sharp tug on her right arm.

The Venetian cocked her head. "She loves me..." she said in a macabre, singsong voice. Artemis tried to buck her off. The Venetian lifted her arm up and pulled.

Artemis screamed as the flesh tore and a sickening popping sound rang in her ears. She nearly blacked out from hot, searing pain as her arm came off in the Venetian's hand.

"She loves me not..." The Venetian tugged on her left arm.

"No!" Artemis yelled.

Suddenly a hand shoved the un-shot arrow sideways into the Venetian's neck, knocking her off balance. Artemis looked in surprise at Alex as she held the arrow tight, arterial blood spouting onto her face and chest.

The Venetian whirled and backhanded Alex with all her strength. She flew into the opposite wall and crumbled to a heap on the floor.

Artemis bucked the now gurgling assailant all the way off. The Venetian rolled to her back, panic fluttering in her strange eyes. Artemis crawled over and sat on her torso, their positions now reversed. Blood ran quickly down her side from the gaping hole in her shoulder, the coppery smell of it thick in her nose. She needed to hurry and get that arm reattached. But first things first.

She leaned over the Venetian, who was barely conscious. "You know, removing an arrow is a delicate procedure," she said breathlessly. "Since they can cause more damage coming out than they do going in." Her fierce blue eyes gleamed as she grabbed the arrow with her left hand, gave it a half turn, and yanked it out.

The Venetian's body stilled as blood gushed out of the now gaping hole in her neck, eddying into a crimson pool on the dark hardwood floor.

Artemis rolled off the body, breathing hard. She stared for a moment of disbelief at her arm, laying forlornly on the floor like it belonged to a doll. It was still covered in a black long sleeve, with the bone sticking out of the top. Artemis' stomach heaved and strangely, Ares' exultation about the old days echoed in her mind.

She gathered it up and tried in vain to return it to its socket. The torn shirt and tendon were in the way, and she was too woozy. She was losing too much blood. She needed help. She glanced over at Alex, who was still crumpled on the floor, unconscious.

Just then two more Venetians filled the doorway. They howled at the sight of their fallen sister and rushed into the room.

Artemis exhaled, totally spent, and waited for her end.

But it never came.

In a blink, Hermes *shifted* into the room, grabbing one the Venetians and disappearing with her. Her partner paused and whirled at the sound of a woman's scream through the window, high in the air. Before she even hit the ground, Hermes had *shifted* back and grabbed the other one.

A second scream was followed by two wet, squishy thumps.

He reappeared and rushed toward Artemis. She waved him toward Alex. "Get Alex first," she whispered. He looked at her in dismay but did as she asked.

The room began to darken at the edges like a vignette, slowly closing in.

Then Hermes was there and her world went blissfully, chillingly black.

51

Alex woke up to find herself laying on some kind of rug in the dark. She felt like a truck had hit her and then also backed over her. Everything hurt—her head, back, and especially her chest. She licked her lips and gagged at the metallic taste of the Venetian's blood.

She waited for her eyes to adjust to the dark then tried to sit up slowly to keep the room from spinning too much. She seemed to be in some sort of cabin. She pulled herself toward the only light in the room—an enormous window several feet away that took up a large section of wall, bending at the corner and continuing up half the ceiling like a massive skylight.

Her thoughts jumbled around like clothes in a dryer as she crawled. She was alive. And hopefully, so was Artemis. She still couldn't believe what had happened. She shivered as she remembered what she'd done to that woman. But she would have killed Artemis, right? She was sure that's why she'd woken up behind the couch instead of on it. Artemis probably did that to try to hide her. At least her arm wasn't off. Oh Artemis. She hoped her friend was okay.

She wondered if she had a concussion.

Alex pulled herself up against the wall and let her head fall forward onto her chest, her eyelids drooping. *If you have a concussion, you need to stay awake,* said a distant voice inside. She forced her eyes open and leaned her head back to look out the window. The Milky Way spanned across the window amid thousands of dancing stars. It was as though she was in the middle of a galaxy. For a brief moment she felt weightless.

"Quite a view, isn't it?" Hermes asked. Alex startled, but her body didn't get the memo. "Why are you sitting in the dark?"

"I couldn't get up to find a light," she mumbled. "Where are we? Where is everyone?" Everything was beginning to feel fuzzy, like she was looking at the world through a dirty film.

"We're at my cabin in Germany. One of the places I go to get away from everything and everyone. It's totally off the grid. I have Artemis being put back together by a doctor friend of mine. Someone we can trust. I dropped Athena, her kid, and the nanny off at her house in London. Once she gets them settled she'll join us."

"Is everyone okay? How did they even know where we were?"

"Yes, everyone will be fine. I don't know yet. I'm going to turn on the light, okay?"

Alex nodded and savored one last look at the Milky Way.

He flipped a switch and a cluster of large Edison bulbs revealed what seemed to be a modern one-room wood cabin with a high A-frame ceiling, two exposed stone walls, and a midnight-green dividing wall that didn't reach the ceiling. She found she was sitting on the floor next to his dining table looking right at the tidy galley kitchen this side of the wall.

Hermes grunted at the sight of her. "I didn't get a good look at you before. Is that your blood?"

"No," she whispered.

"Okay, good. But you look monstrous. Let's get you cleaned up."

Alex tried to stand and stumbled. Hermes rushed over and helped her up. She leaned heavily on his reassuringly solid frame as he led her toward the bathroom.

"Are you injured?" he asked.

"I may have a concussion and I hurt all the way to my bones, but I don't think anything's broken."

Hermes slowly guided her toward the bathroom. "What happened? Artemis was too out of it to tell me, and Athena hasn't told me anything yet. All I got was a message from her to get everyone out. Lucky I started with you two."

"Yes. Thanks for that," Alex said. Hermes turned the light on in the bathroom and sat her on the wide edge of the tub ensconced in a wood trim. He turned the faucet on, feeling for the water to warm.

Alex numbly recounted what happened when she came out of the vision.

Hermes raised his brows. "You stabbed one of them in the neck with an arrow?" He shook his head. "You know, I've known a lot of humans in my lifetime. They are usually predictable, almost to a fault. But you, Miss Alex, you keep surprising me."

Alex smiled wanly.

He leaned over to pull the stopper on the tub.

Alex shook her head. "No, that's ok. I'll just sit in the shower."

"Fair enough." Hermes pulled the shower knob and stood to leave.

Alex just stared at the floor, not quite able to get her body to move. A shower felt too monumental of a task.

"You know, I think let's just do a spit bath for now, shall we?" Hermes said gently.

Alex nodded gratefully. He lathered a washcloth with soap and warm water, then sat next to her and began to wipe off the blood. He had to rinse out the cloth several times as he cleaned her face, hair, and neck.

"I think we'd better just toss the shirt, is that okay?" He studiously kept his eyes on hers. "I have a shirt you can wear."

She nodded, too weary to care. She just wanted it off. He got a soft red t-shirt and laid it on her lap.

Alex tried to pull the shirt off and cried out in pain as she lifted her arms over her head. "I don't think I can do that. Do you have scissors?" she asked, trembling.

Hermes nodded and went to get them, then cut the shirt right up the middle.

"Gods," Hermes whispered. "No wonder."

Alex looked down. An angry forearm shaped bruise was forming across her chest. "That tracks," she said.

Hermes pointed to her glove. "Can we take this off too? It's got blood on it." She nodded, realizing with a distant pang the other one was left behind. But that too disappeared into the numbness that was taking over.

Hermes stoically cleaned only around the edges of where the t-shirt had been, getting the last of the blood. He dried her off with a towel, then helped her into the t-shirt.

It smelled like fresh laundry. She felt clean and so exhausted she wondered how she was conscious at all.

He pulled up her eyelids, checking her eyes. "You're not throwing up, talking fairly coherently. Do you have double vision?" he asked.

Alex shook her head, and winced. It did feel like her brain was loose, but no double vision.

"I think maybe we should get you to a doctor."

"No, I just need to rest."

"I don't know…" he sounded dubious.

"Please," she said.

"Okay, let's get you to bed." He led her around the dividing wall to the bedroom on the other side, pulling back the bedding on the low platform bed.

"I have sweats you can wear if you—"

Alex undid her jeans and let them fall to the floor. "Alright, that works too," he said, helping her step out and into the bed.

"Wait, we better at least get you something for the pain and swelling." He ran for some water then held the glass as she swallowed the pills he'd given her.

Alex felt warm, safe, and so very heavy. She laid on her back and fumbled for the blankets.

Hermes pulled the covers over her.

"Thank you so much," Alex whispered.

"I think that should be my line," Hermes said quietly.

She was barely aware of him watching her drift off to sleep.

52

Shadows danced on Alex's face as sunlight percolated through the autumnal trees outside the window. She stretched without thinking and her body screamed in protest. Hermes had woken her up several times through the night, probably just to make sure she would. She vaguely remembered getting another dose of painkillers too. She didn't notice her body as much if she lay still, so she let the sound of the birds chirping outside wash over her, lulling her back into a deep sleep.

When she woke again it was almost dark. The soft light of a black floor lamp drew her gaze. Hermes sat in a well-worn brown armchair in the corner of the room, typing away on his laptop.

She moved slowly, testing each motion. Her body hurt slightly less.

"Glad to see you awake," he said, without looking up.

Alex sighed. "Me too, I think. Thanks for letting me sleep."

He nodded. "You needed it. Probably still do. But you should eat while you're up. Give your body some resources. Are you hungry?"

Her stomach growled at the thought of food. It felt like years since she'd picked at Nyssa's pancakes.

"I could eat," she said.

"Great. What do you want?" Hermes asked. "I'll go get it."

Alex thought about it. "Honestly? A cheeseburger and fries is sounding really good right now."

Hermes smiled. "Be right back." He put his laptop down and vanished.

Alex sat up gingerly, noticing her head still throbbed slightly. She padded to the bathroom, grabbing her jeans on the way. She stared at herself in the mirror, barely recognizing the person looking back at her. That woman had killed a person. The visceral feeling of the arrow going into that woman's neck came back to her then. How it had pierced the skin and sliced through the muscle. How steaming hot blood had spewed all over her.

Alex's stomach heaved. She ran to the toilet and threw up what little there was in her stomach. It burned her throat.

"You okay in there?" Hermes asked, apparently returned.

"Yeah. Be out in a minute," she said through the door.

She rinsed out her mouth and splashed water on her face. She went to put on her jeans when she noticed there was blood on them too.

"Um, Hermes? Can I take you up on those sweats? These jeans have blood on them. I can't..." her voice wavered.

He opened the door just wide enough to hand her the sweats. She pulled them on and joined him in the kitchen. The smell of hamburger filled the cabin.

"Thanks," she said. "Are my things still at Athena's?"

"Yes. Athena and I decided to intentionally leave them there, since they seem to always know where you are. But I'll throw those in the wash."

"Oh. Okay. Thanks," she said. "What about my other glove?"

"You really need it?"

Alex thought for a moment. New skills or not, it was like asking Linus to leave behind his security blanket. "I don't know, I'll give it a try."

Hermes pulled takeout containers out of a bag. "This is from a little hole in the wall in South Carolina," he said. "One of the best burgers I ever had."

Alex sat and took a bite and sighed, the burst of flavor filling her mouth and helping her forget everything else for just a moment. "So good. Thank you."

"My pleasure."

They ate in silence for a while, for which Alex was grateful. She practically inhaled half the burger.

"How's Artemis?" she asked eventually.

"They got her arm back into the socket and stitched her up so her body could heal it properly. She's been sleeping non-stop too. It will help her heal. I imagine it will be usable in a few days."

"I'm so glad. And Athena and Sophie?"

"They're fine. What about you?" Hermes asked.

"I'll live. I'm super envious of your healing abilities though."

"Yeah, I wish we could share them."

"Me too." She rubbed her temples to ease the throbbing.

"Your head still hurt?"

Alex nodded.

"Do you want to lay back down?"

"Not yet. I need a distraction. Do you have a TV or anything?

"Not here. My laptop has a satellite connection though."

"That's okay, no worries."

"You know, vomiting could be a sign of serious head injury."

"It wasn't that," she said.

"Okay, good." He didn't push.

But she found herself talking around it, realizing she was with someone who had also just done the unthinkable. "I'm assuming that wasn't the first time you've killed people?" It came out as more of a statement than a question.

He grimaced. "No, it's happened more than I'd like. Some were self-defense. Some not. Either way, there's a cognitive dissonance to process through. We aren't meant to kill each other."

Alex sighed. God, she was definitely going to need therapy after all this.

"It sticks with you for a while," he said. "But you better believe you did the right thing. That small cut on your neck says you probably had another narrow escape. It was definitely self-defense."

Alex felt her throat, her eyes wide. She hadn't felt the scab there mixed in with all the other pain.

"You're okay now though," Hermes said hurriedly. "It's okay."

It was all too much. Alex could feel herself teetering on the edge of a total meltdown, a baby's breath would send her over.

"Just use it," he said gruffly. "Use it to remember that you're alive. That it was her or you. And if it came between picking between you versus that masked psycho, the world is much better off with you in it."

Alex took a deep breath and tried to steady herself, turning his words into a mantra she held to like a lifeline. *Her or me and I chose me...her or me and I chose me...her or me and I chose me.*

She pulled herself away from the edge, taking a deep, clearing breath. "Thanks."

He nodded and they took more bites in silence, the tangy dipping sauce for the fries taking much of her attention.

"Can I ask why you're being so nice to me?" she asked through a mouthful of hot fries. "I'm grateful, I just...I thought you didn't like me much."

Hermes cleared his throat as he wiped some ketchup from his mouth and beard. "I never didn't... Ah, well. It's just easier to be an asshole, you know?"

Alex didn't and it must have shown on her face.

"Keeps folks at a distance. I've lost a lot of people I care about over the years. Not interested in losing more."

Alex twirled a fry in her fingers. "I get that." She leaned back and looked up at the yawning window in the ceiling. She could see the brightest stars even through the glare on the glass.

"Where did you say we are again?" she asked.

"Germany. Middle of the Black Forest. Not a town for miles."

"Ah. I've always wanted to go to Europe."

"Ha. *Willkommen.*"

She gave a small smile.

The pounding in Alex's head was becoming more pronounced. "Thanks again for dinner. I think I'll lay down again, if that's okay."

"No problem."

Alex paused on her way around the dividing wall to the bedroom. "Am I taking your bed?" she asked.

"I'm good. I caught a few hours on the couch. I don't need much."

"Okay. Thanks."

Alex took off the sweats and slipped back into the cool green sheets. She lay in bed, listening to Hermes tidy up. She liked this kind, thoughtful, and quiet Hermes. She was struck by the similarities of this situation to the one she'd just been in a couple of days ago.

With Hermes though, she never once felt uneasy or uncomfortable.

Alex realized she felt safe for the first time in days.

lex was pulled out of sleep the next morning by the sound of crinkling paper and whispering.

"Shhhh, you'll wake her up!"

"Look at you being all concerned!"

"Hey, someone had to take care of her!"

Artemis sounded contrite. "I know, I'm just teasing. I really am grateful."

Alex's eyes flew open. *Artemis!*

She sat up slowly, taking measure of the pain. It was there, but not screaming quite as loud. She pulled on the sweats and walked around the dividing wall.

Artemis sat at the hand-carved kitchen table unwrapping a breakfast sandwich with her left hand. Her right arm was in a black sling, barely noticeable against her black clothes. She looked a little frazzled, with hair mostly pulled out of the braid and her makeup a little smeared. She had color in her face though.

"There she is," Artemis said.

"Artemis! Are you okay?" Alex asked. "Hermes said they got your arm back into place?"

"Yeah, I will be." Artemis looked down at her arm. "The new tissue seems to have grown already, but it's definitely weak. Hence the sling."

"I'm so glad."

"Yeah, at least it wasn't both arms. *And* that you came out of your vision right then. Thanks for the save."

"I'd say that makes us even." Alex touched the scab on her neck. "Or maybe I still owe you one."

Artemis grimaced. "Pretty sure I owe you infinity." She watched with concern as Alex sat down gingerly in the wooden chair next to her. "Are *you* okay?"

"Still just achy and sore. I'm lucky nothing broke."

"Show her the bruise on your chest," Hermes said, turning his back.

Alex lifted up the red t-shirt revealing the violent purple-black mark that matched her black bra.

"Jesus!" Artemis exclaimed.

"Yeah." Alex let the shirt drop.

Hermes scooted a takeout bag, a cup of coffee, and more painkillers toward Alex. "For you."

"Thank you."

The sound of a phone sliced through the quiet.

"It's Athena," Hermes said. "She's ready to join us too. Which is good, because I have some news. I'll be right back." He shoveled the rest of the sandwich into his mouth then vanished.

He reappeared quickly with Athena, who looked drawn and weary, though of course more put together than anyone else, with her hair back in a simple, sleek ponytail and casual clothes.

"So glad you are all okay," she said, giving both women a hug.

"What happened to you?" Artemis asked. "I heard a gunshot but that was it, though I think that saved us. It drew most of them toward you."

"Yes, though it seems you two still managed to take the brunt of the attack. I got one of them, though. After getting Sophie and her nanny to the panic room, I was able to sneak into my bedroom to get my phone and gun, which I needed pretty quickly. I sent the message to Hermes after I was able to get back into the walls."

"Do we know how many there were?" Artemis asked.

"Well, we killed five. There were likely more."

"How did they know where we were?" Alex asked.

Athena scowled. "I don't know, but I intend to find out," she said. "What of your news, Hermes?"

"Right. I wanted to wait until we'd re-grouped. I found the video feed to Apollo's lab. The original video had been deleted, but I had it backed up to another storage bucket. It's a little grainy, and there's very little sound, but I found a recording of Apollo's murder."

54

Artemis felt like she'd just been pushed off a cliff and was freefalling through the air, her breathing coming in staccato bursts. Ignoring the others' advice that she didn't have to, she had just watched the video all the way to the bitter, harrowing end. She'd owed Apollo that much. But a scream was building deep within her.

"Hermes. Go back to where she takes out her knife, it was distinctive," Athena directed calmly. Too calmly, in Artemis' opinion, for someone who had just watched her own brother's snuff film. "Can we zoom in on it?"

"I can try," he said, his voice thick with emotion. He captured a still from the video and increased the magnification. "This is the best I can do without more time and better software." The image caught the woman as she drew the blade down Apollo's cheek, catching the dagger in the emergency lights. It was a strange, sleek, aerodynamic knife with what looked like a five-inch blade in the shape of a spearhead. The bottom of the handle had a strange shape as well, though it was more difficult to make out.

"Damn," Athena whispered. "I missed it."

Artemis felt her heart skip a beat. "What? You recognize that or something?"

"Not the knife specifically, but the symbolism on it. Hermes, can you find a still that shows the bottom better?"

He slowly played the video until the Venetian held her knife over Apollo's heart. He paused and zoomed in. The blood drained from his face. "No," he whispered.

Artemis still wasn't sure what she was looking at. "What? What?"

"Hang on," Athena said. Her eyes went unfocused.

"Goddamnit, Athena!" Artemis yelled. But her sister was already in her stupid little memory palace.

Athena surfaced and nodded to herself. "Okay. If I'm right, and I think I am, that knife looks like a spear. A spear with a pinecone and ivy on the end. It's basically a miniature thyrsus."

A vile, pregnant silence followed.

Artemis' blood began to boil as she stared at the knife hovering over Apollo's heart. "I'm going to rip…his…fucking…head off," she snarled.

Hermes lifted his arms. "Now wait, we don't know that it's him."

"Like hell we don't!" Artemis yelled.

"We don't. You don't know him like I do. He cared for Apollo. He wouldn't do this."

"That's one of his symbols, Hermes!"

"No, it's one of the symbols of his followers."

"Are you really going to argue semantics with me right now? They're *his followers*!"

"Yes. I mean, no, not semantics. But if those are maenads, which would make a whole lotta sense, then we have to tread carefully. There are other powerful people involved. I'm just saying we might not know the whole story."

Athena nodded. "Nyssa. And who knows who else in the cult."

Hermes nodded.

"And she just does whatever she wants, and that little turd doesn't know anything? I don't buy it. Why are you defending him?" Artemis asked.

"I'm not. I'm just saying let's not jump to conclusions and start ripping heads off. He's our brother, and I, for one, am skeptical he could pull something like this off."

"No way. He hated Hera more than any of us, and has always had mixed feelings about Father." Artemis gasped. "I bet he has Father there now! We need to go!"

Athena stood too. "Hermes is right."

Artemis barely stifled a scream.

"Only in that we need to make sure. We need to proceed carefully if we want any chance of saving Father."

"Fine, and just how are we going to do that? Let's bring him here so we can confront him."

"That's a terrible plan. He can just *shift* away," Hermes said.

"Then we ask him nicely. Make up some reason. I don't care!"

Alex raised her hand timidly, a stunned look on her face. "Um, I'm pretty sure he wouldn't come right now anyway," she said. They all looked at her in surprise. "I assume since you mentioned Nyssa and the cult that you're talking about Dionysus?"

Athena nodded.

"Well, the Mysteries are this weekend, and he's getting ready."

"He told you about the Mysteries?" Athena interrupted.

"Not much," Alex said. "Just that it's their biggest ceremony, and that it's partly how he maintains his powers. Though it costs him a lot of energy. He invited me."

Each of them gaped at her at that. "Interesting," said Athena. "No one has ever been given access to this ceremony, not even Hermes. In fact… Demeter is the only other person that has ever been involved, and she's missing as well. Hmmm, this really is coming together. They would have known about Alex after the family meeting, so that would account for the first Venetian attack. Not sure about the second one…unless they found a way to track Alex after she left his complex."

Alex paled. "Oh no. They did give me a bottle of wine to take with me."

"Aha!" Athena exclaimed. "A thousand dollars says it has a tracker on it."

"But wait. Why would he save me if he was behind their attack?" Alex gestured to the screen where Apollo was about to be murdered. "And why would he help me with my visions?"

Hermes nodded. "Exactly. There are too many questions. We just don't know for sure."

The scream that had been building within Artemis finally erupted, its raw, heartbreaking sound reverberating in the wood cabin like a wounded animal. The sound slowly coalesced into words. "THEY KILLED APOLLO, HERMES!" she screamed.

Hermes dropped his eyes. "I know. I'm sorry. It's just so unreal."

They all gave the moment some space. Artemis felt like a volcano that had barely begun its eruption. Pools of roiling rage still rose and fell within her. She fought an urge to flip the table and start wrecking the place.

"Wait, Alex, did you have any luck with your vision?" Athena asked finally.

"I think so."

"Anything that would confirm that he was involved?"

Alex shrugged. "I don't know. I saw things that felt important, but I don't have enough context. You would know more. You need to ask questions, and it isn't going to be easy."

"Go for it, Athena." Artemis paced.

Athena began. "You saw the woman who wore the piece of mask you were holding, yes?"

Alex nodded.

"Was she a maenad?"

Alex shrugged. "I don't know what that means. I didn't hear that word."

Hermes slammed his hand down on the table. "No! This is going to make me crazy. It's time to test this curse against modern technology. I'll get my satellite wi-fi up and running."

"Okay, agreed. Just don't use this vision!" Athena said.

"No shit," Hermes said. "We can quickly try several methodologies at once to see what sticks. Come with me." He gestured for Alex to follow him out of the room.

Alex glanced at Artemis as she left, a haunted look in her eyes.

Artemis barely registered it through the sulfurous red in her own.

55

E mily, the technical expert of the Chosen Elite, sat in a dark operating room with three lit monitors in front of her, trying to focus. Normally, she loved serving her god with her systems engineering skillset. Now, she cringed under the weight of the First One's wrath.

"Five Chosen Elites gone. All that talent and training wasted," the First One said from behind her.

And five beautiful women that were my friends, Emily thought, grieving behind her mask and silently outraged at the First One's callousness. She knew better than to say anything though, especially when she had more bad news. "The targets have all disappeared. I cannot find them in any of the places we monitor currently," she said.

The First One exhaled noisily in frustration.

"But you did say to let you know if anyone accessed the feed to Apollo's lab. Someone did."

"Can you tell from where?"

"No, they used an anonymizing VPN."

"It has to be them. You deleted the video feed though, yes?"

"Yes. But..." Emily took a deep, shaky breath. "There was a backup that we missed."

The First One's eyes flared within their porcelain mask. "We?"

Emily trembled. "A backup *I* missed."

"And is there anything in that video that would help them?"

"Possibly." The Chosen Elite braced herself as she turned the monitor to show the First One on the screen. "Please forgive me," she squeaked.

The First One let out a scream and pounded a fist on the table. "That is unfortunate. There is not a universe that exists in which Athena would miss that. Stay sharp this weekend and tell all your sisters to do the same.

"They are coming."

56

Alex followed Hermes outside onto a shaded wooden deck with a thick press of yellowing trees mere feet away. The cheerful birds chirping in the sun were at odds with her mood. She was having difficulty reconciling Dionysus as a murderer. Possessive, yes. Boundary issues, yes. But a murderer? He didn't seem like one. But what if he was? What if she'd just made out with…? She stopped herself from going any further and tried to focus on the test.

Hermes sat her in a wide Adirondack bench, handed her his laptop, gave her a few simple instructions, and left her to it. Easy. But Alex's fingers hovered over the keyboard. The cursor blinked in a slow, mesmerizing rhythm, just waiting for the first key to drop. She felt a little queasy.

What is wrong with me? she wondered. Maybe she just didn't want to be disappointed again if it didn't work. Well, there was more riding on this than her disappointment. She'd been graced with hundreds of unsolicited visions during her gloomy life as a broken Oracle, so it wasn't difficult to select a few to test with. She got started.

The first test was an audio file. Alex created a recording about a prosecutor who had tragically died of a heart attack in the middle of closing arguments. She remembered prepping the body for the funeral, and how she'd set the woman's hair to how she wore it in court—a low, side ponytail—and her family had sent the nicest note. She put the file in a shared folder as directed.

Next, a simple email. She briefly typed up a vision of a girl who had committed suicide in the very hospital room Alex had once stayed in. The hapless girl had held a hand-stitched quilt sewn with love and a note saying she was "just so tired". That one had gotten to Alex, though she didn't include that in the email. She clicked send.

The third test was an image. She was still deciding which one to use when her hands started typing, almost of their own accord. Trembling, she described a vision from long ago—a kind, elderly woman who had run out for groceries, even though she'd promised not to. On that godawful day, the woman, having just crossed the street into the park, was struck by a garish yellow sports car that swerved onto the sidewalk, pinning her to a tree. The woman bled out in minutes while whispering one name over and over, her voice obscured by the unending blare of the car horn.

Alex sent the screen-capture to Hermes. She set the laptop on the footrest and stared at the story in its hideous, pixelated clarity until the words bled into the white space and lost all meaning. The car horn blared in her head.

Then Hermes was there, holding a tablet. She hadn't even heard him come out. "Okay, got 'em," he said. "The first one was a recording of total nonsense, and I don't remember what I heard. So I guess that's out. Fascinating that the curse still worked with a recording of your voice. That's worth digging into at some point."

Alex said nothing, staring at the laptop as though waiting for a guillotine to drop. Hermes didn't seem to notice.

"The second, though. You saw a girl hang herself in the hospital while holding a homemade quilt, right?"

Alex nodded. The first fracture splintered down her heart.

"So that worked! Great. No more excruciating yes/no questions. And god, the poor woman who got pinned to the tree. I assume the asshole was a drunk driver, did he die too?"

Alex's heart was too busy breaking into a thousand jagged pieces to respond. She stifled a sob.

Hermes knelt next to her. "Hey, are you okay?"

She covered her face with her hands and wept as though the sorrow of the whole world was coming out of her. Sobs wracked her body as she pulled up her knees to her chest. She barely registered Hermes hurrying inside.

Moments later, she sensed someone sitting next to her on the bench. "Alex," Athena said softly. "What is it? What's wrong?"

Alex shook her head. She couldn't say it yet.

Athena rested a hand on her back, waiting patiently.

Eventually Alex took a few deep, gulping breaths. "I could have saved her," she wailed, gesturing to the screen.

"Ah," Athena said. She pulled the laptop over and read the text. "I see. Alex, you couldn't have known." She handed Alex a few tissues. "This was someone close to you? You foresaw her death?"

Alex nodded, wiping her face.

"But it was a long time ago, yes?"

Alex shrugged. Did it matter?

Athena unfocused her eyes for a moment. Alex wondered briefly what she could possibly be recalling. When she returned, Athena leaned back into the chair. "I'm going to tell you a story, is that okay?"

Alex nodded, sniffling.

"There was once a little girl who learned the things she saw in her day-dreams really happened. Often truly frightful things. Things little girls should not have to see. At first, her father and teachers were mostly worried about what happened to her physically, but when the little girl started talking about what she saw, the concern spiraled. The little girl would become angry and frustrated when they didn't believe her or remember."

Alex listened in stunned silence. She remembered palpably that desperate frustration, so big her body could barely contain it.

"Her father had her evaluated for psychological issues and being young, the girl was honest. Her honesty was rewarded with long hospital stays filled with drugs and electric shock therapy. Over time, the girl got smart and stopped talking about what she saw. Until one day when she was around eight years old, she foresaw her father's death."

Alex trembled. She did not want to relive this part, but she was mesmerized. Athena continued telling her her own story.

"She did everything she could to convince him, to warn him, to save him. As the time neared, the more desperate she became, and the bigger her behavior issues were until finally, convinced she was having a mental breakdown, he had her committed for a longer stay."

The hospital stay that had very nearly crushed her spirit.

"When she came out of the hospital, she found out he'd died in just the way she had seen, and her little heart was broken. She went to live with her grandmother, who was ultimately, amazingly, able to help her granddaughter find small ways to cope. The girl grew up very close to her grandmother. Then about ten years later, again the worst. The young woman foresaw the completely preventable death of her grandmother."

Alex felt sick, and something else she couldn't quite place.

"She did everything she could to save her, but in the end she grew desperate, and again, she was hospitalized. Ultimately the grandmother died in a horrific and senseless car accident."

Athena looked Alex directly in the eyes. "Now, this in the early 2000s. There were no smartphones. Email was popular, but given the adoption rate of the elderly to new technologies, the grandmother was not likely to have used it. There may not have even been a computer in the home. The young woman could not have known there were any legitimate avenues to convey her warning."

Alex stared at Athena in disbelief, reeling. How had she known all that?

"Amazingly, this girl's story did not end with the devastating death of her grandmother. Alone in the world, she still managed to finish school and, in an incredibly unique and creative way, built a life for herself that worked within her limitations, keeping her safe, though terribly isolated. This woman is exceptional in every way and has done the best she could, having dealt with the dreadful hand that fate gave her with grace and fortitude."

Athena let her last words hang in the air. She smiled. "Was I pretty close?"

Alex wished she could take those shimmering words and bottle them up for later. She threw her arms around Athena's elegant neck and wept the cleansing, healing tears that come from feeling truly seen. "Pretty damn close," Alex whispered. "Thank you. How did you…?"

Athena gave her a gentle squeeze back and let go. "I made educated guesses about the ages and guardians listed in your hospital records, the gaps in between stays, and of course the story you just wrote.

"You really are a remarkable woman, Alexandra Theodoros. Don't ever let anyone tell you otherwise, including and especially yourself."

57

Alex breathed in the clean, earthy smell of the forest as she let her dread and sorrow evaporate into the soft breeze. Athena had returned to the cabin, leaving Alex to pull together the pieces of her heart and finish the task of typing up the mask's vision. She tried to convey what seemed important while maintaining brevity, phonetically spelling out the words she didn't know—Buhkhai, Bahkuss.

She sent the email, still marveling the painfully simple solution. She felt lighter than she had in years.

She floated inside to see what the others thought of her summary. They were scattered around the small living area of the cabin. Hermes sat in the armchair with his ubiquitous laptop, while Artemis and Athena were ensconced in a sage green sofa, reading on their phones. Alex sat against the wall next to a black wood-burning stove and watched. Each gasped at different times as they read at different speeds. Athena finished first, of course.

"Incredible," she breathed. "They still call themselves Bacchae. And that wine! It must account for their speed and strength. And their eyes."

"And there IS a splinter cell within!" Hermes exclaimed. He sounded vindicated.

"But it doesn't say who that splinter group reports to. Did they give any indication?" Artemis asked Alex.

Alex shook her head. "I knew you guys would understand it right away. Can someone please fill me in?"

Athena cleared her throat and put on her professor's voice. "The Bacchae are maenads, famous women followers of Dionysus, the god in the horned mask. The Romans called him Bacchus."

"Oh." Alex kicked herself for not realizing the horned god was, of course, the god she already knew. Her face must have reflected her conflicted feelings because Athena nodded. "Exactly. So, thanks to you, we have more information about our adversary, but we still need to determine who they are ultimately getting their orders from."

Hermes grimaced as he gestured to Artemis. "Maenads were also particularly known for their mad frenzy, often pulling apart the enemies of their god limb from limb."

Artemis snarled and flew to her feet. "Bottom line, we need to get in there. Now."

Athena sighed in exasperation. "Artemis, sit down. I think we all agree, but we have to be strategic about it, yes? Are you looking for another run in with not just one, but dozens or hundreds of impossibly strong maenads? No? I thought not."

Artemis sat down with a miserable whump.

"We do need to move quickly though. Let me think for a moment." Athena looked inward for a several long minutes before resurfacing. Alex breathed a small sigh of relief, her job was mostly done. She could watch the grown-ups do their thing now.

Athena resurfaced. "Okay. We have no idea what to expect, so in order to be as effective as possible and cover the most ground, I propose a two-pronged approach. One in the front, and one in the back.

"For the front, we need someone to be part of the cult, there to celebrate the Mysteries and legitimately search and explore as much as possible. For the back we need to find an ideal way to infiltrate, either just staying stealthy or becoming house staff, or maybe even a maenad. Artemis, I think it makes sense for you to infiltrate from the back. You—"

"Hey, I'm the professional thief here!" Hermes interjected.

"May I finish?"

He gestured for her to continue with mock magnanimity.

"Artemis. Given that the majority of his closest followers are women, you have the most options available to you for getting around. Plus, your stealth and tracking skills are quickly coming back online. Your purpose is to find Father as soon as possible, assuming he's still alive. Which, of course, we're going to assume he is," she said meaningfully.

Everyone nodded, looking grim.

"Hermes, we'll still be making use of your expertise and skills. You and Alex will go in the front and pose as an Orphic couple. There to revel in the Mysteries."

Hermes' jaw dropped.

Um, what? Alex thought, her eyes wide as saucers. She'd literally be the world's worst spy, her face gave away her every emotion.

"You're joking," Hermes said. "He only knows my face by heart. And with her?" He gestured to Alex without even looking at her. "She doesn't know the first thing about…and are we really going to endanger her more at this point?"

Alex didn't really disagree with any of that.

"I was coming to that," Athena said. "It's important you go as a couple. It's less conspicuous than a single man. You can help each other through sticky situations and always use each other as excuses. There are likely to be euphoric elements and other unforeseen things we'll need to handle. A pair makes the most sense.

"Also, and just as importantly, one of our primary goals in sending Alex there is to see if we can get her close enough to a maenad, to Nyssa, or perhaps even Dionysus to discover who our enemy really is and what this is all about."

Alex shifted uncomfortably as a writhing mass of anxiety crawled into her stomach and settled there. The bruise on her chest seemed to twinge on its own.

Hermes pointed to his face. "And this?"

"I'm counting on their need for secrecy. I have a feeling they will wear masks or have other means of protecting the identity of their followers. This is a secret society. They need a way to gather and enjoy the revelry without fear of reprisal or scandal in the real world. If that's not the case, we'll have to go back to the drawing board. Be thinking about what resources you have at your disposal that would best conceal it."

"Got it. Let's hope you're right."

"Now, it's been years since I spent any time on this, but at one point I worked on uncovering what I could about Dionysus' cult. They have an isolated network so I was unable to get a complete roster, but using surveillance and other techniques I was able to compile a list of a couple hundred of his followers. Again, it's outdated but I suspect few people leave once they're in. Hermes, I'll send you the list." She pulled a small laptop out of a bag on the floor.

"Go through it and find a good pair whose identities it makes the most sense to take, then work on confirming they are current members."

He nodded and opened his laptop.

Athena turned to Alex, who wondered if she looked as shell-shocked as she felt. Her voice softened. "Alex, are you willing to go a little further with us? It will be dangerous, maybe especially for you. But you'll have protection." She gestured to Hermes. "That said, if you don't want to, I'll understand. We all will."

Hermes nodded once while still looking at his laptop. Artemis just looked at her hands.

"Artemis?" Athena prodded.

"Of course," Artemis said, smiling briefly.

She could tell Artemis was hoping she'd say yes, but it felt like she was being asked to swim into the mouth of a shark. But she'd come this far. How could she say no now?

"Okay," Alex said quietly. "Though I have to warn you, I'm a terrible liar and a worse actor."

Hermes grimaced. Athena nodded. "Thank you, Alex. We're all so grateful. I'll run the entire thing from nearby. Hermes, I may need you to do some initial recon to find a place that makes sense as I do not think it likely we'll find blueprints for the complex in any county records. We'll have state-of-the-art cameras and microphones and I will be in constant contact with all of you. We'll likely set it up so I'm the primary contact, with the ability to turn entire group communications on and off. I have a feeling the revelry Alex and Hermes will be in the middle of would be detrimental to the quiet infiltration you intend to do, Artemis."

"Good thinking," Artemis said. "Also, when will we know the results of our tests? It seems I'm okay, but are you and Hermes? We need to know how, well, careful to be."

"You should be careful regardless. But we should know within the next few hours. Also, I think it's time you called Ares to give him the latest news."

Artemis looked shocked. "Why the hell would I do that?"

"Let's just say I think we'll need to call in his favor."

"Lovely." Artemis pulled out her phone with a look of distaste. "Shouldn't I wait until I know what the favor is and ask all in one call?"

"No, we proceed carefully with him. Just make sure he's going to honor his bargain before telling him anything."

Artemis nodded as she walked out onto the deck to make the call.

Hermes jumped in. "I made a slight modification to a script I already had that takes names and cities and matches them with potential social media profiles, cross referencing them with each other. It already found a few prospective matches. Two in particular."

"What makes them good?" Athena asked.

"Similar heights and dark hair, so no wigs. I'm working on hacking into their emails now to see what I can find while the script continues."

"If you're able, please search for the invitation and a manual or handbook or something for their faith or the event itself. There is sure to be one."

Hermes nodded, a glint in his eye. "They are both in real estate, so their work email is public. Most people aren't very careful about clicking links in email, and I still have a botnet or two at my disposal. Suffice it to say, they're about to get completely and totally owned."

Alex was still stuck on the no-wigs comment. She was just realizing the ramifications of what was happening, what she was being asked to do. Infiltration. Pretending to be someone else. The risk of failure being a literal loss of life and limb.

She was only human. She should hurry and say no, change her mind.

Instead, she raided Hermes' kitchen for a drink.

58

Artemis strode around the small cabin room as though on patrol, finding it impossible to sit still. It felt as if Hermes had been at it for hours, though it had likely been not even two. Athena was on her laptop as well, buying up the specialized gear they'd need.

"Jackpot!" Hermes yelled from the kitchen table. She bounded over to him in a flash.

"Thanks to Mr. and Mrs. Wade Dalton's use of a simple six-character password, I didn't even need to send them a malicious email. It took my botnet seven seconds to crack it. I just found a save the date email for The Mysteries in Wade's inbox. It also says the invitation with detailed instructions would be sent via registered letter, and that they would need to bring it with them to gain entrance. You were right Athena, it included a reminder at the bottom for everyone to wear a half mask of their choosing. It included a link to a mask shoppe in Venice if they needed a new one."

"Excellent!" Athena said. "Where do they live?"

"Upstate New York, though they hang out in the city all the time. They tag themselves often in social media and even in the photos they didn't, they left the geotagging on so it's easy to pull their location data. We'll be able to find them pretty easy no matter where they are."

"Good. Well, first we need to find a way to have them suddenly unable to attend. And while I loathe the idea, this is where I was thinking Ares would come in. How did that conversation go, Artemis?"

"He was cagey at first, as per usual, but once I told him about... Apollo, he said he would honor his promises." Even just saying Apollo's name stoked the rage roiling inside her.

"Well, I propose we have him use his resources to get them out of the way as soon as possible. Then we search their house for the invitation," Athena said.

"What exactly do you mean by 'get them out of the way'?" Alex asked, seeming worried.

"Nothing as drastic as it sounds, and we'll give Ares strict instructions on that. I'm thinking something like an unfortunate mix-up in identity with some fake money-laundering scheme or something. I have a few resources that could help in those areas, but they need supervision and I don't have time. We have much to do to prepare for tomorrow night. Artemis, I think it would be wise to make the request in person, do you agree?"

Artemis sighed and sent Ares a text. *Need that favor. Where can we meet?*

Artemis' phone pinged back right away.

Meet me at my MMA gym in thirty minutes. Same building, new name —the last owner met an untimely death. Wonder why.

Artemis winced as she thought of the nice muscle head who had helped her, and by extension thought he was helping Ares. She steeled herself for the inevitable bath she'd need after asking this favor.

She hoped they were doing the right thing.

Artemis spotted Ares in the far corner of the airy gym and its red sparring gear and mats. He stood in front of a large punching bag attacking it with fast, rounded kicks over and over.

Artemis approached him. "Hey Ares," she said.

Ares stopped and looked at her and her resurrected look appreciatively. She'd cleaned up and donned her traditional black outfit, makeup, and re-done braid. She needed a new jacket though. "Hello, Artemis. What happened there?" He gestured to her arm, still in its sling. He threw a few punches.

"I had my arm pulled off."

"Funny. Be serious."

"I am being serious."

Ares stopped, a grin spreading over his face. "Really? By those Venetian women?"

Artemis nodded.

"Ha! I love it!" he crowed, punching the bag in delight.

Artemis scowled. "Your concern for my well-being is overwhelming."

"Oh, you're fine." He grinned. "So. What can I do for you?"

"Just something simple, for now. We need you to detain a married couple for a few days. Two high-class real estate agents in up-state New York."

Ares kept punching. "Detain how?"

"That's up to you, as long as they are unharmed."

"More information please."

"We're going to impersonate them and use their identities to infiltrate the Orphic cult of Dionysus during The Mysteries."

"Interesting. To what end?"

"Isn't it obvious?"

He started punching again. "No details, no favor."

Artemis filled him in on what they'd learned from the video and from Alex's vision.

Ares whistled.

She continued. "So we need to figure out who is calling the shots here. Hermes swears Dionysus wouldn't do it. I'm not convinced. We also need to rescue Father, of course." Artemis grimaced inside. *Sorry, Father,* she thought.

Ares saw right through her and chuckled. "But revenge first, right little sister?"

Artemis shrugged.

"I don't blame you, I would too," Ares said.

Artemis felt disgusted. She'd never have said she shared anything in common with Ares.

"Who is going on this little adventure?" he asked.

"Hermes and Alex are impersonating the couple, I'm infiltrating in from the back. Athena is running point."

Ares looked at her as though she'd just said the sky was purple.

"You'd endanger the world's last Oracle for your revenge? Now that, I cannot condone. She should be protected and utilized."

Artemis felt a pang of guilt and tried to bury it. Who was he to judge? It's not like he cared about Alex, in his eyes she was just a tool. But…was she treating her any differently? She shoved the thought aside. "If we can get to the heart of the matter, we'll know who to go after and hopefully even where Father is. She may be our quickest way to do that. She's my friend, and we did not ask her to do this lightly. But we're on a timeline. Speaking of…will you—"

"Not yet. You're holding something else back. I make my living off reading people. Now out…with…the…rest," he said, punctuating each word with a punch to the bag.

Artemis quickly thought back to Athena's parting instructions. She was not to bring up the virus if at all possible. But they'd discussed how to approach it if he pressed.

"Well, I didn't know anything about this until after he died, but we think part of the reason this is happening is because of a gene-altering virus Apollo created. He wanted to become mortal and grow old with Henry, and he figured out how. Hera and Apollo were both infected. They died very human deaths."

Ares slowly turned toward Artemis, his eyes glittering dangerously. "That's a mighty important detail to leave out, little sister." His voice was like the sound of a blade unsheathing.

"Blame Athena, she didn't want you or anyone to know right away." Artemis rolled her eyes, wanting to seem on the same team. Athena's strategy again—she had no issues with Ares hating her.

Ares bellowed and punched the bag so hard it flew off the hook. "Will that bitch ever just stop her conniving and puppeteering?"

"I doubt it," Artemis said. "Though the plan was to tell you along with everyone else after this situation was under control so we can share a complete story."

"Something like that though…it's not her call to make."

"Look. I can't speak for her, but we're all just hanging on by a thread here. We're doing the best we can."

"Yes, well, that's what happens when you become emotionally invested in people. You make yourself vulnerable," he said.

Because you're so happy without them? Artemis thought, though she kept the thought to herself. Someone like Ares was probably incapable of real happiness.

"Alright. You must tell me what you find, and where that virus has been, who has it, and who knows about it. This must be contained."

Artemis nodded.

He started pulling off his gloves. "Why is Athena not handling this couple's temporary disappearance? Surely she has the resources."

"I don't know, she just said to ask you. Between you and me, it sounded like her people would try to keep it above board somehow, which would take more time than we have."

Ares barked a cynical laugh. "God, this family. What a bunch of hypocrites." Artemis started to talk but he raised his hand. "It doesn't matter. You will have your rather trifling favor. They will find themselves on a nice little vacation this afternoon."

"Just make sure they—"

"They will not be harmed," Ares said in a put-upon voice. "I'll text you an email address. Send everything you know about them and I will make it happen. I'll text you when it's done." He gestured to a gym bag sitting on a nearby bench. "And get another one of those drinks out of my bag. It will help your arm heal faster."

"It's okay, it's healing." She hated feeling like she owed him.

"And would you like to be able to use your bow in this little infiltration of yours?"

Artemis sighed and got the drink. "Thank you."

Ares began to walk toward the locker room.

"Just remember about those people—they are truly innocent," Artemis called after him.

"Artemis, there is no such thing."

59

lex followed Artemis into the Black Forest. Athena had chased them outside probably in hopes that the dark energy emanating from Artemis would dissipate in the outdoors. They ate sandwiches as they walked, each absorbed in their own thoughts. It felt a little like their first walk around the courtyard at the hospital. Alex was glad to have some time alone with her friend.

Artemis seemed to be looking for something as they wove silently through a world of color—golden trees spread out before them dotted with oranges, reds, and even an occasional evergreen. Alex took in a deep breath, happily crunching the leaves already collecting on the ground. Hermes had given her a jacket to wear in the cooling weather, and she was back in her own clean jeans.

They stepped into an expansive clearing. "Finally," Artemis said. She found the largest tree at the perimeter and measured out twenty long-legged steps. She slipped her right arm out of the sling and manifested her bow.

"Do you think that's a good idea? What if you aren't healed all the way?" Alex asked.

"I think I'm ok to do a few rounds. Probably good to start building the muscle back."

"Do you usually practice a lot?"

"I used to. For a long time it was the one thing that made me feel like me. But…it's been a little while." Artemis held the bow up, aimed and winced as she slowly pulled the string back. She held it close to her cheek, then exhaled slowly. At the bottom of the breath, she released the arrow. *Thwip!* It whistled through the air and landed with a thunk in the center of the tree. Another arrow appeared when she put her hand on the string. She pulled, breathed, and released again. It split the first one.

Artemis rolled her shoulder. "This is starting to feel good." She shot a few more times, starting a new grouping higher on the tree. "I'm going to kill you," she muttered in time with the shots. *Thwip, thwip, thwip, thwip.*

Alex decided to wander slightly around the meadow as Artemis practiced. The sound of the arrows flying mixed with the crunching leaves as she enjoyed this momentary refuge. The pleasure in something so simple. When she rejoined Artemis, she looked at the tree for a long minute before figuring out what was strange. "Shouldn't there be a lot more arrows?"

Artemis shook her head. "They disappear after about fifteen minutes."

"Ah. Smart."

"Yeah, I'm proud of that little detail. No searching for lost ones, no need to clean them. No need to pull them out of enemies, unless you want to. It's perfect."

The only sound for several minutes was of arrows thunking into trees. *Thwip, thwip, thwip.* The burnished silver bow glinted in the light. It was the first time Alex got a good look at it. It seemed to be a single piece of…whatever it was made of. Its smooth limbs curved sinuously into two waves, meeting in the middle in a rounded dark gray grip. Alex noticed there were soft white patterns etched on the inside and wondered at their meaning.

She was about to ask when Artemis spoke. "You know, even though I feel certain he did it, I just can't figure out what his angle would be. He's already won. He stayed in power while we became shriveled husks."

"Well, you said he had a chip on his shoulder the size of Kentucky. Why?" Alex asked.

"It built up over millennia like shale, layer upon layer. In her usual appalling way, Hera took out her rage on the woman pregnant with her husband's son. She pretended to be her friend and slipped her something that would end the pregnancy. Somehow Father found out about it and saved the baby.

"The myths say Father sewed the baby up in his thigh, which I always thought was so weird and gross. Homer and his poet buddies made shit like that up all the time. Anyway, in reality he gave the baby to Hermes to raise.

"When Dionysus was old enough," Artemis continued, "Hermes introduced him at Olympus. To say Hera was furious that he was alive is an understatement. She denied Dionysus entry, grabbed him, and disappeared. I don't know what happened to him next, but apparently, it was bad. All she said when she returned alone was, 'He has been robbed of his soul's judgment.'"

Artemis lowered her bow, looking somber. "You know, I've never forgotten that phrase. I suppose it's probably one of the worst things that can happen to a person. I've thought a lot about it over the centuries as I've struggled myself." She shook herself and began shooting again.

"Afterward, she forced him to wander the world, not to return unless he had proven himself worthy. So he did. He planted his precious grape vine wherever he went and grew quite famous among the peoples of the world far beyond our Greco-Roman roots. Places like Egypt, India, and China. He gathered intense, dedicated followers everywhere he went, even in cities that were against him and his ways. They loved everything he stood for—the arts, freedom, an uninhibited life."

Artemis snorted, but Alex thought it didn't sound so bad.

"It took decades, but by the time he came back to Olympus he was easily as powerful as the rest of us. He was grudgingly admitted to the home of the gods and included in our canon. But the chip on his shoulder had well developed by then and he never did assimilate with us or make it easy to be around him. He and Father were especially complicated."

To Alex, it seemed that the chip on his shoulder was well-deserved. "That makes sense," she said. "He saved him as a baby, but also let Hera do…whatever she did."

"Exactly. In the end, only Hermes stayed close to him. I'll admit that I wasn't the nicest to him, nor he to me. Apollo was always kind to him though." She choked up. "Which. Makes. This. Even. More. Maddening." In quick succession, a dozen arrows flew fast and true. "I'm thinking beheading by arrow."

The arrows were arranged in two short, double lines.

Alex gulped. "Well, I suppose it's a good thing we're making sure about him then, before you do…that."

"I suppose," Artemis said tonelessly. She shot several arrows into a small grouping underneath, where the heart would be.

They walked back in silence. Alex was grateful for the chance to sift through her feelings after hearing the rest of his story. Dionysus had been kind. He'd changed her life. She'd never forget that moment or the freedom she'd felt, and her cheeks warmed at the thought of some of their time together. And now his callousness towards his family made more sense.

But what if he *was* what she said? What if he saw her there, having infiltrated his home on the arm of Hermes, of all people? She shuddered.

Hermes stood on the deck, waiting for them. "I was about to come find you. While we wait to hear from Ares, you and I should do some prep work," he said to Alex.

She grimaced. "Okay."

Artemis squeezed her arm in encouragement.

"In my experience," Hermes said, "the more time you take to choose your clothes and accoutrements, the more comfortable you feel. The more comfortable you feel, the better you're able to perform."

"Makes sense," Alex said.

"I popped over to that shop in Venice and, um, borrowed some of their masks. I want you to pick the one that you feel will suit you the most. Artemis, they didn't have any that looked quite like those Venetian ones."

"What about the ones on the bodies at Athena's?" Alex asked.

"I checked, they were already gone."

Artemis shrugged. "Thanks for checking. I'll figure it out when I'm there." She wished Alex luck and strode into the cabin, her energy having merely dissipated from pitch-black to charcoal.

Alex followed Hermes into the bathroom. On the black granite counter sat four bejeweled half masks, sparkling in the light—red, silver, multi-colored, and black.

"These look ridiculous," she said as she put each one up to her face.

"Well, they're going to look ridiculous now when you're wearing jeans and an oversized t-shirt. But we'll dress to match the mask. I'm certain at least part of this will be formal attire."

Alex looked again and found herself staring at the silver mask the longest. It had a filigree design delicately encrusted in diamonds on the sides of the eyes and around the edge. She was going to ask if they were real then decided she didn't want to know. If it was, it probably cost more than her apartment. She picked it up and tried it on again.

"I guess this one, then. It will go with anything. And I do love silver."

"Excellent choice. It will complement the mask I picked as well." He showed her a masculine, slightly longer than normal half mask. It had black with black diamonds and black swirls that came down to points on his lower cheeks.

"Okay, now I can get us some clothes to try on. You're what, a size six? Eight?"

"Eight," Alex said, perplexed at how he would know that.

Artemis poked her head in. "Actually, Hermes, hang on. Ares just called and the Daltons are out of the picture. I need you to drop me off at their house so I can find that invitation and whatever else."

"Then I need you to pick up some of this communications gear!" Athena called from the kitchen.

Hermes rolled his eyes. Artemis gave Alex a bemused look just as Hermes grabbed her arm.

They vanished.

Alex walked into the kitchen where Athena sat with her laptop. "Hey, when you said Hermes would be utilizing his expertise and skills, what skills, exactly, were you talking about?"

Athena glanced up from her laptop only briefly as she typed away. "Oh, our Hermes used to *live* for the con. He's lived hundreds of different lives, more than all of us together probably, but for much shorter amounts of times. Kind of like a hermit crab—he picks up and discards various personas and lives as he goes. For a long time he found satisfaction in the game, the score, and the tech, always looking to hone his skills."

"Does he still do it?" Alex remembered how easy it was for him to pretend to be her boyfriend at the morgue.

"No. Apparently, it stopped being fun. I always thought he used it to avoid having to live his own life. I'm not sure it ever made him happy actually."

"What does he do now?"

"Other than the hacking stuff? I don't think anything."

Athena's phone rang so Alex went to sit on the deck to wait, imagining the life of a human hermit crab. She thought of Artemis' struggles and Apollo's wish to live one precious life with his husband.

How *does* a person fill an eternity of time?

From what she could tell so far, immortality seemed to mostly kind of suck.

60

lex stood in awe at the quantity of garment bags and sacks on the cabin's low platform bed. "Formal dresses and nice casual clothes," Hermes said. "See if there's any you like. I made sure they were all high necked to cover your bruise." He vanished.

Alex sighed and started with the gowns. She pulled each one out with a frown. They were *very* formal, each more lavish than the next, each causing more anxiety than the next. Finally, she pulled one out that felt doable. Navy blue velvet with a simple but form-fitting cut. It had a boat neck, no sleeves, and a back with draping that opened down almost to her lower back.

She put it on and looked in the mirror. It fit well, but she felt like a fraud. A Pollyanna in a less-busty Jessica Rabbit dress. But it felt more like her than the rest, and she had to admit that while drafty, it did bring out her hazel eyes. She tackled shoes next, choosing the shortest, simplest ones she could find. They were silver, and three inches high. Her ankles wobbled dangerously and she pulled them off as quickly as possible.

The casual clothes were easier. She settled on a pair of black, slightly flared soft pants and a black top with a high, draped neckline.

"Athena, I found it!" Artemis suddenly exclaimed on the other side of the dividing wall. Hermes must have just picked her up.

Alex ran around to see. Artemis held a medium-sized wooden box in one hand, and a large envelope made of parchment paper in the other.

Athena took and opened the box. It was lined with burgundy velvet and had three compartments just the right size for each of its contents. A small bottle of wine with an Orphic snake and egg on the label was nestled into its place on the right, and a pair of white candles were nestled into the compartment on the left. In the middle lay a smaller antique silver box, engraved with the same snake and egg symbol. It had no obvious way to open it.

Artemis pointed toward a small pinecone on the bottom front of the larger box. "Push the pinecone." Athena did so and a thin drawer popped open. Inside, a handbook with the same Orphic symbol was neatly cushioned inside.

"Good work, Artemis."

"Thanks. The invitation was in there too." She handed Athena the envelope, which had a golden bull-horned mask printed on it. The invitation inside was elegantly simple, its tone somehow striking a delicate balance between religious sacrament and masquerade ball.

Come bask in the illuminative and transformative presence of Bacchus as can only be experienced during our most intense and extraordinary ceremony—The Mysteries. Under the light of a blood moon eclipse, you will go through the rites and rituals of our faith that allow you to free yourself from the barriers in this life, and experience your True Life here and now. All fully Initiated are welcome.

The Mysteries will be held on Friday, October 2, through Sunday, October 4, at the Orphic Temple (please refer to the back of this invitation for travel instructions). To attend:

1—Send the Orphic secretary a $100,000 USD tithe, per person.

2—Bring this invitation and your personal box of sacrifice. Without them, you will not gain entrance to the Orphic Temple.

3—Leave all electronics behind. Any phones, cameras, or any other personal electronic devices will be confiscated.

4—Wear a mask. This will protect both your privacy and our family, and must be worn throughout the entire event.

5—Refresh your memory on your rites and prayers, as you will be required to go through them again in a symbolic gesture of your journey and as a way to purify yourself to be in the presence of your god. We will say the prayers often throughout The Mysteries.

6—Prepare a sacrifice. Blood sacrifices are the most powerful during a blood moon and will reap the biggest rewards, though a sacrifice of anything loved is sufficient. Refer to the sacrificial guidelines in the Orphic Handbook if you need help in this area.

7—There will be a mandatory Initial Ceremony requiring formal attire at the very beginning. Attire for the rest of the weekend, if you wear any, is completely up to you, though we request it be tasteful.

We look forward to seeing you as you savor and revel in your True Life. Praise Bacchus!

"Wow," Hermes said, glancing at Alex. Her stomach had twisted more with each sentence. Sacrifice. Memorized prayers. If she was nervous before, now she was terrified. And it was tomorrow.

Athena began pouring over the handbook. Alex watched in awe at the speed at which she read. Each dense page turned about every fifteen seconds, often mumbling words like "fascinating", and "so clever".

In order to distract herself, Alex picked up the silver box and held it to the light. There were no seams. She looked again at the top of it. It had to be in the design somehow. She tried pushing down on several different parts of the engraving to no avail. She handed it to Artemis who closed her eyes and felt all over it with light fingers. "Hmpf," she said. "Tricky."

Athena took it and set it on the table. "We'll figure it out. I'll work on highlighting the sections of this manual I think will be helpful to you and Hermes."

"Great, thanks," Hermes said. Alex nodded, not trusting herself to speak.

"Can we go pick up my gear now?" Athena asked. Hermes nodded and they disappeared.

Alex stared into the space their bodies had just vacated, the words of the invitation seeming to float before her eyes.

"I guess I should try to be more patient with him," Artemis said, gesturing to the same space. "Hermes expresses about as much emotion as a mushroom, but he's probably pretty upset about all this. All of his children have passed. Most were mortal, and the few immortal ones he had quite literally lost their heads in various ways back in the old days. Then came the Pact. Dionysus is all he has left, though I don't think they interact often."

"Makes sense then why he doesn't want to believe it's him," Alex said.

Artemis ignored this and plopped into a chair. "You know, I actually wonder if Hermes is secretly miserable. As far as I know he has no connections, no real sense of purpose. So come to think of it, he's basically me but with life skills." She laughed bitterly.

"You've got skills, Artemis," Alex said.

"I mean useful skills," she said, "but thanks."

"Well, I know I haven't known you long, but you seem more alive now than ever. Maybe when this is all over you should go into bounty hunting, or kidnap resolution or something along those lines," Alex said.

Artemis waved the idea away. "Oh stop."

"I'm serious! You know what they do, right?"

"I mean, I've watched enough TV to know generally, but there's no way that's real life."

"When we're done with all this, we're going to look and see. What do you have to lose? Maybe we can do it together. I'm not sure I want to stay in mortuary work now that I can control my life. And you can't go back to before either. Maybe we can start a vigilante group!" She laughed.

"Ha. I don't know about any of that, but thanks. Regardless, I'm looking forward to hanging out in normal times after all this." She grinned and pulled Alex in for a hug.

Alex felt a knot in her heart relax she hadn't realized was there. She and Artemis were going to stay friends.

Hermes and Athena reappeared carrying two oversized black canvas bags.

She turned to Artemis. "Okay, one of these bags is for you. You need to become familiar with the vest camera and microphone set. Since you won't have a face mask for us to embed a mic into, you'll wear a minimal earpiece. Which reminds me. Based on the brief recon Hermes did, I believe the old carriage house turned garage on the grounds separate from the temple will be a good place for me to run the op from. Close, but not too close. But it means these need to work from a distance of several hundred feet. They're supposed to, but will you help me test when we get back to my house?"

Artemis nodded as she pawed through the bag, making sounds of appreciation.

"Alright," Athena said. "We all have lots to do, and I need to get home to Sophie. I think everyone should get a good dinner and go to bed early. It's going to be a big day tomorrow. We'll regroup in the morning. Hermes, will you please take Artemis and I home?"

"A *please*, how nice," he said, poker-faced.

Athena's mouth twitched into a smile.

"See you in the morning, Alex!" Artemis said, grabbing the biggest black bag.

"Alex, you like sushi?" Hermes asked.

Alex nodded. They all disappeared. She turned on the cabin's lamps and sat down at the kitchen table to wait, laying her head in her arms.

Hermes reappeared holding a plastic bag with Japanese writing on it. It had been a long time since Alex had sushi and she found her appetite returning at the smell of soy sauce and tempura. She attacked it with gusto and chopsticks.

Hermes picked up a piece of spider-roll and dipped it in the soy sauce. "Did you find something to wear?" he asked.

"Yes, the navy one."

"Good choice. I have you scheduled at my friend Anton's tomorrow. He'll get you all ready in the morning."

"Okay." Her appetite waned again and Hermes finished the rest of the rolls.

"I'm going to get going so you can get to bed. You good?"

"Honestly, I'm just trying not to freak out. I don't know if I'll be able to sleep much."

Hermes grunted. "You'll be fine."

"I hope so. I'd just like to say I'm sorry in advance if I mess it all up." Her voice trembled.

"Alex, don't worry. It will all be okay." It looked like he was about to say something else, but he ended up just giving her a nod before disappearing.

Alex sighed. The cabin suddenly felt very quiet.

She got ready for bed and laid down. Sleep was a long time coming.

Tomorrow she was joining a cult.

IV

Whom the gods would destroy they first make mad.

—William Anderson Scott

61

Alex woke to the glorious smell of coffee brewing. Bleary eyed, she threw on her clothes and went around to find Artemis in the galley kitchen making eggs. Her hair was in a new, intricate braid and she wore her signature black outfit.

"I didn't know you cooked," Alex said.

"Only eggs. It's a new thing. Want some? It's brunchtime," she said.

"Yes, please." Alex poured herself a cup of coffee and watched Artemis stir the eggs.

"How are you feeling?"

"The bruise is still a little tender but not too bad. The other aches are minimal now. Thanks for asking. How's your arm?"

"Good enough. There's some notes for you to read while you're getting ready so you can start getting into character. Read it out loud."

Alex picked up the paper. "'I'm Jennifer Dalton. A thirty-five year old real estate agent to the rich and famous of upstate New York. I am married to Wade, also a real estate agent. We most likely have an open relationship and it's the only way we've stayed married for as long as we have. We make a ridiculous amount of money and are probably arrogant in-your-face assholes about it.' Wait, who…?"

Artemis chuckled. "Hermes wrote it."

"Ah. Of course. It goes on. 'We have no children and lavish all our attention on overly pampered greyhounds that we dress in ridiculous sweaters. We joined the Orphic cult in 2009 and have been members ever since. This is our second Mysteries.'"

Alex sighed. "I just hope no one really knows them there."

"Eh, even if someone recognizes you, just prepare a line about not being ready to talk, that you're basking in the 'light of Bacchus' or some such nonsense." Artemis made a face. "Ugh, even saying that makes my skin crawl. I don't know how they can love him so much."

Athena and Hermes popped into the kitchen. She also wore all black and looked bright-eyed and excited. "Morning. I know how to open the box. The prayers in the manual made me think of it. We're forgetting that Dionysus is still a god."

She picked up the silver box. "Their ideology is intriguing," she said as her fingers felt along the engraved serpent and egg. "It's all about rewards in this life and the next, based on the ancient writings of Orpheus, who waxed lyrical about Dionysus and his triumph over the Underworld. He praised Dionysus as the only way to access your True Life, which is revealed as you shed this life, both figuratively and eventually literally. But while you're here on earth you do that using Orphic wine and sacrifice."

Hermes rolled his eyes. "What a load of heaping codswallop."

"What does it say about the Orphic Wine?" Alex asked. "There's no way it's just regular wine."

"Not much, other than it's a conduit to your True Life," Athena said. "They're supposed to drink it on a weekly basis, during a little home sacrificial ceremony. The more they worship, the more rewards they receive, though there is no mention of what the rewards are. They're also instructed to do a bigger sacrifice every six to twelve months, more if they like, and they'll find 'rejuvenation therein', whatever that means."

"Smart," Artemis said begrudgingly. "Keep them connected, in contact, maybe even addicted, and the money and prayers just *rolllll* in."

"Exactly. It's brilliant," Athena said. She pulled out the manual, now fully highlighted. She flipped to a page. "It says to begin your sacrifice, pray to your god with the common prayer." She showed it to Alex and handed her the box. "Read this."

Alex obliged. "Praise the God of True Life, the God of the Vine, the god who has transformed our lives now and in the afterlife. Praise Bacchus!"

The lid snapped open. Athena gave a small triumphant smile.

Inside were two small silver daggers. Each had a three-inch blade that spewed out of the hilt of a gaping snake's mouth. Its eyes were closed and its coils carved down around the handle. The blade itself was wicked sharp and had a deep groove with vines engraved into the side.

Alex groaned. "I'm going to have to cut myself or something, aren't I?"

"Quite likely, yes," Athena said.

"I mean, at least they aren't sacrificing animals," Artemis said.

"Well, we don't know that—I suspect the larger sacrifice would be something along those very lines," Athena said, trailing off as she followed a train of thought.

"Guys, I am NOT cutting a goat's throat or anything," Alex said.

"I doubt that's part of the mainstream cult, most people in America would not have the stomach for it," Hermes said.

"You'd be surprised what people do if the benefits are substantial enough," Athena said. "And it is, I suspect, why they took Father."

The woman seemed to relish dropping single sentence bombs.

Artemis looked stricken. "Do you really think so?"

"Why else? Why not just kill him with Hera and Poseidon?" Athena continued. "He would make a powerful sacrifice. Even if he were mortal, he would still be a three-thousand-year-old healthy man."

"This is insane," Artemis muttered. "Should we go in earlier then? Like now?"

"No, we stick to the plan. In the chaos of the ceremony you will likely have more success staying under cover. I highly doubt it would happen right at the beginning."

Artemis set the not-quite cooked eggs in front of Alex. She forced some down for the energy and gave a thumbs up to her friend, who grinned.

"Alex, just a heads up you're due for your hair and makeup in an hour," Hermes said. "Take the manual with you so you can read it while you get dolled up. Bring the dress and mask too."

"Have you read it?" she asked.

"I skimmed it, and we'll have Athena in our ears, so I'm not worried," he said.

"Of course you're not," Alex muttered. She paged through the handbook; there was no way her brain could handle reading these religious stereo instructions right now.

She was showered and ready when Hermes came for her. In short order, Alex sat in a vanity chair surrounded by bright bulbs that illuminated all her pores and was introduced to Anton, a friendly British makeup artist.

He seemed to be able to tell she was totally out of her element as he creamed and brushed and painted. "Just relax and let Anton do his magic," he said. His accent soothed her nerves a little. The manual sat in her lap unread.

He turned her around so she could see her face before he put the mask on. She gasped in spite of herself. The woman in the mirror was glamorous, with accentuated cheekbones and eye makeup that somehow both highlighted her eyes and would complement the dress. Her lips somehow looked thicker and pouty with a shimmery, but not too bold color. It barely looked like her, and yet it did. She turned her head left and right, looking at all the angles.

She wouldn't want to do this all the time, it felt more like a mask than the mask she was about to put on, but she couldn't help but feel beautiful. "You've done a lovely job. I'm going to consider it my war paint. Thank you so much," she said to Anton.

He looked confused and flattered at the same time. "You're welcome. Wait until you see what I do with your hair!" He separated it into sections and put the silver mask on her face, tying it under the top half. The inside of the mask was soft velvet and none of the edges dug into her cheeks. The eyeholes were wide enough they didn't interfere with her new long lashes or hamper her peripheral vision. Her worries about wearing it for hours disappeared.

Anton worked on her for another hour, brushing, pulling, curling, and pinning, and spraying. He wouldn't let her see until she was also in the dress, wanting her to see the full effect. He turned around so she could slip into it. She zipped it up from the bottom and felt it hug her body, her skin prickling at the open back.

She walked to the full-length mirror and stood in silent disbelief. Her hair was pulled up into a gorgeous pile of twists and small braids, leaving a few tendrils around her face and mask. The cut of the dress accentuated her waistline and bust, and she was surprised how much she appreciated seeing her collarbones peeking out over the boat neck. The makeup looked more subtle with the mask as it sparkled next to the navy blue.

"I am a master, am I not?" Anton said, beaming with pride.

"Yes, Anton, that you are. You're amazing."

He bowed. "I don't know what this is for, but whatever it is you're ready for it now," he said. "I shall take my leave of you."

"Thank you!" she called as he left. She did not take her eyes off the mirror.

Hermes popped into the room next door. "Are you done and decent?"

"Yes, be right out." Alex felt butterflies as she walked into the other room.

Hermes stared, momentarily speechless. "You're stunning."

Alex smiled and curtsied. "Thank you."

"These are for you…you know…just in case." He handed her a pair of silver arm-length gloves. They matched the silver of the mask and complimented the dress.

"Oh, thank you!" Alex clasped them to her chest, relieved. There was too much at stake for newbie skills.

He just nodded. "How do you feel?"

"Like I might just be able to do this."

They *shifted* to the cabin.

Artemis circled her. "Oh, Alex, you look gorgeous!" she said. "It accentuates your curves and is sexy without being slutty."

Athena smiled. "You look perfect."

"Thanks, everybody. Artemis, you look like a badass."

She wore a black vest with a body cam and lots of pockets, a small wireless earpiece, a small backpack, a black hood, and a cowl she could quickly pull up over her face as a mask should she need it. She wore no makeup and looked like she was about to invade enemy territory. Which she technically was.

Alex slipped out of the dress into jeans and a t-shirt while she waited the day out and tried but failed to read the manual. They all ate a late lunch together, talking through various scenarios and testing the tiny mics and earphones embedded in the masks. The energy in the room heightened as the time drew nigh and the afternoon light stretched into the room.

Then it was time for Hermes to take Athena and Artemis to their positions—Athena in the garage, Artemis on the roof.

The little group gathered together in the living room. "Alright everyone, stay in contact with me," Athena said. "We can do this."

Artemis gave Alex a big hug. "Thanks for this," she whispered. "Good luck."

"Of course, and you too. Be careful." Alex squeezed tight.

"You too." She waved as Hermes vanished with her.

Athena gave her a hug as well. "Yes, thank you, Alex. And just remember, bravery cannot exist without fear."

Alex scoffed quietly. "Well, then I'm the bravest person in the world."

"That, you are. I'll be with you," she said, pointing to her earpiece. Then Hermes took her away too.

Hermes returned back to the cabin after just a few minutes. "Okay, time to get ready. According to the directions we're supposed to pick up a limo in Napa in an hour." He headed to the bathroom to shower and dress.

Alex donned her velvet armor, refusing to wear the heels until it was absolutely necessary. She sat at the table in the kitchen, tapping her fingers until she couldn't take the wait anymore. She started rummaging in the kitchen for a drink.

She was taking her second sizable swig of beer when Hermes came out. He looked striking in his black suit and mask. The points of the mask hovered just over his trimmed beard. She felt a tug in her chest.

"You look rather amazing yourself."

"Ready?" he asked.

"No."

He held out his hand. She took it.

The Daltons were off.

62

Alex watched the setting sun kiss the vineyards of Northern California as they flew by in the limo they'd picked up in Napa. They were arriving as early as the invitation allowed, giving them sixty minutes to settle in before the Initial Ceremony.

Her heart felt like a caged bird trying to escape.

"Artemis, have you found a suitable entrance point from the roof?" Athena asked, her voice clear but slightly tinny in their concealed earpieces.

"I believe so. There are a few open windows that seem to lead to unused rooms."

"Perfect, let us know where you end up."

"Roger that," Artemis said.

"Also, I just received confirmation that neither Hermes nor I have been infected by the virus," Athena said.

"Oh, thank god," Artemis said.

"Fantastic," Hermes said.

"Still," Athena said, "do not forget who we're dealing with. Please be careful. I'm switching to individual comms now. Good luck, everyone."

The limo finally turned down a short road that ended at a tall brick wall with a wide cast-iron gate, lit with landscape lights. There were two security guards posted in front of it holding tablets.

One of the guards approached the limo and opened the door for Alex and Hermes.

Here we go, Alex thought.

"Please show me your invitations," the guard said.

Hermes pulled them out of his jacket pocket and handed them over.

"Thank you, Mr. and Mrs. Dalton. Do come in." He opened a smaller gate where another guard did a metal check on them and their bags. After finding only the sacrificial box, he had them sit in one of a dozen golf carts all with drivers waiting. Hermes helped Alex into the cart while their bags were stowed in the back.

The cart ambled up a long, meandering path lined with tall, fiery torches. From this distance, Alex could see the Parthenonic temple as it dominated from its elevated base in the back of the cult's sprawling complex. That was soon hidden behind the brilliantly lit, prodigious white building they were nearing. It sat atop an expansive staircase that reached up to a platform where six Corinthian columns sat on either side of a soaring arched entryway.

Alex exhaled slowly as they saw masked Venetians in blue robes standing between each column holding tall thyrsus staffs with their pinecones and ivy on the top in place of a blade. Maenads. According to the handbook, when in their blue robes, they were the Chosen.

A strong hand grabbed her gloved one and squeezed it. She glanced over at Hermes but was unable to see his eyes in the torchlight of the path. "Doing okay?" he whispered.

Alex nodded and looked away but let his hand linger, willing some of his confidence to seep into her.

At the top of the marble steps was a short line of elegantly dressed people waiting to talk to the Chosen standing in front of the open doorway. Her Venetian mask was cat-like with gold and blue colors and a knowing smile. When it was their turn, the Chosen greeted them warmly and asked for their invitations.

Upon finding their names on her list, she opened her arms wide. "Welcome to The Mysteries. Your room is on the third floor." She handed Hermes a small brass key. "The number is engraved on the key. Your bags will join you there. Now, as you enter the sacred buildings of our faith, you leave behind your old life, and your names. Praise Bacchus!" She gestured them through the open door.

"Praise Bacchus," they replied in unison.

Hermes grabbed Alex's hand again as they entered the large arched corridor. It led to a massive reception area, with trees, candelabras, and Chosen scattered along the walls. Its vaulted ceiling seemed to be filled with a midnight sky, with small twinkling constellations and larger floating spheres providing extra light.

Any bit of wall not covered by foliage was filled with the art of their faith—paintings of Dionysus, Nyssa as priestess, and sculptures of the serpent and the egg—the Orphic Egg—which Alex had learned from the handbook represented life, creativity, and the Orphic Mysteries.

"Well, this is impressive," Athena said in their ears, though surely the micro-cameras embedded in their masks were not doing the room justice.

"It's gorgeous," Alex said. It was clear she had seen so very little the last time she was here.

They wove through the light crowd to a set of ornate elevator doors, with golden engravings flickering in the candlelight. They emerged onto the third floor and walked down a comparatively normal hallway with cream walls and greenery until they found their sizable room, which had a similar feel. Everything looked expensive and luxurious, with a richly upholstered red sofa and a king-sized bed with a red velvet coverlet. A spread of tapas and chilled champagne sat on the entrance table.

"And we're in like Flynn," Hermes said with a smile. "Easy."

Alex scoffed.

Hermes tapped her arm to get her attention. She looked at him suspiciously when he pushed the small button on the edge of her mask, turning off the microphone and camera. He did the same to his.

"I should have done this before, but there's something we need to talk about before we go back out there. And I can't do it with my sister in my head." He took a deep breath and ran his hand through his hair.

"You're doing an amazing thing here, sticking your neck out for me and my family. Again. I know it's scary after everything we've seen. But we've got this. Just like we did at your work."

Alex made a wry face. "Ha, yeah, I guess. The price of failure is a little steeper here though than fooling one poor old security guard."

"That's true, but it's the same game. Look, I have to ask you a question. I know you were recently with Dionysus—"

Indignation flashed through her. She stepped back. "I wasn't *with* Dionysus," she interrupted. "And I barely know him."

"Ah, okay, good. But...do you want to be?" he asked. "With him, I mean."

Alex stared. "Seriously? Aren't there more important things to be worried about right now?"

"Absolutely. But I have two reasons for asking. First, he clearly likes you. And if you like him, and he has a chance to be happy, I want that for him. And for you, for that matter."

Alex shook her head, completely mystified. "Look, I like him, and I'll be forever grateful for what he did for me. But he also gave off some weird vibes—and that was *before* I started worrying whether he was a murderer. So let's just say the jury is out. Way out."

Hermes seemed to relax a little. "Fair. Sorry for putting you on the spot. I had to though, because of the second reason." He closed the gap between them, pulling one of her gloved hands into his. He lifted it so they were palm to palm, their fingers entwined.

Alex's heart skipped a beat. What was he doing?

"For this to have the best chance at being successful, we need to look like we've been together a while. We can't seem so stiff with each other. Only as far as you're comfortable, and within reason, of course." He stroked a finger down her cheek. He seemed to be waiting for her.

"Okay," she whispered, nodding. Anticipation at his touch tingled throughout her.

Hermes lifted her chin with his hand and kissed her softly. His spicy aftershave was as stirring to her blood as the mix of his soft lips and scruffy beard. His tongue was gentle, sending electric pulses into her body with each touch.

He pulled back. "Well, that was even more delicious than I'd imagined," he said with a rugged, roguish smile. "If it was going to happen, I didn't want it to happen out there with all those people."

Alex felt a little breathless for more than one reason. He'd been imagining that?

"One more, then we better get back online and get out there," he murmured. "Athena is probably freaking out."

He leaned in and brushed her lips with his.

A light flashed.

No! Alex thought. She tried to prevent it, to close the book.

But it was too late. The vision consumed her.

Hermes knelt in the grass over a man's prostrate body. They were in a wide, circular room, open to the sky, lit only by the light of the full moon as it reflected on the tears streaming down his face. There were other bodies scattered around and a strange keening filled in the air. Across the room, just inside a doorway, lay a tall, lithe body in black, with a long blonde braid splayed behind her.

No! Anguish pierced Alex's heart. This couldn't happen. She wouldn't let it. She tried to manifest the Thread but couldn't focus through the despair. The old, familiar feeling of helplessness crept over her as she failed again, and again.

The smell of licorice and cat pee interrupted the struggle. She sat up spluttering.

"Oh, thank god," Hermes said. "It took me a minute to find this." He held up the vial.

Alex swallowed a sob, trembling. "How long was I out?"

"Maybe five, six minutes," he said. "What did you see?"

She looked at him wordlessly.

"About me? Or about tonight?" he asked.

She nodded in answer to both. "It wasn't good. We're not going to let it happen," she said.

He looked at her for a long moment, as if trying to decide whether to push it. "Why don't you just—"

Suddenly, the sliding glass door to the balcony opened and a black-clad figure leapt in, landing with soft feet. They whirled to find Artemis, her breaths coming in heaves. She was clearly perplexed to see them both just standing there.

"What the hell do you think you're doing turning off your cameras and comms for so long?" she asked. "Athena has been freaking out—well, as much as she does—and sent me to come check on you."

"Oh shit," Hermes said, touching the button on his mask. Alex did too. Athena was already speaking. "…and I see they are unharmed," she said dryly.

"Sorry, Athena," Hermes said. "We needed to chat in private for a minute. Then she had a vision and I forgot to turn them back on."

"Hermes, the time for chatting was *before*. Do not turn them off again. We have bigger stakes here tonight."

"You're right, sorry," Hermes said.

"Sorry, Athena," Alex said, quietly.

Artemis shot a dark look at Hermes. "I'm sure it wasn't *your* fault, Alex," she said. "But I'm glad you're okay. I better get back up there." She slipped out to the balcony and was gone.

Suddenly the room filled with the sound of ethereal chimes, signaling everyone to gather in the courtyard for the Initial Ceremony.

"We've got to go." Hermes opened the door for Alex. As she walked through, he grabbed her hand and pulled her back, kissing her briefly but thoroughly one last time. "For luck," he whispered, smiling.

She gave him a weak smile back, feeling even more butterflies and knots in her stomach than before.

Which, frankly, she really didn't need.

63

Alex and Hermes headed back to the large reception room where a throng of masked Orphics were slowly filing through five doors in the back, a blue-robed Chosen posted at each one. There was an excited, almost palpable buzz in the air. They slipped into the rear of the group to wait their turn.

As they neared the doors, they noticed the Chosen were handing each member a small glass of red wine. No one got through the door without saying a prayer and drinking. Alex glanced at Hermes, trying not to panic. He took her hand again. "It will be okay, it won't affect me much, if at all, or if it does it won't be for long. And I'm not letting you out of my sight."

Alex nodded, but she also knew he couldn't possibly know that for sure, even with his immortal metabolism. The drink was, after all, created by the literal god of wine.

Suddenly a portly man stopped at the door a few people ahead of them, already seeming a bit drunk. He took the small glass and raised it to the crowd behind him. He spoke in a slurred voice. "Praise the God of True Life, the God of the Vine, the god who has transformed our lives now and in the afterlife. Praise Bacchus! Woo!" The crowd laughed and responded in kind. "Praise Bacchus!" He drank and stumbled out the door.

All too soon it was her turn. She took the cup from the Chosen and looked right into her eyes. Alex stifled a gasp. The Chosen's pupils moved fluidly in her irises. She tore her eyes away, raised the cup, and said the prayer with Athena's guidance. She drank. It didn't taste like anything too special.

"Welcome Orphic, please keep your glass," the Chosen said. Alex nodded.

Hermes followed suit, and then they were out under the burgeoning stars.

Alex sighed in relief. First hurdle cleared.

They walked under a flowering arbor full of fairy lights into an expansive courtyard, or agora, if it could even be called that, it was so big. Trees and bushes lined the edges of a colonnade lit with soft light. The space easily held the hundreds of people milling around. Ambient ethereal music filled the air, somehow not drowned out by the crowd's low rumble. On the far side of the courtyard stood the temple, lit entirely by a seemingly otherworldly white light. It smelled woodsy, like they were walking into a forest, not a throng of bodies.

"Wow," Alex said. She saw a massive pile of shoes by a nearby tree and after a quick look around, realized with delight that most of the guests were barefoot. *Oh thank god,* she thought. She tossed her heels into the pile with relish.

The courtyard slowly took on a warm glow, giving all the lights a small halo. She began to feel everything very clearly, the silk fabric of the gloves on her hands and arms, the pressure of Hermes' hand, the velvet on her bare legs and chest—it all felt luxurious. Her skin was alive. The sensations seeped into her, smoothing her raw nerves into warm, creamy butter. All was now well with the world. She started smiling at everyone she passed, and they all smiled back.

Hermes was watching her. "You okay?"

Alex beamed and nodded slowly.

He chuckled and squeezed her hand. "Ah. I guess you are." He led her to the side, away from the people still entering the courtyard.

"You're not feeling anything? You're really not?" Alex asked.

"A little, I guess. I think not as much as you," Hermes answered.

She reached out to touch the sleeve of a woman wearing a particularly inviting silk dress, wanting to touch the softness. The woman smiled warmly at her, continuing down her path.

Her gloves were getting in the way. Handing her glass to Hermes, she peeled them off and dropped them on the ground. She touched along the velvet boatneck of her dress. It felt like magic on her bare fingers.

She moved to follow another woman who wore a black satin gown as she conversed with other Orphics. She desperately wanted to mingle with them. It wasn't even sexual, this pull. Just people who were clearly enjoying the sensations of closeness and touching.

She was a woman starved for physical contact, and before her was a feast.

Dozens of Chosen wandered through the crowd with their thyrsus staffs, nodding sagely at the guests. The crowd respectfully parted and came back together after they passed, murmuring prayers and thanks.

"The Chosen seem to command respect among the Orphics. I presume they are all maenads, would you agree?" Athena asked in their ears.

"Yes," Alex whispered at the same time Hermes said, "Possibly."

"The one at the door had eyes like you described," Alex said. "So strange, with the pupil moving like that. Like a lava lamp!" She exclaimed the last part louder than she intended, happy at finding an appropriate analogy.

"Not so loud!" Hermes whispered, even though the nearest Chosen was several feet away. "I have not noticed that, Athena," he said. "It's possible not all of them are maenads."

Alex felt a flash of annoyance, but it puffed away like a dandelion. She looked up at Hermes as he scanned the crowd. She could see his jaw clenching. He seemed to be fighting it. She reached up to turn his face toward hers, massaging his jaw with her fingers. "Relax," she said. "It's okay. You said it would be okay, and it is." She slid her fingers to the back of his head and kissed him.

Firelight filled her body. If her hands felt like magic, the sensitive skin of her lips was rapture. Hermes pulled back just as it was becoming urgent.

"We can't," he whispered.

"Right, right, sorry," she said. Disappointment flared and puffed away. She looked around and saw the crowd's energy taking a similar turn, with significantly more masked couples kissing than there were moments ago.

Just then, the music changed, from ethereal and light to deep and throbbing. Across the courtyard, several of the Chosen swayed out onto a dais atop the temple's marble steps. The crowd turned, and the air thickened with anticipation.

Hermes pulled her in that direction, moving quickly so they could see better. It was a striking sight, with large marble columns framing the blue of the Chosen as they created a single speared line, leaving a space in the middle. They stopped swaying in time with the very last beat of the music.

All was quiet.

They raised their hands in the air, the long sleeves of the robes draping down onto the floor. They chanted, "Now we are dead, and now we are born, thrice blessed into our True Life. Bacchus has redeemed us. Praise the God of True Life, the God of the Vine, the god who has transformed our lives now and in the afterlife. Praise Bacchus!" They hit their staffs on the floor in time with the last two words.

The crowd erupted. "Praise Bacchus!"

The throbbing music started again and another hooded figure in wine colored robes swayed to the empty spot between the Chosen. She pulled her hood down, revealing her unmasked face, and the music stopped.

Nyssa.

"Praise Bacchus!" she said. Her alto voice echoed more than it should have in such an open space.

"Praise Bacchus!" exulted the crowd.

"Welcome, fellow Orphics, to The Mysteries. You are here to celebrate your god and receive his blessings. Shed away the drudgery of this life and reveal your True Life. The life that, through the grace of your god, you can claim both here *and* in the afterlife! The power of the blood moon amplifies all sacrifices made here tonight, so be generous with them, pray hard to your god, and he will bless you. Tonight, we are as one, and the lifeblood of our faith will join us together."

She pulled an empty glass from her sleeve and raised it up. The crowd raised up all their empty glasses in response. Alex and Hermes quickly followed suit.

She chanted along. "Praise the God of True Life, the God of the Vine, the god who has transformed our lives now and in the afterlife. Praise Bacchus!" With that, all the raised glasses in the courtyard filled anew with Orphic wine. The crowd cheered and yelled "Praise Bacchus" yet again, before drinking.

Alex gasped, thrilled to have more. Hermes pushed it away from her lips. He leaned in and pretended to nuzzle her. "We shouldn't have more if we can avoid it," he whispered. He subtly poured their glasses out into the bushes behind them. She frowned.

The cups disappeared from his hands. All the cups did. Alex gasped again and clapped appreciatively with the crowd.

The Chosen began to chant in low voices as Nyssa spoke. "Our god is near," she said, her voice low and booming with energy. The crowd erupted in cheers. "He will join us if we pray. If we beg him to share his exalted self with us."

The crowd chanted. "Praise Bacchus, praise Bacchus, praise Bacchus." It started slow and crescendoed, with people in gowns and tuxedos kneeling on the grass and waving their arms, a look of rapture on their faces.

Alex felt her heart race in anticipation. Something was coming. *Someone* was coming. Even the haloes of light seemed to pulse as the crowd chanted his name. She didn't even realize she was on her knees until Hermes joined her. He put his arm around her waist, seeming to watch her carefully. She couldn't tell what he was feeling—his body seemed relaxed but his jaw still clenched.

The chanting reached a peak and at that very moment thunder boomed and the center of the dais in front of Nyssa erupted in a pillar of brilliant white flame. Out of it walked Dionysus, resplendent in a black tuxedo with a black shirt and tie. A crown of verdant ivy sat atop his golden mask with two large bull horns curving up at an angle from his forehead, bringing out the gold in his mane of red-gold hair.

He looked every inch a god.

The pillar of fire disappeared, but the glow around him remained brighter than anything else in the courtyard.

He was magnificent.

The crowd stood and erupted in cheers.

"Oh, Dionysus," Alex breathed. She stood and took several steps forward, pulling free of Hermes. Her mind was full of her god. She needed to be nearer to his glory.

"Wait!" Hermes whispered. He tried to grab her, but the crowd closed quickly behind her.

The Orphics cheered and everyone chanted again. *Praise Bacchus, praise Bacchus, praise Bacchus.* Many were clutching their chests and weeping. Alex understood. This man, this god, would change her life, *had* changed her life. And nothing was ever going to be the same. He grinned at the crowd and the sound of *ahhs* rippled through the air. He lifted his hands and the crowd quieted.

He spoke.

"My friends, my family, I rejoice in you as much as you rejoice in me." His tenor voice was smooth and resonant in Alex's ears. The crowd cheered, "Praise Bacchus!" He raised his hands again for quiet. "This is an evening for revelations, where you may be delivered from your old life, and experience your True Life in all its peace, joy, and glory. The glory of the afterlife, as you will receive through me and through your sacrifice. This will be a deepening of your worship, for the blood moon pulls us toward it, enriching us, magnifying your sacrifices, and allowing your True Life to manifest more completely here in this world. And it will be glorious!"

The Orphics cheered and chanted. He raised his hands again.

"Now, my family, tonight is a night of exploration, jubilation, and pleasure as you explore your True Life. My home and all its mysteries, experiences, and sensations are open to you." The crowd murmured in excitement. "A reminder. You will respect each other as completely as you respect me. Anyone found to be causing anything less than peace and joy will be removed and will lose access to their True Life, perhaps permanently. This is a place, *we are a family*, of love and rejoicing!"

The crowd cheered. They threw their arms around each other,

swaying in lines as they chanted. Alex found herself next to a large man in a tuxedo with a crow's mask that only heightened the look of ecstasy in his eyes. He grabbed Alex's side and grinned at her. She grinned back and slid her arm around his waist too. To her right, a woman in a white horned mask and a crimson gown slipped her arm behind Alex's back and gave her a big squeeze. Odd how comfortable she felt with these strangers. And yet not. They were her family.

"Now, my family, go. Go and sacrifice yourselves, go and celebrate in the name of Bacchus. Go, and live the life you are meant to live in eternity and I will be among you as you do. The Mysteries commence now!" He raised his arms and gold fireworks filled the sky, raining down their shimmering light for what felt like forever. The crowd erupted and Dionysus disappeared in another blinding pillar of white fire.

An energetic, thumping music swelled and the Orphics began to dance. Alex felt the vibrations come up the grass through her feet and into her soul. She was deeply aware how glorious it was to have a body, to be able to move it the way she wanted, and in rhythm to such music. She felt more free, more alive than she ever had in her life.

A grinning woman in an iridescent mask and a green jeweled gown came up to dance with her. The woman moved in close, touching Alex's shoulders.

A woman's wry voice buzzed in her ear like a fly. "Well, he certainly does know how to put on a show." Alex shook her head, trying to shake it off. The iridescent woman was beautiful. As they danced, they constantly brushed each other's faces, necks, and hips.

The voice didn't go away. "Hermes, do you have eyes on Alex?" Athena asked. "I can't see very well."

"Yes," he said. "I'm trying to get to her now, but it's proving difficult."

Hermes' voice, thick with some unidentifiable emotion, slowly penetrated the rhythms of the music. Alex turned and saw him elbowing his way through the crowd, looking more like a bouncer than an acolyte. She turned back to the iridescent woman, smiled at her, and brushed her lips ever so briefly with a light kiss. The woman hugged her and started dancing with someone else. Alex headed back toward Hermes.

"She's heading toward me," he said. He backed up toward the edge, keeping her in his sights. "I'll get her inside the temple and begin searching."

"Excellent. I need to talk to Artemis, be right back," Athena said.

Their words floated atop the rhythm until they melted into nothing.

She danced her way through the crowd, though it took several minutes as people kept pulling her in to dance, or swing her, or just touch and celebrate the movement of bodies together. It all felt so safe, so beautiful, so wonderful. She wanted Hermes to feel it too. Everyone deserved such happiness. Finally, she squeezed through the edge of the throng and stumbled to where Hermes stood. He caught her in his arms before she fell and looked down at her with inscrutable eyes. He let her go quickly but grabbed her hand, almost crushing it, perhaps for fear she'd run off again.

"You look like you're having fun," he said in a flat voice.

Alex laughed delightedly. "That, my sour friend, is an understatement. I can honestly say I don't think I've ever been so happy."

He arched an eyebrow at her. "Aren't you worried one of them will trigger a vision with all that touching?"

It was the first time she'd thought of it. Her face filled with surprise and wonder. "No!" she said, laughing. "I'm not worried about that at all! How wonderful!" She laughed again. She went on her tiptoes and threw her arms around his neck in a long, tight hug, their bodies touching all the way down. It took him by surprise and he stumbled back, his arms snaking around her, his hands brushing against the bare skin of her back. It was exhilarating. The music changed and she started bouncing on the pads of her bare feet to match the beat.

She stepped back and pulled on his hands. "Come dance with me," she said, her eyes sparkling. "Please." She pulled on his hand.

He stood still, unmoving, as though he didn't trust himself. "No, we have to go. Really. Also, I don't dance," he said gruffly.

"But I want you to be happy, pretend husband," she said, swaying back into him. "I know you're not. But you deserve it. You deserve to be happy." She kissed him again. He returned the kiss, but kept it reserved.

"Just let go," she whispered in his ear. She kissed him more ardently, trying as hard as she could to tear down his wall. She pulled his arms around her so his hands settled more firmly on her open back. He exhaled and she felt something in him crumble. He kissed her back then, matching her eagerness. His hands moved down her back, sneaking beneath the folds of her dress. Alex sighed as he moved his lips down her neck, his dark beard leaving tingles along her skin. The crowd surged around them suddenly, swaying to the rhythm of the music. She needed to be part of it. She pulled him again toward the dancing. This time, he followed.

"Hermes, Alex…" Athena's warning voice rang in their ears. "Remember why we're here. I know we put you in the middle of this, but try, please, for Father." She repeated herself again, "For Father, we have to find Father. Remember what these people did. To Hera, and Poseidon, to Apollo. What they're going to do to Father."

Hermes stopped dead in his tracks and pulled a confused Alex back to the edge.

Athena's voice darkened the edges of Alex's euphoria like burning paper. She shook her head, desperate to hold on to what felt like the first true joy she'd ever had. She tried to pull away, wanting to disappear into the crowd, but his hand was a vice on hers. She looked at him in consternation.

Hermes held her gaze with his intense brown eyes. "I'm sorry," he said. "I want you to be happy too." He kissed her roughly one more time. A kiss full of fire and regret. He pulled back. "But we have to go."

He didn't wait for her to respond before turning toward the doors, pulling her behind him.

Alex stopped fighting and watched his back as she tried to reconcile what was happening. The profound loss she felt at leaving. Tears leaked into the velvet of her mask as they headed up the marble stairs of the temple, away from the crowd, through a large ornate metal door.

Alex watched the door close behind them, the music becoming as muted as her joy.

64

Artemis stood on the balcony trying to decide what to do. The exterior of the building was lit only with the occasional ground lanterns and light emanating from uncovered windows. She'd been able to easily drop down between the staggered balconies and wide window sills, but there were few footholds for going up. The ground didn't look promising either. Masked women in blue robes walked the perimeter in pairs, laughing and chatting while they walked in long, easy strides.

"Damnit, I don't think I can get back up to the roof, Athena. Unless Hermes can come get me, I'm just going to have to wing it. I'll wait until I see a decent-sized gap and try to stay between them. Maybe I can find a window on the ground floor."

"Hermes can't, and I don't like it. Too risky," Athena said.

"Do you have any other ideas?"

She waited for several Chosen to walk by, trying to sense a cadence. Then she saw it. A gap. A pair had rounded a couple of minutes ago and there was still no one else behind them.

"I see an opening. I'm going."

"Be careful!"

Artemis climbed down the rest of the balconies all the way to the one just above the ground, waiting for the Chosen to pass underneath.

"Just a few more rounds and it's time to celebrate!" one of the Chosen said.

"I know. It's been a long time coming. I am so excited," said the other. "Do you think you'll try to find an Initiate to revel with?"

"Definitely. You?"

"Definitely." They both laughed.

Artemis counted to thirty then jumped down to the soft grass. She crept along the ground while trying to stay in the shadows, looking for an open window. She heard more voices coming from behind her. Another pair of Chosen turned the corner, heading toward her. Artemis picked up her pace, trying to stay equidistant between the two pairs.

Whenever there was a window within a shadowed section she'd dart in to test it, keeping her feet as silent as possible on the landscaping. She was starting to worry she'd never find one when a smaller window a little higher up caught her attention. It was open and it looked like she could fit.

She darted in and tripped over a hidden sprinkler. She fell to her knees onto some decorative river rocks, the crunching sound reverberating in her ears. She saw with chagrin the two Chosen ahead of her stop and cock their heads in that horrible way they had. They turned around. They were still twenty-five yards away or so, but that meant she only had a minute. Unless they decided to run. If they ran, she was screwed.

Her pulse sped up significantly.

She pulled herself up to the window, dismayed to discover a screen. She began to push on it as hard as she could with what little leverage she had. They were almost on her when it budged. She pulled herself up and wriggled in. Her backpack and hips caught on the frame, but she pulled hard and fell in, bringing several cans and cardboard boxes to the ground with her.

She was in some kind of pantry. She rolled back up against the bottom shelf under the window and froze, her heart pounding. She heard shoes on the rocks beneath the window.

"Ah, it looks like one of the pantries. Probably raccoons again," said a Chosen. "We'd better—"

"Do nothing. Right? Otherwise it's going to be even longer until we can get to the Bacchae celebration and ceremony. The raccoons can have their feast. We need ours more."

"Hmmmm. This is true," her companion said, laughing. "Very well, we go on."

"I wonder what, exactly, is the point of those patrols," Athena said disdainfully, once they were gone. "But either way, well done, Artemis."

Artemis held a thumbs up to the vest camera. She waited for her eyes to adjust to the dim light, grateful for the cacophony coming from the next room that masked her fall. She cracked open the door to listen.

"How are the small plates coming?" a booming in-charge sounding male voice said.

"Good!" answered a woman. "The stations have all been set up and about a third of them have food already."

"Great, keep it going, and keep me apprised if any are close to running out."

"Yep, on it," a second woman said.

Artemis peeked out of the door. A woman in an apron stood at a kitchen sink in the direct path of the only way out, her back to the door. Artemis held her breath and went for it, crouch-walking out of the pantry.

Another aproned woman walked in right at that moment. Artemis dropped down out of sight behind the island. The woman plopped down a pile of plates next to the sink to be washed. "Don't you wish you could be out there?" she asked, her voice young and wistful.

"Yes and no," the seemingly older woman said. "I mean, I wish I had a hundred grand to blow on a single weekend of euphoria. But I also like knowing what's real and what isn't."

"I know, but it looks so glamorous."

"But it's not glamour," the first woman replied. "Or at least, it's short lived glamour."

"Well, we don't really know that." The girl sounded unconvinced. "We just haven't been raised to that level yet. Bacchus will bless us with that experience eventually, I'm sure of it."

"Bacchus has taught us to also be grateful with where we are now, and that every True Life is different. If we were supposed to be out there with all those hoity-toity people, we would. But we're his true worshippers, the ones that work for him and serve every day. We will ultimately be blessed greater than they will. Don't worry." The first woman side hugged the younger woman. They turned to the sink, the rest of their conversation lost to the running water.

Bewildered and slightly repulsed by their devotion to her half-brother, Artemis slipped out of the kitchen into a long hallway immediately to her left. It quickly became a maze. She couldn't quite get her bearings as she tried one hallway after another, ducking into open doorways whenever she heard someone approach. Finally, she came to a dark wooden staircase going up. *Up it is,* she thought. She kept her senses on high alert, testing each step before putting her weight on it. When she was a few steps from the top, she laid down and peeked above the edge of the floor.

The stairs opened up into what could only be described as a long forested corridor of rich green ivy and soft grass along the floor. The leaves rippled in a breeze and the damp smell of forest filled the air.

What the...? Artemis thought, perplexed. One of the ivy walls seemed to spring apart, and a maskless, facially tattooed maenad scampered out. Artemis got a quick peek into what looked like a semi-normal bedroom before the door closed. The maenad wore a cream tunic with fringe and nothing else but her facial tattoo. She looked happy and excited. She was joined by two others and they headed down the forest hallway, laughing.

They looked more like hippies than murderers.

"Artemis," Athena came back to her ear. "What are you seeing...? You have me in the dark."

Artemis rolled over and raised a finger in front of the camera, indicating for Athena to give her a minute. Her mind raced. They had weighed the risks of assuming the identity of a maenad. Did they all know each other? Would they pick her out quickly? If found out, would she immediately be torn apart? It was impossible to know. But the benefits were compelling—they would likely have access everywhere.

Now the choice was before her.

She waited until the maenads were out of sight, then found the doorknob amid the vines and slipped into the bedroom of the one who just left, closing the door quietly behind her.

65

Alex and Hermes entered a long, shallow room with yet another set of ornate doors all along the opposite wall, also guarded by Chosen. It was almost painfully quiet. They stood still for a minute, unsure what to do.

A Chosen wearing a jester's mask approached. "If you are ready to enter the Rooms of True Life, you will need to perform your sacrifice," she whispered. "You may do it here, or you may do it in private. Just show the evidence to one of us, and you will be allowed entrance. More comfortable clothes are recommended and masks are still required, of course."

"What evidence?" The words flew out of Alex's mouth before her brain could stop it.

The Chosen cocked her head and looked closer at her.

"She had a lot of wine even before the ceremony," Hermes said, rolling his eyes. He pulled Alex back toward the door they'd just come through. "We shall return, thank you."

The Chosen nodded and Alex felt her eyes on their backs as they left the temple. Hermes found a small alcove just off the top of the stairs, looking over the pulsating courtyard.

"Don't say anything at all if you're just going to say whatever comes to mind," he snapped.

"I'm sorry," Alex mumbled. "I told you I wasn't good at this." Her voice trembled. She was having difficulty pulling herself together. She felt drawn toward the Orphics and the rhythm below, and the world around her still had its soft halo.

"I think I better *shift* us back to the room, I don't want to go through that crowd again," he whispered. He pulled Alex behind a tall bush and they vanished.

Once back in the room, Alex grabbed her bag and ran into the bathroom, locking the door. Her ears rang loudly in the quiet.

Alex sat down on the toilet and tried to compose herself while tears leaked from her eyes. What the hell was she doing here?

"I finally saw what you meant about their eyes," Hermes said through the door. "That is crazy."

Alex didn't respond.

"I'm sorry, I didn't mean to criticize you. And I'm sorry we couldn't stay at the ceremony and, well—"

"…be happy for the first time in my life? Me too," Alex said, under her breath. She took a tissue and dabbed at her eyes, thanking her stars Anton had used waterproof eyeliner.

"It wasn't real," Hermes said, suddenly next to her.

Alex jumped out of her skin and backhanded him in the stomach. "Don't *do* that!"

He grabbed her and pulled her up. "I felt it too," he said. "But it wasn't real."

"How do you know? How do you know what's real?"

"Because we didn't feel that way before the wine—"

"But who's to say how we felt before was any more real? With all our inhibitions and the layers of fear and anxiety and whatever else we put on ourselves. I mean, I'm not a total idiot, I know the wine was keyed to Dionysus or whatever—god, the rush of emotion when he appeared—but still. I just wish I'd never felt it. Any of it. I didn't need anything to compare to. My stupid little life was already empty enough."

"I know a little about that," Hermes said quietly. He enveloped her in a strong, solid hug.

It felt good, comforting. "I'm so sorry about down there in the ceremony," she said into his lapel. "I know there's a lot at stake tonight, I just couldn't stop. And then I didn't want to. It was so consuming. And it was just so nice to have…joy." She buried her head in her hands, feeling the loss and the shame equally deep. "I am a ridiculous person."

"It's okay, Alex," Athena said warmly in her ear. "We knew there was a significant likelihood something like this would happen. Hermes has stimulants to help you feel more like yourself, but only after you sacrifice. Just in case it's important to have that wine in your blood."

Alex froze. Somehow she'd forgotten about Athena, who had of course just watched and heard the whole conversation. And she realized Hermes had also heard her muttering to herself. Alex put her head in her hands. *Oh god, oh god, oh god.* What was wrong with her? Her cheeks felt hot, and the real world settled around her like a heavy, wet blanket.

She grabbed her bag and slipped past him into the bedroom. She pulled out the sacrificial box and set it on the bed, wanting to just get on with the horrendous night.

"Just give us a minute, Athena," Hermes said.

"If you're not back in five minutes, you'll be very, very sorry."

"Roger that." Hermes turned his mask off, then strode over to Alex and turned hers off too.

"What are you doing?" she asked.

"Just making it you and me again for a minute. Regardless of the existential discussion, that was some potent stuff. For me to have felt it at all for as long as I did…I can't imagine what it was like for you. And during all of that, of all the things you could have been doing right then, you thought of me. You tried *very* hard to get through to me."

She flushed. "Please don't. Don't mock."

"Mock?" He sounded mystified. "I'm definitely not mocking you."

"Then what are you saying?"

"I'm saying that I don't know the last time anyone's particularly cared about what happens to me…with or without magic wine. And for myself, I can't think of the last time I've given a shit about anyone like I've started to give a shit about you."

Alex blinked at his way with words, and their meaning was slow to sink in.

"Watching you dance like that…" he shook his head. "You are not ridiculous, and you weren't alone. I really wanted to be there with you." He pulled her to him and flashed a rugged smile. "And I hated…that we had to stop…so abruptly…" He punctuated every pause with a kiss.

Alex's heart flip flopped unceremoniously as a rush of unidentifiable feelings filled her.

"We really should get changed," he murmured. His hands moved down her neck. He started to push the thick straps of her dress off her shoulders.

His hands left warm, magical trails on her skin. She could feel herself being sucked back in. But the shame of moments ago was still sharp and palpable.

"Hermes." Alex pulled back and crossed her arms in front of her to catch the dress before it fell. "I think maybe you're still feeling the wine too."

"I don't think so." He stepped back and ran his hands through his hair. "Man, I don't know. Maybe."

Alex sighed regretfully. "I'll be back." She grabbed the black casual outfit and ran to the bathroom to change.

When she came out he was already changed as well, wearing dark jeans and a black polo shirt to compliment his black mask. It was strange to see him look so preppy, but he could make anything look good. He gestured for her to sit down across from him on the rug at the foot of the bed. They turned their comms back on.

Athena was singing their names, ever so slightly off-key. "*Hermeeees, Aleeeex.*"

"We're back, we're back, stop singing," Hermes said quickly.

"Shall we get this whole sacrifice nonsense over with?" Athena asked. "I fear time is a limited commodity. We need to get moving to find Father."

"I agree. What's the word from Artemis?"

"She's assumed the role of a maenad and just now found their ceremony."

Oh be careful, Artemis, Alex thought. The image of her laying prone amid maenads flashed across her mind with a pang of anxiety that took longer to puff away this time. She pushed it away and tried to focus. She had her own problems.

Hermes put the silver box on the floor between them and grinned at Alex. "Let the bloodletting commence!"

Alex looked balefully at the box and did not smile back.

66

The Chosen named Hope walked the perimeter of the Initial Ceremony, keeping an eye out for anyone getting too carried away. She enjoyed watching the abandon of the Orphics. It resonated with the Madness pulsing inside her, making her eager to join her sister Bacchae in their celebration. She looked at the clock hidden at the top of the stairs. It was almost time for her shift to end.

Just then she saw a couple slip out onto the side of the dais. He whispered in her ear, then pulled her behind the decorative bush. The woman had looked unhappy.

She cocked her head to the side. They probably just wanted privacy, but it was her job to make sure there was nothing untoward happening.

She moved closer and stopped in surprise to see the space was empty.

There was literally nowhere else they could have gone, and she'd had her eyes on the spot the entire time.

She wondered if she should report it. They'd been warned to be on the lookout for anything strange. Stranger than usual, anyway.

She decided she'd better.

Just in case.

67

rtemis looked around the tiny, spartan bedroom with curiosity. A small window let in just enough moonlight to see the bare white walls, a tall bunk bed with unkempt bedding, a nightstand with a lamp, and a doorless closet. The closet seemed fairly desolate, with only a few cream fringed tunics and simple black clothes within. Not a single family picture or any other personal belongings were visible, other than a Venetian mask and blue Chosen robe hanging on the wall. Next to those sat an alcove containing what appeared to be a shrine. It held a picture of the horned god, an embossed silver box, a metal goblet, a small bottle of wine, and a wide white candle.

The air was heavy with the smell of sweat. She turned on the lamp. "Athena," she whispered. "I'm in one of their rooms. There's an extra mask and robe here. They also seem to be wearing some sort of hippie tunic. Have you seen anything like that out there?"

"No, I've only seen the blue robes and thyrsus. No idea what they are wearing underneath," Athena said.

"Okay."

"Are you sure about this?" Athena asked.

"Yes and no," Artemis whispered back.

"Okay. Stay sharp."

She swatted away a spark of annoyance and gave another thumbs up to the camera. She put her backpack on the bottom bunk and pulled out the temporary tattoo sheet Athena had printed, modeled off the maenad from the video. It was cut into four separate sections to allow for easier application and required water to attach to the skin, like a high-quality Cracker-jack prize. When it was complete it looked real enough. Unless someone got really close. But if someone was that close, she probably had bigger problems on her hands.

She pulled out one of the spare tunics hanging in the closet, fingering the soft material. She shrugged off the vest along with the rest of her black clothes and pulled it over her head.

It felt breezy, vulnerable, and a little too short, but it fit.

"Is there anywhere to secure the camera?" Athena asked.

"No," Artemis said. She stowed her own clothes in her pack.

"Do try to keep me apprised of what you're seeing then, when you can," Athena said. "I don't like being blind."

"Will do. Applying tattoos now."

She took out a small water bottle and cloth and got to work in front of a little mirror on the back of the door. It didn't take long to finish the application and closed her eyes to spray it with a setting solution. She checked her angles in the mirror. She would pass.

She looked at herself again and felt something was still not right. But what? She thought back to the maenads she'd seen in the hallway, they'd been so minimal in every way.

Then she had it. Their hair. From what she'd seen so far, the maenads had hair of varying lengths, but they all wore it down.

Artemis loosened her hair from its braid until it hung in long crinkled waves down her back. She squirted the rest of the water from her water bottle into the length of it to help calm it down.

In the corner of her eye something moved. She turned slowly. A small maenad with short brown hair sat up in the top bunk wearing a sweat-filled white sleeping shirt.

Artemis berated herself for not checking the top bunk more thoroughly given how heavy the sweat smell was. Not to mention making a colossally stupid assumption that the mask and robe were extra. She reached quickly for the light and turned it off.

"Forgive me, Sister," she whispered. "I did not mean to wake you."

The maenad barely looked at her. "Sister," she panted. "Sister, I am dreaming terrible dreams."

"I'm sorry," Artemis whispered. "They will pass."

The maenad squinted her eyes and cocked her head. Artemis' stomach dropped. "Why are you here and not out with the others?"

Artemis thought fast and kept her voice low. "I just came back to check on you."

The maenad fell back onto her bed. "That is kind, I haven't been ill like this in years. But the wine of the Bacchae cannot protect from all."

"True," Artemis said. "Feel better, Sister. Praise Bacchus."

"Praise Bacchus," the sick maenad murmured. She was already turning away onto her side, heading back to her fever dreams.

Artemis picked up her pack and grabbed the mask and robe. She peeked into the hallway. It was mercifully clear and quiet. As she slipped out of the room, Artemis was again struck with the oddity of grass underfoot while indoors. She stowed her backpack behind a particularly lush fern and turned towards the music she heard in the distance.

"Nice work," Athena said.

"Thanks," Artemis muttered back. "How are the others doing?"

"Doing okay. They had a rough start, but they made it through the Initial Ceremony and are about to do the sacrifice."

"Okay, good. Game on for us all then."

Artemis followed the music through several more forested hallways past a staggering number of bedrooms. There's no way this many people could all know each other. It made the odds in her favor. On the next turn she nearly ran right into three maenads standing together, laughing like school girls.

Okay, keep cool, she told herself. They all looked up at once and cocked their heads to the side slightly. They smiled as they nodded at her. Artemis smiled and nodded back. One of them spoke, "Are you heading out to do your shift?"

Artemis slowed but did not stop. "Sorry?"

The maenad gestured to the robe and mask in her arms.

"Oh! Yes," Artemis said simply.

"Do keep an eye out for anyone that might want to revel later," she said with a mischievous laugh.

"Of course!" Artemis laughed back and kept walking. *Whew.*

The music was throbbing as the last hallway opened into an outside courtyard area so big the surrounding columns were several meters away.

It was chock full of wildly cavorting maenads.

68

Alex sat cross-legged on the floor with Hermes, the silver box, wine, and a couple of hand towels between them. Hermes said the prayer in a flat, annoyed voice. "Praise the God of True Life, the God of the Vine, the god who has transformed our lives now and in the afterlife. Praise Bacchus. God, I hate saying that."

Alex picked one of the previously disinfected snake daggers and grimaced.

Hermes picked up the other one. "Okay, what do we do, Athena?"

"Pour yourselves some of the wine, then cut yourselves and say a prayer as your blood runs down the groove into the mouth of the snake." Athena spoke as though describing how to change a lightbulb. "Then something happens in the knife. Once it does, drip the blood into the wine and say another prayer, which I'll walk you through. Then something else happens, but it's not clear what. It just says, *reap your reward, and carry it with you.*"

"Figures," Hermes said. He poured the wine into two wine glasses found in the room. "I'll go first." Alex held one of the hand towels underneath his left arm as he held it out over the floor. He stoically pierced a vein at the crook. Blood bubbled out and he angled the knife to ensure the blood flowed down the groove in the blade. They watched the knife carefully.

Blood dripped off the handle onto the towel. Nothing else happened.

"The prayer!" Athena said. "Repeat after me. 'I offer a sacrifice of my life's blood to the lord god Bacchus. May he see this as a sign of my obedience and dedication, that I worship him with my entire body and soul. Praise Bacchus.'"

Hermes repeated and at the last word, the snake's eyes flew open revealing a glowing pearly white light within. They gasped as the blood started to move faster than gravity alone allowed. As though the snake was hungry.

"The handle is warming," he said. After what felt like a long moment, the snake closed its eyes.

"I think that means you can stop," Athena said.

He pulled the point of the knife out of his skin. Alex covered the crook of his arm with the towel. When he took it off, the wound was already healed, with no sign it had ever existed other than the blood on his arm.

Alex shook her head. "Must be nice."

Hermes nodded. "Definite perk."

"Okay, now hold the knife over the wine," Athena said. "Repeat after me. 'May Bacchus accept this offered sacrifice and in turn, grant me metamorphosis, health, wellness, and eyes that see his glory. Praise Bacchus.'"

The eyes of the snake opened again, this time shining gold. But nothing else happened.

"Alright, here goes," Hermes said dubiously. He angled the knife downward toward the glass. The blood had been transformed. Out poured a trickle of pinkish gold liquid that shimmered as it dripped into the red wine, turning it to a golden rosé.

Hermes lifted his glass to Alex and chugged the wine in three swallows.

They waited.

"Do you feel any different?" Alex asked.

Hermes shook his head. "But maybe it doesn't work as well on me. I do see a soft halo around things, sort of like the wine from the Initial Ceremony."

"Okay, well let's do it on Alex and see if there is any difference. We need to know this will get you through the doors," Athena said.

Alex picked up the knife, placed it at her elbow and pushed, but not hard enough. Her hand shook.

"Do you want help?" Hermes offered.

"Yes, please."

Hermes held her elbow in one hand and the knife in the other. Alex looked away and hissed as the blade pierced her soft skin. Athena walked her through the prayer and she looked down at the bottom of the knife as the blood slid into the snake's mouth, studiously ignoring the sharp part still in her body. The snake's pearly eyes opened until it drank its fill. Alex took the knife from him, said the prayer of metamorphosis, and poured her own golden blood liquid into the wine.

"Here goes nothing," she said. Her stomach fluttered at the thought of drinking even transformed blood, and for whatever else would happen next. "Please forgive me for anything I say or do after this."

"You're fine, Alex," Athena said. Hermes nodded encouragingly.

She drank the wine and waited as the warm liquid slipped down her throat. It filled her stomach with a radiant warmth, as though she was being filled with soft, afternoon sunlight. She closed her eyes, feeling it seep into her limbs and up to her face.

"It feels amazing," she whispered. "An immense sense of well-being. Like I can do anything." She opened her eyes. "And these colors!" She looked around the room. "Everything is so vibrant and rich." Alex took a towel and wiped the blood off her arm. The wound had healed completely, without even a hint of a scar. She looked down her shirt and the arm-sized bruise on her chest was gone too. She grinned.

"Incredible," Athena said. "And brilliant. There is no fatigue with the sacrificing and they are motivated to continue. The weekly ceremonies have sacrifice and prayers, and the group ceremonies have a series of doors and checkpoints that require worship and sacrifice in order to get to the next. No cutting corners. No wonder Dionysus has remained power-ful. Any idea yet how you prove you've completed the sacrifice?"

Alex looked at herself then up at Hermes with a shrug. "I have no idea!"

Hermes leaned forward, peering into her eyes. "I do," he said.

"What?" Alex said.

"It's your eyes. Your pupils are gold, and there's a ring of gold around your irises."

"What?" Alex ran to the bathroom to see. "Cooooool," she whispered.

Hermes joined her to examine his own eyes. The gold was there, but fainter. "Hrm," he said. "Hopefully that'll be enough. Worse case, they turn me away and I just *shift* in there."

Athena piped in. "Good. Go get out there. It's getting late and the blood moon eclipse peaks at 2 am. Also, I would be shocked if there were not some upper echelon you can attain after a certain amount of years, sacrifices, and level of tithe. They'll likely reap more benefits. Keep an eye out for them."

"Got it. Okay, let's go," Hermes said. "Do you want these?" He held out Alex's gloves; he must have rescued them from the ground. "They may make you stand out a little."

She eyed them. "I guess not. I'm here to intentionally have visions anyway. But you have the stimulants and the smelling salts just in case, right?"

Hermes nodded and reached out his hand. She took it, deeply appreciating the simple act.

They walked quickly back toward the temple, picking a different door and Chosen. The Chosen peered into their eyes, first Alex then Hermes. She paused, squinting.

"It's so stupid, but we ran out of wine at the end," he said apologetically. "Can you see it at all?" He leaned forward and widened his eyes.

"Ah. It is faint but there," she said, nodding. She had them hold out their wrists and put on a simple black paper bracelet with the Orphic symbol. She opened the door and ushered them in. "Welcome to the Great Room of the Temple of Bacchus."

They both stopped short upon entering a cavernous, forested room surrounded by yet another Corinthian colonnade.

Alex breathed in the earthy fragrant air and stared. "You have no idea what this looks like through my eyes right now," she said. It was like what heaven would look like if it were on earth. She didn't even want to try to describe it. Opulence and nature mingled together in a breathtaking blend. Crystal and ivy chandeliers hung from soaring ceilings, and all the trees and plants had crystal bright fairy lights on them. There were even a few similarly lit wide swings with ivy woven down the chains, which several Orphics were already enjoying.

In the center was a large clearing containing an idealized marble statue of Dionysus holding an urn out of which vibrant red wine poured into a fountain below.

It took a moment for Alex to notice the doors. Recessed behind the colonnade, well over a dozen ornate alcoved doors were spaced around the entire room, lit by some sort of otherworldly light. Each had a wide lintel and unique carvings. "What do you think?" she asked quietly, gesturing to them. "Just start going through the doors to see what we see? Do you think Dionysus and Nyssa are just wandering around?"

"I suppose so, and I have no idea," Hermes answered.

They walked to a door that didn't have anyone actively standing in front of it. The door itself was lustrous white nestled between two dark marble columns holding up a lintel with an intricate carving of what looked like a wave. Hermes tried the silver handle, but it wouldn't budge.

"Say the prayer," said Athena.

He rolled his eyes as he said it, but the door clicked. They squinted as they stepped onto a white sand beach, turquoise waves breaking softly nearby. There were already Orphics frolicking in the waves, some in swimsuits, some not. Not too far down the beach others were doing another kind of frolicking.

The beach looked like it went on for miles.

After a moment of stunned silence, Hermes asked, "How many doors were out there?"

"I counted at least fifteen," Athena said in their ears.

He sighed. "This is going to be more difficult than expected."

69

Artemis skirted around the edge of the maenad's lush courtyard. There were at least a couple hundred of them, all maskless and dressed in their matching tunics and bare feet, dancing to the thumping music with wild abandon and laughter. Mixed in with them were dozens of men and women wearing regular clothes who looked both happy and completely mystified to be there.

Occasionally a maenad would see Artemis and try to pull her in, but Artemis would just lift her cloak saying she had to do her shift soon. The maenad would nod and without fail wish her luck, asking that she keep an eye out for any men or women who should come join them. Artemis would laugh and nod, but wondered what the criteria was. There seemed to be no common denominator among the regular Orphics already there. She noticed maenads occasionally led them to more secluded spots in pairs or small groups, laughing and teasing as they went. She chuckled, assuming they were going to 'revel'.

She continued to walk the perimeter until she came upon a large stone fountain of wine nestled into a corner. It looked like it came straight from the streets of Rome. Maenads would occasionally break from their dancing and come get their fill. Each said a prayer before drinking, then closed their eyes as the wine seeped into their bodies.

Just beyond the fountain, Artemis noticed two in-charge looking

Chosen holding clipboards. They stood in front of an arbored corridor that led out of the courtyard. To their right were several long tables of sandwiches and other finger food. Artemis was wondering why they were just standing there when a loud bell resonated in the courtyard three times. A group of about twenty sweaty, wild-haired maenads separated themselves from the larger group and made their way over.

Artemis sidled up to the fountain and pretended to drink the wine so she could listen.

"Group Three, yes?" yelled one of the Chosen with clipboards.

"Yes!" the maenads said eagerly.

The Chosen pointed to the food. "Eat quickly. You're to relieve your counterparts in the outer courtyard and rooms of True Life in fifteen minutes. You will be relieved by Group Four an hour later. Do any of you need reminders on where to go?" Several of them raised their hands and they all laughed. The Chosen had them line up and started giving out their assignments from a clipboard.

"Remember, you only answer questions if asked directly. You do not get involved in anything unless you see someone disturbing the peace, causing fear, or hurting someone. And then what do we do?"

"Remove the offending person without harm and as quietly as possible," they intoned together, most with their mouths full.

"Good. And where do we put them?"

"In the quiet rooms, until they calm down," they replied, still in unison.

Quiet rooms? Artemis thought. That sounded promising.

"Good," the Chosen said. "Be sure to partake of the sacred wine of the Chosen and pray before you leave. Our god and our Priestess need us tonight." Murmurings of "Praise Bacchus" went through the women. "We are their eyes and ears, and the Orphics see us as their hands. Respect that position and honor it. Keep your own frivolity under wraps until you're back here. Am I understood?"

"Yes! Praise Bacchus!"

"One more thing—a reminder this year—please keep your eyes open and share anything out of the ordinary you see."

"Like what?" one of them asked.

"Just something or someone that doesn't belong. That is all we were told."

They nodded, shoveling food into their mouths for a few more minutes. The maenads gathered their hooded robes and masks from nearby hooks just inside the corridor.

Artemis was already moving when Athena muttered in her ear. "It appears you'll have more access wearing the mask and cloak. I think we should find those quiet rooms."

"You think?" she murmured. Artemis put on her borrowed mask and blue robe and began to follow when a maenad came up and rested her hand on her arm.

"Sister! I thought you were unwell?"

Fuck. "Uh, I'm feeling a little better now. I just wanted to serve and see at least some of the night." Artemis tried to sound ill, making her voice crack slightly. It was difficult over the loud music.

"I understand, but are you sure that is wise?"

"Probably not, but it will be worth it!"

"Ha! That's true, I suppose I would do the same. Though you cannot expect to enjoy *all* of tonight's deliciousness, you don't want to make anyone else sick."

"I know, I will not. Thank you, sister. Praise Bacchus." Artemis coughed and turned to leave.

"Praise Bacchus!" the maenad replied. "Feel better!"

Artemis exhaled and strode down the hallway to catch up to the rear of the quick moving group ahead of her. She glanced behind her. The maenad was still watching her walk away, her head cocked to the side.

Artemis held her breath until she turned the corner. She was surprised to see a wide, utilitarian hallway, with simple cream colored tile and far less greenery.

She caught up to the group just as they began to disperse. She tapped one of the maenads on the shoulder. "Sister, I am embarrassed, but I am forgetting—can you remind me where the quiet rooms are? I can't seem to remember. I haven't been well." Artemis made her voice crack again.

"No need to be embarrassed, forgetting is a blessed part of being Bacchae. The quiet rooms are two floors down. Take the stairwell in the next hallway to your right or if you are taking an Initiate who is in need of one, take them via the south elevator."

"Many thanks, sister. Praise Bacchus!" Artemis exclaimed.

"Praise Bacchus!"

She slowed until the rest of the maenads had gone a little further away, then slipped down the next hallway and ran to the stairs. Her breath echoed in her mask. She heard a small sound behind her and whirled, sure there was someone there.

There was no one.

She took the steps down two at a time.

She had a feeling she was about to find Father.

70

lex and Hermes opened the door to yet another room after muttering another godforsaken prayer. This one had a jellyfish on the lintel and the Orphics within lounged on chairs embedded in a vibrant coral reef. Somehow they were under water without being under water. Everyone's hair floated like a mermaid, there was soft sand underfoot, and there were hundreds of colorful sea creatures swimming around for people to interact with. Alex sighed as they shut the door, wishing they could stay in any number of these rooms.

"Imagine the amount of power this is taking," Athena said.

"That's assuming he didn't create each room to be a relic, so it could exist without him," Hermes said.

"True," Athena said. "To construct all of these rooms as relics would have taken centuries given the amount of power I estimate he has, even with boosts from ceremonies like these."

"Well, he's *had* centuries."

Athena sighed. "Obviously, Hermes. I was just saying."

Occasionally they would see Chosen walking through, watching carefully. They were treated with deference and were only spoken to if they spoke first.

"Should I be trying to get close to one of them?" Alex asked.

"No, everyone seems to give them a wide berth," Athena said. "I think someone touching them then going into a catatonic state would certainly catch their attention."

"Good point."

The following room was full of sound and color. As in the sound *created* the color. Wide swirls darted and undulated into the air whenever anyone spoke, sang, or played the myriad of instruments within.

The next room held the depths of space. But in this cosmos, the stars moved when they were touched, as if the universe itself was a massive bioluminescent bay. The stars eddied around any movement, rippling together to make brilliant swaths of light as people walked or moved their arms. The bigger the movement, the more brilliant the light.

But Alex's favorite room by far was a labyrinth of dark, wooden shelves, filled with books of all color and size, arranged alphabetically by author. She pulled off an antique edition of Jane Austen's *Sense and Sensibility* and opened it to a random page. The room around her faded and she was suddenly surrounded by an English countryside with carriages and women walking arm in arm in empire waist dresses. "Oh, Miss Dashwood!" a voice called behind her. Alex whirled to see a young woman rushing up to her. But she, and the rest of the scene melted in front of her, returning her to Hermes.

"Where did you go?" he asked, holding the book. "You just went all blank. Almost like you were in a vision."

"Oh god, I think I was in the book!" Alex said, grinning. A closer look down the long winding aisles revealed other people sitting on the ground, ostensibly lost in the story they held. Hermes had to quite literally pull Alex away.

At first they were puzzled by the next room, it was filled floor to ceiling in a strange, vibrant red material, molded into various shapes they could walk around. Alex pushed on one of the shapes and it moved to however she formed it. Once she let go, it stayed in that shape. They ventured in a little further around and found dozens of people having sex, all using the material for extremely creative positions.

Well, it was only a matter of time until we found something like that, Alex thought, her face burning. This time she was the one to pull Hermes away.

The following room was a vast green meadow with very few people. They looked at each other in consternation when Alex saw movement out of the corner of her eye. "Look!" She pointed to the cloudless blue sky. Orphics were literally flying through the air, rolling and wheeling in atmospheric acrobatics. The ground felt springy and somehow she knew if she tried, she could use it to launch into the air.

Everyone they saw seemed ridiculously happy, in every room.

"So far none of these scream human sacrifice to me," Hermes said. "And we're not seeing any evidence that Dionysus or Nyssa hang out in them."

"I agree," said Athena. "We're losing time and this is proving fruitless."

They returned to the Great Room to find tables of rich food and small plates strategically placed next to each door.

"I'm starving," Alex said, picking up a balsamic caprese stack. She paused. "Think the food has anything euphoric in it?"

"Doubtful," Hermes said. "It's probably all about the wine. But I'll taste it first just to see." He pulled the food out of her fingers and popped it in his mouth.

"Hey!"

"I think it's okay," he said, smiling with his mouth full.

"Great." She picked up a few more morsels from various tables and gobbled them down.

A brilliant light flashed and the sound of thunder rolled into the room. The Orphics turned to find Dionysus, still in his horned mask, standing on the edge of the wine fountain. Alex gasped as she gazed on him with her golden eyes. He had an aura so bright she wanted to squint, as though he were too glorious to behold.

"My family!" His voice echoed in the Great Room.

Everyone dropped to their knees. Alex and Hermes followed. "Praise Bacchus!"

"I hope you are enjoying The Mysteries!"

The crowd cheered.

"Know that I, your god, love you."

The crowd cheered again and started chanting. *Praise Bacchus, Praise Bacchus, Praise Bacchus.*

He grinned as his eyes scanned the crowd. Alex froze as they passed over her. She couldn't believe how such a big part of her still wanted to run up to him. She tried to focus, to sense his Thread, but felt nothing but awe and reverence.

His voice boomed again. "You will continue to be blessed just for being here and your dedication to me. Carry on and be well as you live your True Life!" He disappeared in a pillar of flame that left an after-image in their eyes.

The crowd cheered again.

Alex and Hermes rose and moved toward a set of doors on the opposite side of the fountain, trying to decide what to do next.

"Just pick one randomly and go. It's the best!" said a busty woman sashaying by in a short, strappy green shift dress and emerald half mask. Her blonde hair was up in a bun. She closed her eyes, pointed her arm in front of her, and spun in a circle. She stopped and laughed as she headed toward the door nearest to where she pointed. It had a snowflake on its lintel.

Hermes sighed. "That's essentially what it feels like we've been doing. I just don't—"

"Wait, did you see that woman's back?" Alex interrupted.

"Her back? I'm going to go with no," Hermes said.

"She had a tattoo of the Orphic Egg."

"So? That seems like it could be common for an Orphic to have that," he muttered.

"Have you noticed it on anyone else?" she asked.

"Well, no," he admitted, "but I haven't been looking."

"It seems like in a society like this it could have meaning. Similar to how the mae…the Chosen have face tattoos."

"There is logic to that argument," Athena said. Alex smiled, taking that as a great compliment. "It could even be looked down on to get something so plainly demonstrative unless you've earned it somehow. Either way, I agree it's time to forego the rooms and start focusing on the people. Perhaps that's how they mark their upper echelon. Go!"

They followed her through the door and found themselves in an exquisite ice hotel, warm and yet not melting. It was snowing outside, and Alex could see people skiing and snowboarding in the powder, wearing only light, non-winter clothing.

Alex and Hermes scanned for the tattooed woman amongst the dozens of revelers lying around in strangely comfortable looking ice chairs and couches. They found her in a small hexagonal room, lounging in what looked like a foaming ice bath. She sat with her back to the entrance.

Alex gestured for Hermes to stay in the doorway. She walked up next to the woman and dipped her toe in. "Oh! It's warm!" she exclaimed.

"Yes. You should get in, it's glorious," the woman said.

"I don't know if I want to get all wet."

"Oh, well you dry off right away." The woman stood to demonstrate. Her dress looked as dry as it had before, no evidence of water whatsoever. "It's amazing. I love this room."

"It *is* amazing," Alex agreed. She sat and put her legs in, pants and all. "This is all so incredible. It's my first Mysteries."

"Oh, enjoy it, honey, it only gets better from here. This is my seventh!" the woman said conspiratorially.

"Seventh!" Alex was genuinely shocked, quickly doing the math given the Mysteries only happened every seven years. "That's incredible! You don't look a day over thirty!"

"Exactly," she said, grinning. Like that explained everything.

"Fascinating," Athena said in Alex's ear.

"Any tips?" Alex asked as she stood, marveling as she pulled dry legs out of the water.

"Nope! Just explore until you find what brings you the most joy. Praise Bacchus!" Alex could tell the woman wasn't interested in a longer chat. She concentrated, trying to sense her Thread. It was there, invisible and vibrant, reaching out from her heart.

"Thanks! Praise Bacchus!" Alex said. She looked meaningfully at Hermes then squatted to touch the woman's shoulder in farewell.

Flash.

.   .   .

Alex blinked as she entered a vision of the woman in a lavish wedding on a beach somewhere. She immediately manifested and grabbed hold of her Thread. She slid the vision forward past some blush-inducing moments in the True Life rooms until she got to the end of the evening. She skipped through, watching with wide eyes and a curdled stomach. She paused it at the end, staring at the awful scene and the people in it, fear rising like a flood.

She'd seen what she needed to, it was time to get out. They were definitely running out of time. She manifested a book and tried to close it. It went right through the Thread with no result.

Again, and again.

The frustration at failing in this moment flooded through her until she thought she would scream. She stared at the rapturous face of the woman and fear began to turn to anger, which quickly morphed into rage. Rage against the helplessness she felt now and had felt her whole life. Rage at all the horror she'd seen; at what she was seeing now.

She took the rage and focused on it, concentrating. She screamed. The sound was still reverberating when she manifested a book with the Orphic egg on its cover, blood seeping over the serpent's coils. She opened it and lit the pages on fire, watching the paper crackle darkly and furl in on itself. She held up the burning book to the Thread and slammed it closed.

She felt something as the vision disintegrated. Something new.

For the first time, she could tell that someday, maybe soon, she would no longer need her constructs at all.

rtemis paused at the bottom of the concrete stairwell and peeked around the open doorway. It led out into a long simple hallway similar to the one she'd just left, though much narrower. There were doors all along one wall with glass windows and slots at the bottom, ostensibly to slip food trays into. The first few she checked were empty, though to her surprise they looked like posh hotel rooms inside—with a queen bed, mounted TV, lamps, and ensuite bathroom.

"This is weird," Artemis said quietly.

"What are you seeing?" Athena asked.

Artemis described the hallway and its strange rooms.

"I suppose it makes sense. If they were going to keep rowdy Orphics down here, they'd still need to keep it nice," Athena said.

"I guess," Artemis said quietly. "Still, there's a weird vibe down here."

The next room she peered into contained an older, pot-bellied man passed out on the bed in nothing but his mask. Artemis wrinkled her nose and moved on. The next occupied room had a woman in a gown sitting on the edge of the bed with her masked head in her hands.

She picked up the pace. Her pulse raced a little as she approached each room, wondering if this would be the one. But each one disappointed. The second to last door was the last room with a light on. She took in a deep breath and peered through the window.

She gasped.

"What? What do you see?" Athena asked, clearly annoyed she had to keep asking.

"Demeter."

Demeter was pacing the small room muttering to herself, the bed unmade behind her. There were stacks of plates on a nearby dresser. She'd been here a while.

Artemis tried the door, it was locked. She tapped on the heavy glass of the window.

Demeter backed away with her arms up.

"It's okay, it's okay, it's me!" Artemis said, pulling off her mask.

Recognition and shock registered on Demeter's face. "Artemis! Man, am I happy to see you."

Artemis could barely hear her through the door, so she knelt on the floor in front of the food slot and put her cheek on the cold hard stone.

"Demeter!" Artemis whispered. "We were worried about you! How long have you been here? Is Father here? How do I get you out?"

Demeter lay on the floor too.

"He is, I'm sure of it," Demeter whispered back. "And I don't know, one of the Chosen have always unlocked the door from the outside."

"Damnit, okay. I don't have the lock-picking kit with me. Athena, you there? Thoughts?"

Athena didn't answer.

"Artemis, stop. Your father is the one in danger tonight. We must save him!" Demeter's voice caught. "And watch out for the maenads, there is a small group of them who—"

The sound of thyrsus staffs on the tile stopped both of them short. Artemis froze. She quickly pulled down her mask before standing up.

Two Chosen in blue robes and masks stood several doors down the hallway.

"What exactly are you doing, Sister? Why are you speaking to her? You should not be here."

"Forgive me, I was just doing as I was told," Artemis said, lowering her head. She rapidly ran through her options. None of them were good. She was cornered, the only exit was the stairs or elevator at least fifteen yards away behind the Chosen. She knew she would lose if they got close, should she just shoot now? She was fast, but they were faster. So fast she might miss. But like Athena said, better to contend with one than two. But how to know if they were part of the Chosen Elite? She wasn't particularly interested in murdering innocents, if there were any.

"You are lying. The First One asked us to ensure no one spoke to her. Show us your face." The second maenad turned and cocked her head at her companion, seeming perplexed.

"Of course." Artemis lifted her hand toward her face as though to remove the mask, and hoped she'd read the situation accurately. Instead, she flicked her wrist and crouched, firing off two arrows in a matter of seconds. They found their mark, the first fatally piercing the chest of the maenad who had spoken. The second maenad screamed as the other arrow flew into her shoulder. She dropped to a crouch and lunged forward toward Artemis, robe flying behind her, staff thrown to the side.

Artemis threw herself backward, shooting off arrows as she went, but the maenad moved too fast, dodging left and right until she bowled Artemis over, throwing her to the ground and knocking the bow out of her hand.

The maenad sat on top of Artemis, pulling off her mask and pinning both of her arms down.

Not again, Artemis thought, panicking.

"You will now be torn apart in the name of Bacchus for killing one of his Chosen," the maenad hissed. Artemis looked at her lava lamp eyes surrounded by her white and red checkerboard mask.

"Well, to be fair, your sisters killed my brother and uncle," Artemis wheezed.

"That is not true," the maenad said.

"Like hell it's not. I have it on video."

"Mention the Elite and the First One," Athena whispered in her ear.

"I take it you're not part of the Chosen Elite? The inner circle of Chosen that follow the First One?" Artemis asked.

"I don't know what you mean," the maenad said slowly.

"I think you do. I think your friend here was part of it, was she not?"

"I don't know, I am not usually paired with her." Doubt started to creep into her voice. "She just grabbed me to come down here, saying she needed help with an Orphic."

"Well, that's my aunt you have in that cell over there, and I have a feeling you crazy bitches are about to murder my father in some hellish sacrificial ceremony, so let's either finish this or get off me so I can stop it."

The maenad didn't move for what felt like ages. Finally, she pulled off her mask, her tattooed face full of confusion. "The Harvest Sacrifice is a willing participant," she said. "One who has chosen to seek out their True Life in the hereafter. Those who wish to provide for their family forever, as compensated by our god. It is a beautiful thing they do. It is not…what you make it sound like."

"If you say so. Look, it seems like maybe you're a good one. If you want proof, let's ask Demeter, she was just about to tell me." She gestured to Demeter's room down the hallway.

"That is…Demeter?" The maenad sounded awed.

"Yes, you know her?"

"Of course, she is an integral part of our sacrificial ceremonies. But I have never seen her up close."

Artemis felt like she'd been punched in the gut. Demeter was involved? "Well, I guess I'll just have to ask her about that. Like I said, she's my aunt. I am Artemis. Dionysus, or Bacchus as you call him, is my brother."

The maenad scrambled off her as if she'd been burned. She laid down prostrate, hissing in pain as the arrow came in contact with the ground. "Forgive me, I didn't know."

Artemis sat up. "It's okay, I wasn't sure about you either. But I hoped, which is why I aimed for the shoulder. I'd help you pull it out, but it will actually disappear in another twelve minutes or so. That'll be the best for your body."

"Truly? Wonderful. Then the wine will heal me," she said.

The maenad on the floor made a ghastly gurgling sound, startling both of them. Artemis scrambled over to her and yanked off the dying Chosen's mask. "Where is Zeus?" she growled.

The Chosen smiled, her teeth covered in blood. "Hmmm, a large mortal man with black hair and a black beard?"

"That's the one," said Artemis.

"Mortal," Athena breathed.

"You are too late. He is being prepared."

"No," Artemis said.

She coughed. "You will not interfere, the First One will not allow it."

"Sister, who is the First One?" the second maenad asked.

The Chosen Elite's eyes vacated and her head lolled. She was gone.

"Does she have a key for Demeter?" Athena asked.

"Do you have a key for these doors?" Artemis repeated.

"Yes," the Chosen said, her voice thick with emotion. She pulled a chain from around her neck. "I don't understand what is happening."

"That makes two of us. Just don't get in my way." Artemis held out her hand.

The maenad gave her the key. "I will not. I will also not stand by and allow an unwilling sacrifice to happen. It is not who we are. Plus, it seems likely to taint the wine and ruin us all."

"Maybe the sacrifice isn't for wine this time," Artemis said.

"But that is the primary purpose of the Harvest Sacrifice, though there are other benefits. It allows our god to bless both the wine already barreled, and the entire valley for many years, so the grapes grow well. It ensures we have enough to last us until the next blood moon."

"Well, it seems like things aren't always as they seem around here," Artemis said. She ran to Demeter's door.

"Yes. That seems true," the maenad said quietly, looking at her dead sister.

Demeter was peering through the glass and smiled in obvious relief at the sight of Artemis.

Artemis' face was like stone. "Sounds like we need to have a little chat, Demeter."

Demeter's smile faded.

72

A lex came back to her senses to find Hermes kissing her neck. She was sitting on his lap while he held her upper body. She curled her arms up around him.

"Oh thank god. Keep it up," he said. "There's a Chosen coming right towards us. I must have failed at not looking creepy while holding a non-responsive woman."

Alex chuckled. She pulled his face up and kissed him.

The Chosen walked up to them and paused to look down, scrutinizing. They stopped to smile and nod at her, and went back to it.

The Chosen moved on.

Alex pulled back and breathed a sigh of relief.

"Nice work. Did you see anything useful, Alex?" Athena asked.

Alex frowned. "Yes. And we have no time. Right now we need to figure out how to get our own serpent and egg tattoos. It should be about the same size as that woman's. Three or four inches."

"I can scan the symbol from the handbook," Athena said. "I have the temporary tattoo paper I used for Artemis. I can print it out, you'll just need to *shift* over to get it."

"You have a printer with you?" Hermes asked, incredulous.

"A small portable one, yes," she said simply. "It was an eventuality easy to foresee—"

"Okay, okay, great," Hermes interrupted. "Let's head back to the room," he said to Alex.

Alex shook her head. "No, we need to keep an eye on her. It's how we'll know when we need to go."

"Okay, then you'll have to stay with her while I go to Athena."

"I'll let you know when they're ready. Give me about ten minutes," Athena said.

"What else do we need to be doing?" he asked Alex.

"Watch her. That's it," Alex said.

They followed the woman as she left the winter room and headed back to the courtyard. She refilled on wine and sat in one of the swings. Orphics were starting to fill the area, eating, drinking, and dancing to the light and playful music.

Alex and Hermes sat on some soft grass against a large tree strung with crystal lights. Hermes started asking questions while they waited. "Could you see who performed the sacrifice? Was it Nyssa or Dionysus?"

Alex shook her head. She wasn't sure who the other person was, actually. But no one in that room had been innocent.

"Okay, it's ready," Athena said in their ear.

"Are you going to be good here?" Hermes asked, squeezing her hand.

"Of course."

"Ok, I'll be back soon." Hermes headed to one of the rooms to *shift* where no one would see.

A group of revelers burst out laughing, drawing Alex's attention. When she looked back, the swing was empty. She caught a glimpse of green in the crowd but it closed behind her, making it impossible to see where she'd gone.

"Damnit, I lost her!" Alex said, plunging into the crowd anyway.

"Alex, wait," Athena said. But Alex pushed on. They couldn't know how desperately they needed that woman.

But she was gone.

Damn damn damn! Alex thought back to what she'd seen in the vision. The door to the Harvest Ceremony had been in a room of perpetual fall. Maybe she should just start trying to find that.

"Hermes has the tattoos," Athena said, interrupting her thoughts.

"Since following the woman is no longer an option, pick a room for him to meet you in so you can find a private place to apply them. We'll go from there."

"Okay," Alex said. She had her hand on the door with the jellyfish on the lintel when she noticed a knot of Chosen surrounding a maskless woman in a wine-dark hooded robe.

"Nyssa," Alex whispered. She moved to the side and watched as Nyssa gave directions to the Chosen. One knelt in front of her. Nyssa beamed at her, raised her up, and gave her a big hug. She seemed warm and loving, like a mother hen. Alex could see in that moment why Dionysus and the Chosen liked her so much. The Chosen dispersed and Nyssa stood with a silver thyrsus watching the frivolities with a small, private smile.

"I'm going to see if I can get into her Thread," Alex said under her breath.

"No, Alex, not while you're alone," Athena said quickly. "If you're successful you'll go into your catatonic state with your white eyes. She *will* recognize it. We'll be exposed."

"What if I can do it as I'm walking by her? Just brush her hand so I'm facing the other direction when it triggers?"

Athena seemed to think for a moment.

Nyssa was approached by a few Orphics who seemed to be thanking her profusely. Nyssa gave a wide, welcoming grin and gestured for them to return to the evening. It seemed like she was going to move on any minute.

"I think I can do it. There is a door behind her and to the side a little. There are people going in and out of it and I could just act as though I was going there."

"Perhaps, but wait for Hermes, he's coming."

Nyssa turned and started to walk slowly around the edge of the room as she watched the crowd, passing doors as she did. Alex's heart was pounding. "I'm going to lose her. This is our chance, the one we were looking for. The reason you brought me. I'm going to go for it."

"Alex, wait!" Athena said.

But Alex was already moving. She ran back through the crowd then turned so she headed toward Nyssa at an angle. She started to sway to the music as she walked.

Nyssa greeted more Orphics then glanced Alex's way. She turned back and stared at Alex. She cocked her head ever so slightly, not taking her eyes off of her.

A chill went up Alex's spine. There's no way she recognized her in the dim light and mask right?

"Alex, stop!" Athena said. "Something's wrong!"

It was too late. Alex was only a few feet away. She couldn't change directions now without looking even more strange. She swayed toward the door behind Nyssa, already concentrating harder than ever to feel the woman's Thread. She could feel it, but it felt different, strangely tenuous, like it was further away somehow.

She nodded at Nyssa as she walked by. Nyssa nodded back, her eyes boring into her.

Alex reached out and brushed Nyssa's hand, willing herself into the distant Thread as she took two big steps past her.

She hoped she'd gone far enough.

Flash.

lex was surrounded by a vast, silent, darkness, with nothing but a faint, luminous Thread as far as she could see. She started to panic. Something was wrong. She'd felt different as she'd slipped into this vision, it had felt so far away. She touched the Thread and slid the vision backward, jumping when it suddenly filled with light and sound.

Nyssa and Dionysus were eating dinner and talking.

So strange, Alex thought. She swiped a little more, passing by more black spots in the Thread then more Nyssa and Dionysus. The pattern continued several times and she wondered how she was ever going to find out who had planned all of this. At the thought she felt a tug and the vision skipped backward.

Dionysus paced in the kitchen, arguing with Nyssa.

Alex stepped into the vision.

"It is a burden, and it no longer brings me any pleasure. What's it to you if I don't want to do this anymore?" Dionysus sounded as though this was a well-worn argument.

"Same as it was last time we talked about it," Nyssa said crossly.

"You owe it to the people you have cultivated as your family. You owe it to me. I don't want to stop."

"I have given the family plenty. For centuries," he snapped. "I owe them nothing. As for you, I want you to be happy. Truly. We just need to find a way for your happiness to not be hinged on me maintaining everything. There has to be a way to take me out, but leave you in."

Nyssa smiled, seeming slightly exultant. "Actually, I think I found a way to do that very thing. I just hadn't figured out how to talk to you about it yet," she said.

"How?"

"Well, remember how I told you I have been keeping an eye on your family?"

"Yes, though I still can't fathom why," he said.

"Well, now you will. You have likely not heard of it, given your aversion to news and things of this time. But there have been great strides in science, genetics specifically. The humans have discovered a way to edit their genes, a tool. Apollo has utilized this tool and created a virus."

"His successes do not interest me!"

"Patience, Dionysus. Let me finish. It is a special virus. A virus that can turn the immortal, mortal."

Dionysus stared. "You're not serious."

Nyssa smiled. "I am. Very."

"Why would he want to do something like that?" he asked, mystified.

"He has found someone he does not want to lose, or some such nonsense. Someone he wants to grow old with."

Dionysus furrowed his brow, clearly trying to process this. Anger clouded his face. "Why are you just now telling me about this? This could put us in danger!"

"The point is," she continued, "it solves our problem and provides us means of a truly perfect revenge against those who have harmed you most."

"That's not an answer. But how so?" he said.

"If we had that virus and turned one of them mortal, we could use him or her as our Harvest Sacrifice in the upcoming Mysteries. Imagine the

power such a long life would give us, give our valley. We would have a rich harvest for decades. You could have your break."

"But it has to be a willing sacrifice," he said, confused.

"Says who?"

Dionysus thought. "Us, I guess," he said finally.

Nyssa nodded. "And either way you have the power to make it look as though they willingly walk to the altar."

"Will that work? If the mind is not truly willing?"

"I feel certain it will," she said firmly.

"But you cannot know for sure, we have never tried it."

"It's worth trying," she said. "We can keep a backup."

"Who in my family, exactly, do you have in mind?" he asked, sounding wary. "And what is the revenge you speak of?"

"Who has hurt you the most?"

Dionysus was silent for a long time. Nyssa waited, seeming to know he needed to come to these answers himself.

"Hera," he said, in a voice so full of acid it could have eaten a hole in the world.

"And who let her do that?"

Another long silence.

"Father."

Nyssa waited, then reached out and grabbed his hands in her own. "Dionysus, you do deserve a rest. And if we do this right, they can be the ones who give it to you. And I would say they owe it to you, do they not?"

Dionysus sat still, looking at the floor.

"Do they not?" she asked again.

"I suppose. I mean, Hera, yes. But with Father it is complicated. And he was a different person then, we all were."

"No! It is not complicated! You may have had a few moments when you felt he cared for you, but he has never cared for you the way a father should care for a son. And worse, stood by while you were cruelly—"

"Stop," he said in warning.

She did.

"So what, exactly, are you proposing?" he asked.

His eyes remained on the floor while Nyssa laid out a high-level plan of theft, torture, murder, kidnapping, and mortal sacrifice. When she was done she stopped and waited. Dionysus sat still for a long time, until finally he looked at her, his face full of warring emotions. "You would do all that for me?"

"I would do anything for you," Nyssa said. "You are my family."

"How?"

"Maenads."

He looked at her pointedly. "You mean your little band of Chosen Elite?"

Nyssa's face clouded slightly. "I did not know you knew about them," she said cautiously.

"Then you think me a fool," he said.

She did not answer right away, her mind seemed to be racing. "Of course not. But I and my Elite have always taken care of the things you find distasteful."

"Like the massacre," he said flatly.

"Like your victory over The Fall and your rotten family."

Dionysus sighed. "It will hurt Hermes and the rest of the family. They love Father." His voice was wooden.

She shrugged. "The hurt it will cause Hermes is regrettable. The rest of the family is of no concern."

"What of Demeter? We need her and her sickle for the sacrifice. She will not go for this," he said.

"No, we need only the sickle," Nyssa said.

"She has shared much with us and been our ally. We will not hurt her," he said forcefully.

Nyssa tried unsuccessfully to hide a smile. "Agreed. She will simply be detained, and we will borrow her sickle. We will make it up to her."

Dionysus was silent again for several minutes. "So," he said slowly. "How many years do you think a mortal sacrifice of Father's caliber will bless the valley and allow the wine to flow?"

Nyssa's eyes flashed in triumph.

. . .

Alex felt sick and exultant at her success at the same time. They had both done this. She moved the vision forward to see what was supposed to happen tonight when suddenly she was spluttering and coughing, the smelling salts in her nose.

Hermes was kneeling in front of her, waving the vial in her face.

"That was a fucking ridiculous stunt you just pulled!" Hermes whispered, a vein throbbing in his forehead. "Nyssa had turned to follow you right when I got there. Luckily I pulled you into the room and then *shifted* to this one. She may be looking for us now."

"But it worked! I saw it. She planned it but he went along with it. He knew everything." Alex gasped. She covered her mouth with her hands, watching in horror as his face went slack and eyes unfocused, a wave of disbelief washing over him, just as it was surely washing over Athena. The realization of what she'd just done sank like a stone into her stomach.

Hermes shook his head. "What do you mean? That's impossible." He pulled her up and then paused, the second part of the curse kicking in, forgetting. "Wait, what were we talking about?"

Alex wanted to cry. "Nothing," she whispered.

"Athena?" Alex asked. But she didn't answer. She hoped against hope that Athena had been talking to Artemis and didn't hear.

"Okay, let's *shift* back to the room," Hermes said. "We have to apply these tattoos." He pulled her behind a wide pillar and *shifted.*

Back in the room, they applied the tattoos to each other, using the finishing spray to set it and make it look more real. Alex barely registered the warmth of his hands on her skin. "Look," she said. "You need to know, I fucked up. Pretty bad. I talked about my vision of Nyssa right when I came out of it and it affected you. It was important."

"You did? I don't remember that."

"I know."

"Well, that explains the face you've had for the last several minutes," he said. "But it's done, so we'll work around it. How long does the curse usually last?"

"I don't know. Probably forever."

"Okay. Alex, it's okay."

"I don't know if it is, it was a pretty bad one to mess up on," she said miserably.

He kissed her briefly. "It's done, let it go. We'll figure it out. But no more stunts. I'll go get my laptop so you can tell us what you saw."

He *shifted* away and back quickly and handed her a small laptop. She typed up a short description of the autumnal room. "Do you think you can pop in and out of the rooms quickly to try to find it?" she asked. "The Orphics might be so preoccupied they don't notice."

"Yeah, I'll give it a shot." He disappeared.

Alex began to pace, the evening feeling more ominous with each minute. "Athena? Are you there?" Athena still didn't answer.

"Found it," Hermes said as he popped back into the room.

He grabbed her hand and they *shifted*.

74

Artemis studied her aunt as she spoke, realizing how little she really knew about Demeter even after all the time she'd spent at her farm. But had she ever really asked? *Everything was always about me when I stayed there*, she thought with a twinge of guilt. Demeter had just finished quickly telling how the maenads had kidnapped her after using the yelping of the poor, tortured dogs to force her into giving up her sickle. Tears fell on her cheeks as she spoke. The maenad wept with her.

Artemis had already shed all her tears. "But…why do you take part in all this?" she asked.

"We're two sides of the same coin, he and I. Both tied to the earth, both tied to The Mysteries. They have changed over time, but the heart remains the same. After The Fall I was at his mercy and just grateful he was going to continue. Especially when he agreed to still ensure it was a willing sacrifice. There is always enough to bless his valley as well as my farm and gardens."

"Ah, so that's why it always looks so amazing, even in seasons with little rain," Artemis said.

Demeter nodded. "I'm good, but I'm not that good. Not anymore. After they put me in here, Dionysus came to apologize. He said he hadn't known about the dogs until after, and he was sick about it. I demanded an explanation, and after I wore him down a little, the whole thing just rushed out of him, like he was desperate to talk about it. He didn't say, but I got the impression it was Nyssa's idea. Anyway, right now all that matters is they are definitely planning to use my brother as a sacrifice in the Harvest Ceremony."

"Then we must go," the maenad said, her face conflicted. "The Harvest Ceremony comes soon. I…I will show you how to get there, but if he knows what he is doing—"

"What's your name?" Artemis asked.

"Sarah."

"We're so grateful for your help, Sarah. Will you be out of place if you take us?"

"No, we usually take part. Along with a few dozen of the Orphic Inner Circle."

"Athena, have you gotten all this?" Artemis asked.

"Yes," she said quietly.

"Athena is here?" Demeter asked.

"Yes, along with Hermes and Alex," Artemis said.

"Who's Alex?"

"A friend of mine, an Oracle. Also, Hera and Poseidon are dead." Artemis felt only slightly bad for dropping it on her like that. Demeter's face went from baffled to horrified.

Artemis turned to Sarah. "Okay, what do we need to do?"

Having already dragged the dead Chosen's body into Demeter's room, they pulled off her robe and mask, then rushed up the stairs.

Sarah took them to the temple through one of the simple underground hallways, explaining how the Chosen would eventually stop their rounds among the Orphics and all go to a separate part of the temple for the ceremony. "Bacchus calls the Inner Circle by warming the serpent and egg tattoo they wear. They join us through a passageway from one of the True Life rooms. This way the rest of the Orphics don't notice them leaving."

Athena jumped in. "Alex and Hermes are already in the room of perpetual fall. Ask her if she knows which tree it is."

Artemis relayed the question.

"Yes, it is a tree with all gold leaves to the right of the door after entering, about ten yards away. There is a serpent and egg carving on it which must be pressed for five seconds and a door will open. The Orphics in the Inner Circle love having a secret passageway. Tell your friends to prepare for another sacrifice," Sarah warned.

"What kind of sacrifice?" Artemis asked.

"I'm not sure, I have not yet been a part of an Inner Circle ceremony. But it's likely another blood sacrifice."

Demeter nodded. "I believe it's a significant amount, actually."

"Lovely," Athena said dryly. "Passing all that onto Hermes and Alex, hang on."

"Is there a sacrifice required of the maenads as well?" Artemis asked.

"Yes, we also give of our own blood," Sarah said. "It is the most powerful sacrifice."

Artemis smelled the greenery and breathed in the warm night air well before they turned a corner and entered the maenad courtyard, where there were even more of them dancing than before. The energy in the room crackled and they seemed more frenzied than ever.

She noticed there were no longer regular Orphics among them.

The time was near.

75

Alex and Hermes walked hand in hand through a golden afternoon that shone through autumnal trees of all shades. Trees whose leaves fell without leaving the branches bare.

They had been looking in vain for a secret door, while watching for any Orphics heading off alone or in a small group.

"Alex, Hermes, sorry for the radio silence, we had a bit of an intense situation," Athena said suddenly in their ears.

"Is everyone okay?" Alex asked.

"Yes. And I know where you need to go." She relayed the information. They looked at each other in dismay when she explained about the next blood sacrifice.

They retraced their steps and found the tree, its golden leaves glittering in the light. Hermes covered the Orphic egg carving with his palm for five seconds. Sure enough, a square door swung open, revealing a circular ivory marble staircase heading down. He gestured for Alex to go first.

Groups of soft white candles embedded in alcoves guided them all the way to a vacuous candle-lit antechamber. Dozens of Orphic Inner Circle members whispered excitedly. Alex and Hermes stayed to the back, waiting and watching. It wasn't long before four Chosen walked in and banged their staffs on the floor twice.

One stepped forward and spoke in a resonant voice. "Inner Circle, it is time. Let us begin our preparation for the Harvest Ceremony." The whispers escalated as the men and women looked at each other eagerly.

One of the other Chosen opened a cleverly concealed closet in the wall to reveal a row of soft dark brown deerskin tunics. A second closet was full of small empty cubicles.

"Please form a line to select a tunic. Remove your clothing and stow them in the cubicles. You may leave your masks on, but nature is the only thing allowed to touch the rest of your body. You will put on the tunic and one of the Chosen will tie up the back after checking for your sacred tattoo. You will perform your sacrifice in two groups. Now please, come prepare."

The Orphics created a line. Alex looked at Hermes in alarm as the first several disrobed in front of everyone.

"It's fine," he said. "No one seems to really be watching or care." She looked around and saw that was true. Those with their tunics on had already gone through a door on the opposite side of the room. The rest were just talking amongst themselves.

It was Alex's turn. She took off her shirt and pants and dropped them to the floor, quickly pulling the soft tunic on. Using the tunic as a shield, she pulled her arms in and slipped off her bra and underwear, then put all the clothes into a cubicle.

Suddenly she stood in front of a Chosen. She'd forgotten to worry about the condition of her fake tattoo until just this moment. Alex quickly turned away from the maenad's lava lamp eyes before they could see the fear in hers.

She held her breath, but the Chosen simply tied up her tunic. She moved forward and waited for Hermes, who had no problem dropping everything to the floor as he pulled on a tunic. She whirled away and waited, catching only a glimpse of a solidly muscled body. He grabbed her hand and they went through the door together. It opened into another candlelit circular chamber with an immense black stone bowl in the center. It had a deeply grooved brim leading to a strange pattern carved into the bottom.

Everyone stood in a circle around it. More Chosen entered, one carrying chalices of wine, and several carrying trays with serpent daggers and towels.

Each Orphic was given a chalice. "Now we drink, chant, and perform the sacrifice required to enter the Inner Sanctuary," the lead Chosen said, her blue hooded robe and white Venetian mask stood out amongst all the brown tunics. "Behold, the sacrificial wine, the one most sacred to our lord god Bacchus. May it serve its purpose and prepare your bodies to accept the gift you are about to receive."

Everyone raised their chalices. "Praise our lord god Bacchus!" They drank. Alex waited anxiously to see what this wine would do, but felt only warmth and an eerie sense of tranquility.

Each Chosen came to stand next to an Orphic as they performed essentially the same ritual as before, but with significantly larger daggers, and slightly different prayers.

Alex completed the ritual and poured the rose gold wine into the chalice and drank. It tasted of glory and love and sacrifice. It was warm and tingly as it coursed down her throat, flowing into her body, limb by limb, filling her with light. She found herself looking to see if any was leaking from her skin.

"Thank you for your sacrifice," her Chosen whispered, then left to stand with her fellow Chosen. They were all holding chalices still more than half full of rose gold wine.

The first Chosen spoke again. "May the sacrificial blood of the Inner Circle, the Orphic followers closest to Bacchus, allow them to bask in the light of the blood moon and the full presence of their god. May their blood mingle and may their sacrifices and promises be fulfilled this night. Praise Bacchus."

"Praise Bacchus," the group responded.

As one, the Chosen carefully poured the rest of the golden wine into the wide brim of the black basin. The group watched as it filled the grooves carved into the bottom, slowly forming the shape of a horned bull's head. Once the design had filled completely, the basin began to move, stone grinding against the stone, turning and twisting into a narrow circular staircase lifting to the floor above.

"Your sacrifice has been accepted. Go and prostrate yourselves before your god."

Alex followed the Orphic next to her up into a vast circular room open to the stars and the moon, lit with smokeless torches. It smelled lightly of pine and was comfortably warm, even though it was outside. Even the grass beneath them was warm.

It was the room from the vision. Seeing it in person felt like déjà vu, each detail a stone of dread skipping across her wine-filled lake of serenity. An eight-foot-long stone altar sat in the center of the room, carved with intricate vines. Just beyond the altar stood a dais. Dionysus sat unmasked in a large silver chair. Nyssa stood next to him in her robe and feathered Venetian mask.

Alex realized belatedly the Inner Circle members she'd come up with were almost all prostrate. She knelt quickly and bowed forward.

Dionysus stood and spoke. "Welcome, my most precious friends. Tonight you will be rewarded for your faithfulness and dedication. Please rise and look on the face of your god."

"Praise Bacchus!" they said as they stood. Most of them were grinning and nodding to him.

Alex couldn't stop staring at Dionysus sitting in his transcendent golden aura. It was the first time she'd seen his face since she'd left his house. After he'd helped her. She thought he looked tired.

"The eclipse is upon us. Please make yourself comfortable while we wait for the rest to join us and we prepare our willing sacrifice." Dionysus gestured and large cushions appeared at their feet. The group murmured appreciatively and sat or laid down.

Dionysus sat back down in his chair and took a long drink out of a golden chalice of his own.

Alex felt a familiar hand grab hers as Hermes led her to one of the large cushions furthest from the altar. They sat down shoulder to shoulder, fingers entwined. Alex leaned her head onto his shoulder.

"Jesus," he whispered. "That was quite a thing. Did you see all of that in your vision?"

"More or less."

"How do you feel?" Athena asked.

"Good. Better than good," she said. "Like the sacrificial wine from before but more intense. Not euphoric though."

"Good. Nice work getting through that, you two," Athena said. "Artemis is coming the back way now, with a maenad named Sarah. And she's bringing Demeter with her."

"*What?*" Hermes asked.

"It's a long story. In short, they found Demeter but not Father, and she confirmed he is the sacrifice. So this ceremony is our only chance to save him."

They quietly discussed a plan. Hermes would simply *shift* over to Zeus when he was brought in, *shift* him away, then come right back for Alex and Artemis. Easy. They stood and slowly meandered to not quite diametrically opposed positions in the room, to make it less obvious when he left.

The second half of the Inner Circle joined them, lowering themselves before their god and receiving the same message. Maenads also began filing into the room, forming a circle at least six women deep around the outer edge.

Nyssa moved next to Dionysus and placed a hand on his shoulder. "Please rise," she said. "The blood moon is upon us."

The air in the room was electric as Alex and the rest of the Inner Circle formed a crescent in front of the altar. Behind them stood a circle of quiet maskless maenads who had a feverish energy of their own. It was difficult to make out faces. Alex wondered if Artemis was already among them.

"Witness the earth devouring the moon, taking its energy and giving it to us," Nyssa said.

Everyone looked at the sky and watched as the moon's shadow made its journey, now more than three-quarters of the way across. The night slowly became darker.

"Now behold, our willing sacrifice." Nyssa gestured to a doorway behind the dais. A large man wearing deerskin shambled into the room, bracketed by two pairs of Chosen.

A murmur of appreciation went around the room. Alex could tell Zeus had once been a force—tall and broad chested, with black hair and a thick black beard. But his eyes were vacant, his soul robbed of judgement.

Nyssa raised her hands to the group. "Let us express our thanks."

"Honor and gratitude to our willing sacrifice," the room chanted together.

"This is a special one for you tonight, brothers and sisters. The valley will be blessed and protected for years to come, and the aftereffect, your rejuvenation, will also be as never before." Another murmur of anticipation and excitement.

Dionysus stared forward unseeing, not looking at Zeus.

Alex kept glancing at Hermes, wondering when he would make his move.

Zeus walked up to the altar and willingly climbed on, laying prostrate. The Chosen went to stand on either side of the dais.

Now, Hermes, now! Alex thought. Surely he would disappear any second. But nothing happened. She looked at Hermes. What could he possibly be waiting for?

Hermes looked at her and shook his head, looking alarmed.

Oh no! she thought. *He can't do it!*

Nyssa picked up a golden sickle from a small table, its curved blade glinting in the torchlight. "Now, the presentation of the golden sickle, and the preparation of the sacrifice." She used the sickle to cut a line in Zeus' tunic from his neck down to his navel. She carved several symbols directly onto his chest, murmuring prayers as she cut. Small rivulets of blood rolled down his sides.

The anticipation in the room swelled and Orphics and maenads alike raised their arms and started chanting as well.

"Praise Bacchus, praise Bacchus, praise Bacchus."

NO! Alex screamed in her head. Her heart was pounding, she did *not* want to watch this.

Nyssa finished carving and waited for the now darkened moon to turn blood red. She raised the sickle in both hands. Alex felt a scream building inside her. But Hermes yelled instead.

"No! Don't do it, brother!" Nyssa looked up sharply and the chanting stopped. Consternation flooded the room.

Hermes stepped forward and pulled off his mask. "This is not a willing sacrifice!"

Nyssa nodded to the Chosen next to her. They were on Hermes in flash, forcing him to his knees. The group created space around them.

Dionysus shook his head, as though trying to bring the room into focus. "Hermes?"

"Dionysus, do not be distracted," Nyssa said fervently.

Hermes bellowed as the maenads pulled on his arms and head.

Dionysus flew out of his chair. "Don't hurt him!" he yelled to the Chosen. They looked to Nyssa first, who reluctantly nodded.

They stopped pulling but kept Hermes immovable.

"Dionysus, please," Hermes croaked. He nodded to their father. "I know he failed you when you needed him the most, but—"

"Exactly," Nyssa hissed. "His death is our redemption. It is an appropriate sacrifice, giving his son the rest he deserves." Her eyes gleamed and she raised the sickle again.

Thwip! Thwip! Thwip! The room gasped as three silver arrows appeared in Nyssa's neck. Her mouth opened, gurgling as she fell. The golden sickle dropped to the ground with a loud clang.

Dionysus looked down at her in horror.

Alex's heart soared at the sight of Artemis standing at the inner edge of the circle of maenads in a deerskin tunic, bow raised. The nearest maenads converged on her, yelling and pulling on her limbs.

"Dionysus!" Artemis yelled. "Please!"

Dionysus looked at her in confusion. He raised his hand to still the maenads. "Artemis? What are you doing? Why did you do that?" He spoke woodenly and gestured to the floor where Nyssa's body lay.

"They killed Apollo! I'm here for him!"

"No," he said, sounding confused.

Alex was bewildered as well. She knew for a fact Dionysus was aware of Apollo's death and who had done it. How could he forget something like that?

"Dionysus! They did!" Artemis' voice cracked. "I held his body in my arms. I have it on video. I watched your maenads slide a dagger into his heart!"

A ripple of confusion and fear went through the maenads.

"NO!" he screamed, a deafening sound that emanated from him like a blast.

The room quieted.

Into that silence, a harrowing sound came from behind the altar.

Nyssa slowly stood. A low, resonant laugh coming out of her impossibly perfect throat. There were no arrows, no blood. Her mask was off and she had a wild look in her eyes.

The room gasped and started chanting. Their god had worked a miracle. *"Praise Bacchus, praise Bacchus, praise Bacchus."*

The torchlight glinted off the golden sickle as Nyssa raised her arms up to the blood-red moon. "May the god of the afterlife accept this sacrifice, and may the valley, the vines, the wine, and the bodies in this room receive its blessings!"

She plunged the blade into Zeus' heart.

76

As the golden sickle found its grisly mark, a blast of energy exploded from the altar, knocking Alex and the others off their feet and blowing all the torches out. The circular room was now illuminated only by the stars and the white crescent of the moon as it began its journey out of shadow.

The room was silent as the Orphics and maenads pulled themselves up from the floor with a look of rapture on their faces. Alex felt strange. Alive. The energy of the sacrificial wine seemed paltry compared to this. It was as though she was a young girl again, a kid. A kid with no worries, no cares, and a body that could do anything. She stood, bouncing on the pads of her feet and flexing, feeling as though she could leap out of the room. Her eyes were wide and rapturous.

Zeus' body lay dark on the altar; the golden sickle glowed in its deadly resting place.

Nyssa spoke. "Inner Circle, go now. Rejoice in your blessing. As always, be careful as you move through the world. Do not betray your secret. And, on a personal note, please forgive the drama. Even gods have family. Praise Bacchus!" She motioned for one of the Chosen to lead them out of the room.

"Praise Bacchus!" they responded. They hurried down the stairs. Part of Alex wanted to flee with them, but she couldn't leave yet.

It was time to toss her pebble. She stood alone.

Nyssa noticed and cocked her head at Alex in recognition. "Remove her mask and hold her," she said to the maenads closest to her. They moved quickly, snapping the ribbons.

Dionysus' face went through many expressions—concern, bewilderment, finally settling on anger mixed with sorrow. "Alex? You're here?" He sounded normal again, more like himself. He took a step toward her, as if to see if it was really her.

"Yes, I came to help. I was hoping you weren't involved in…" She nodded toward the altar.

Dionysus grimaced, still not looking at his dead father. "Alex, you don't understand." He took another step toward her.

"Dionysus, stop! She cannot be trusted!" Nyssa yelled. She gestured for the maenads to squeeze Alex.

"No!" Dionysus bellowed. "You will not harm her! Step away!"

The Chosen Elite looked to Nyssa who shook her head, but lifted her finger to stop the squeezing.

Thunder rolled across the room as the god's voice boomed. "I am your god! You will do as *I* say!" He lifted his arm, ostensibly to force them to move.

He froze, mid-gesture, eyes panicked. "I can't move," he whispered.

"I'm sorry, Dionysus, I never wanted to do this to you," Nyssa said.

"Nyssa? What's happening?"

"Dionysus, my boy, honestly, what do you think is happening?" she asked. Her face looked almost maternal as she approached him.

"I don't know," he said. "Everything is so fuzzy. Why can't I move?"

"You should sit down." Nyssa motioned with her hand. His body jerked back and sat on the horned silver chair. Shock filled his face. She raised her hands and all the candles in the room lit at the same time.

Nyssa sighed. "If I had my way you would never have found out. But I suppose if you must know, it's only appropriate your family hears it as well. Then maybe they can appreciate the magnitude of what's been done to you. And why we have done what we have."

She came up the steps of the dais and knelt next to Dionysus. "Who, exactly, do you think I am?" she asked softly. She held his hand.

"You're my priestess, my protector, and friend. The sister I never had," he said. "I love you." He sounded confused and miserable.

"I am all those things. But I am not a god, not immortal. So how have I lasted this long by your side?"

Dionysus looked flummoxed. "I did that," he said. "I gave you the gift of long life."

"But when?"

"I don't know, sometime before The Fall."

"Think back, Dionysus." She paused. "Do you truly remember such an event?"

The room was as quiet as a confessional.

Dionysus massaged his temples. "I don't know," he said finally.

"Think!" she said sharply.

Dionysus jolted up. "No. I guess, I guess I don't remember doing that," he stammered.

"Because it never happened." She squeezed his hand. "I have never needed it."

His face stayed cloudy. "I don't understand."

Nyssa sighed again. "No, I suppose not. I shall guide you more plainly then. When did I become part of your life? Start walking beside you, protecting you, planning with you."

His eyes became haunted. "Before Olympus," he said warily. "When I was wandering."

"Yes. Do you remember the first time you heard my voice?"

He looked at her and nodded.

"When?"

"I…I don't want to do this," he whispered.

"We must. When?"

Dionysus buried his head in his hands, his body trembled. "In the dark."

"Yes," she said. "I'm Hera's unwitting gift to you as she shattered your mind."

"No," he whimpered.

"Why do you think you forget so much, especially when I am strong?"

Dionysus shook his head.

"I come from you," she said. "And you, a god, are able to give me, *an alter*, form. But I'm not real, not truly."

Dionysus began to weep.

"It took a long time to realize what was happening myself, who I was, how I was connected to you. As I became more aware, it also became clear that you did not know. Did not understand. And I thought it safer, healthier, to leave it that way. To use your power on your behalf, protecting you, as I always have. I'm so sorry," she whispered. She cradled his head against her as he sobbed.

Alex watched in shock and her heart broke for him. She glanced at Hermes and Artemis, who both looked stricken.

"So. Do you remember? When the opportunity came to utterly destroy Hera, we were compelled to take advantage."

Dionysus didn't answer. He kept his face buried in her robe.

"You were on the fence about including your father, but when I told you he could give you the rest you needed, the rest you deserved, you agreed."

He nodded again.

"But Apollo? Poseidon?" he asked, his voice muffled.

"That was necessary as well."

"Bullshit!" Artemis said, shattering the moment. "Apollo would never have used that virus on anyone other than himself."

"You cannot know that," Nyssa hissed. "And you cannot know that someone else, one of you, wouldn't have found it and used it on him. And now no one can. Now that the creator and his lab are destroyed."

Dionysus pulled back. "Nyssa, you presume too much!" he said angrily.

"It was necessary to protect you," she said. "It's what I do. I'm the only one who ever has. But I see no reason to harm any more of your family. Our family." She gestured for the maenads to let Artemis and Hermes go.

Hermes rushed to Dionysus and pulled him into a tight embrace. Dionysus continued to sob.

"I'm so sorry," Hermes said. "I didn't know."

"Me too. I didn't either," Dionysus said.

"I don't know what to think," said Artemis. "But, oh, Father!" She ran to the altar, tears of sorrow and rage flowing down her cheeks. She lifted the golden sickle out of his chest and threw it away with disgust. It landed with a metal thud in front of the doorway.

Alex saw a figure peek around the corner and disappear again. Athena! She squirmed against the maenads' grip. They squeezed harder and she yelped.

Artemis looked up sharply through her tears. "Why have your maenads not released Alex?"

Dionysus and Hermes looked over as well.

"I haven't decided what to do with her yet," Nyssa said simply, as if Alex was a piece of furniture to either keep or discard.

Alex's blood froze.

"What do you mean?" Hermes demanded. "You're going to let her go, of course."

Dionysus nodded. "Nyssa, we have to. I care about her. She's a good person. And I can't live with another—"

"Don't finish that sentence," Nyssa warned.

He set his face. "With another Oracle murder on my hands. Especially hers."

Hermes and Artemis stared, open-mouthed. "So it's true!" Artemis said.

Dionysus nodded. "It was Nyssa's idea. If we got rid of the Oracles, it was much less likely you would find out about the pending religious revolution. By the time you realized, it would be too late. We would reign supreme."

"They were our friends! You murdered children!" Hermes said, his face pale. Artemis shot daggers out of her eyes at Nyssa, who returned her gaze coolly.

"I know. I didn't know it was going to be that...thorough," Dionysus said miserably.

"You all treated him so poorly," Nyssa said with contempt. "He deserved to come out on top."

"And your wife?" Artemis asked, incredulous.

Dionysus hung his head. "It never occurred to me she would be included."

"It was necessary. It would point back to you too clearly otherwise," Nyssa said with a put-upon air.

"So you have said," Dionysus said woodenly.

"The same problem is present today," Nyssa said. "This girl, broken Oracle though she is, is a threat."

"God, you are just full of bullshit," Artemis said. Nyssa turned to her, eyes ablaze. "There's nothing Alex could see that would be a threat to Dionysus or anything you've built here," Artemis continued. "The real threat is that he cares about her. She's a reminder of his wife and all that he's lost. She's a chink in the armor you've built up around him. Of his dependence on you."

"Nonsense," Nyssa said.

But Dionysus looked thoughtful for a minute. "She's right, isn't she? I can feel it."

"Look, we have a lot of healing to do now," Nyssa said, moving her body so as to obscure Alex from his view. "So many more important things to figure out together and focus on."

"Dionysus, please, I just want to go home," Alex said in a small, panicked voice.

"Nyssa, let her go," Dionysus said.

"I can't yet," Nyssa said. "We'll just put her in one of the quiet rooms until we can figure out—"

"LET HER GO!" He pushed Nyssa out of the way and headed toward Alex. The maenads squeezed tighter.

Nyssa's face paled. Or did it become just a little translucent?

Dionysus stopped moving again, clearly struggling against an unseen force.

"Please, Dionysus, please listen to reason," Nyssa said.

Dionysus was incredulous. "Reason? You and I are clearly the least reasonable people in this room!" He took a deep breath. "Let go of me." He stared daggers at her.

Nyssa shook her head. She looked at the maenads holding Alex. "Do it."

"NO!" Hermes and Artemis both yelled.

Alex's vision swam as the breath was crushed out of her.

Thunder filled the room. "I. SAID. STOP!" Dionysus boomed.

Nyssa was suddenly nowhere to be seen.

Dionysus gestured with his hands and the maenads holding Alex were thrown against the wall. Alex fell to her knees, gasping.

He turned to the Chosen Elite he'd just tossed. "How dare you. How dare you disobey *me*, your god, the benefactor of your glorious Madness. No longer are you welcome here, no longer will you receive the wine of the Chosen. No longer are you my faithful servants. Be gone, Chosen Elite, those of you who served her more than me. Go now and I will spare you your lives!" he roared.

Over twenty maenads separated from the group and scurried out of the room. The remaining maenads seemed mystified and murmured amongst themselves.

Dionysus stumbled over to Alex and knelt down in front of her. He lifted her chin up so she could see his face. It was filled with anguish. "I'm so sorry," he said.

Alex nodded. "It's okay," she whispered. "Thank you."

Then Dionysus bent over and moaned, grabbing his head.

Artemis ran to Alex and dragged her away.

At that moment, Athena walked into the room holding the golden sickle down at her side. "Dionysus," she said gently. She touched his back. He lifted his face to her, tears streaming.

"Athena! You're here too? Did you hear all of that?"

"I did," she said, her face full of sorrow.

"How could I not have known? How could I be so stupid?" he asked through clenched teeth. He groaned and leaned forward.

"Dionysus, there's a reason the people who study this condition today call it a hidden system," she said. "The alternate identities are designed to protect you. It often does that partly by staying concealed from the person who has it."

Gratitude flashed through the grief and pain on his face. "Thank you," he said. "I hope that is true."

He groaned again, his hands clenching his head. "I don't know how I made her go away, but she's screaming to come back. It's deafening. I don't think I can stop her. She is—and always has been—stronger than me."

Hermes rushed to his brother. "You *are* strong, Dionysus!" he said. He glanced at the sickle and glared at Athena, shaking his head. "You have conquered so much in your life. Built so much. And done it all on your own. You're incredible. And we failed you." Tears began streaming down his face. "*I* failed you."

"Not you, Hermes. Never you. If anything, I failed you. I did not stand up to her, I let her convince me of such vile, twisted things."

Dionysus looked at Athena and nodded. "Do it," he said. "I don't want this. Any of it. I don't think I can fight her. And truthfully, I don't want to. She has always been there for me. But...the massacre has haunted me for millennia, and now our family will as well—Father, Poseidon, Apollo. And now even Alex? When does it stop? Who will our next enemy be?"

Dionysus groaned and leaned forward onto the grass.

"No!" Hermes said. "There is medication for this. We have that virus now, we could turn you mortal and get you help, we have options! Please don't give up!"

Dionysus screamed in pain. He spoke haltingly. "I don't want...a mortal life. And...I'm tired. Tired of all of this." He waved his hand, gesturing at the room. "And I understand now, why she...will never truly let me leave it."

Hermes was silent, holding the man he'd raised from a child as he waged his inner battle.

"Athena, please," Dionysus begged. He shoved Hermes away and pushed himself up onto his knees. He lifted his head to make his neck accessible.

"Athena, no!" Hermes yelled.

Athena looked at him, tears also running down her face. "We cannot fail him again."

The fight left Hermes like a ghost. He sank next to Dionysus, grabbing him tight. "I love you, little brother." Then he leaned away, still holding onto his forearms. Dionysus would not face death alone.

"Dionysus, I'm so sorry," Athena said. She held the sickle up in the air.

"Hurry," Dionysus whispered. He closed his eyes, trembling.

Athena's arm shook. She faltered.

Dionysus opened his eyes. The silver gray of Nyssa's looked out of them.

He began to rise.

Athena gasped as a strong hand grabbed the golden sickle and shoved her away.

Wielding it deftly, Demeter swung.

77

Alex stood to the side of Apollo's well-manicured lawn watching the ex-Olympian family as they quietly drank and talked in the early evening. The birds were chirping as a slight breeze drifted by, making it seem an almost cheerful wake, if there was such a thing.

The dead sat on a tall pedestal, in five separate urns, each one representing the person whose remains it held. Apollo's was a burnished gold, for the sun he loved. Poseidon's, a deep aqua hue. Zeus' was the color of a summer sky. Black for Hera, and a deep burgundy etched with vines for Dionysus. There would be mortal ceremonies for each of them later, but for now, what was left of the family wanted to be together. For once.

Athena and Artemis had planned it. Demeter, Aphrodite, and Hephaestus showed up, and even Ares deigned to come. It was a little stilted at first, but the beauty of the evening and the rivers of alcohol helped smooth everything over. They were soon regaling each other with stories of their fallen family. The only one missing was Hermes. And Henry, who said he couldn't bear to socialize.

Alex sat on the stone edge of a small raised koi pond. She felt heavy as she stared at the burgundy urn. It had only been a few days since the devastating events at the Orphic Temple, and everyone was still reeling from the revelations and outcome. Most of the maenads had wailed and scattered, and she'd heard that half the True Life rooms had gone dark, causing pandemonium and confusion amongst the Orphics.

Hermes had disappeared and hadn't been seen since the moment he'd been covered in the blood of his brother.

Athena had arranged for everyone to travel back to Apollo's. Some of the maenads, including Sarah, stayed and helped carry the bodies out the back, avoiding the crowds.

Everyone had insisted that Alex stay at Apollo's, though she felt distinctly out of place. Artemis said at this point she may as well be family. Alex appreciated the sentiment but wasn't quite sure how to feel about that.

Demeter wandered over and sat next to her, holding a glass of white wine. She was wearing her curly golden hair up in a high, loose bun and a simple black dress. She smiled warmly. "Hi. I'm Demeter. I thought we should meet properly."

Alex gave her a small smile in return. "Hi. Alex." She was having difficulty reconciling this warm, lovely woman with the woman who had so expertly wielded that sickle. An image she'd had difficulty forgetting over the last few days. That said, it could have been worse; she was deeply relieved her vision hadn't come to fruition. She wondered how many pebbles it had taken to change it, or if her small one had been enough.

Demeter pulled her into a side hug. "I hear we have much to be grateful to you for."

"Oh, I don't know about that," Alex said thickly. Her emotions were close to the surface lately.

"Nonsense," Demeter said, still holding her close. "We would have never been able to save Dionysus, if not for you."

"But—"

"No buts," she said firmly. "Dionysus had been not so secretly miserable for a long time. He had nothing other than his wine. From what I've heard, you were the first thing that drew his interest in a very long time. And it's what gave him strength to fight her."

Alex pulled away. "It's all just so awful."

Demeter nodded. "It's heartbreaking. I'd seen glimpses of Nyssa's power and potency over the years but had no idea the depths it went to. Knowing what I know now, I think eventually she would have taken over completely."

Alex nodded. "That actually makes me think of one of the questions I've had as I've replayed that night in my head. Why couldn't Hermes *shift* out of there?"

"Ah. Nyssa was always worried about Hermes popping in unannounced. There were several rooms where Dionysus had ensured that particular relic wouldn't work. Nyssa was paranoid, as you can tell. And, I suppose, rightly so in the end."

Alex nodded. "Well, I'm so sorry you had to do…what you did."

Demeter grimaced. "Thanks. I wish I could say it was my first time, but…" She shrugged. "It's been a very long time though. Nyssa has been doing the Harvest Sacrifices for centuries. And I've certainly never…with family," she said. Her voice caught.

A door opened behind them. Henry came out onto the lawn, his face a mask of grief.

"Henry! I'm so glad you decided to come." Artemis ran to him. They held each other and sobbed, having both loved Apollo more than anyone. Titus ran up and jumped on both of them. They laughed and sobbed and hugged more.

Alex felt an urge to get out of there. "Thanks for coming over, Demeter. It really is nice to meet you."

"You too, I hope to see you again. Hang in there."

Alex wandered into the house, not sure where to go. She finally decided to head to Apollo's study, where she'd first met Titus. She wondered what would happen to this house; was it Henry's now? Would he want to stay here? What about Artemis? She was still lost in her thoughts when someone blocked the light in the doorway.

She turned to find Hermes standing there with his hands in his pockets, looking at her. She ran over to him and threw her arms around his neck. "I'm sorry, I'm so sorry," she said.

He held her tight, burying his face in her neck.

They clung to each other for a long minute before letting go. "Look," he said. "I can't stay. I can't be around them," he thumbed toward the lawn, "or anyone, right now. But I wanted—needed—to make sure you were okay. That you knew this was not your fault. And that, more than anything else, I think you staying is what saved him in the end."

Tears brimmed in her eyes. "That's not what it feels like," she said.

"I know. I'm still processing it too. But I'm coming around to the idea that it was, in the end, probably what was best."

"I hope so," she said.

"I hope so too."

They were silent for a moment. It was strange to stand there with him, having just gone through so much together, but in the end, still barely knowing each other. She didn't ask any of the questions rattling around in her head, she didn't really want to know the answers. He was just one more thing to be confused about.

He pulled her close again and kissed her gently. Alex's heart started pounding.

"I don't know when, but I'll be back," he said. "If you want?" He arched a questioning brow.

"I guess that depends, are you going to be an asshole?" she asked, half smiling.

"Heh, probably," he said. "But I'll try to keep it to a minimum."

She kissed him. "Then I want," she said simply.

He gave her his now familiar rugged smile, stepped back, and disappeared.

Alex was laying on the grass outside in the front when Artemis came and laid down next to her. They lay in companionable silence looking at the twinkling stars. The family had all left over an hour ago.

"How are you?" Alex asked her friend eventually.

"Shitty," Artemis said.

"Yeah, hard day."

"Hard week."

Alex nodded. They were silent again for a moment.

"Out of curiosity, why did you include Hera in this? Knowing everything we know?" Alex asked.

"Athena and I debated about that. Hera planted the seed that ended up destroying half our family. But ultimately, it felt wrong to leave her out. She was a terrible person, but she was still family. And Father loved her."

"Makes sense. Sorta."

"Heh, right. As much as any of this makes sense. By the way, I've been meaning to ask if you're okay? Like from the ceremony? Have you noticed anything physically yet?"

Alex stretched her body. That feeling of vitality hadn't left her, and she said so. "I wonder what that means though." She lifted her head up onto her elbow.

"Well," Artemis said, lifting her head onto her elbow too, "from what I gather from Demeter, I think you just got an extra life."

"You're joking. Like, how long?"

"She had no idea, since it was the first and only time they used someone as old *and* healthy as him. But, to give you an idea, she said that when they used someone in their forties or fifties, often unhealthy in some way, it usually gave the Inner Circle increased vitality for about five years or so."

Alex's eyes went wide. Zeus had been over three thousand years old. She fell back onto the grass, stunned, unwilling to do the math. "I guess we'll just have to see," she said finally. She actually felt fairly sick at the thought of her current life stretching out into time unknown.

Then again, her life was changing. She had control. She had friends. Immortal friends.

Artemis had similar thoughts. "Look, it won't be so bad. You're on your way to conquering your curse, and now we have each other." She squeezed Alex's hand.

"True." Alex smiled and squeezed back.

"And the rest of the family, of course. I think you're stuck with all of us. Or at least me, Athena, and Hermes. Which, by the way…you and Hermes?" Her eyes glinted in the dark.

"Gah, I don't know," Alex said. "Possibly. Is that okay?"

Artemis chuckled. "Yeah, it's okay," she said. "I like Hermes. Plus, if you're together maybe I'll get more free rides out of him."

Relief flooded through her. If forced, she would have chosen Artemis over Hermes, but she was glad not to have to.

Alex noticed the constellation of Orion as it crept up over the horizon. He'd always been one of her favorites, it felt like home whenever she saw him in the sky.

She was startled by the sudden remembrance that his story was actually entwined somehow with Artemis and Apollo. She chuckled to herself. She'd have to ask Artemis about that sometime.

Artemis, former Goddess of the Hunt. Ex-Goddess of the Moon.

Her friend.

"I just don't know what I'm going to do now, without Apollo," Artemis said.

"You could come work with me at the mortuary," Alex teased. Though she couldn't really imagine going back to that world of death now that so much life was ahead of her.

"God, no way," Artemis said. "Vigilantes sounds better."

"You'd have to teach me to shoot," Alex said.

"Deal, you'll love it. It's so satisfying."

"Seriously, though, I still want to help people. People that can't help themselves," Alex said. "That was the thing I liked most about my work."

"Yeah, that would be…good," Artemis said.

"But right now, I think we're the ones that need help. Drinks and a show?" Alex said.

"Definitely. Something comforting. Beer with Bob Ross?"

"Perfect. And fitting, given that our entire friendship is just one happy little accident."

Artemis smiled. "Best. Accident. Ever."

They rose and walked arm-in-arm into the house.

EPILOGUE

Athena cut open the box and carefully removed the cold packs surrounding the hermetically sealed container within. She lifted the container up to the light.
Two glass vials were encased inside.
Athena smiled.
Her daughter Sophie played happily in the background.

SUPPLEMENTAL MATERIALS

Ancient Baalbek, Lebanon—known in Greek and Roman times as Heliopolis. Dionysus used this temple complex as a model for his own.

source: Wikimedia Commons

Visit heidikallen.com/supplementals for more supplemental materials including a cast of characters, pronunciations, and more!

WANT MORE MYTH & MADNESS?

Join my monthly newsletter to get a free copy of
The Sea Blue Mane, a contemporary mythic fantasy novella.

*Poseidon, desperate to reclaim his lost trident, must infiltrate an island
cloaked in perpetual storms, contend with a long-forgotten sea nymph,
and survive a series of brutal trials inspired by* The Odyssey,
his least favorite book.

You'll also receive book updates, occasional special deals, and bonus
content for fellow book and word lovers. Connecting with readers is one
of the greatest joys of an author and I look forward to
chatting with you there.

Visit heidikallen.com to sign up and start reading today!

PLEASE LEAVE A REVIEW!

Thank you for reading *Where Madness Lies*. If you enjoyed this book, I would be so grateful if you would please leave a review.

Reviews are essential to me as independent author—they help me gain visibility and bring my books to the attention of other readers who may enjoy it as well. They also help me get special promotion deals on certain sites.

Please visit heidikallen.com/reviews for links to leave a review on your retailer of choice or on Goodreads.

Thank you so very much!

ALSO BY HEIDI K. ALLEN

Visit <u>heidikallen.com/books</u> to see my complete list of books.

Also if you're interested in reading more, please consider purchasing future books directly from me. You'll still able to read in your format of choice, and you'd be supporting me in a meaningful way.

Selling direct allows me to build relationships directly with my readers, cut out the perilous ups-and-downs of the big-brand stores, and of course provides me with more resources to give you what you really want…the next great book.

ACKNOWLEDGMENTS

This book has been a part of my life in one way or another for fourteen years. Thank you Lindsey, for encouraging me to write a book. I wish you were still here to read it.

As I struggled to find my footing as a writer, this story went through two disastrous NaNoWriMos, three titles, four styles of outlines, countless revisions, a supportive writing group and other forgiving alpha readers (thank you Rachel, Beth, Marc, Dan, Shari, and Marci), many long pauses when life, work, and motherhood conspired to get in the way, a smart, no-nonsense writing coach (thank you Angie Fenimore), a year of querying literary agents, and finally, after choosing to take its fate in my own hands, two detailed editors (thank you Corwin Zahn, and especially to Megan McKeever, whose thoughtful insights, kindness, and encouragement were of great consequence and deeply appreciated).

All that to say, I'm thrilled and so proud to finally be putting this novel out into the world.

I'm especially grateful for the support of my loving family—my siblings, Darren, Arianne, and Rebecca, my father Jack, and my aunt Shari, thank you all for cheering me on for so very long. Abby and Kate, my darling girls, thank you for your patience through the busy times, and for all the supportive snuggles. I hope what you remember most is what it looks like to work hard for a dream.

My most tender and heartfelt gratitude is reserved especially for my mother Marci, in whose lap I became a reader, and who was my biggest and most constant source of solace, support, encouragement, and validation throughout this entire endeavor (and all my other ones as well). Thank you for shoring me up when I needed it, for not letting me quit, and really, for everything.

$$\infty$$

KICKSTARTER ACKNOWLEDGMENTS

This book began its manifested life in the real world via a special platform called Kickstarter. To all my wonderful backers, I thank you from the bottom of my heart. It was a thrilling campaign. Thank you especially to those of you who backed early and earned a place here in the acknowledgements!

Thank you so much to: Jack, Marci, Arianne, Darren, Rebecca, Danielle, Robert Gooch, Joye Whitaker, Ben, Kristopher Ecklof, Beth Dove, Shannon Smith, Shari Baker, Laura Whitney, Dean Winter, Robert Luettjohann, Herman Steuernagel, Steve Sawaya, Larry Gilley, Josh McGillis, Amanda Hansen, Gina Weaver, Simon Wilkins, Marshall Hunsaker, Stef Tidwell, Marcellus van Lent, Kaitlin Ciminelli, Leesha Baker, Esa Eriksson, Jason Katzenbach, Ben Jacobson, Scott Casey, Rachel Bush, Aimee Roy, John Dilts, Catherine Nalder, Brandon Greenwood, Bryan Conner, Mark McIver, Alexa Thomas, Edward Varra, Nate Auwerda, Garrett Seibt, Monica Kim, and Anna Layton.